The Great Story of Lolly Pobs

Natalye Benitez

The Great Story of Lolly Pobs

Natalye Benitez

RIVER BIRCH PRESS

Daphne, Alabama

For my adoring family.
Thank you for being patient with me
while I followed my dreams.
I love you!

Table of Contents

Acknowledgments

I want to thank the beautiful Creator (Elohim) for inspiring me to write this book. I was only a songwriter and usually only wrote a few paragraphs on one page. But You, God, allowed me to write an entire manuscript with just YOU. And I love how I woke up to the main character "Lolly" on my mind one morning and couldn't let it go until I drew her, not knowing she was a protagonist in a book that I would write. I'm so grateful.

A big thank you to my agent, Keith Carroll, for reading my extra-packed manuscript and still coming back for more and still giving his wonderful advice. He helped shape my book in a way that enabled me to deliver the message I wanted to convey successfully.

Thank you to my publisher, Brian Banashak at River Birch Press, who took the time to talk with me about the vision I had for my book. Even though we're a million miles apart, I felt like he walked with me through a park, listening to my ideas, then brought them to life with a big splash of his own creativity/imagination. Brian and his team birthed an awesome "stare-at" worthy book with a matching beautiful inside that I am so proud of.

Thank you to my editor, Kathy Banashak, for understanding my voice and keeping it mine, adding pops of her cleverness that carried my thoughts across wondrously.

Thank you to my generous-in-love best friend Amanda for never leaving my side and for giving me the support and love I needed to continue my journey.

An eternal THANK YOU to my little one, Robyn Lyn, for being patient with Mommy while I dove into the world God took me into to write *The Great Story of Lolly Pobs*, and then came back to make a quick/late dinner! Mama loves you, baby.

Thanks so much to my brilliant siblings, Claudia and Jonathan. What would I do without your advice and love?

Thank you to my caring mother for praying for me and believing in me! I love you.

And to my aunt, Katherine Elizabeth, a 10+ year survivor of lupus, thank you for inspiring me to write about it. You always wanted people to know how serious lupus truly is, and I hope I did you proud. I love you.

Preface

I fully gave my life to Christ in 2014. In 2018 God called me to do a set of amplified exercises that would prepare my mind to put *The Great Story of Lolly Pobs* together.

He had been molding me since 2014, giving me instructions on how to deal with certain situations through His Word. I surrendered my life and time to Him, and in exchange, I sacrificed a lot. I wasn't able to hang out with old friends or spend a large amount of time talking or being with family. I wasn't allowed to go to certain events or say certain things. I was in four walls for years as His servant, happily captured, and a captive of God's love. Although it took great sacrifice, I've come to realize that life is not about living. It's about being used by the Creator to carry out His will. That devotion allowed me to write TGSLP's manuscript in 2021, in only eight months. To God be the glory!

Because I answered God's call, I was able to successfully give all the teachings God gave me to others around me. They benefited greatly from that advice repeatedly. I then found myself wanting to share my life with them, almost walking with them through every struggle because I hated to see them suffer. But I knew I couldn't.

It was deep in my heart that I wanted to have a way to show people how God can greatly transform one's life. (And to my surprise, God made it enjoyable—a FICTION/CHRISTIAN/FANTASY.) I couldn't walk everyday with every person, but I could show them what God taught me through a personal handbook, *The Great Story of Lolly Pobs*. I learned how He's the one that walks closely with us, causing us to get the victory EVERY TIME.

Thank you to all my "love captured" readers! I adore you!

1

Wild Child

Character—something I unknowingly lacked. Who knew I was supposed to be kind, meek, and mild? Although I had spurts of these characteristics, God wanted me to encompass the nature of all three, then incorporate them into my daily living, choices, and mannerisms. Being oblivious to this truth didn't justify me any more than it made me a criminal. Only grace had a say in that. Put simply, my behavior stunk more than a week's worth of trash being hauled to the nearest landfill *with me in it*. But God had a plan to change it. At the time, I could only process it as this: you can wear nice clothes, but they don't dress the soul.

My alarm wakes me early, and my perfectly polished nails hit the button atop my periwinkle alarm clock. I get up and dress, throwing on my go-go boots and pairing them with a short khaki plaid skort and white long-sleeve top. I shuffle in front of the mirror, admiring my outfit, which was simple yet cute. I walk to my vanity, apply makeup, then pick through a selection of lip glosses. My hips faintly sway to the soft music playing in the background.

"Lolly? Are you ready for school, sweetheart?" I hear my mother's groggy voice when she breaks through my swinging door, and I roll my eyes.

"Mom, I told you to knock before coming in my room!" I shoot her a glare, then turn around to continue my gloss application.

"Oh right, I'm sorry, honey. Do you want breakfast? I'm making pancakes, your favorite."

"Mm-hmm," I say to get her to leave.

I grab my black tube of pink blush and apply the shimmer to each cheek. My mother still stands at my door, staring. Annoyed, I narrow my eyes at her. "What?" I ask.

"I just can't believe how much you've grown! You're a pro at makeup and so gorgeous!"

My eyes shift from her to me in the mirror, and I smile. "I'm no pro, but it does look good, doesn't it? Thanks, Liz!"

Her eyes widen at my mention of her first name, but I ignore it and am thrilled when she finally leaves. I brush my long, straight brown hair into a ponytail. Then I gather my bag containing a few books for school, since seniors don't need much, and fill it with oodles of makeup. I blow a kiss at myself in the mirror and depart.

I pull out my phone, go to favorites, and call Addison. She's been my best friend since we moved back to LA four years ago. Daddy finally let me start and finish a school without sailing us across the continent, *yet again,* for his real estate business. Wherever the market is banging, he wants to be. So my first week of high school, I knew no one. Thankfully, I met Addy during first period when she told a boy to get up from a seat she saw me eyeing, and the rest is history.

Now, graduation is only a few weeks away. The stability makes me feel like I've accomplished a great goal or something. My heart pounds at the thought of walking across that big stage, but the daydream gets interrupted by my best friend's voice: "Hey, babe."

"Headed your way," I say.

"Cool," Addy says. "Almost ready. Can I borrow that pretty blue eyeshadow you wore to Auston's party? It'll make my outfit pop!"

I circle around.

Daddy, Mother, and my little brother are all at the kitchen bar, watching me scurry back and forth.

"Ugh. Of course! What are you wearing?" I ask in my voice's highest pitch. My best friend and I are the talk of the school. We definitely set the bar high.

"The blue corduroy overalls dress I got from MADE. I love it, Cher. Leena's stuff is so high quality."

I love that she always calls me by my middle name, Cher. I reach my room in a snap, grab the squared jar, and then head back towards the front door. "True! I'm wearing her boots right now!"

"Lolly, your breakfast is ready, hon!" my mother calls.

As if . . . "No thanks. I'll grab something to go. Bye!" I say, then hear her gasp. The front door slams behind me harder than I intended, cutting her off before she can complain. As I make my way to my car, I giggle. The bubblegum pink paint glistens on the convertible, catching my reflection perfectly. After I unlock it and put the top back up with one easy click, I get in. I smudge the blue on Addy's eyelids, saying, "Thanks for letting me get some practice in."

"Of course, Lolly, you always slay!"

When we're a little closer to school, I put the top back down so everyone will see us, although they already know me by my car. We park in senior parking and walk out, bags in arms. Time seems to move in slow motion as we head inside with all eyes on us, as usual.

"Lolly, I love your shoes!" says a little freshman from fourth period.

"Ew, why are you speaking to me?" I say flatly and roll my eyes.

"They are really cute, Cher. You're bound to get attention

from all kinds of people," says Addison, flipping her long blonde plaits off her shoulder.

"True." I shrug and flutter my lashes as we continue our walk.

"Lolly, nice threads!" says Kyla Martin, whose parents are some of the richest in the area.

"Thanks, girl, they're from MADE, by Leena." I smile at her good taste and keep it moving as she does.

Me and Addison O.M.G. to each other. We're popular, but *she's more.* We reach the courtyard alongside everyone and wait for the bell to ring for first. Chatter fills the air, and I hope no one touches me because we're all so close together. Just then, a girl grazes my shoulder with hers. *Ew.* I pat invisible cooties off me.

My mood lightens at the sight of Carter Garcia. Addison is watching some boy bump into everyone instead of me, and irritation floods me. I clear my throat. "Oh my gosh! Carter Garcia!"

"Where?" asks Addy. She ten-huts.

I signaled in his direction with my eyes, and she spotted him just as the bell rang. Our feet move, and Carter happens to be walking toward us.

"Hi, Lolly. Sup, Addison," he says.

"Hey Carter!" Addison finally lets out. Realizing I'm stunned, she nudges me.

"Hi, Carter!" I say and shyly smile.

As we walk on, Addison says, "He couldn't keep his eyes off you, Cher!"

I gasp. "Oh my gosh! Do you think he'll ask me to prom?"

"Um yeah! He'd be crazy not to." We both giggle.

At lunch, we sit in the courtyard at our usual table, with our Ray-Bans on, basking in the sun. I see Carter again. This time he just smiles at me, and I wave coolly. Could there be a more gorgeous creature in the world? *I think not!*

"What guy are you dating right now?" I ask Addy.

"*Right now?* You say that like I have a small yellow bus filled with boos, girl. As if!" She scoffs. "Just because I'm not on self-lockdown *like you*, doesn't mean I'm out here or something."

"Stop! I just lost track. You broke up with Anthony, Marcus, Shawn, and Luis, right?"

"Luis is still around . . ."

I swipe at her arm. "You said he was gone!"

"Yeah, but that list is seriously horrible, babe. I'm just picky. If they're not what I expected, then I fall back."

"*Okay,* but you know what I meant."

"I did. I was just being difficult." We giggle.

"His name is Chris."

"Do you think he's *the one*?" I ask.

"Yeah," she says, but her tone is questionable.

I raise an eyebrow.

"What? I do!" she says.

"Do you think Carter could be *the one?*" I ask.

Addison shrugs. "Maybe."

"Addyyyy?" I cry for clarity.

"Guys are lame, and you just never know," she says. "That's why I said Luis is still around. I like Chris a lot, but you gotta have options."

I have no idea what she means. I've never had a boyfriend, and the word makes me cringe. I just woefully stare at her and she says, "Okay!" Then she asks, "How does Carter make you feel?"

I think hard. "I get really shy when he's around. It's weird."

"Lolly! I love your shoes!" Maranda Lewis's voice barges in.

"Thanks, Maranda. I got them from MADE," I say nervously. Maranda is the popular girl everyone is afraid of, or should I say *the bully.*

She and her friends giggle. Addy and I look at each other, wondering why Miss Prissy and her assistants are in our presence. She doesn't particularly like me. Why? I will never know. I had been sitting tabletop with one leg crossed over the other, but her demeanor made me sit up straight, and my feet went flat on the bench Addison was sitting on.

"I was thinking about asking Carter to prom. How should I?"

My jaw drops. Maranda's thinking about taking *my crush* to prom! One word: don't! Steer clear of Carter Garcia while I have my eye on him because he may very well be *the one* for me. Furthermore, why would *she* ask *him? Ew* . . . Aren't guys supposed to ask girls? I wish I had the nerve to say all these things to Maranda, but I don't.

When I don't answer due to a rush of thoughts, she blurts out, "You have gym with him, right?"

I search for an exit door, but none appear. "Yeah."

"And... that's your next period, *isn't it?*"

Her eyes fixate on mine, and I nod.

"Could you relay a message? I would be too shy to give it to him myself." She hands me a folded paper, and I stare at her in defeat. "Thanks, girl," she says. "Bye!" Maranda walks away, cheery as ever, with her friend trolls.

I push myself off the table next to Addison and pout.

All changed into my gym clothes, I walk the plank to Carter while everyone is stretching. I can't believe how much this day has changed from the promise of his *hello,* to now having to say, *"Bye-bye date I wanted for prom."* But prom is right around the corner, and *maybe* he wasn't even going to ask me. I cheer up and decide to say yes to the next boy who asks.

"Hey, Carter," I say confidently after my pep talk.

"Lolly? What's up!"

Adorable must be his middle name, gorgeous, or both. His

brown curls droop on top of low-cut sides, he has olive skin, and his eyes are a beautiful brown hue. *Just give it to him and walk away quickly!* I tell myself before I melt.

"Maranda wanted me to give you this." I shrug. He's confused but opens the paper in front of me. *Oh gosh.* "See you later," I say, quickly turning around and forcing my legs to walk as swiftly as possible without jogging.

"Lolly! Wait up!" I turn around. How did I get myself into this mess?

"I appreciate you delivering the message, but I was gonna ask you to prom. I guess Maranda helped me out." He bites his bottom lip in the most charming way.

My mouth opens to respond, but I have nothing. Carter's features change from confidant to uncertain.

"Yeah . . . yeah! I'll go with you," I manage, trying to keep it cute.

"Cool," he says, balling up the note and walking away, smiling.

That did not just happen! I practically run to my locker to text Addison.

On our way to my car after school, we imagine ourselves in dresses. Maranda stops me in my tracks, wiping the smile off my face. "Lolly! Did you give it to him?" She's in suspense, awaiting my response.

"Yeah," I simply reply, hoping she'll just leave it at that.

"Well, what'd he say?"

Ugh. "He's already taking someone."

"He is?"

I nod. "See you around," I say, yanking Addison. I continue on cloud nine.

2

Oh, the Drama

Aside from a few male subjects asking me to events, I've never dated. I always ended up friend-zoning them because I believe in true love and love's *first kiss*. I suspect most guys think I'm a complicated Daddy's girl, but I don't mind it. Cause when the time is right, I'll make that memory with someone special who's worth it. Perhaps I was being too rash, *maybe* a bit too particular, but Carter might be the answer to this maybe crusade.

I close my eyes and imagine what it'd be like to dance with him. Will I know how?

I change my school clothes, pull out my computer, and start designing flyers for prom. I was the founder of an all-girl editing group, "The Glitter Editing Committee." On the bottom of the purple paper, I add black lettering with the words "Got a date yet?" and "Fellas, get your gals!" Then I fill it with heart-eye emojis and hit print. Laying on top of the lavender comforter on my bed, I flip through my *Cosmopolitan* magazine, my eyes big, admiring every girl until I get my fill of wonder, planning to do makeup this summer. Of course, that's interrupted by my mother yelling that dinner's ready. *Ugh* . . . I hurry out before my mother annoys me with another shout.

As we sit speechless at the dining room table, I dip my broccoli in my mashed potatoes. I look up to see everyone watching me. I clear my throat and reposition myself in my chair.

"Lolly, is everything okay?" My parents look concerned, but I smile.

"Yes." I dramatically pause, swishing my hair over my shoulder, and cheerfully announce, "I got asked to prom!"

"That's great, honey!" my mother says.

"Wow, okay . . ." says Daddy.

"Who would take you?" my brother, Josh, says.

"Shut up!" I yell, throwing a piece of freshly baked bread at his head, which he dodges.

"Lolly, baby!" says my mother. "Why would you—"

"As a matter of fact, Josh," I interrupt, "*Carter Garcia* asked me!" I stick my tongue out at my childish brother.

"The most popular boy at school?" Josh seems surprised, and I smirk in victory. "Yeah, well, I'd be surprised," he continued, "if dude's not dead from glitter poisoning by the time it's over." He chuckles and Daddy laughs. So annoying. Liz and I shoot him a glare, and he clips his laughter.

"Joshua, that's enough! Carter is very fortunate to be taking your sister to prom. Have you picked out a dress?" Mother asks, seeming so interested and a bit nosy.

"Oh, yeah! Daddy, can I have your American Express to have my dress designed? Pleeeeease?" I plead and bat my lashes, but I always get what I want.

Before long, he pulls out his wallet. "Honey, we're cutting back on expenses. Can you just go out and buy a dress?"

Distraught, I say, "But Daddy, it's prom!"

I've never heard him complain about money. "Tim, let her get what she wants," says my mother. "Sweetheart, I'm sure she can find a decent dress for two hundred dollars."

"*Two hundred dollars!* Half of that won't even cover tax,

Daddy!" I whine but grab the heavy black credit card anyway.

Josh interrupts my pity party. "At least you're getting something. They told me I couldn't get the *Call of Duty* that just came out. That sucks!"

"Josh, language!" says Mother.

"*Ugh.* Can I be excused?"

My parents nod, and I can't believe I just asked that. After this betrayal, I may exonerate myself from being their daughter and find more favorable guardians. I go to my room and immediately call Addison.

"Sorry, babe," she says. "I used up all my cash paying off my dress and getting my nails done. I would've spotted you the rest."

"I know." My head goes deeper into my pillow . . . my best friend is about to kill at prom.

"Oh my gosh! What about a thrift store!"

"Huh?"

"Babe, a thrift store! They have like, hidden designer in there!"

Ugh, what has my life come to?

I arrive at school and get The Glitters together to hang and pass out flyers in our sparkling Glitter jackets. Adrian Henry, a football player on Carter's team, grabs one.

"Lolly, wanna go to prom with me?" he asks.

"I'm already going with Carter Garcia."

"My loss." He walks away with undeniable swagger.

Maybe I would've said yes had Carter faltered. I was feeling myself before Maranda marches up to me with her friends. I gulp.

"You're going to prom with Carter!" She's ballistic. If this were a cartoon, steam would be flowing from her ears.

"Yeah." It took all my strength to declare a four-letter word, but it's not my fault he wants to take me, not her.

"So you didn't give him my letter then?" she asks, fuming.

"I did, but he said he wanted to ask me for a while now." I tread lightly because I've heard she spreads rumors that people actually listen to.

"Of course he did! Look at the way you dress. You're easy and he knows it, everyone does." She looks around and smirks, knowing she's done her worst to offend me before haughtily walking away.

At a loss for words, I look down at my short dress and then at everyone's scrutiny. Did Maranda really just start a rumor about me *to my face?* This is exactly why I've been on edge around her, to avoid the drama I knew she'd bring my way if pushed. When lunch hits, everyone is giving me the side eye and whispering.

Addison rushes towards me. "I am going to slap her!" she says with her hand up, declaring war. I'm sure by now Carter heard too.

After school, I run to my car, hoping I don't see Carter. I try to back out of going to prom. Still, Addison talks me out of it, reminding me we are creating significant memories. I agree.

With Daddy's credit card, we head to the thrift store. Addison cheers me up and crosses her heart that she's gonna confront Maranda. I tell her it's not worth it. I'm gonna finish out the school year without princesses putting me out of the castle.

Inside the infamous discount store, it reeks of the musty smell of feet, highlighted by linen air freshener, someone's attempt to cover up the odor, I presume. My amiga gags, letting me know she's caught a whiff of it too. With caution and a thorough inspection of the used goods, we loosen up and try on costumes, shoes, and funny hats. Then we get down to business and shuffle through a heap of dresses.

It feels like we've been here for hours with no success. "Sorry we couldn't find anything, Cher. We can definitely go somewhere else."

"Yeah," I say, feeling defeated. I pray to Jesus we find something soon.

I throw one more glance in the distance for good measure. Something pink and shiny catches my eye. I run to it, dig through the material in the way, and snatch it! It's a beautiful shade of pink and sheer, with a long split from thigh to toe. It looks like it's never been worn and reads "ninety-nine dollars." I can't help but jump up and down.

"Lolly, it's gorg!" Addison looks at the price tag. "You'll even have enough left for shoes!"

"Let's go to MADE!" I say with a lifted spirit and proceed to the register.

I hear her gasp and spin around. "It's from MADE!"

No way. I look at the tag. Sure enough, it says, "MADE by Leena." I cheerfully walk out, bag in hand, super satisfied with my purchase and even happier I listened to Addison.

Outside, my phone rings. Liz's face pops across the screen. Why is she calling me?

"Hi, sweetheart. Where are you?"

Seriously! "Mom, I don't need you checking in on me! I'm not a baby!"

"Well, when you didn't come home after school like you usually do, I got worried, hon."

I hang up on her. I can't believe she's keeping tabs on me like I'm some child. I turn off my phone, thinking, *Find me now, Elizabeth Pobs!* I tug my dress down after sitting and sweep away the unpleasant energy my mother just threw my way.

At MADE, I try on all Leena's shoes and accessories. I find the cutest silver heels to go with the silver detailing on my dress. I buy everything for seventy bucks, and I'm still on budget!

"Really? You found one of my dresses in a thrift store? Can I see it?" Leena, the Asian twenty-nine-year-old shop owner, asks.

I would love to do her makeup one day. She's so beautiful, as is her elderly mother, who now sits aloof behind the counter. You would think she wouldn't hurt a fly, but I occasionally hear her arguing with Leena. Witnessing the Chinese language being thrown between the two in battle is intense. For some reason, I always wonder if they're talking about me. Aside from a few, "She's crazy," Leena hints at, I will never know.

"Oh yes, I remember. I made it for Cindy Vew last year for prom. She's your size and was very beautiful in it. I'm sure you will be too."

"Thanks, Leena. How much did she pay for it?"

"It was very expensive, over five hundred dollars."

Our jaws drop, and I have a thought to snatch it from Leena. She says something to her mother in Chinese, her eyes widen, and the quarreling begins. As we watch, my head and Addison's go back and forth from one to the other. I watch my dress being yanked back and forth in horror, with Leena using it as a pointer towards her mother.

"It's her dress *now*!" It seems Leena takes the gold, all dialect comes to an end, and I gulp. Thankfully, she hands it back in one piece.

"Enjoy," Lenna says.

We all smile as if we've just been in a western brawl. I thought Leena's mom would confiscate it for sure.

I pull into my driveway at 10:00 p.m. sharp, an hour before my 11:00 curfew, with the rebellion against my mother officially only in my head. I soundlessly inch inside. I expected to find my intrusive mother sitting on the La-Z-Boy, waiting to assail me or verify I had kept the law. It's a total shocker when I find nothing. Instead, I see a dim light illuminating the kitchen. My belly rumbles. Leftovers await me, and without hesitation, I thumb in two minutes on the microwave, then shortly thereafter fork down her homemade barbecue chicken, yellow rice, and candied yams.

She can cook! I can't take that away from her. After the day I've had, this is the perfect comfort food. I knew my tummy agreed when I climbed into bed and fell asleep in no time. Somehow, I felt a warm kiss on my forehead, instantly knowing the source. But I'm too drowsy to fight off my interfering, over-protective mother. *I am not five years old,* but I press into her endearment. It would appear right now I need consolation, and maybe that's why I let it slide.

The weekend flies by. On Sunday, I go into the living room to hand Daddy his card and tell him how much I strategically spent. He's surprised but says he knew I could do it. I head back to my room, but he stops me, saying he has to talk to me and Josh about something. With crossed arms, I pout to the couch. Josh turns off his game system and sits next to me. I roll my eyes, wondering how long this will take. I was thinking about designing flyers for makeup gigs this summer. But then, Maranda's rumor hits me, and I push pause on my new endeavor, hoping the hearsay dies down by then.

He calls my mother into the living room, and I actually look at her today. She's been sporting this same robe more than usual, with black rings around her eyes, and she seems fatigued. I wonder if she's been working. I guess she hasn't been, and maybe that's why Daddy is "cutting expenses." She's so selfish.

"We've told you that we're cutting expenses but not why. I think it's only fair that we let you in on what's going on."

He takes a deep breath that rubs me the wrong way, then wraps his arm around her. "Mom's been feeling a bit weak lately. She's been going to the doctor, and they've diagnosed her with an autoimmune disease named Lupus."

"What?" me and my brother say in unison and glare at each other.

Daddy continues. "We've uh, found a hospital willing to treat her in Manhattan." *Manhattan? Like New York? So we're moving? Again!*

"Lolly, I know you have prom and graduation coming up, but you might have to miss, sweetheart. I talked to your principal, he said we can have your diploma mailed."

Is he out of his mind?

"But Daddy! I just bought my dress!" I stand, fists balled at my side. I know I sound like a brat, but *I don't care.* I'm too furious to hide it.

"Mom, are you okay?" Josh interrupts, making my claim less-than, and my anger ignites.

"Is she okay? She's fine! Me, on the other hand, am about to miss the best days of my life because . . . because she's not feeling well?"

"Lolly!" Daddy yells. Seeing my words have no weight here, I start towards my room, and my mother grabs my arm.

"Lolly, it's okay, baby." I snatch it away. I don't see how it's all right when I will miss the ending of what I've worked so hard for and won't be able to enjoy it with all my friends.

The friends that are currently spreading rumors about you? Imaginary friends? I hear a voice inside I'd never heard before. I ignore it.

"Yeah, it will be okay if you would just stop . . . *dying,* long enough for me to go to prom!" I hurry to my room, knowing the words will have serious consequences.

"Lolly Cherice Pobs, come back here, young lady!" Daddy demands, trying to sound authoritative, but he can't. He's never talked to us that way, and it frightens me for the first time ever.

"Let her go," says Mom.

3

The Shift

Monday comes, and I'm numb. I go to school and couldn't care less what everyone is saying about me. I won't be here much longer for them to feed off me anyway. But judging by the gigantic sweater I threw over my outfit this morning, I can't decide if that's true.

I avoid Carter as long as I can until he approaches me in the hall. "Lolly, you ready for prom?" he says. His eyes look right into mine, and I get bashful.

"Of course," I say, knowing I'll be gone in a little while.

"Good," he says before walking away. I wonder why he didn't comment on the rumor.

One Week Later

My mother catches me in the kitchen, washing my plate, which never happens. The only reason *it is* happening is that I've been avoiding them at all costs. She comes too close for comfort, and I avoid eye contact.

"Lolly, sweetie, the last thing I want to do is take your high school experience away. I talked to your father and to the doctors in New York and persuaded them to hold off on my treatment until after graduation."

I stop washing my over-washed dish, and it hits the metal of the sink so hard I thought it would break.

I desperately look into her eyes. "You can't do that!" *Will she be in danger if she doesn't hop on this treatment plan?* I don't know why, but tears start to fall. Was it because I'd get to go to prom and graduation? Or is it just that I need my mommy? Stranger things have happened.

"It's already done, sweetheart." She pushes my hair out of my face and wipes my tears.

Without a second thought, I cave into her chest.

"Lolly baby? It's okay . . ."

I can tell she doesn't know how to handle me in this state because I've never been in it. She instinctively rubs my back. I think everything happening has finally taken its toll because right now, me being barricaded into her bear hug feels like a shelter. Then it automatically floats to strange. I pull away and run off to my room once again.

I now sit in the freezer that is my third period class. Mr. Franco, who stepped out to have papers copied of assignments due this week, gets hot flashes and sets the AC to very low temperatures that should be considered child abuse. He demanded we conduct ourselves as adults while he was away. His words hold no weight here. Chatter started at a whisper and has now escalated to a healthy roar. There's no way I am getting caught with these bozos, so I finish my assignment and slide my sketchbook out of my bag to draw up makeup ideas.

Out of the corner of my eye, I see wavy hair walk past our door. *Maranda!* She looks at Franco's empty desk, takes a few steps back, and walks into our classroom. An evil grimace comes over her face, and everyone grows quiet.

"Get out!" says the class clown. We giggle.

"Shut up, Jamal!" Maranda says, then asks, "Are y'all behaving?"

"Of course!" says Jamal. "You, on the other hand, can't afford to miss a class."

The class oohs. I play with my pencil and chuckle, knowing Jamal's right—*she needs ta go!*

"Whatever . . . It's my free," says Maranda. She bites her top lip, and her eyes shift to mine, then back at the door, looking out for our teacher.

"Lolly, did you choose a dress for prom yet?" Maranda walks towards me with a blue paper in her hand, a mean look on her face.

"She started the rumor," I hear someone whispering behind me.

I finally get the nerve to speak up. "Yeah, so?"

"Oh, you know, since you stole my date for prom," Maranda says.

Yikes, she went there. I proceed even though I'm feeling an urgency to stop.

"Awe, how sad. You're upset that Carter asked me to prom even after you asked him in that letter you wrote him." *Checkmate.*

"She asked him?" "She wrote him a letter?" my classmates whisper.

I look around and hear the sound of the rumors they'll soon spread, and false confidence comes out of me in a single chuckle. But I didn't want this . . . maybe I should've listened to that nudge, 'cause this makes me *just like her.*

"I . . . I didn't . . ." Maranda takes one step back.

"Miss Lewis, can I help you with something?" Mr. Franco walks in, and the intensity in the room weakens.

"No, thank you, Mr. Franco," she says in her sweetest voice

ever, covering her red horns. "I just had to give this to Lolly." She hands me the folded blue paper and walks out.

Mr. Franco continues teaching, and I open the paper. It's a flyer The Glitters and I posted this morning for graduation. Why would she give me this? Probably just to get herself out of trouble. I look at the bottom where it should say, "Flyers created by Lolly Pobs Glitter Committee." I smile in disbelief. It seems as if she'd scribbled over my name with a well-sharpened pencil.

Could anything more ridiculous be occurring in the world at this very moment? I think *not.* I never had an enemy *until now,* and I wish I had repellent for it.

At lunch, Addy has a huge grin stretched across her face, and I smile. "I dunno who you are anymore," she says. "You know with you waging war and all."

"I did not! I feel so bad about it."

"She had it coming, and you stood up for yourself."

I hug Addy, knowing I'll miss this when I'm gone. I haven't told her yet, holding out as long as I can. I'm still thinking about the voice I've heard lately and the tug I felt before I confronted Maranda.

What am I experiencing?

"Can you write me a letter next, Maranda?" A group of boys is circling her.

"Stop!" she screams and pushes through them.

It's horrible. Yes, I stood up for myself, but I know how it feels to be the one in the hot seat and don't wish it on anyone.

Prom Night

In front of my body mirror, I admire the swirls in my brown hair. A silvery headband lines the crown of my head, perfectly complementing the silver imprints on my powder pink gown. The top is haltered, the split on my thigh is high, and my bare leg peeks out. I clip on the necklace I got from MADE that matches my thin headband, which is made of wings.

Seven p.m. rolls around, and a knock at the front door prompts me to finish my makeup. The prom doesn't start till 8:30, but Carter says he wants to take me out for a spin. *Could he be trying to spend time with me?*

I hear my parents go to the door. I try to hurry down, not wanting Carter to know my mom's sick. Plus, sometimes Daddy can talk for ages. When I get there, my mother isn't in her robe. She's wearing a lovely dress and had applied makeup that's so pretty it could've been done by me. I smile in approval.

Everyone oohs and aahs at my dress. Carter places a silver corsage on my wrist, and pictures click for several minutes. My side view catches mom getting weak. She's holding on to the couch, and thankfully Carter's back is to her.

I hurry over and whisper, "Mom, are you okay?" before helping her onto the couch.

"Yeah, sweetie, I just—"

"Mom, please don't ruin my night!" I say bluntly before walking back to Carter and signing for Daddy to stop talking so we can leave. Mom's teary-eyed, and even though I know they're just crocodile tears, something inside me wants to go back and soothe her like she comforted me. But I look away because I don't have time for her theatrics.

We get in the car and drive off. I stare at the front door, hoping she'll be okay while I'm gone. Carter looks very handsome in his suit and tie. He goes through different neighborhoods before stopping at a pier. I look around and see it's super dark. I gulp.

"It's so quiet," I say before he leans over to me. I immediately back away.

"Whoa, Carter!"

"I know you want me, Lolly. Everyone knows you want me." He comes at me again.

So you mean to tell me he thought the rumor about me being easy was true? *That's why he didn't mention it.* The realization cuts deep.

"No I don't!" I yell and get out of the car and slam the door.

"Lolly, wait!" Carter's voice startles me.

I step away from him but hear him say, "I probably read things wrong, but you always flaunted your body around, looking for the attention. I mean, you're showing it off now."

My hand immediately cuffs the start of the slit revealing my thigh, the other around my shoulders to cover me up. "I'm not like that," I say, holding back tears. I had worn all my outfits for fashion, not to be seen as an object, but obviously, that's what others saw.

He sees the sadness in my eyes and exhales. "Let's just go to prom." He points at his car, and I look at it like it's an escaped gorilla. I shake my head no and pull my phone out.

"Who are you calling?" Carter panics, and I start to walk on the sidewalk. "Lolly, are you gonna tell people?"

That's what he's worried about right now, his rep?

He runs up next to me, reaching for my phone. I stumble back and whimper.

"Just get in the car!" he shouts.

I turn away, digging my heels into the pavement, trying to create space between us. I wipe my tears quickly, so they won't mess up my flawless makeup. It's hard, though, and new ones fall. Carter's critical words affected me. I'm starting to think of myself in a way I'm not proud of. I hear his car start and briskly reverse, and my heart leaps in fear.

"Lolly, get in the car please. I'm sorry, I'll take you to prom."

"No, Carter."

He thinks a moment. "Fine!" Then Carter speeds off, leaving me stranded. I'm in complete awe, and I laugh in astonishment. Through my tears, I call Addison and tell her what happened.

We go into the bathroom when we arrive at prom, and Addison helps me wipe up my ruined makeup before applying a new layer. My hands are shaking too much to hold anything straight right now.

"He's such a jerk, Lolly! I so didn't think he was like that! He and Maranda deserve each other!"

I smile, trying not to generate more tears but sniffle. Somehow, Addison always finds a way to defend me. "Is it like my fault? Maybe Maranda *was* right about me?"

"Lolly, you don't seriously believe that, do you? Maranda's wrong; Carter's wrong!" She says, "No more crying. He's not worth it!" I nod in agreement and then look in the mirror. It looks like nothing ever happened.

Chris is waiting for Addison. He's the boy from another school because, obviously, all the guys at *our school* are lame. Another guy is standing next to him, and they're both good-looking.

"This is Chris and his friend Bryan," says Addy.

I look at Bryan, wondering if he'll be cool playing the plus one. We're immersed in talk and laughter.

"Let's dance," Chris says, taking Addy to the dance floor, but not before she winks at us.

"I thought I was gonna be the third wheel," Bryan confesses.

"I thought I was gonna be at prom dateless." I smile, but he grows serious.

"Huh? Addison said you had a date."

"Yeah, he ended up being a jerk!"

Bryan laughs. "Well, you can't let him see you just sitting here. You gotta show him what he's missing out on." He stands up and puts out his hand.

"True!" I say and insert mine into his as he leads me to the floor.

He yells over loud music as we two-step.

"Nice dress. You're really beautiful."

I smile shyly. Bryan seems sweet, but Carter's words throw daggers my way. I step closer to Bryan. His heroic efforts make me feel comfortable enough to ask, "It's not . . . too revealing?"

He scoffs, "No. I've seen girls wear far less. Your dress is perfect." Bryan twists me around, and my confidence grows. There's a hint of something else, an extra barrier that wasn't there before. I hope Carter didn't ruin my outlook on guys. I happen to look up, and my eyes meet Carter's. He's with Maranda but staring intently at me. I disconnect my gaze and warn my bones not to move since I refused to let him intimidate me.

A slow song comes on, and we go limp, but Bryan moves quickly, putting his hand out and bowing. I take it, and he sweeps me off my feet.

"See 'em?" Bryan asks.

"Yeah, he's at table eleven, with the girl in the purple dress."

He swings me around and takes a look for himself. "Serious eye contact," he says, and we laugh. I feel like a princess the way he's carrying me across the ballroom.

The song changes again, and Addy and Chris find us. We're all jumping and enjoying the music. Prom turned out to be totally amazing.

Graduation Day

Bryan asks for my number, and I don't see the harm in giving it. After all, he saved my prom night, plus I know nothing will come from it because I'm leaving in a few days. We're actually graduating on the same day. He sends a selfie, and I reciprocate with my cap on, wearing the black dress I begged Daddy for. I put on my graduation gown and arrive early with The Glitters and Addison to set up.

We created the banner hanging near the stage for graduation. The gold lettering over a white background and a splash of maroon flowers was impressive. It simply said: "Happy Grad Day, We Made It!"

We did make it—even Maranda, even Carter. After a while, people got over the rumor. Maranda seemed more reserved and humble and never bothered me again. Carter just always stared at me. He seemed to want to say something, but he didn't. It was probably for the better.

My name gets called. I walk up in victory, then across the stage, waving my diploma in the air, feeling fulfilled! My classmates cheer, and my mother and father stand. Suddenly, my mom faints and my smile is erased as I run off stage. Everyone is confused and whispering. We get to the back.

"Mom, are you okay?" I ask.

Next to me, Addison says, "Lolly, what happened?"

I don't answer because this is not the way I want her to find out. I grind my teeth. "You just had to take the spotlight, didn't you? You're so embarrassing. We might as well pack up and go to New York right now!"

"New York?" Addison is lost. "Lolly, don't start!"

I can't take Daddy's newfound tone. I start to sob and run out, and Addison follows.

"Cher!" she calls.

I turn to face her once and for all. "I didn't want to tell you, okay? Not yet . . . but we're leaving. My mom has Lupus, and she needs to get treatment in New York, or she'll die."

"Oh no, Lolly!" Addison pulls me into her tight embrace. "This is huge. You should've told me, Cher. You know you can tell me anything!" She starts to cry.

"I'm sorry. I just thought if I didn't say it out loud, it wouldn't be true."

Addy's hands wrap around me, and we sob together.

4

A Small Push

Fortunately, Grand races down the shortcut he found one day when he was about to be late for school. He swiftly glides into his seat right before the last bell rings for late students.

"Grandpa can run!" calls out a classmate, and the class roars in laughter. Grand slouches in his seat.

"That's enough, class," says Mrs. Blake. Grand is used to it because of his name and albinism, a condition that causes very pale skin and orange hair that makes him stick out in crowds.

Rachel Simon flashes in his mind, and nothing else matters. She'll be in his next period, and he watches the clock tick. The bell finally rings, and students rush to the door. Three paper balls fly in the air, striking Grand's head. He looks back at the culprits, Luke Nelson and his two tagalongs, Mark and Cam. They rip past Grand, who huffs but remains quiet. He continues his stride to Rachel. He longed to see her long dark hair that made her pink lips stand out. He could watch her talk for hours. Not only is she beautiful, but she's a humanitarian, always working on projects to help the needy. The late bell rings, but Rachel is nowhere to be found. He declares it's gonna be a long day.

Lunchtime hits, and Grand walks into the cafeteria, spotting Rachel midway. His mood brightens. *Why wasn't she in class?*

"In your dreams," a girl's voice rings through. He hazily looks toward the redhead leaning against the wall. "That's Rachel Simon, and she only dates athletes." How does she know he was looking at Rachel *specifically?*

"I wasn't loo—"

"You're albino, aren't you? Your skin is so white, but I love carrot tops."

Who is she? Grand wondered. She just called out his insecurities in such a smooth way.

"Huh?" is the only thing he can get out before she starts talking again.

"I'm trying to save you some embarrassment. Why don't you try for an easier catch, *like me.* The name's Ci, short for Jessica, 'cause Jess is so overrated."

The statement stuns him. Is Ci saying she's not on Rachel's level?

"Here's the plan . . . I'll buy you a slice of pizza, we can sit together, *and* talk about Rachel." She puts her arm around his neck and drags him towards the express line.

At the end of lunch, his head is swimming with information about girls he doesn't need to know. About the number of times Rachel broke up with a guy, Ci's thoughts on skipping college and moving to California to live a Hollywood lifestyle *on a bus* and with romance. The more he studied her, the more she looked like a hippie with a colorful headband squeezed around her dark red, messy yet still straight hair.

Second period hits the next day, and a breathless Rachel runs in just before the last bell. She hands a letter to Mrs. Jan.

"You were working on a school project during my class, Ms. Simon?"

"Yes, Mrs. Jan. I'm sorry I missed, but Mr. Glover approved it."

"We're not worthy to breathe your same air, Rachel. Take a seat."

Grand wondered why Mrs. Jan was being so rude to her. She had a note from the principal himself, which is excusable to a T. Grand is overcome by Rachel's presence and doesn't retain a thing Mrs. Jan teaches.

At lunch, Ci makes him sit with her again.

"So last month, Rhonda hooked up with Rachel's dude, he's a basketball player, *obviously*. Anyways, she just found out after last period's bell."

Grand jumps up. "What? We gotta find her!"

"And say what? You're not exactly in her circle, boy wonder."

"But you know her . . ."

"I went to middle school with her."

He looks over at Rachel, surrounded by her friends.

"So, I was thinking, after she gets over *said* basketball player, you can swoop in and make your move," Ci says.

"What are you talking about?"

"You're like, in love with her."

"She doesn't even know who I am!" Grand says, annoyed.

"Introduce yourself," Ci says like it's no biggy, but he ponders it. "Wait," she continues, "have you ever kissed a girl?"

Grand shakes his head.

"Here, try it on me." Ci leans forward and puckers up, and Grand backs up abruptly. "You got some learning to do," she says, plugging her number in his phone and telling him to call her for tips.

Early the next day, Grand spots Rachel at her locker. He whispers what he is going to say to her. "Hi, Rachel, I'm Grand," he says, extending his hand. *No.* "Hi, Rachel, did you do the homework?" *She's smart. Of course she did!*

"Grand, hey, what's up?" He looks up, and it's Rachel. He hadn't noticed his black shoes had been making their way to her like magnets.

"Hi Rachel. I . . . was just . . . I was just . . ."

She looks at him patiently.

"Rachel! Come on!" her fellow cheerleaders call from down the hall.

"Coming! I'll see you in class, Grand, okay?"

"Okay." Grand blinks a thousand times. *She knew his name.* Grand scans the lunchroom for Ci, but she's nowhere to be found. He completed step one and it worked, but he needs to know what to do next. Grand turns around, and Rachel's standing in front of him. He freezes.

"Hey, Grand, you needed something?"

He draws from the confidence he had earlier. "Yeah, I just wanted to know if you completed the homework. I was gonna offer to help." He mentions one of the questions he'd thought of, baffled he chose that one.

"Did Mrs. Jan say something?" Rachel crosses her arms and looks down. This is more than he bargained for.

"No, I just assumed . . ."

"It's okay. I just don't have time, you know, with cheerleading and projects. But if I fail her class, I won't be able to stay in my honors programs."

She starts to tear up; this is the opportunity he wanted to comfort her, but how?

"I can help. We can have study sessions. I can call you, help you stay on top of things?" He pulls at his collar to help him breathe.

"You'd do that for me?"

Of course I would. I'd do anything. "Yeah . . ." Grand says out loud.

She grabs his phone, and he peeks to see if this is really happening. She hits *save* and hands it back. "Thank you so much, Grand." She hugs him and walks away.

He's stunned as Ci walks up. "Was that Rachel Simon? What'd I miss?"

At home, he stares at his phone, wondering if he should call Rachel.

"Grand! Dinner is ready. Come eat!"

"Ma, it's early!"

"I said, come eat!" They sit at the dinner table, and she says, "Boy, what are you doing with yourself?"

"What do you mean, Ma?"

"You need to get a job to help me pay bills,"

"I didn't know you needed help, Ma. I'll start looking."

"You need to take care of me like I took care of you."

"Of course, Ma. I got you," he says. He finishes dinner quickly so he can call Rachel.

"Hello? Rachel? It's Grand." She was probably too busy saving the world to remember he'd call.

"Grand, I've been waiting on your call!"

"Really? I'm sorry, I should've called sooner. Um . . . You got your textbook?"

After helping Rachel with a couple of tricky problems, she says, "Hey, you made that fun. Thank you."

"You were an easy tutoree." *That isn't even a word!* He slaps his forehead, but Rachel just giggles.

"You're really sweet! I'm having a fundraiser for girls in group homes who wanna go to college but don't have funds to. Do you wanna come?"

Grand is even more amazed by Rachel. "Of course, I'm coming," he says.

5
A Plug for an Outlet

Pain. The kind that's still relevant even after a while and recedes beyond being patient for something to *eventually* change. Pain that doesn't have an easy fix or way out. The kind that has a chain around a person's neck, giving them inner blisters and bruises.

That was William's reality. Misery followed him, replacing his own shadow. He'd been looking for a remedy, some sort of outlet that made him think about anything other than the suffering he'd been inflicting on others. He'd like to think he wasn't all bad and had good in him. Memories of his life before this one flashed in his head as proof.

He had parents who adored him and gave him the world. They'd taken him to church every Sunday when he was a child. On one occasion, he made his way up to the altar and accepted Jesus into his heart as his Lord and Savior. He smiled at that memory. But somehow, that didn't save him from the furnace he was now in, and his fists tightened with grief, not caring if his nails dug in deep. They plucked out blood, but the pain was satisfactory. He looks at his injured hand. The incisions he created quickly heal before his eyes until they are completely gone. A pity, that high never lasted.

They had a happy little life, but true happiness seemed so far away now. All that was left was the life he'd been implanted into— a world full of wickedness, killing, and monstrous behavior.

William gets up from his oversized bed, grabs his keys, and heads out of the front door. He couldn't sit surrounded by four walls and remain sane, enduring haunting thoughts mixed with beautiful memories that made him hope and wish his life had gone differently. But it hadn't, it wasn't going to, and nothing could separate him from this exasperating life. He had to get to his hiding place to find tranquility and peace.

He drove to his usual spot in a wooded area and walked through the trees. The air had the aroma of fresh rain, and the foliage hovered over him, providing shade and just a bit of renewed sun. He sat down on the grass, leaning on the trunk of his usual tree, and closed his eyes. The wind swiftly blew against him, his soul finally at rest. Nature sounds filled his ears, followed by an all-too-familiar vibration sound in his pocket. Annoyed, he grabs his phone.

"Hello?" His voice was groggy from not speaking until now.

"Hey cowboy, I got that stuff. Usual spot?" said a female voice.

"Yeah, sure, just give me a minute."

"Lemme know when you're on your way."

The receiver disconnects, and William enjoys where he is a little longer. The silence blends with his spirit. *The serenity . . . The not having to control it all* or have it all own him. He hears the butterflies' wings fluttering instead of his victims' screams. He sees the fish's fins flapping as they jump out of the water instead of limp limbs falling to finality. He notices birds' beaks ripping worms out of their socket instead of cracked necks on cold bodies.

William looks out at the dark lake with hopeful eyes. It calls him like a zombie consumed by the urge to spill blood. He makes his way to it, shoulders slightly slumped from the pressure of the burden he bears in agony.

He stares at the lake, seeing it as a lifeline, before bending to his knees and placing his trembling hands in a puddle of New York water. He then runs his fingers through his dark hair, letting the excess drip onto his face and neck for relief. His superhumanity could cause his hair and skin to burn at temperatures above four hundred degrees Fahrenheit. But the cool water wakes him, reminding him he was human *first*. He sucks in a sharp breath, then clears his throat at the shock of the freezing douse. Then all his crisp white teeth arise because it could still burn him.

He wipes the water droplets off, then calls to the One who owns it all: "Where are You? I can't feel You anymore *Gaw . . .*" *God,* he means to say, but his Maker's name can't fasten onto his lips.

He sobs. "Gaw . . ." he chokes on the word. William would scream His name into the forest, then into the whole world if he could, but his invisible chains refuse it. He lets up numb, as usual. The torment in his being scrapes at his bones, not letting him think straight. He knows if he could reach the Almighty, he *would* get relief. Defeated, he puts off his call to God once more, knowing it is sin that separates him from the Father. He moves forward to the phone call.

"Tams?" he says, and a curvy figure emerges from behind computers in a dark office.

"Ore or William? Which is it today?"

"I never like to be the monster, so William it is."

"William it is . . ." Tammy winks.

"You got the goods?" He pulls a stapler from across the room. It flies and drops into his hands.

"Yeah, you think you can transport them fine?" she asks.

William says, "I've taken bigger cargo." He grins as he clamps down on the tool and flings staples about for sport.

"Okay, but this is sensitive cargo," Tammy says in a low,

seductive voice. She retrieves the delicate merchandise from behind a desk, then walks toward him as carefully as possible. "One blueberry pie recipe and two homemade pies to hold you over, *William it is.*"

He chuckles. "Thanks, Tams."

With power, he swooshes each staple he caught back into the stapler, then grabs the pies and stuffs the recipe in his pocket.

"It's Grandma's recipe, so don't you go sharing it with no one but Elo, ya hear?" She gets closer, using a tender voice.

"Top secret mission, the highest rank," William says and walks away from her.

Tammy follows, with her curly blonde hair swaying as she walks. "Good. Wouldn't wanna use my gadgets to come to look for you, cowboy." She doesn't hide her flirtation and bites her bottom lip to emphasize it, but he doesn't seem to notice her advances.

"Don't wanna mess with the FBI," William says. His colorful eyes cause her to buffer, but she finally loads. Tammy frowns, knowing her friend may never see her as anything but.

"What mission does kata have you on as of late?" she asks.

"You know, the usual—assassination, murder for hire, abduction, and over and over again. Just helping to carry out the destruction of the world."

"Whoa . . . pre-tay deep."

"Yeah, got a shoulder to lend?"

"You got my shoulder anytime, you know where my place is," Tammy says.

William looks at his comrade, knowing he could easily get in. But *one*, she was one of his only friends, and *two,* she was his deep connection to the government. He wasn't the type to catch feelings; if Tammy did, it would be a big mess. He calms the thoughts she manifested and pretends he didn't hear her.

"Thanks for the recipe. You won't make them for me on a daily basis, so I'll have Eloise make 'em."

"Who has time to bake? Oh yeah, people whose jobs consists of cooking and cleaning all day, like Eloise!" Her country accent carries her words. "You know, I breathe, sleep, and eat the government. I keep this place running. I'm only twenty-three, with no boyfriend, a two-seater, and an orange cat named Noodle. I just don't have time, and you eat them thangs like clockwork." Tammy is ranting with girly emotions, and William doesn't know how to respond at first. His eyes twitch.

He doesn't get what the commotion is about. Tammy's problems are typical and fixable. His challenges are . . . not so much. He heard once that if people threw their problems into a pile and saw everyone else's, they'd take theirs back.

"I get it, you're busy," he says and puts his hand on her shoulder. Her eyes radiate, and he removes it. "I, on the other hand, wait around to carry out orders that lead to a bad day and a funeral for someone's family."

A light bulb goes off in her head. "You need something to fill your days? What about that tournament going on at Scoffs Warehouse on Eighth and Main?"

William is intrigued. "What tournament?"

"You don't know about Scoffs! Oh, you should go! You'll win the whole dang thang with Ore's power."

"Details?" he asks, something coming alive inside.

"Warriors from different planets come here to fight for the number one spot and win money. It's only happening for seven days. Starts today." "

Eighth and Main," he mumbles and walks to the door.

"Well, you goin'?" Tammy yells.

William is gone before she gets an answer.

How could he have missed this? He puts on sweats and a tank top, then packs a duffle bag. Could this be the outlet he'd been searching for to untangle all his frustration? He gets in his car and plugs in the two streets. Twenty minutes later, he pulls up to a massive sign on the gray building that says *Scoffs Warehouse* in orange and red. His eyebrows raise, wondering about the lot's emptiness. His motor rumbles as he pulls up and climbs out. If Tammy says there's something here, *there's something here.*

A green ring of light bounces off him, and he penetrates a forcefield that came before sliding doors. He looks around in search of any danger. Sensing none, he continues his stride. The doors smoothly roll away, granting him access to another world.

His eyes grow wide at all the different creatures casually walking around. He'd seen a few supernatural beings on earth before, but they were scarce because God didn't allow them to roam the planet. Those here had a strict decree against showing themselves to humans. If it happened, they'd be punished by banishment from the earth for good. So far, he was an exception to that rule.

"Tickets, please!" A husky, rough-looking guard in the form of a large pig man holds up hooves in demand at the entry booth. A stench fills the area. The dirt marks and dried hay matted on his skin proved why. William gagged at the recipe and resisted the temptation to block his nose.

"I don't have one," William managed to say, and a ripped frog, smaller than the pig man, speaks.

"What do you mean you don't have one, kid?"

William's attention shifts to the frog, and others behind him complain about the smell.

The frog pulls William away from the smell, saying, "Yo, how does he still work here!"

Appreciative, William breathes the fresh air.

"He gets the job done, kid, but did you register?"

William's attention is on strange-looking people coming in through flashing portals, but he still answers, "Nah."

The frog sizes him up. "No registration, no entry, no exceptions."

Still staring at them, William shrugs. What could they be? He then walks off. Not getting his way irritates him.

"Aye kid! Wait up." The frog runs. William continues on.

"Look, can you throw down?" asks the frog.

"Waste of my time," William says.

"I can get you in," says the frog.

William stops. Now the frog is speaking his language.

They get to the frog's desk with a lengthy window held open by two sticks on each side.

The frog whispers, "I could use your help."

"What?" William asks, puzzled. What could the frog possibly want from him? He doesn't even know him.

"The last Game, my brother lost to this cat named Akeem, and I got it in for him, ya know. He's undefeated, but you got somethin' no one else's got. I see it."

William scoffs. "That's how I get in? I can do that." Again, the frog is speaking his lingo. He got used to these types of rendezvous all of his adult life. But he can't help thinking being used gets tiring. It followed him around. Nevertheless, he wants this, so he agrees.

"I knew you'd be the one. I'm Peen. What's your name?"

"Ore." The frog takes out paperwork for William to sign and then faxes it.

"Do you know about the fight, Ore? Do you have wheels?" Peen asks.

"Do I . . . have a car?" William says.

Peen sighs and says, "God himself must be on your side, kid, because I'm not usually this helpful."

William thinks about how he tried to pray at the lake. Could this be an answer? *From God . . .*

"Fights are picked at random that require a cycle. It's a game of tag. Whoever pulls the flag from the other's bike throws the first hit."

"Oh, I don't have one."

"Just in case, come through the door." He presses the loud buzzer that sounds until William opens the door.

"Why do I get myself involved? Oh that's right, my hot-tempered brother!" Peen says.

A heap of two- and four-wheelers sit for selection. They're colorful and have metal all around as protective gear. Nothing ever really excites William, but he looks around in awe. He comes across a blue two-wheeler that says *Royal* and gets on.

"Of course you pick Royal. Akeem won with that one last year," says Peen, his face turning sour. "You know how to ride?" asks Peen.

"No, but I'm a fast learner."

Peen gulps. "How old are you?"

"I'm twenty-one."

"Oh boy."

William kicks the stopper and carries the hunk of metal to a better position. Peen was deceived by his slight, lean, muscular build that hid his strength. He takes Ore to the back for practice. He jumps on the bike, immediately taking off like a natural, only stopping a few times to adjust. He pulls a wheelie.

"Wow, I gotta see what you can do in the arena."

"Oh, it's over," says William.

"I'm betting money on your first fight," says Peen, his eyes twinkling.

It was tough for William to put the bike back. It made him feel alive and free.

"What's the meaning of this, Peen!" A tall, muscular man with a Russian accent sweeps a paper across Peen's desk.

"Mr. Scoff!" says Peen. He scurries to grab the paper. "It's a late entry!"

Scoff puts his finger on the desk, "No registration, no entry, no exceptions!"

6

Let the Games Begin

"No, Mr. Scoff. I am simply just putting it in; it was my mistake."

Nathan Scoff looks at William, then back to Peen. "You think this is acceptable, do you?"

"No sir, but he's a great fighter."

Mr. Scoff eases up. "I assume you're Ore?"

William looks at Mr. Scoff's slacks, collared shirt, and Rolex. As a businessman, he can respect his prerogative to run a smooth-sailing business.

"Yeah."

"Peen, your brother's defeat has you very . . . *emotional*. I run a tight business, but Jonathan isn't here." He chooses his words carefully. "Let him through, and don't let this happen again."

"Yes, sir," says Peen. Mr. Scoff grabs the paper he initially threw.

"Make sure! I'm in charge of these goons, and anyone out of place falls on my head."

Peen nods.

"Has he paid the registration fee? I have yet to see the funds."

"Uh . . ." Peen realizes he forgot about it. *My brother does have me emotional*, he thinks to himself.

Nathan's annoyance grows.

"How much?" asks William.

Nathan answers, "Fifteen hundred."

Nathan's Russian accent mixed with anger almost makes William laugh, but he doesn't.

"No problem," says William.

Scoff looks at Peen. "I expect to see it paid and processed immediately." He steps away.

Peen gives William the account information.

"Done," says William.

"What do you mean *done*? Done what?"

"I transferred it over."

"You were just standing there staring at a piece of paper," says Peen. He looks at his computer. "*You transferred it over . . .* it's done," he says in amazement. Peens excitement lessens. "You shouldn't be able to use your gift in this building." He whispers even lower, "Don't let anyone see you use it. It should only activate in the arena. Who are you, kid?" Peen curiously asks.

"Peen!" Scoff yells from across the room.

Peen quivers, knocking down a cup of pens.

With a big smile, Scoff gives a thumbs up, okaying the transfer.

Peen crosses his arms. "You're a wonder, kid. You pin your opponent down in the red circle at the center of the arena for sixty seconds, or make them surrender. Everything goes, so don't die out there, kid!"

"Not possible. I tried it," William says nonchalantly. Peen looks puzzled but doesn't comment. "What happen to your brother?" he asks Peen.

"He surrendered. Akeem's a vampire, and he was gonna rip out his throat with those teeth. After you surrender, you can't show your face around here again. You kapeesh?"

William nods.

As they sit and wait for Ore's name to be called, a strange-looking group dressed in preppy attire walks in. A huge guy with golden dreads leads them. A girl with a plaited skirt, matching jacket, long socks, and white-collared shirt holds his bulky arm. She notices William's curious eyes and rolls hers at him. He chuckles.

Three other guys and a girl with short blonde hair are with them. One of their arms hangs around her shoulders.

"Vampires. The one with the dreads is Akeem," says Peen.

"I figured," says William.

"I'm fighting who?" says someone from around the corner, which captures everyone's attention.

William and Peen speed walk to see what's happening. A crowd builds around the vampires. The brunette with the plaited skirt stands in front of him, trying to keep him from pouncing on the person behind the information desk.

"Akeem, calm down," she says.

"I'm not fighting some newbie, Von. They need to give me one of the champs. Get me Scoff, now!" he yells.

Peen and William walk back to their spot. "Someone on their team wins every year. They will probably draw straws to decide who'll get it this year," says Peen, laughing.

"He called me a newbie," says William, who laughs like a toddler taking a toy that doesn't belong to him. "Hope Akeem didn't draw it this year."

Peen pats William on the back, "Like I said, my money's on you, kid." Peen chooses the best spot for Ore to glimpse what's to come.

William looks at the crowd, "What are they? They look like humans."

"No humans are allowed here," says Peen. "The group of people that has antlers and glossy skin are called the 'Similory' because of their resemblance to the human race." They're the people he'd seen exiting the portals.

"They're from Planet Vaimos," he says. "Like the contestants, they get teleported here. We have separate quarters that house them for seven days. They're sent back after. The Big Guy upstairs won't let them stay longer."

They turn back to the arena as the warriors switch off. William squints. The orange fighter has explosives in all sizes everywhere. He grins, deciding it will be wild.

The announcer says, "On one end is 'Tremor the Barbaric' from the tribe of Acula, weighing in at two hundred and fifty pounds."

The crowd cheers and Tremor raises both fists. "I am my people's champ, and today I seek victory on their behalf."

A cluster of cheering lizard people share a small area in the crowd, and they're louder than anyone else.

"I'm gonna make you tremble, enemy!" Tremor declares with a deep voice. The crowd roars.

"On the other side, weighing in at two hundred and seventy pounds is Cannon, the one they call 'The Great Warrior.'"

"Cannon! Cannon! Cannon!" they cry out and clap for him.

"Thank you; thank you," says Cannon. "I don't particularly care to speak, other than to say I'm gonna whoop some lizard tail tah-night!"

His country accent makes William chuckle. It's thicker than Tammy's. The crowd roars again, still neutral to their choice of the winner.

"Fight!" The announcer calls. Cannon is on all fours, rushing to his enemy. His hair extends out, turning into a fierce black and orange lion. The lizard creeps on the ground, his large tail swinging from side to side. Black and blue smoke pumped up with lightning surround the lizard. He disappears, then reappears above the lion.

Cannon doesn't see his opponent. Tremor wraps his slimy

limbs around him, sending rounds of unrelenting electricity through him. The lion wrenches in excruciating pain, and he lets out a colossal roar.

Cannon rolls around, pounding and scraping the lizard's body into the ground. He reaches back, pinches Tremor's skin with his claws, and launches him into the air. Tremor finds the land, the air hits the abrasions on his back, and he twitches. Tremor angrily repositions himself before the lying lion and charges at him. The shock dust he provided Cannon should've demobilized him by now.

Cannon's breathless from fighting the electric shockwaves. He can feel it in each of his organs as they continuously contract and grow to remedy the internal turmoil. He gathers the strength to stand, watching the reptile speedily squirming towards him. His insides have become entwined within him, and he backflips to stretch them, landing far from the desperate lizard to recuperate.

Tremor's confusion grows. "How can Cannon still be mobile!" he says in dismay.

Before he can turn back, Cannon makes his hands grow ten times larger than usual and wraps them around the lizard's over-sized neck.

The crowd goes wild, rising to their feet. Cannon chokes Tremor and is repeatedly whacking Tremor's entire body against the arena wall. Cannon throws him to the side like a rag doll, then takes time to catch his breath again.

The lizard doesn't get up, and the crowd screams in delight. Cannon grabs the grenades at his side.

"What are you doing?" Tremor asks and cocks his head to the side.

Cannon's mouth fills with pins. He throws multiple grenades and runs off. They combust on the creature, and smoke fills the air.

William is exhilarated. He stands to see if the lizard made it or not, and Peen pumps his fists in victory. Dust begins to clear, and the crowd is quiet. Cannon breathes heavily, awaiting the results. The Similory people are amazed!

The lizard's limbs and tail are detached from its center. Cannon raises his arms in victory. "You should've shut your pie hole with all that bragging, buddy."

Tremor grunts while pushing and pushing, sweat building on his skin. Two arms plunge out of his sides, followed by two legs, but he's exhausted.

"You mangy mutt!" calls Cannon.

"Wait. I have a debt to pay. I need the prize money to pay it off in American currency," Tremor says between breaths.

"And? If you can't beat me, what makes you think you can beat Akeem? The good Lord says I'm winning this year, so surrender now or you're toast!"

"We do not surrender in Acula! I have already used most of our group power. They won't stand a chance against the Obsidian."

"Sounds like a personal problem," says Cannon.

Seeing the lion is unwilling to help, Tremor attempts his master move. He draws spit from the pit of his stomach, then, with a big breath, splashes it on Cannon. Green sewage-like slime covers the lion.

It starts to burn his skin, and he yells, "You wretched thang, you!"

Tremor pushes Cannon down as his digestive compounds do their work. He opens up his mouth as wide as it will go and positions it over Cannon. His consumption of Cannon is at fifty percent. Cannon wiggles around, his wails muffled. Blood rolls as Tremor's teeth cut away at Cannon's flesh. Cannon quickly grabs more grenades and shoots them into the open pockets of Tremor's mouth.

Tremor feels each metal weight drop in, and he pulls back in an attempt to spit them out. But Cannon's hands swell and clamp down around Tremor's nozzle. Tremor's eyes grow wide as he receives the bombs into his abdomen.

"Attah boy. It's a big meal, isn't it? Enjoy," says Cannon.

The lizard fights to move, but Cannon is too strong. "I'll win this tournament and help your family; you got my word," he says, but it doesn't ease Tremor's torment.

The grenades go off in Tremor's stomach, and the green goop erupts in every direction. The crowd cheers and the announcer says, "Cannon for the win!"

William is pleased and ready to go, but Preen explains that more will come. "The winner of each round will go against each other until there are only two. The last contestants will face off, and the winner takes home twenty Gs."

"Twenty Gs? That's how much a life is worth?" William asks.

The cleaners come out and remove the residue and grime.

Next Round

Announcer: "Vonvex is up, weighing in at one hundred and twenty-five pounds." The crowd goes wild. "Her opponent, weighing in at one hundred and fifty pounds, is Nora Escobar!"

Some cheer; most boo. Still, Nora confidently extends her hand. An anxious look flashes on her face, but she blurs it with a smile.

"Why are they booing her?" William asks.

"Vonvex is Jonathan Scoff's daughter, the owner of this arena. Anyone who goes against her is disliked by the people."

Vonvex, the chick that was walking with Akeem, William thinks.

Nora's long white braided ponytail hangs down her back, her black clothing presses tightly against her exquisitely dark complexion. Her family is from the snowy mountains far away. They stay away, making her a rare contestant. Her family's strict boundaries caused her to rebel against them, seeking fun at The Games.

"Begin!" the announcer calls. Vonvex twists her way to her counter, only stopping to pull on her hoodie. Nora's pupils glow green as she runs towards Vonvex, pulling her blades and twirling them in her hands. She'd mastered hunting, and this was no different.

The girls have a heated battle. Von takes off her hoodie. She didn't think she would have to put in any effort, but this year's competition is killer. Vonvex exposes her teeth a bit, but Nora doesn't flinch. In record speed, she kicks Nora's knives out of her hands with a turn, then backhands her.

Nora holds her mouth, blood rolls down her chin, and it calls out to Von. Von is breathing heavily, veins protruding from her neck. Nora backs up, sensing her predator wants to eat. Nora starts to twitch, marble hair sprouts from her skin, and her bones pop. Her eyes turn an aqua blue.

A werewolf now growls at Vonvex and charges at her. A whip of her claws rips the skin off Von's chest. She wails, glaring at the wound, knowing her gang won't be forgiving if she loses. Vonvex quickly goes behind Nora and chokes the wolf, pinning her to the ground. In the blink of an eye, Nora turns back into a human. Vonvex opens her mouth so wide that her face is transfigured. She pulls out her teeth to bite Nora's neck.

"No! My family!" cries Nora, raising her hand in surrender.

Peen leans over to William to explain. "If bitten, she'll be a vampire and won't be accepted back into her clan."

"Vonvex takes the crown!" the announcer yells, and the crowd cheers.

"Ore, you're up!" the coordinator calls. Peen and William walk toward the arena entrance.

7

Up To Pitch

Peen and William pass Nora yelling at the coordinator, "I told you no vampires!" Then they step by Vonvex walking out of the arena doors. She sniffs the air. William wondered if he was seeing things.

"Best wishes, stud," Vonvex says, smirks, and cuts her throat with an invisible knife.

Ore ignores her. *That's what she thinks* he decides.

This will be an awesome distraction, just a getaway from having to do the devil's dirty work all the time. He walks onto the dirt ground and mounts the motorcycle labeled *Royal*.

The announcer says, "On one side lies Akeem, weighing in at two hundred and ten pounds." The crowd cheers. "On the other stands Ore, weighing in at one hundred forty-five pounds." The crowd laughs at the difference, and Akeem joins them.

William stands his ground. *I'll show 'em.* A cleaned-up Von walks onto the field and stands by Akeem's side as he jumps onto his four-wheeler. Von's arms are crossed, and they look like they're arguing.

William looks around at the waste of his time. Akeem dodges Von's kiss and pushes her. Defeated, she walks off the battlefield. A thought about having someone someday flashes through William's head, but he quickly dismisses it.

The two men start up their motors.

"Begin!" says the announcer.

Each fighter circles around the lining of the arena. They head toward each other at full speed when they hit the center. They dodge one another, but Akeem comes too close, grabbing for Ore's tag. He laughs when William slides his wheel away from him. "Ready, newbie? I'll take it easy on you, don't worry."

Akeem tries to tease him. "I don't know . . . your girl did that and almost lost."

William grins."Funny, man. I'm gonna wipe that smirk off your face!"

Akeem puffs and races towards him, and William does the same, neither man backing down.

At the last minute, William unnaturally slows his rate. He backs his bike up to the side, using his ability to control metal. Done so swiftly, Akeem unknowingly zooms right by him.

William snatches his flag with ease. Akeem turns around with a smirk on his face at Ore's retreat. William holds the red tag up, then ties it to Royal's handlebar. The dark red cloth sticks out amongst the bike's silver, purple, and blue.

They stand counter to each other; Akeem is fuming. He takes off his shirt, his eyes never moving off William. He's sure Akeem doesn't feel like he did earlier at customer service. "That was a child's game. This one won't be so easy," Akeem says.

William is amused. He finally has something to feed his enthusiasm.

He powers up, and his once perfectly combed black hair now burns with blue, yellow, and orange flames on his head. His skin is pale, and his teeth and fingernails turn a pearly black. No one knows his make is undefeated. *"A distraction, just a distraction. Take it easy on him. Don't lose control. You got this . . ."* he says to himself, trying to keep a steady mood.

If he doesn't, it'll be over too soon, although his fists throb with eagerness to hit something. He stares at this fool of a vampire who has no clue what will happen. He isn't used to fighting for sport. William is one thing and one thing alone in the form of Ore, an assassin.

These last few days were draining, having to kill several people that owed the devil. They had died before they ever got a chance to repent, sealing their fate in hell forever. All the lies the devil told them so they'd continue to sin and live a life pleasing to their flesh, turned his stomach. And Satan always sold it to them on a silver platter, but they were all lies! He clenches his fists even tighter.

The crowd oohs and aahs at Ore's appearance and starts to cheer for him. Akeem's smile evaporates. Ore looks at the people blankly, and his eyes twitch as anxiety fills him. He's used to people screaming in horror, not in admiration.

"Fight!"

Ore blinks out of his thoughts, his eyes dancing around as if he doesn't know where he is. He remembers—he's up to pitch. He disappears and reappears before Akeem. He turns and kicks him in the face and follows up with a hook. Akeem falls slightly, then swiftly brings his body up as if he's resurrected.

Akeem goes in with a right hook, but Ore blocks with his forearm and then shoots a glance at Akeem, sending him flying. Akeem catches himself in the air and darts back toward his opponent. Ore jumps up and kicks Akeem in the chin. As he passes around, Ore captures his head and hurls it into the ground face first. The crowd ignites. Ore backs up and lets Akeem regenerate. Akeem rises up and clears his face of sand, breathing heavily.

Akeem receives a brutal beating as Ore sends him to the ground repeatedly. "Are you tired of getting beat up? Or wait, you seem like the type that just likes to give it," he says about how he just pushed his girl.

"Shut up, hair fire. I'm just warming up." Ore chuckles and moves so fast he can't be detected. Akeem frustratedly scans the area. He receives a jab to the face, and his eyes turn red. He's wild and quickly moves for Ore, putting him in a headlock.

Ore breaks it and turns to grab him. With super speed, Akeem flexes his teeth, bites down on Ore's wrist, then zips to the ground. Ore analyzes the marks, slowly descending to the ground. Akeem lightly laughs.

The two wait to see what this means. The crowd cheers, and Akeem hypes them up. "This is who you cheer for? So quickly defeated and on the way to his grave!" He laughs and raises his hands to push the crowd even more. They appease him.

"Don't worry, you'll be my pet. I know exactly where to put you . . . *with the girl vampires!*" He laughs, and the crowd goes wild.

Akeem spits out blood mixed with his saliva and wipes his lip. "First, you'll get the sweats as my fluids push out your own, making way for the new DNA. Then, your body will go into shock, and you'll be a zombie, standing in command of your new master."

Ore thinks about Akeem's words, which annoy him because the devil did just that to him, infecting him with rules and regulations since the tender age of nine. They remind him of his chains to *that monster.* The red string around his wrist that kept him entangled with the evil one, in comparison to the bite alongside it, looks intriguing to William. It has a matching necklace he'd tried to break more than once. They turn to metal and wrap tighter against his flesh. If they killed him, his soul would be stuck in hell forever.

But there's no way in hell . . . *literally*, that he could be enslaved to another commander. He smirks, knowing the capacity of hell's hold on him couldn't be overpowered by a mere bite. *No way!* His boundaries were indeed set in stone long ago, although this is an excellent way to test the waters, to measure his potential or . . . limitations?

He draws in a quick breath as he feels the sting of the venom crawling through his veins, and possibility floods him. He looks at his cocky, watchful opponent and back to his wrist as his veins tighten.

More pressure comes, and he lightly grunts, unfamiliar with defeat. It's sharp, out of order, and freeing. Could this be a way out? Hope lingers for a second, and a dark smirk appears. The crowd anxiously awaits to see the transformation, and whispers are heard. If this works, Akeem will have to be disposed of, the old chains will fall off, and he'd do whatever it took to free himself from this *puny* vampire and his whole clan if need be. The sting slowly subsides and now feels like Kool-Aid compared to the acid of legitimate power.

He can feel the liquid in his veins loosening, returning to the original canal. Ore is disappointed and a bit weary. He lightly sniffles in exasperation, another escape attempt lost. The moisture drains out; it's a yellowish-brown toxin only he can see at this angle. He snaps back to reality, generously bothered by the waste of an injury and his time. He grabs his wrist, his annoyance turning to humor. *His rival's gonna pay.*

"What, you mean this?" Ore says, lifting up his wrist. "I've never had a vampire bite before. It's cool and all, but my body just rejected it!" He chuckles, then sucks at the bite, spitting the rest of the poison onto the ground. The two holes heal, and he wipes his mouth.

"What! That's impossible!" says Akeem. "Not ever, not in a thousand years!"

Oh, it's possible when it comes to his situation, Ore thinks. The crowd roars louder than they did for Akeem.

"This is gonna cost ya!" says Ore, shaking his pointer finger at Akeem. "But I'll cut you some slack because it didn't leave a mark." Ore grins. His eyes are empty, his heart broken from yet another denial. The self-control he pledged to at the beginning of this gets lost in the wind.

"Who are you?" Akeem asks.

William lets down his disguise, then puts it back up, deciding to keep the madness in Ore's hands.

"That's not important. What *is* important is my curiosity. You're a vampire . . ." He puts his hand to his chin. "I've seen the movies, and you know, I wanna see if stakes and fire really kill you."

"You little pest!" Akeem says, his voice sounding strained. He tries to move to Ore but can't.

"What are you doing to me!" Akeem yells in terror.

Ah . . . there's that sweet sound Ore's used to. He smirks, closes his eyes, and enjoys it. Maybe this is him, who he is now, *who he truly is now.*

"Let me go!" Stuck in place, Akeem watches Ore.

Ore drives out wood from the arena wall and shreds it into a thousand small pieces. He looks up at his friend, Peen. Mr. Scoff's standing right beside him. They both look concerned. He'll gladly pay for the damages, *maybe.*

Akeem's eyes grow wide as Ore makes the needle-sized pieces go into his arms. Akeem screams as blood streams from them, and he falls to his knees.

"Oh," says Ore, "I have to mention for . . . advertising purposes, this is for Ping."

"What does that loser have to do with this! Ahhhh!"

"Where to next?" says Ore, sending more wood pieces to both of Akeem's legs. He hollers in agony, and Ore crams them into Akeem's chest with his eyes. Blood squirts to the ground, and Akeem's suffering spreads to the crowd. Even they are alarmed. Akeem's eyes fill with dread as Ore lights the pieces of wood in his body on fire, which now resembles a birthday cake with extreme candles.

Ore can hear Peen say, "Yeah! Attaboy!" He chuckles for a second, then proceeds to . . .

"Noooo!" A door slams, Von runs across the floor and gets over to Ore quickly. She kicks him in the back of the head.

Ore falls to the ground and spit flies out of his mouth, angrily wiping it. He then rushes over to Von, gripping her head tightly, wanting to snap it out of place, but he has to know what makes her love Akeem the way she does. Even when he's not up to par. Maybe someone could love him like that.

"You shouldn't have done that," Ore tells Von. "Now you're gonna die with your boyfriend," he says softly in her ear.

"He hurts my family!" Mr. Scoff says to Peen.

"He won't hurt her," Peen replies.

But Peen doesn't know if his words are accurate. Scoff gives it a moment more.

"Please . . . please don't hurt him," says Von.

"Why do you defend him after treating you so poorly?"

"Take them out!" Von plaintively yells as she sees Akeem coughing up blood. Ore won't press his curiosity. It's not that important to him.

"He has to surrender first," Ore says, smiling.

"Never!" Akeem says.

Ore intensifies the flames and Akeem howls.

"Akeem, please surrender, love." Ore can't help but think about it again when the word *love* leaves her mouth. William never had it, and he'd never drag someone into his mess of a life. He couldn't give a girl his entirety; that was already consumed.

"I surrender!" says Akeem. And Ore shifts his eyes from

Von's hair back to his subject. William powers down, takes the wood out of Akeem, restores it to its original color, and returns it to the arena wall.

Von rushes to Akeem's side. Ore is announced the winner, and he walks off the floor, hearing Vonvex's cry in his heart.

William is cleaning himself off in the bathroom when Peen walks in.

"Gotta hand it to ya kid," says Peen. "You did real damage out there. And the 3G's I won doesn't hurt either." He rolls out the money from his pocket.

"Think so?" William says and grins.

"Know so." William gets his duffle bag out of the locker.

"I'm out," William says, walking past Peen.

"Where you going? You gotta finish all the rounds kid."

"I'm good."

"Are you kidding me? You were amazing out there!"

William shrugs. Another hit is calling his name, and it's a priority.

He goes back to his peaceful spot for rest. More blood and pain have been caused by his hands—another assassination gone perfectly. His hands quiver as pulses of memories from the hit make their rounds. *Why does it feel so wrong if this is what he was built for?*

William looks out at the water. He'd do anything for his life to be as still as the lake. Something in him wants to hurt people, but a small voice tells him it's not right. It confirms that's not who he's supposed to be, that God had other plans for his life no matter how destructive he felt as Ore. *Well then, why doesn't God change it?*

"In time," the voice replies. *But that answer hurts.*

Something tickles his ear. He scratches it and catches a brown ring of hair blowing in the wind. He looks at its owner.

"Hi," she says.

He grins and looks away. "How did you find me?" He says dryly. Von really came after him? *Bingo.*

"I have your scent and so does Akeem."

William chuckles. "And what? You're here to warn me?"

"I blocked your scent, but not before I found your spot."

He walks off without looking at her, but she catches up to him, saying, "You should be careful, though. We live just up the mountain." She points up in the direction of home. "Can't promise you won't run into him if you stick around."

"If he finds me, he's dead."

"Why are you all alone?" she asks, batting her eyelashes at him.

He stops and says, "Look, I'm not interested in making friends. Go back to your . . . clan."

She stops and watches him walk away, then zooms in front of him, putting her hand on his chest.

"I don't want to be your friend," says Von while looking into his eyes.

"Vampires aren't my thing," he says.

"It's funny 'cause I love fire head boys."

She uses that word again, *love,* and he can't deny the curiosity it brings. He considers this, deciding she'll be a great addition to the distractions list he's creating. Still, he detests vampires. They're dead and gone, pretending to still have life. If he died, he'd want it to be final. No one could control him then.

She follows him around for the next few hours like a lost puppy until she gets his full attention. They go into the forest and fight for fun, but she's no match for him. She gets to kiss the angry boy. "Aren't you gonna give me your number?" she asks him.

"Nope, you know where to find me," he says before leaving.

Hell

"Where have you been, William?" says a creepy voice.

"Busy," William says to his opposer.

"That's not a coordinate, boy!" the devil says, his beady eyes now coming into view. "Need I remind you whom you belong to?"

"Nope." William leans up against hell's wall and crosses his arms.

"Good. I like the new blue suit—crisp and *assassiny*. I got a new hit for you."

"What's new?"

"Are you annoyed with me, William? Because I give you your freedom. You can roam the earth, come and go out of hell as you please, as long as you do what you're told. But you can stay down here with me *permanently,* if you'd rather that?" he says, threatening him.

William plays with the red thread on his wrist. "Nah, I'm good. Just tell me what you want." The thought of losing his freedom alarms him.

The low ghoulish voice taunts him, saying, "I don't want to be a burden."

"What's my assignment, kata?"

"That's more like it! Colton Scoff."

"Scoff?" William is caught off guard.

"Yes, do you know of him?"

"No."

"Very well, I want him off the face of the earth by this afternoon."

"I just did a hit this morning. Don't you ever get tired of this?" It comes out as more of a whine, and Satan disapproves. Ore is his most valued soldier, and he needs him primed and ready for war at all times.

"*Never.* But I didn't create you to ask questions."

"You didn't create me at all."

Satan forces Ore's power. "You belong to me! Isn't that evident?"

William powers down, saying, "Is there anybody else I can grab for you to torture for eternity?"

"You've never been this rebellious, William. Maybe the New York air is making you soft."

"I'm not doing it." If he's right, Satan wants him to kill a member of Vonvex's family, and if he does, he won't hear the end of it. *Or is it that he cares for her?*

Thick gold chains band around his neck, wrists, and ankles, forcing him to his knees. They clink together, and the noise makes William's ears rattle.

"I think you need a time out," says Satan, laughing.

The familiar feeling of entrapment returns as he remembers being bound without chains as an ill child, unable to play with other kids. The sickness brought about by the thing that stood before him, keeping him in remembrance.

"I'll do it!"

"You are not willing." The devil's red color burns for a response. Scoff owes him big time and can't be touched by him, but Ore could.

"I said I'll do it! I'll do it, right now!" William's' chains disappear at once, but he can still feel their heaviness, and he checks to see if they're really gone. He stands to his feet, trying to erase the agony that was just caused.

"So there's no problem, right?"

"No," says William, exiting hell.

8

The Similory: Vai Forest

The Similory people live on planet Vaimos, which has three pieces of land and is made up of mostly water.

Ládi Mountain, meaning "oil," only housed the wealthy and reflected earth's cities. It contains tall buildings, houses, electricity, hospitals, and clean water. The middle-class Similory, Imerians, are essential to Ládi and include builders, utility workers, doctors, framers, and boat and drill operators. They can submit a temporary visa for approval to King Vasiliás to live in Ládi. This keeps Ládi from being overpopulated.

Other Imerians can apply to work for businesses on Ládi Mountain. Boats are discharged to Iméra every morning to pick up laborers. They're sent home at sundown when all work stops on Ládi. There is very little crime. The Megálo Army, run by a wizard, Du'Jomi, keeps the people in line. Laians bask in royalties and look down on the poor and middle class. They have a money system called Vairos, made with leaves from a unique tree, only grown in Ládi, saturated with oil.

Iméra means "day" and is where the overwhelming population of people with essential professions reside. They apply to Ládi Mountain but are waitlisted or denied to keep numbers low. They can keep the status of the middle class because of trade. They sell Ládi Mountain cement for buildings, etc., and their land is richly filled with its vital ingredient, limestone. Although Ládi has some cement, without the elements from Iméra, they would run out eventually.

Imerians work all day and all night to keep their estate grounded, which is tiring for the people. They often dream of living in Ládi, a place that only works until midday. Iméra is run by a mayor. Crime is not tolerated, and law enforcement has a heavy hand on its people.

Vai Valley was the first place the Similory people lived as a whole before the expansion of territory. It has few resources or professions, and only one or two doctors live in the area. The people cannot pay for medical help, so most die or wait days for a doctor to travel to their homes. Their work is to search Vai Forest for artifacts their ancestors left behind in an attempt to negotiate their findings as trade with Iméra.

Greta, poisonous creatures that live in the Vai forest, make it almost impossible to find a trade. Without proper medical attention, if people are bitten, they die. They are also in danger of being eaten by the creatures. Vaiens wake and live to hunt; if they don't gather, they can't trade. They'll die if they can't trade for food and clean water. Vai Forest has a unique red fruit named Ju Fruit, but it is scarce and eaten by the Greta. They cannot apply for work in Ládi and will not be considered under any circumstances.

Vaimos is self-generated and does not need any help from outside forces.

"Papa, tell us of The Games on earth!" says Pinelle.

Her big sister, Deylou, listens in, excited to hear the stories she's heard a million times. Their limping father sits on the wool couch he'd crafted. He'd been scratched by a Greta a few days ago and awaits a doctor's arrival from the village ten miles away.

"Well, the scorpion man had my vote! He battled against the

tarantula with a mighty tail!" he says as Amai, their mother, brings in the tiniest bowl of fish soup for dinner, sadness in her eyes. Deylou looked at their supply of clean water. They had about three days left, but their father's injury prevented him from returning to the forest.

They finish dinner after their father's story about the extraordinary creatures in Vai Forest, ones that aren't dangerous. Still hungry, Deylou goes into the kitchen where her mother is cleaning, but she would never say it.

"Mama, will we one day have enough?"

Her mother tries to hide her discouragement. "I believe one day God will give us more than enough, Dey."

Deylou nods. "I am gonna have a bath," she says.

"I will boil water, love."

Deylou makes her way to the darkened bathroom, daylight breaking through between sticks on the ceiling to light her path.

She gets into the dented iron tub and sits knees to chest, thinking about *more than enough*. She turns the lever to run the water. Her father had run a line from the ocean. Her lip shivers, and she hugs her knees to keep warm. Deylou places a rubber stopper over the drain, and the tub begins to fill. Her mother knocks on the wooden door and brings in a large pot of boiling water. She pours it into the tub, and relief hits Deylou.

"Thank you, Mama."

Her mother smiles, fetches a lit candle for her, and closes the door. Deylou leans her head against the tub's rim and dreams of a day she'll no longer have to rely on salted, boiled seawater for bathing.

She reaches for soap made of plants and carefully measures the tiniest amount from the already small bar. She rolls it on a small piece of fabric, then attempts to scrub the dirt off, but the suds aren't coming.

She never really felt clean after every bath except when Papa brought home the nicest smelling soap and shampoo packaged in the most beautiful wrapping gifted to her father one glorious time for working for the island of Iméra. She lays in her cot, her stomach growling, next to her snoring thirteen-year-old sister.

The next day, she and Pinelle walk along the seashore. Deylou picks up stones and ricochets them across the water. They'd given the doctor room to work on their father. She had been generous enough to offer her services for free after their father had fixed her piping last year. The scorching sun makes the Vaiens' throat stick together with every swallow.

"I am thirsty, Dey!" says Pinelle, dancing around. The girls go inside, and Deylou pours a third of the water into each cup, her mother watching.

Pinelle chugs it down. "I need more, Dey!"

"Okay, but no more, Nel!" She pours her the same amount, and Nel takes it with a sour face. She drinks hers while hearing the doctor say it'll be another week before her father can return to the forest for trade. Deylou's eyes widen as she looks at the loaf of bread they're dividing for dinner.

Early the next morning, Deylou and Pinelle stand before Vai forest. Deylou's bulging eyes scan the area for danger. Dozens of vines fall from each tall tree, making it difficult to see beyond the entrance. White stones make up a perimeter around the forest, protecting the Similory from the Greta. She exhales, deciding to move forward and into the green web of leaves. The girls look around, and despite the gloomy terrain and the dim light of the new day, they see its beauty.

"Deylou, I am scared. Father will not like that we are here. Let's go back!" "Pinelle, we need to find dinner, okay?"

"What if we are eaten by the Greta! And are never found like the others?"

"Do not say that, Nel. Look!" Deylou points to a tall tree that reaches beyond the clouds. The girls love to climb. Nel gets excited, and Deylou helps her into it. She grabs soot and a vile of seawater and pours them into her hands.

Vines grow out of the mixture and wrap around the tree's branches, helping her up.

"I will get you!" Deylou whispers to Nel. Her papa told them the Greta are drawn by the noise.

"You will not!" Nel whispers back.

At the top, the girls giggle. Deylou loved the fresh air the trees gripped as the wind blew. Small drops of leftover rain bring chills as they sprinkle on their faces, and their tiny antlers recoil. Deylou's tunic and loose sandy hair go with its beat. There's a salty aroma carried in its rouse, birthed from the sea. Her eyes part. From here, the forest is soundless and beautiful but also dark and murky. She can't make out the clouds, and mist hugs the twigs of trees.

If she hadn't heard stories about Vai Forest, she wouldn't believe beasts dwelled here. She didn't see the danger, although it was without movement and void. Where were the lovely animals her papa talked about? Had they been eaten by the Greta? And how did plants grow here without the sun shining through? She heard the forest was so ill-lit because the sun refused to let out its radiance to the forest's wickedness.

"Look what I found," Nel says, holding a red fruit that fills her entire hand. "Ju fruit!" Deylou hugs her and packs it in their pouch. The girls climb down.

"Do you know of my master?" says a voice.

Deylou's head snaps to attention, and Pinelle latches on to her torso.

"Who speaks?" asks Dyelou.

"Why, it is I," says a long-stemmed sunflower in a small bed of her own kind. "I have asked you. Do you know of my master?"

The sunflower twists its head to meet Deylou's scrutiny.

"You talk?" Deylou says in delight.

"Yes, and so do you, Deylou Mar Similory. I am a living, breathing, talking organism, just as you are."

"But you are just a flower."

The flower laughs in amusement, and her accompanying posies follow.

"I am more than just that. I am intelligence."

"Is that how you know my name?"

"I am familiar with most things on Planet Vaimos. I can be *any* flower, though I am not *every* flower."

Deylou inspects the flower. Her petals are flowing like hair, her eyes are large, and her teeth are sharp.

"Now, do you know of my master?"

The girls shake their heads, and the sunflower lowers her mane.

"Do you have a name?" Nel asks timidly.

"I am called Vema,"

"Vema, why do you not know of your master?" asks Deylou.

"He is not yet, but will be," says Vema, looking off into the distance. "It is not safe for you to be here. You must leave."

"We cannot leave without food." Deylou moves around the bed of flowers, pulling Pinelle.

The sunflowers turn as one, watching every step the girls take. "Very well, but you've been warned," they say in unison, although Vema's voice rings over the others. They turn back to a neutral state and flow with the wind. The girls hurry away.

"Deylou, she was frightening!" says Nel.

Deylou looks at the journey ahead and gulps. A sparkle catches her eye. She gets soot for Nel and herself, and they swing in the trees towards it, watching their surroundings. Their boots hit the ground, and they run towards it. Nelly trips on a tree stump, screeching on her way down. It echoes, and Deylou runs to her. Worried the sound may have drawn beasts, Deylou looks into the forest, but it's clear and quiet. "Come," she says and helps Nelly up.

A bizarre call erupts from behind them, and their bodies stiffen. Branches shake in the distance. Four creatures with frog-like bodies, pointy ears, and long rat tails crawl out. Two jump through trees and the others dig their claws into the ground, aiding their thrust to a quick meal.

"The Greta!" says Deylou, and they take off. Deylou pulls Nel into a large hole in a tree and signals for her to be quiet. They can't see the Greta, but they hear its breathing. The mucus from its nose and mouth rubs against its throat, and its tongue flickers from licking its lips, ready to eat.

At length, it creeps down a tree coming into view, its face sinister. It seems to laugh at the game of cat and mouse.

Beauty captures the girls' gazes as a petite, brilliantly blue fox with a tail that glistens at its tip runs by. Pointing at the fox, Pinelle opens her mouth to speak, but Deylou moves quickly to cover it and brings her back into the hole as the creature chases after it.

"Deylou, a Lunar Fox!" Nel whispers. Deylou is still on alert but says, "I know . . ." She motions for Nel to keep her voice down. She understands Nel's excitement. She felt it too. It's one of the rare animals their father spoke of, saying it was most beautiful, next to a highly dangerous creature named The Arkin.

"Come, they are gone," says Deylou after peeking. They crawl out, and Deylou spots the silver. She goes and picks it up. It's a chunk of gold. Her eyes light up, and the girls cheer. Out of nowhere, two men covered in mud spring up from one of the many craters in the ground and step out, axes in hand. Nelly screams and runs.

"Nel!" Deylou yells. Right before her eyes, Nel steps into quicksand and is pulled down by a little boy that has a blanket of mud around him.

Deylou blinks rapidly in disbelief and is stone still. She circles around but doesn't see her sister. She pushes herself to run as the Mudwor gets closer, jumping on each patch of grass, steering clear of mud puddles. They're catching up quickly. She passes a sign that says, "Mud," and the mud men stop, unable to pass into Greta territory.

Deylou lets out a shrilled whimper. "Nelly!" She hears a familiar rattle and gasps, looking in every direction for the Greta. "Vema! Help!" she calls and sees colorful lights explode.

"Deylou?" says Vema, but a flash of blue light overpowers her light before her system goes down.

"Nelly!" she yells in horror.

Hands pull her into a bush. Deylou starts to panic, but a blue-haired girl brings a finger to her mouth. Deylou looks between the two girls dressed in Vaien attire, but they are too clean.

The girls now ride on a small boat.

"I'm Taj," says the blue-haired girl, holding her hand out. Deylou shakes it.

"Starm," says the other girl, who sticks her nose up.

"You are not from here," says Deylou.

"No, we're from Iméra," says Taj.

"Why have you come?"

"To study your people and to help hunt." She takes out a Ju fruit and hands it to Deylou.

Deylou doesn't like that they're here to dissect her people when they're fighting to survive each day. But sadness overpowers dislike. *What will she tell her mama and papa?* Three girls aren't strong enough to defeat the Mudwor, mud men her father told them about.

"Do you know of The Games?" asks Taj,

"Of course not," says Starm.

"I do!" says Deylou, and the girls jump.

Taj smiles and hurriedly takes out thick golden tickets. "I'm delivering these to customers. I have an extra. Would you like to come?"

Deylou looks at the bunch of tickets in Taj's bag, thinking about the stories of fighters her father told them about. If she could get three, for her and her family, she could distract her parents and go to The Games to find a fighter willing to come back and rescue Nelly. Deylou nods and Taj hands her a ticket, placing the rest in her bag.

"Goldfish jumping out of the water!" says Starm.

"Gold! Where?" Taj goes to the other side of the boat.

Deylou immediately snatches two extra tickets from the pack. Her heart pounds. She'd never stolen anything before, but she folds them into her bag beside the chunk of gold she found before going over to the show in the water.

"Thank you for your help," says Deylou.

"You're welcome! The portals start tomorrow at daybreak."

Deylou nods and runs down the path home. She whimpers, opening her bag and running her fingers over the gold tickets. The weight of losing her sister and how she'd obtained the tickets pours over her like a flood. Shame fills her. No matter what the circumstances, taking something from someone isn't right. Being disobedient to her parents by going into the forest set off a string of unthinkable events, even if she was just trying to help.

She walks up the worn steps to their hut and composes herself, wondering if her papa will be well enough to go to The Games. When she opens the door, her father walks by without a limp.

"Papa! You are better?"

"I am." He hugs her.

"Good news! Nelly won a contest! Girls from Iméra came to explore, and they sell tickets to The Games." She spreads the tickets on the counter. Her mother walks up as she's talking.

"What?" She grabs a thick ticket, and her eyes glow.

"Eh! Where's my winner?" asks her papa.

"She had to go with them!" Deylou stutters, hoping her parents don't see her shaking.

"Is she safe?" asks Amai.

"Yes, they are very nice. We will follow tomorrow!"

The next morning, Deylou's mother gives her clothes only Imérians wear. "I have been saving them for a special day," she says.

Deylou puts on the beige silky pants and shirt with pearls beaded along the sides. She and her parents are all dressed in new clothes. They board boats to Iméra. The happy Mars flash their tickets to the Imérian guards. Deylou holds her breath until they're let through. Iméra is so clean and colorful that they light up in delight. Three lines form for the portals to planet earth, and they stand in one.

Deylou spots the girls. They're angrily headed right for her.

"I see friends; I will meet you there!" she says to her mother.

"Go on!" her mother says, happily standing with her healed husband.

"You stole two tickets from my bag!" Taj yells.

The wizard patrol hears Taj and walks towards them. Deylou sees her parents' hands get stamped and then disappear into the portals. She takes off, looking back to see a scary Du'Jomi coming after her. She lets them stamp her hand and rushes through to the portals.

"Stop that Similory!" He points while she's teleported to earth.

9

A Step in the Right Direction

On leaving day, Addison helps me pack. She said she'll visit, but I know she'll be busy with nursing classes. Daddy handed me new keys. As promised, he traded in my convertible this morning for an older model jeep with no payments. I kicked and screamed like a child as he confiscated my bunny head keys. I eyed mother but decided to shut it because Daddy looked like he was just daring me to say something.

Nevertheless, I wasn't excited about going from Barbie to Cinderella, the one in rags. My mother is not some evil stepmother, although that's up for debate.

My jeep is tan, and the inside is all black. Addison loved it, but I scoffed when I saw strings sticking out of the steering wheel—it's so secondhand! When I turned on the radio to see if it even worked, it filled the car with neon hues.

"No way!" We smack our hands together and intertwine our fingers. When we pulled off, Addison followed on the freeway with her pretty blue VW Beetle, a grad gift from her parents that suits her oh so well. She honked a hundred times before taking the exit, and my heart cried with every wheel roll away.

A few hotels, restaurants, and a forty-plus-hour drive later, we pull up to our new home, if that's what you call this. I scrunch up my nose. It's old looking, not like falling apart at the seams or anything, but not like our modern home in LA. It's one of the only houses on the street. Next to it are tall buildings joined together, and I have no idea where they start and finish. I overhear Daddy telling Liz his real estate friend was selling the jewel for an older woman, which was nothing to brag about. This has to be the twilight zone and not my real life.

I go in and see my mother standing in the kitchen. She motions for me to come over, and I roll my eyes.

"Isn't it beautiful?"

The kitchen is newly remodeled, and it is lovely. I smile as my mom smiles, but if she thinks just because we had a moment in our other kitchen, this is suddenly our thing, she's wrong.

"You only like it because you cook. I don't. This house is so old, and the only reason we're here is because of you, so don't try to play bonding time." I stomp away and don't look back because it's the truth, but why do I feel terrible about it?

My feet follow this rhythm all the way up the twirling stairs. I turn and admire the winding, white railing. But I back away from it before she sees I'm enjoying the new scenery... *I am?* I see my brother lying on the ground of a small room and run to the only other one up besides the bathroom. If he thinks he's gonna get the best room, he's wrong! I open the door, and sunflowers with vines line the top of the walls. This is why he chose the other room. This room is definitely bigger!

The moving company Daddy hired finally arrive with all our stuff. I fall asleep, staring at the brown cardboard stained with black marker.

When I wake up the next day, my mother stares at me from my doorway. "You still look the same sleeping like you did when you were little."

"I see you're *still* coming through closed doors without knocking."

"Lolly, I know you're upset, sweetheart, but it's hard for me too."

"Sure it is." I turn my back to her. It's too early for this.

"Baby, come down for breakfast soon. I made pancakes." She shuts the door. *Why is she so nice to me even when I'm so mean to her?* It's annoying.

I go to the table and see that my brother looks as if he's ready for summer school, and Daddy is dressed in a suit and tie. *Great!* They're leaving me with *her*. Liz hands out stacks of pancakes, then suddenly grows weak. Daddy runs to her. Josh and I shoot out of our seats.

"Mommy?" I call out, and everyone stares at me. I turn to run, but she grabs me.

"Baby, don't go. Please eat. I just lost my footing." Her feet are firmly on the ground, and we return to the table.

"Lolly, I wanted to talk to you about something." She grabs Daddy's hand.

What now? My fork and knife roughly tap at the plate as I cut my cakes.

"Josh and Dad have school and work and . . ." She looks at Daddy. "I'm renting out space to start my own antique shop. Would you like to help me? I know you're not sure about college, so of course you would get a paycheck."

Wha?

"Sweet!" Josh says.

"Pretty sweet!" Dad adds.

Are they serious? "Mom, you're sick. How are you gonna work?" seeps out of my mouth.

My mother worked at an antique mall for years back home. She had her own booth, filled with special items she'd hunt down at discounted prices, only to sell them for three times as much at her table. Coworkers would be jealous of her numbers; she always sold out of all her merchandise. *But could she still do that in her state?* I can't picture it, especially with this morning's episode.

"Baby, that's the reason we came, for me to get treatment so I can get better. I'm not just gonna give up," Liz says.

I ignore her. "Daddy, are you really gonna let her do this?"

Josh's head bobbles between us. He nods, deciding mother will win.

"You heard her, honey, I'm not the one to get in the way of anyone's dreams. We already put the deposit down. The better question is, are you gonna let her do it alone?"

I look between them in disbelief, but it's surprisingly not a bad idea, especially when money is involved. "Fine! But I'm not gonna work for minimum wage."

They cheer. I get up and carry my food upstairs because I don't feel like partaking in their happiness. After all, I'm so far away from home and miss my bestie already.

"Lolly, she's gonna pay you? That's so rad, Doll!"

"Girl, this is all a sad scheme to get me to bond with her," I say.

"Why not, babe?"

"I'm just mad at her for dragging me out here! Well, we never really got along honestly."

"It's not her fault, Cher. I think it's because you two are so similar."

"No, we're not!"

"Yes, you are! I mean, you're really sweet to me. But you're different towards her because you love her so much."

That's so backward. "I don't get it."

"Okay, it's like when you like a boy, and you're really mean to him because you're trying to hide the fact that you like him so much. Same thing."

I think about her words and realize she could be on to something. "Maybe? I don't know."

"It's gonna be okay, babe. Just take your time with her."

"I will, thanks."

"Of course. How is she?"

"The same."

A little later, while unpacking, mother shockingly knocks on my door, yelling that she's off to an appointment.

"Okay!" I say, unsure of what to do with myself. *She really knocked this time.*

The Shop

Monday comes, and Liz knocks on my door. Still freaked by her new behavior, I open it, brows raised. The beauty before me stuns me. Her hair is straightened, long, and luscious. She has on heels, a sweater that reaches her knees, blue jeans, and a white shirt. Her radiant dark complexion shines through, and she even has on eyeshadow. I'd burn her robe if I could.

"Mom!" I say, awestruck.

"I know! I feel really good today. Ready?"

My face turns up in confusion.

"You forgot? The shop!" She shakes the keys.

"Oh my gosh!" I hug her and then pull away. We clear our throats.

"Let's roll," she says.

I love how she didn't make a big deal of it. *Similarities,* something whispers in my spirit.

We pull into the shop, going under a giant neon flashing sign that says, "Big Barns." It's so whacky. Multiple shops are connected to one another.

"Wow, the pictures are dull compared to this."

I can tell she loves it. She parks out back in the large parking lot, and we walk past all the shops' back doors.

We go in, and she immediately complains about the off-white color on the walls. She wanted a crisp white. She moves past it for now and takes me to a door on the side.

"This is why I picked it out, ta-da!" she says.

I look at the empty space, puzzled.

"Lolly, you have an eye just like mine. I want people to see your talent. And of course aside from your 'more than minimum wage request,' all the profit that comes from this room will go straight to you."

I smile and walk further into the small square to hide it. "I dunno. I really wouldn't know where to start."

"You will. Let it come to you."

We go to the shop every day for a whole week to sweep, dust, and paint the walls her crisp white. We receive multiple dark wooden tables she ordered and throw lace tablecloths over them. People curiously peek in, she's thrilled, and I'm so happy that she's happy.

We walk around the ring of shops, noticing the weird names on the buildings. Mom is trying to decide what to call her shop.

An older woman stops us, saying, "Hi there. I'm Carol. You're opening the new antique shop, right?"

"Hello, Carol. Yes, I'm Elizabeth Pobs, and this is my daughter, Lolly Pobs."

My mom shakes her hand.

"Lolly? What kind of name is that?"

Carol is a little too blunt for me . . . I mean, I know my name is unique, but *geez*.

"She's actually named after my great-grandmother, Lollian Jones. She was a famous singer back in the day."

I've seen pictures of her. I favor her a lot, but she was an absolute beauty. Mom says she has records of her somewhere, but I've never heard her sing. My family calls her "The Disappearing

Goldmine" because she ran off with her true love against the record label's wishes.

"Oh, that's beautiful, hon. You two are beautiful."

"Thank you. We're checking out the area," Mom says.

"Oh! Let me give you the grand tour," says Carol.

For the next hour and a half, we walk around with Carol, and she gives us the full scoop. There's a pawn shop named "Massive Pawn." The name sounds like a lie to me. She says they think the owner used to be a millionaire but struck a bad deal and was kicked out of his home. But not before he got the chance to retrieve all the stuff he is now selling to survive.

"Oldies" is a tattoo parlor famous for recreating portraits of legends like Elvis, Michael Jackson, Marilyn Monroe, and others on people's skin. It's owned by a couple and their triplet sons, all covered in tattoos except one. "Slash Clip" is a barber shop, but why would anyone get their hair cut *there?*

There's a hair salon named "Pin It Up." A jewelry store called "IV Ice Therapy" is owned by a couple and their five girls. But who has that many girl babies? There's an arcade named "Surreal Play," a boxing ring called "Supreme Boxer," and a thrift store named "Shirt's Out Thrift" because they're always sold out of their poppin' merchandise. It's owned by an older couple. The final building is a theater that's "Coming Soon."

Despite all those goofy names, Carol has a 70s diner named after herself. *What a surprise.* She said it also has a gift shop in it with "BARNS" souvenirs and a jukebox. Carol said the other shop owners give her grief because they wanted all the stores to have weird names. So she uppercased the "R" in "CaRol's," but they're still unsatisfied. She says people come from all around to shop in the unique stores and to experience the very distinctive owners. At first, I questioned why they would want to meet ordinary people, but judging by Carol, I doubt they are ordinary.

By the time she's done with us, our heads are spinning, and back at the shop, we take a minute to recover.

"She's sweet for doing that, but she can really talk," Mom says, rubbing her temples.

I'm too weak to form a coherent sentence to respond.

"Something good came out of it, though. I have a name for the shop!" She is excited.

"What?" I manage to ask, checking my ear to see if it's bleeding.

"Pobs Pop Antique."

My jaw drops. "Mom, that's an awesome name!" The name now hangs atop the store. I helped her design it, and it has gold lettering with a pink rim. She also hangs a sign that says, "Coming Soon."

10

A Turn for the Better or Worse?

Rachel waves at Grand as the bell rings for lunch. Mrs. Jan looks confused as she turns in her assignments. Grand watches her walk with her friends. She hasn't said a word to him since the fundraiser. As usual, Luke, Mark, and Cam each slam Grand's head into a locker.

"Stop!" He finally speaks up for himself, drawing from the confidence Ci stirred. Luke turns around and gets in his face.

"Or what?"

"Don't you have something better to do than harass me!"

"What's better than messing with you because of your big mouth?"

"Get a life!" Grand yells.

Luke punches him, and Grand holds himself up on a locker, wiping the blood from his lip.

"You had enough yet?" Grand asks Luke.

"No, actually."

"Oh, you know how to use big words?"

Everyone laughs, and Luke goes in for another punch, but Rachel grabs his arm. "Luke, stop!"

He quickly pushes her, and she falls to the ground. Suddenly he realizes it is Rachel. "Ray? Baby, I didn't mean to . . ."

Luke tries to help Rachel, but Grand pulls him back and throws a fist at him, and a popping noise bursts out of the silence.

He looks at his fist. *What did he just do?* So Luke's *the* boyfriend who cheated on her?

Grand gets home after being suspended for a week and wallows in his sorrows. His mother showed no mercy, her bickering starting from the moment of pick-up to drop-off. She doubles his chores and takes his game. He can't shake that Luke called Rachel "baby." How could a sweet girl like that be with a jerk like him? It fires him up again, and he concludes it's the main reason he punched Luke.

A week later, after receiving a warning not to get into any more trouble, Grand walks his usual path to school. He kicks a rock in frustration. The moment he finally got somewhere with Rachel, it got shut down. He texted her during his suspension to make sure she was okay, but she never responded. It seems everyone's against him, and no one is for him. He looks to the sky and yells, "Give me a break!"

In second period, Rachel doesn't even look at him. Grand would've taken a hundred punches for her, and yeah, they would've hurt, but this hurt so much more. At lunch, he searches for Ci, the only one that bothered to call during his suspension.

"Grand, are you okay?" It's Rachel, and he almost falls from the weight of her aura.

"Yeah, I texted to check on you but—"

"You did? I'm so sorry. My parents took my phone because of Jan. She told them I was skipping, and she was concerned about my grades."

"Did you tell them I was helping?"

"Yeah, they just had to prove a point."

"Sorry."

"Don't be. I wanted to say thank you for sticking up for me. Luke is such a jerk!" They chuckle. "I broke up with him for good this time."

Grand's eyes flutter with hope. She stands on her tippy toes, kisses him on the cheek, then says, "Gotta go!" and scurries away.

He puts his hand on his cheek to cover her kiss so it'll stay longer. He sees Luke and his friends staring at him with cold expressions. *Were they there the whole time?* He takes his hand away. Luke's scowl makes it seem he wants to punch him again.

Grand then happily walks to the cafe. If that's not the break he asked for, then he doesn't know what is. "Thank you, God!" He pumps a fist at heaven and can't wait to tell Ci. Her methods are not recommended, but they do work.

He walks home, thinking, *could this lead to more if he kept trying?* He strides confidently on the sidewalk. Rubber moving over gravel behind him catches his attention. A black car is creeping up. This street is pretty quiet and deserted most times. Luke gets out with Mark and Cam, but Cam stays by the car.

"What are you doing out here by yourself, Powder?" says Luke.

Grand gulps.

"So you're kissing my girl now, huh?"

"Bro, she broke up with you," Mark says.

"Shut up!" Luke fires back.

"She kissed me," Grand says.

"You still mouthy I see, Turosi," says Luke. "We're gonna have to fix that."

Luke nods at Cam, who gets a bat out of the car.

Grand takes off.

They go after him. Grand trips, landing on his knee, and he holds it to soothe the pain. They jump him. He tries to push them off, but their blows are too heavy.

Luke grabs the bat and swings it, hitting Grand's shoulder, which knocks him back to the ground. He swings it again, and blood splatters all over the sidewalk. Luke wipes the sweat off of his forehead. All they see is blood.

"Is he . . . ?" Cam asks.

Mark rakes his fingers through his hair and fidgets. Luke is breathless. Anger had gotten the best of him. He looks around for a quick solution. "Grab his legs!"

They run across the street with Grand's limp body and kick the old, tarnished lock off the gate to an old military base that's been shut down for years. They quickly bring him in.

"We need to hurry up before they see my car!" Luke yells, twisting every doorknob, looking for a place to hide the body. One finally turns. "In here!" Inside, a tall cylinder tank reads "Z71" in big, bold letters.

Mark lets go of Grand's legs. "Bro, I don't want anything to do with this. I'm out." He leaves.

Luke looks at Cam, saying, "I can't do this by myself, bro."

Cam nods, placing the cigarette he was about to light behind his ear. They both head up the long staircase.

When they reach the top, they put the body down and remove the thin, flimsy lid. Grand's fingers move, but they don't notice.

Luke looks at the dark water. Reality sets in, and he freezes.

"You good bro?" asks Cam.

Luke has to get himself together before Cam bails. He coughs and says, "Yeah, come on." They put Grand into the water and head downstairs. Cam reads the label, "*Zionzetic* Type: 71, an Acid Chemical. Caution." His eyes open wide and he hurries downstairs.

Mark is in the passenger's seat, staring at his phone, as Luke goes into the glove compartment and grabs zip ties. He seals the gate, and they drive away in silence.

11

Conflicting Duty

William goes home and rests his head on the couch.

"Whatever is wrong, dear boy?"

"Long week, Eloise."

"Why so long?" the main housekeeper asks.

"It just is."

She knows better than to press any further. "Ah," she says.

"Elo, when I was younger, did my parents have any idea what I'd become?"

Finally something, she thinks, and walks further into the second living room. "You used to put on Dad's big ol' shoes, pick up his briefcase, and wait for him at the door."

William lightly chuckles.

"He felt honored by what you did, broke down, and took you to that busy office one or two times." She sighs. "They wanted you to take over the business and to follow God. You're well on your way. You pray, you—"

"I haven't been able to pray lately," says William, interrupting. "There's a lot going on."

"He hears you, child. Even when you're on the go, he still hears you."

"But Elo, what if I've done bad things?"

"Oh William, God forgives you. All you have to do is ask. I mean, it's not like you've killed anybody," she says, laughing.

He gets up, buttoning his tux abruptly.

A concerned expression comes over her face. "But even if you had . . . he'll still forgive you."

"Thank you, Eloise." William walks out of the living room, leaving her there. He paces back and forth in his study. He can't even talk to God, let alone ask for forgiveness. There's a block because he's *still* taking heads off *God's people*. His actions were deplorable. Well, they *are* sinners, thieves, and liars. But still, it wasn't his or the devil's call to make.

"He hears you, child . . ." Her words linger. He saves those thoughts for a better time. He's on assignment, and although God is in his heart, the devil is his master. He walks towards the door, disappearing before he reaches it.

He checked Scoff's, *no vampires*. He departs and goes to the mountains where Vonvex directed him. She had unknowingly laid out her brother's death sentence. Either way, he would've found it, but she made it easier. He finds himself passing the line between pavement and wet dirt. He swiftly moves up until he sees a red brick mansion. He walks through their closed gate, melting metal behind him in the shape of his entity.

Ore looks back. He was so hasty to shed blood that he didn't make himself invisible so he wouldn't leave evidence. He rebuilds it with a swing of his hand, then vanishes.

He slips into their walls undetected. He hears loud opera music playing in the background. He slowly steps towards a large open door.

"Daddy, I almost lost to a puny mountain wolf. I had to take out my teeth to scare her."

"I'd think you stronger than that. Maybe it's Akeem throwing you off your game."

Jonathan Scoff. He wasn't familiar with their family. Some supernaturals are free to roam the earth, but they are well hidden here.

He peeks in but can only see the back of Jonathan, his dark hair like stone, not a string out of place. They stand by the fireplace.

"Akeem lost," she says, looking down.

"Oh, he did, did he? To whom, daughter?" he said, his voice calm and inviting. He could put a person into a trance before they knew it. "Ore. He's new to The Games," her voice chimes at the mention of his name.

"Ore? beat . . . Akeem? And he's new?" He laughs. "How preposterous. Akeem is getting weaker by the second."

"No, father. Ore is invincible. We've never seen anything like him."

"Do not speak out of turn, child. Akeem is a hothead, nothing more. It will be his ruin. I love our kind, but some should be more humble." Ore detects sincerity in his voice.

In walks a male with long green hair. "Father, you're back."

"Ah, for example," Jonathan says, turning and pointing a cup of wine at the vampire.

Ore is thrown off. Jonathan Scoff looks like he could be Vonvex's brother, not father.

"Hello, Colton."

"What example do you speak of, Father?"

"That some of us should be more humble, not spending the fortune we've earned off dead corpses through the past centuries on worthless things."

"What good is money if you can't spend it?"

Jonathan's face deflates. "It's what you spend it on, son, that makes it good." He takes a sip of his wine.

"I spend it on girls, booze, and a *good* time. It makes living more . . . bearable," Colton says and sticks his hand out. A human girl comes and sits on his lap.

Jonathan turns to the fireplace, "You are corrupt and out of control!" His tone is harsh. Unlike the mildness before, he breaks the wineglass in his hand. "I am ashamed to call you my son and regret the day Alina and I brought you into this world. You are nothing like your sister and brother, Jax!"

"Father?" Vonvex's voice cracks. Jonathan walks out.

"Maybe your standards are so high, I don't care to meet them!" Colton says to his father's back.

"He's right, you know. All you do these days is party. Mom would've expected more from us."

"Well, she isn't here, is she? She chose to stay human and live out her short years till her human heart stopped. She didn't care what would become of us because we . . ."

His bottom lip quivers. "We have to live out forever without her, even if we're half human!"

"That's why you're lashing out? Because she's not here and you get to live when she had to die?"

"Chose to die!" he says.

"Can you blame her for wanting to live a regular life! You're four hundred; I'm three hundred ninety-nine. All I wanted to do was go to a regular school, have regular friends without trying to rip their throats out all the time! I stopped aging at eighteen, but sometimes I wish I were like her. Just live out my sixty to one hundred years and be done with it. But you, you bask in it, living it up because you're self-centered!" Vonvex storms out.

Colton scoffs, pushes the girl off him, and then walks up the long, unforgiving stairs. William follows.

Maybe they won't miss him after all, William tries to tell himself. But in some ways, he was comparing himself to Colton. If his parents were alive, they'd probably feel similarly. They reach his room and stumble inside, rolling with laughter.

"Wait here," Colton instructs. The girl nods.

William rolls his eyes at the oversized picture of Colton hanging over his bed and smaller ones spread throughout his room. Colton goes into the large bathroom and uses it. The door creeks behind him and closes. He looks over his shoulder. "I told you to wait! Is she under my spell? How did she . . ." He finishes and turns. "Oh, it's you . . ." Colton's eyebrows raise. Ore grins.

William thinks about Colton's downfall and, in his heart, desires that he could have a second chance to make things right. But he knew people, and Colton Scoff wasn't the type to make a change. That's precisely why the devil wanted him. So he had to put feelings aside because, in the end, it wasn't his choice anyway.

"Why are you in my stall?"

Ore recites his usual death sentence: "Your number's up. Satan wants your soul."

Ore drags Colton's head on the white blood-stained tile. It pours out from his brow, nose, and mouth.

"I've seen you show mercy before. Can you do something for me?" Colton asks.

Ore has seen men bargain, beg, and plead for their lives. He's used to it all. "Sure."

"Can you tell my father and sister I'm sorry for making a mess of my life, and . . . I love them?"

William's heart swells. He didn't get to tell his parents good-bye either.

Ore answers, "Yeah, man."

"Do it quickly," says Scoff.

Ore snaps Colton's neck and tears his head from his shoulders. It rolls to the other side of the room, blood running everywhere.

Ore summons flames and burns both ends to a crisp. He stares at his stained hands, which shake uncontrollably. He rubs the blood between his fingers. He loves the way its thickness feels and its unforgiving vibrant color. He runs through the forest and hears the girl in Colton's room screaming, not knowing Vonvex picked up a tiny trace of his scent.

Hell

"It's done."

"Oh, I know. I watched you do it."

"You're following me now?"

"No, I just had to make sure your outburst wasn't going to be a problem. But you didn't even flinch." Satan was filled with glee. "I can see I have no worries. His ask was touching, but no matter."

The tall red figure stands over Ore. "I see you're in your natural form today with red horns and a pitchfork?"

"Yes," says Satan. "Red is my style. My dark hole form is fitting on land, making it more tolerable."

Humming erupts from afar. Ore and Satan straighten up.

"Daddy? Daddy!"

"I'm here, rose petal." Beautiful legs surface, and wings wiggle as the girl steps to them.

"Daddy, I'm bored." She yawns, her red lips forming a perfect *o* behind her silky black gloves. "Oh, hey, Willie," she says sweetly.

"Divina," says Ore.

"Daddy, make Willie take me flying."

"I have something to . . ." Ore stops as they both stare at him, knowing they won't permit insubordination.

"See, he's not busy." An evil smile spreads on her face.

"Take her, Ore, and bring her back in twenty minutes."

"*Twenty minutes?* Daddy, that's not enough . . . I think I'm angry." She crosses her arms.

"Divina, I am not moved by your threats. If I let you out of my sight for too long and anything happens to you, Divina, I—"

She starts flapping her wings wildly, and gusts of wind flood hell, making its lava splash.

"Divina, your pouting is not getting to me. I have said what I said."

Ore casually dodges goo and raises an eyebrow at the devil's smoking skin.

She makes a whirlwind, attracting rock and fire.

"Ore, take Divina out for thirty minutes, no longer." The underground hurricane stops, and the lava falls back into its proper area.

"Yay!" She lands on her feet and struts past Ore, blowing a piece of ash off of her wing. He follows her as she scratches at the skin below her necklace.

They fly, and Divina flips, twirls, and dives as if she were a fish in water. She extends her wings and allows the sun to give them natural warmth. She lands under bunches of trees, and William closely follows as she skips along.

"I feel like more of a bird than an underground thingy. It's so moist and dark down there. I'd rather have wind flowing through my hair and the sun's light warming my wings, not lava." She sighs. "Sometimes I don't understand how he could be my daddy. We're so different."

When she was a baby hawk, Satan stole her from her nest because she's rare. Her power is unmatched. They try not to anger her because she could destroy the world if pushed.

She wraps her arms around his neck. "Willie, do you have a girlfriend?"

"I don't."

"Why not? You're very handsome."

"I don't want one."

"Oh well, I guess what I feel will always only be a crush."

She frowns. He forces a smile, and distastefulness comes to him at the thought of the destruction she could cause.

He studies Divina. Her beauty is immeasurable. No other being could hold the delicacy of her features or drink from the same cup she held to her exquisite lips.

Her structure was perfectly picked like flowers by the Creator, each part colorful. Her arms and legs are long, and her skin is bright, like a shooting star. And her pastel gray-green feathers, while beautiful, pale in comparison to her eyes.

She's a masterpiece, but he knows although she claims to be nothing like her father, as soon as she gets her claws into him, he can add another set of links to his chains. To her, they're invisibly already there. She has loose screws, but he senses it's because she's not with her true people and feels emptiness, not knowing how to express herself. He'd only been with the devil a few years, but Divina's been since she was a chick and no doubt questions the chain around her neck. She loosens her arms and says, "Let's go. Daddy will be waiting." She walks a few steps and then blasts into the air. William follows suit.

12

I Think I Adore You

A few weeks go by, and shipments come in daily with stuff Mom ordered online. It's better than her going out to find products, although I know she'd like that. They're mostly used, but she always buys them "like new" and is an excellent bargain hunter, always negotiating on the phone. It's super funny to watch.

"That's too much! I'm not paying thirty dollars for used candleholders. I don't care if they're zebra-shaped and printed! I'll put my order in right now if you give them to me for fifteen dollars!" She pauses, telling the delivery guy to set the boxes behind the counter.

"Twenty? No, eighteen! Final offer!" She awaits a response, worry flashing in her eyes. I can tell it's something she doesn't wanna lose.

I sit by anxiously as she hangs up, drooling to know what happened already! "Well?"

"I got them for eighteen dollars!"

We jump in victory. Mom goes on to say, "I'm gonna sell them here for thirty dollars! They're gorgeous. Wait till you see them, honey!"

I can't believe I just witnessed her cleverness. She acted as if it didn't matter, even though she really wanted them, which is what snagged her the sale. I find myself hoping to be even a fraction of who she is. She's *incredible.* I blink away my newfound adoration for her. Something in me wants her to interact with me further, but I push it back.

Her tables are almost full, and she decides to open her doors to wandering customers. She greets them with a smile, and I roll my eyes. If they think I'm as sweet as her, they're in for a rude awakening because I am not. I hide behind the register and plug in headphones as I watch her cheerfully help people and check them out. She taps my shoulder, and I take out an earbud.

"Baby, can you help out Mrs. Baker here?"

Is she serious? I grumpily follow her instructions, pounding down on every button till the very end. It surprisingly goes by smoothly. I even say, "Thank you and have a nice day," to the customer and write down the purchase in the books. I could possibly get used to this.

"You okay, sweetheart?"

I nod. She's sweating a little as she shows a man plastic flowers. It seems today is taking a lot out of her.

"I'll take the whole box if you say they'll look good around the church's pulpit," the man says. He and my mom laugh as they stroll to the register, and if I wasn't sure about my parents' love, I'd be concerned.

"I can do it, Mom. Sit." I grab the box, partially wanting her to rest and also because I want her to get away from him.

"Thank you, love." She smiles at me. *If only she knew.*

At home, I see her take a bajillion pills, which shocks me. Days go by, and I watch her even closer. Maybe I'm hallucinating, but it seems she has pain in her body that she's hiding.

A guy comes in one day and tells my mother his name is Julio, and he owns a boat. Says he travels the world and looks for extraordinary pieces and would like to bring her some to sell.

"I would have to see the things you have, Julio. I know good stuff, and so does my sweet daughter." She's bragging about me again, and I don't know if it's true. He agrees and shows her pieces she's completely in love with, including a glass flower from Japan and vases from Alaska.

She negotiates a deal with him to make a profit from what he brings her, and days go by before I see him again. He finally stops by, and now my mother has created a whole table for his items, almost like she did for me. However, I have an entire room! I look at it and smile at her generosity I hadn't seen before. Maybe I was too stuck in my teenage drama queen madness to notice. Now that it's just us, things are so different. I kinda get what Addison meant.

He pulls out necklaces from his bag, and I strain my neck to look at them. My mom notices and motions for me to come over. He places them in my hands.

"Where'd you get these?" I say in amazement.

"India." He has an Hispanic accent.

"Do you want them for your room, baby girl?"

"Please?"

"Of course! Take them."

I bring them to the register. They're beautiful, but I know I can add my touch somehow.

I go to craft stores with the money I've earned and look online for trinkets I could possibly add. I was so focused on creating them that I barely noticed my mother was getting weaker and weaker.

One day Julio brought a whole bicycle from Italy. He said his crew found it at the bottom of a river. My mother shook in excitement, but her store is way too small for it. I thought maybe he could bring it to Shirt's Out, the thrift store. But she thought it had spunk. It was brown with fake flowers tied to it, and although it had been submerged in water, the effect it created made it look vintage somehow. She bought mint-colored paint, and we painted it together in the back before the store opened, in our overalls. Laughter filled the space as she told me stories of Josh when he was a baby.

The color set it off, and she added more flowers by the handlebars and a silver bell she found online. We let it sit in the back to dry for a few days while considering how to price it.

"What do you think?" she asks me.

My eyes get big, and I shrug. She's the price expert.

"It should be more than a hundred, I know that much!" I say sarcastically. She nods and writes the price on a tag without telling me, leaving me to wonder. She then starts to bring it into the store.

I run to where she placed it along the wall. It reads two hundred dollars! She doubled it!

"Mom, they're not gonna buy it at that price. I didn't mean it!" I would be so embarrassed if people walked by thinking, *That's way too costly!* Ugh!

"I think your instinct is right, and the right person will buy it—even if it were labeled a thousand dollars." She winks at me and continues to straighten up the shop before opening.

That night, I lay in bed thinking about that ridiculous bike. Not just about the price but about how much fun I had with my mother.

"Lolly!" she yells. I rush downstairs.

"Mom!" *Is she okay?* She's in the kitchen, ingredients scattered throughout the countertops.

"Wanna help?"

I smile. How much more fun could we have? "What are we cooking?" I am antsy to see what she'll say.

"Pot roast."

Daddy blesses the food, and we eat. They love it, and Daddy

cheers me on for learning. Josh even says I finally did something right, and I *whatever* him. I grab Josh's and my plate to put them in the sink.

"What's wrong with you?" says Josh. "Mom, Lolly's sick!"

"What?" Mom says and studies me.

"Am not!" I yell like a child, then turn around to wash dishes and notice *I'm washing dishes!* Ew, maybe I am sick? I touch my forehead to confirm. I'm normal temperature. Thank you very much, Josh!

"Aww, baby, I'll do it! Your nails will get ruined."

"Got it, Mom, not a big deal." I throw her attitude that hasn't been around lately, and it feels like I'm backtracking somehow.

Everyone is gone when I'm done cleaning the kitchen, and I've worked up a sweat. I wipe at it and walk into my parents' room.

"Just wanted to say goodnight." Don't know why I did. It just felt right.

They look like they've seen Bigfoot. "Um . . . yeah, honey . . . we uh, goodnight."

I turn to walk away, but my parents' words make me stay. "Thank you for cleaning up, sweetheart. It really helped your mother!" Daddy says.

"Don't mention it. Bye!" I sweetly say and walk out. I lay in bed looking at my nails. Sure enough, they do have chips. It sucks, but it was worth every fragment.

As I am getting ready for the shop the next morning, I hear a heavy pounding at my door. I run to open it, and Josh stands there, looking scared.

"Where's Mom!"

"Dad took her to the hospital. Said she had a fever that wouldn't break. Can we go?"

I scramble to find my keys.

"Come on!" he shouts.

"I'm trying to find my keys, Josh!"

"They're on the hook in the kitchen like always . . . Did you forget?"

He's right. I made a habit of it ever since we moved in. *What's wrong with me?*

"We don't have time for this!" he says, in panic mode.

"I just don't know what to do," I whisper, trying to catch my breath.

"What?"

I gather strength. "Nothing! Let's just go!" I try to sound well put together because he's already freaking out. I don't wipe my tears until I pass him.

13

Up-a-Sale, Down-a-You

Mommy hated that we had to close the shop for a whole week while she was recovering. She spent three days in the hospital in a feeble state and went home for the rest, gathering her strength. I went by the shop a few times to decorate my room and to keep from thinking about her. My brain couldn't comprehend how one moment she could be running around the shop so vibrantly, then restricted to a pillow and blanket the next.

A tall dresser I asked her to order for my necklaces finally came in today, and I found myself wishing she could be here. It was oldish, but the wood looked so chic. I placed a laced table-cloth over it to match her style. I sent pictures to Ady, who adored it. She'd been so busy with school and I with the shop that we barely spoke. I missed her so much. Tears were beginning to well up in my eyes, and I had to get out of here. I walk the aisles of *Shirt's Out Thrift* and find a mannequin for ten bucks. Who would've thought I'd be a thrifter?

The shop owners, the Franks, ask about her. I really don't want to answer the question, but all the shop owners love her very much. When mom has time, she visits and buys from them. I would hate to be the one to not inform them about her progress.

"Well, we sure are praying for her!" says Mr. Frank, dressed in a superhero costume and taking pictures with the kids. Mrs. Frank wears a matching set, which makes me giggle. I thank them before walking out of their door and find myself searching for new air to breathe.

Back in our shop, I wipe tears, then look over at the notorious mint bike. "You never really got a chance, did you?" I say and head home.

The next day I heard a knock early, and I hurry to it.

"Ready for work, babygirl?"

I jump to her, nearly knocking her down, then remember I have to be gentle.

"Sorry, Mom!"

"I missed the shop too, sweetheart."

Well, I meant I missed you most, Mama, my heart says, and I keep it under lock and key. She tells me she experienced a flareup for the first time, where her symptoms worsened temporarily. I don't fully understand, but I listen. She looks tired and like she tried to cover it with makeup, but she is still so beautiful. We open the shop. So many customers are there throughout the day, but she handles herself very well. I do see her go into the back a lot, though.

I catch her eyeing something very closely and look. A guy is checking out the mint bike. I gasp. It seems as if she's thinking about going over to him. His eyes dart to us, and we quickly act like we're in full-blown conversation.

"I'm interested in purchasing the green bike," he says. He has no knowledge about the specifics of colors. *The bike is mint!* I roll my eyes, thinking about the effort it took to decorate, and get irritated. Mom said it would be for someone special. He doesn't seem exquisite to me, and I pout.

"Yes, of course." Mom rings him up, remembering the price very well.

"It reminds me of home. I miss it very much." I now realize he is speaking with an accent.

"Really? Are you from Italy?"

"I am."

"It was shipped from Italy, and it's been waiting here just for you."

Mom winks at me. I'm sure there's a twinkle in my eye. He pays the two hundred dollars plus tax with no problem, and we watch him walk out a satisfied customer.

Our hands fly up. "We did it!" Mom says. "See, sometimes you have to take that risk!" I nod. This seems like something I'll hold on to forever.

We spent the first three months with everything pretty normal. We even finished my room in the shop, and I decided to paint the walls "Bike Mint Green" because I couldn't stop thinking about its success. Sometimes I see the Italian customer riding by, making great use of it. He seems happy, like he's connected to home somehow.

We decided to call my room at the shop "The Lolly Pobs Collection." It had a ring to it, and I thought it was perfect. And the best thing about it was Mom.

As I sit at my mother's funeral, staring at the large picture of the beauty before me and thinking about the last three months of her life, I wonder how I let so much time slip away before we formed our . . . *connection*. Like beach sand I tried to hold within a clenched fist that still escaped due to crashing waves, she was ripped from me. I wonder why I was so mean to her for so long when she was a complete angel to me. I spent only six months adoring her, admiring her, wanting to be like her and with her. She was available to me like this all along, but I took her for granted. I sob. Pain is in my chest I had never experienced before.

Josh and I knew she was undergoing radiation to help her stay alive, but our parents didn't tell us they'd only given her six months to live. My mother was slowly slipping away, but Josh and I had no clue. At the end, when it was clear she wasn't going to make it, I asked her why she didn't tell me. She said she didn't want me to be sad and only wanted me to remember the good parts.

I look at Josh across the room. He catches my glance, and I look away. He and Mom had always been so close. Now I know why he felt that way for her, as I experienced it myself. I think he took her passing the worst, resorting to punching walls and throwing things around the house. I could hear him crying at night, his room so close to mine.

At the funeral, Daddy seemed confused, like he didn't know his left from his right. I could tell he tried to be polite to all the people gathered to remember Mom, but it seemed he just wanted to be alone. Everyone from Barns came, and family I hadn't seen in years came too. They were the ones who acted like they cared so much for her but barely even checked on her when her life was normal or when it wasn't. I was kind, remembering she called me "sweet" and didn't correct them when they said they loved and missed her.

Everyone was gone now except for an emotional Julio and us. He'd really taken a liking to her. He seems more like family than the others, and I hope he will stay around. We sit there a little longer just to be with her. Addison and I sat silently, two girls in black dresses, hand in hand.

My brain sunk deeper into the rabbit hole.

Her body had been fighting itself, attacking her organs, and they were failing. She was always so tired, losing significant amounts of weight at a time, and losing her hair. They pumped her with pain meds and steroids for the swelling her body underwent. She changed her eating habits to healthier choices, which was the hardest because she loved to cook, and we loved her food. Even Josh gave up the sweets he loved so much. I would be lying if I said having steamed carrots five nights in a row didn't leave me permanently damaged.

She was back in that bed for good this time and asked me to take care of the shop. I hesitantly agreed, wondering now if it made her go faster. We didn't know what would happen then, but deep down, *she knew*. It was in every word she said, the sadness behind her eyes. She told me I was the most beautiful young woman in the world and that she knew I'd make her proud. She told me that it made her so very happy that we built a relationship and to never forget that love. She also said to keep God close and trust Him even through hard times. If I didn't feel it before, I sure felt it then too, the deep pressure of goodbye . . . and I hated it.

I then found myself skipping her room to avoid all her final *farewells*. It wasn't right that she said those things like she felt she didn't have a chance. I was so confused. She was always a fighter. I sat outside her room crying, barely being able to breathe, gasping to catch even a tiny bit of air.

Light research suggested I was having panic attacks, and a few symptoms confirmed it. I didn't tell anyone because I didn't want to worry them. I just wanted to be near Mama for once and not think about what would eventually occur, which was devastating. I prayed for Jesus to keep her here for longer. Maybe for a miracle, but I wasn't sure what words to use.

After it had been a bit since I had checked in on her, I did go to visit her.

"Where's my precious girl?" Mom said. I breathed deeply to stop the compulsion of my chest and wiped my tears.

"Right here, Mommy."

"Lolly, I haven't seen you, my beautiful girl. I need . . . I need to see your smile. Please don't go away," she said gently.

I nodded, looking at the tubes in her nostrils helping her breathe. "I won't, Mom. I'm sorry, I . . . I . . ." I never knew how to explain myself. I didn't know how to not hurt her feelings and keep mine a secret or what the right words would be to use for such an unsure future.

But I realized I was being selfish. I was worried about the hurt Mama was causing me by looking at her this way when she was always so full of life instead of just being with her. From that moment on, I spent every waking moment with her unless I was at the shop. I hadn't realized the agony I was causing myself by staying away. I got instant energy from just being near her. I understood better why God made us to love one another. I reduced the standard hours for the shop to be with her more. I ran it by her, of course, and she said I would be an outstanding businesswoman. I knew her shop meant the world to her, and I had to keep it going to somehow summon the strength to smile at new customers and handle the questions of known ones.

We came up with "Cookbook Fridays" for fun at home. She sat in the kitchen every Friday in her wheelchair as I read the cookbook she'd written before her fingers stopped working properly. I cooked most of the stuff by myself with her guidance because she was too weak, and I even made her lasagna by myself when she couldn't get up. We tore it up like cavemen because we ate healthy the rest of the week. Mama had some, and she approved it, and that would give me the push I needed to make her recipes for years to come.

I didn't want to let her go. Was that selfish of me? What if I have questions that no one else could answer *but her?* I apologized for all the years I'd badmouthed her.

She said, "I don't know what you're referring to. Every word you spoke came from my sweet, beautiful babygirl. All I know is I love you beyond words." I cried so much that the riverbeds couldn't hold my tears.

Hospital trips became routine then until they weren't . . .

"Daddy, when can she go home? Hopefully not after two weeks like last time." I chuckled, but Daddy shook his head at me. "Daddy! I'm sure she'd rather be home. It's too cold here." I rubbed my arm to soothe the bumps that had risen from the air, or maybe it was a feeling telling me something more serious was going on, something more . . . *final.*

"She's gone, Lolly."

At first, the words wouldn't register, upload, or ring through that she wasn't coming home for sure. And so this time, Mama, I had to say farewell to you.

14

Mother Dear

Grand's body slowly floats downward. It jerks, fighting to stay alive even in its worn state. He reaches the bottom of the blue water, and tiny bubbles ring out as Z71 comes into contact with an object. He's there all night.

In Heaven

"Go!" says God, who sits in majesty.

And out of heaven dispenses a troop of winged angels to earth. Two groups of six burst into the metal doors, wrapped in white material, barefooted with outstretched arms. They run up flights of stairs found on each side of the tank. Two of them focus on retrieving the treasure from the bottom of the watered burial, and the rest are waiting and singing a hymn to the Lord. Grand's body slowly rises and has now peaked. They grab him, and the surrounding angels gently clap. They raise his body out of the grave and descend to the ground.

They stand and wait for the Father's verdict. It comes: "My child, rise up!" says the voice from above, and the angels dance in praise and song at what the Lord has done. They prance to their home in heaven. The room returns to darkness in the absence of their light.

At eight a.m. sharp, there's a knock at the door. "Grand?" His mother walks in and pulls the comforter. He yanks it back.

"Hmm!"

"Where have you been? You think you can party and come back just like that?"

"Not now, Ma."

"Not now? When is a better time for you?" she shouts and swats him on what could be his head.

"Stop, Ma!"

"What about school, Grand?"

"I'm not going today." He groans.

"We're gonna talk about it, Grand. I am not tolerating this behavior in my home!" His Latina mother walks out, slamming the door.

The growling of his stomach wakes him before the day does, and he pulls the sheets off and stretches. He instantly remembers what Luke and his boys did last night, and flashes of angels pulling him out of the water come up. He rushes to the mirror, flinching at the blue tint covering his face.

"Ma?" he calls into the house but receives no answer. He showers, scrubs his body, and finds that every inch is covered with this blue stuff. He whimpers, thinking about all that had occurred.

He walks back to the mirror and studies himself. His body still has a blue tint but is ripped with good-sized muscles, although he'd never gone to a gym. He flexes his muscles, turning to each side. His hair is not orange anymore. It's a light brown hue, and he likes it above everything. Was some kind of dye in the water? He can't go to school like this, and his smile disappears. Maybe he could wait on the color to fade in the next couple of days.

He eats leftovers, thinking of Rachel. She'd be at lunch right now. He looks around. His belongings are gone, and he huffs in anger before picking up his house phone, trying to remember her number. It rings.

"Hello? Rachel?"

"Grand! Where are you?" She sounds excited.

"Home, I'm . . ." He looks at himself in the mirror. "Sick."

"Oh gosh. Is it that bug that's going around?" she whispers.

"Yeah," he says because there's always a bug going around.

His muscles give him confidence, mixed with a bit of Ci's teachings. "I miss you." But he shakes his head, deciding that's too big of a plunge, and adds, "I just called to check on you." He puts his hand over his face.

"Grand, I . . ."

He readies himself for the rejection he's used to, but she says, "I miss you too."

He picks up his head. "I'm finishing up a project. Can I call you later?"

"Of course." They hang up. Grand jumps in a cheer, and the top of his head hits the ceiling, creating a hole. Debris falls like snow. *Did he just fly?* He goes for it again. He springs high but can't hover, no matter how hard he tries. He looks at his face in the mirror. *Who is he kidding?*

He'll never see the light of day again, let alone Rachel Simon. He thought he was getting picked on before, but this is undeniably weird.

He manages to avoid his mother for three days.

"Grand! Open the door or I will call the police!"

He panics. She beats at the door, and he places his back on it, saying, "I can't, okay!"

"Why?"

He slides to the foot of the door. "Cause I can't, Ma." Tears well in his eyes, her silence pushing them out and onto the ground. A sizzling noise followed by smoke coming from under him captures his attention. He scoots over. Is she smoking him out? He squints, seeing tiny dents where his tears had fallen on the ground.

His hands quiver as he wipes at his eyes with his T-shirt. Holes build into it. He removes it and throws it across the room. He feels wetness around his eyes and wipes at it. The liquid is now on his fingers, and nothing happens. *Was he imagining things?* He grabs the shirt he threw, wipes the rest of his face, and it tears wide open. His eyes dart from side to side, fear ripples through him, and for the first time, he feels alone.

He drops the shirt, wipes the sweat from his forehead, twists the doorknob, and runs out. "Ma, help me!" He grabs her wrist, and she squeals and snatches it away.

Shivering, she pulls her eyes away from the blue figure. They now focus on the burn mark of his handprint he's left on her.

"Diablo!" she yells and runs into his bathroom, locking herself inside.

He goes to it. "Ma!" Unwanted tears come. He tries to catch them before they fall, but they hit the ground. Smoke fills the area, and his mother wails in terror. He rushes to his room, throwing the door behind him. It burned her but didn't affect his skin at all? He's ashamed. He'd never intentionally hurt her. She stays there the rest of the day and night.

In the morning, he hears the bathroom door, and his eyes shoot open. He races to it, but his mother makes it to her room and locks her door.

"Ma, please, talk to me!" She doesn't. "I'm sorry, Ma!" He resists the urge to cry and stays at her door for hours just to be with someone other than himself in that room. He eats and leaves a plate and water at her door. He barely hears his mother and misses her even if she *is* domineering.

His days are filled with containment, Call of Duty, and enchanting calls from Rachel. He notices his toothbrush, although holding up a bit, is melting. His spit and pee are going down the drains fine, but the pipes are beginning to squeak as if his liquids are doing a number on them. He starts waking up to evaporated sheets and halved pillows. He realizes his sweat is melting them, and the AC isn't keeping him cool enough. He gets cardboard boxes from the garage, puts them on his hole-filled mattress, and makes a boarded pillow with string. He's now sure the blue is a part of him, and all liquids in his body make things dissolve.

He hears his mother in the kitchen but needs to pee really bad. He doesn't want to scare her, so he runs to it. He still hears pots and pans moving around and rejoices. He walks out and attempts to talk to her, but she runs and hides in the pantry. He goes into his room, deciding on baby steps like Ci instructed.

His orders of anti-sweat clothing finally arrive. His face is entirely masked, except for his eyes, which have a dark netted film over them, along with long sleeves, pants, and gloves. The next day, he jogs down his familiar empty path to catch Rachel leaving school. He had to connect the voice with the beauty. She gets into her father's car, and they ride off, leaving his heart on the street.

"I saw you today."

"You did? Where?"

"Leaving school."

"Why didn't you say hi?"

"I should've." He melts.

"Maybe we can hang soon? I haven't seen you since you went to a different school," she says.

Soon sounds so far away . . .

15

Hellbound

William needed to stay away from his favorite place until things cleared up at the Scoffs. All he did was sleep and sit in the dark while victims' faces flashed in his head with no relief. Colton's irritated him the most. Sharing that moment with his family and then getting rid of him scarred him. He rose from his bed shirtless and raked his fingers through his hair. Would they always have this power over him? His knees dig into the carpet, and his elbows follow. "Get out of my head!" he says.

Eloise walks in and draws back the shades. William pulls the blanket over his head.

"Mornin' Elo." His voice sounds raspy.

"Time to get up, William. You can't sleep all day."

"I don't know, El. I think it's possible."

"It very well may be, but I'm making the recipe you slipped me, and I'm sure you won't want to miss it."

William turns towards her, saying, "You're right."

Elo then says, "But first, breakfast." She moves out of the way and allows the maids to bring in trays.

They set it up at a small table, far away from his king-sized bed, which was Elo's strategy to get him out of it. After they leave, he looks at the door left open, raises his hand to shut it, and closes the blinds in one swoop. Elo doesn't know about his power, none of the housekeepers do, and he intends to keep it that way. If God decided to banish him because he showed humans his ability, maybe he could escape from the devil. But whatever God had in mind for the banshee would probably suck worse than chains.

With that thought, he closes his eyes and doesn't wake until the power of coffee and blueberry pies stirs in his nostrils. He climbs out of bed and follows the scent to the kitchen. He grabs a pie cutter and walks toward the two crusted deserts. He raises the metal to cut.

"Not so fast, William Blue Junior!"

He closes his eyes and flinches at the way she just called his whole name. He turns to look at the British woman who has cared for him since he left the womb.

"Those have to cool!" They watch the maids bring in his stale breakfast he didn't touch. "Table, now!" Elo points.

He pushes off the counter and drags himself to the long dining room table. The girls immediately bring him new food, swooning over his lack of a shirt. He grins, flashing his eyebrows at them. "A shirt wouldn't hurt!" Eloise snatches a Polo shirt from a peeking maid and hands it to him. He scoffs at her block game and throws it on. "Enjoy," she says.

He rips breakfast apart, glad he let Elo force him to eat. The girls come back to retrieve empty dishes and lightly whisper about him. He grabs one of the maid's hands and pulls her close, making sure Elo is nowhere in sight. "Could you do me a favor?" he softly whispers in her ear. He can feel her trembling.

"Anything, sir." He barely hears her tiny voice.

"Would you bring me a pan of blueberry pie, sweetheart?"

"Right away sir." She quickly runs to the kitchen, and he hears them squealing. *That'll teach them to keep their eyes to themselves.*

After spooning it down, he goes into his home gym and works out. He stares at the cameras and decides to go into his power room, a metal room he built with his own hands. He turns into Ore, forms small fire flames, and throws them at the walls. Some evaporate, and others bounce back at him. He dodges, running on the steel walls. He flips off after they're gone and summons black fire rings burning with lava. He throws them, and they dart at him with no mercy, too many of them fill the box. He counters them with more rings. They create a spark when they touch, then disappear.

Two cut at each arm, ricocheting from the wall behind him to the other wall and coming back for more. The wounds throb, but he doesn't keep his eyes off his aggressors. He powers up and blows the rings out one by one. He tenses up, trying not to let the pain drive him, his devices causing him to heal slower than usual. "You can't get sloppy!" he says to himself.

Soft metal calls to him, and he watches a single ring bouncing horizontally between walls.

"You want me?" His brows lower, his eyes squint for concentration, and his lip twitches. "Who doesn't!" He roars and sucks it toward him. He tightens his fists and shoots his left foot in the air, catching the ring with it, and smashes it underneath his foot. It crackles into pieces and disappears.

With clenched teeth, he melts into normal skin, wiping angry tears he didn't know were there until their coolness rolled down his hot skin. Black marks line the metal walls now. He grunts while closing his eyes, restoring them to their original strong and shiny solidity.

He showers and dresses in a black shirt, blue tailor-made suit, and black dress shoes. Later, William walks around the burning inferno. Rock shakes under his feet, and a different type of heat fills the area.

"Look! It's the pretty boy," a ghoul says.

William rolls his eyes.

"I guess you're too good to talk to hell folk now that you get to go up to the surface."

That gets his attention. "Nah, I just don't like talking to you."

"Master, he's gonna start to think he's a regular human when he's just like us!"

"Hold your tongue, Ashaka! You're commissioned to dwell in the dark. William *is* a human in duty to me."

What a pleasure, William thinks but still grins at the tall ghoul. "Nevertheless, one of us," the devil finishes.

William scoffs. "And what's my duty today?" he asks the giant dark matter dressed in Indian clothing.

"Today you come with me. There's a debt I need settled."

"I don't do back up," William says, his fist tightening.

"Hmm, I can just taste the metal around your throat in a cell guarded by Ashaka."

"You don't have to threaten me with chains every time I say no to you!" William says.

"I'm sorry, did you think this was a negotiation?" The devil pounces towards him, but William puts his hands in his pockets and looks away. He knows what this means—he'll have to sit by and watch Satan talk someone into lying, stealing, killing, or worse . . . *suicide*. He didn't want any part of it.

The devil grabs William by the collar and throws him into a small, lit cave. His necklace and bracelet turn into iron. Links form one by one, chaining him to the wall. Leaky lava bars close his prison, and the devil laughs down the hall as Ashaka peeks in. "See, you're no better than us," he laughs. William tries to break the chains but feels them tugging at his soul.

16

Babygirl's Got God

Addison accompanied me to the shop to clean up the way Mommy would've wanted. She cried with me and told me, "It's okay to cry, best friend. Let it out." I did. I poured out my heart while I still had my bestie. She finally saw my room at the shop and loved my mannequin. Mommy and I had picked out a large-striped black and white flared dress for it. Addy and I matched it with one of my colorful necklaces and talked until the sun went down. On Sunday, I accompanied her to the airport.

After Addison left, I couldn't sleep and wouldn't eat or pick up any calls from her. Daddy and I closed the shop since he said I had to get myself together before I tried to run it again. Josh's grades dropped, and he put football on the back burner. Coach gave him time but warned him he'd be off the team if he wasn't back ASAP. Daddy tried talking to Josh, but he wasn't hearing it. I lay at the top of the stairs, with a blanket and pillow, to cry with Daddy. I knew he wouldn't do it while I was around. One time, he poured orange juice into his cereal, bit into an orange instead of an apple, then continued to chew, staring into space. I saw this and strangely understood, not once attempting to stop him. She had left us in bad shape. *She had left us.*

That's when the sleepwalking started.

I see her open my door without knocking, motioning for me

to come with her. It's so foggy, but this is so like her. I get up, admiring my beautiful yellow dress, and follow her down those spiraling steps. I see her long sweater, pants, and heels go into the kitchen. She turns on all the burners for us to cook, and they play a trick on my eyes, dancing in the darkness.

She's leaning on the counter quietly. The heat from the burners carries through the air, stinging my eyes, and I place my arm over my face, blocking the radiation.

"Mama?" I call, but she's gone. Instead, I find a grave with a stone and ugly dirt knitted into the kitchen floor. I fall to my knees, grab my mother's apron hanging from the oven door, and clinch it to my chest.

"Mommy!" A horrifying screech escapes my mouth.

Lolly's father stumbles into the kitchen, and Josh follows. They turn on the light and see her on her knees. Then they see the whole stovetop lit up in red, including the oven.

He hurries to Lolly. "Josh! Turn off the stove!"

Josh carefully reaches the knobs, and the heat can even be felt under his long sleeve.

"Lolly, honey? Wake up!" Her eyes are tightly closed, and beads of sweat are beaming on her forehead, making her hair stick to her face. Her father pulls at the apron. She grunts, not wanting him to take it, and tightens her grip.

"Shake her!" Josh commands.

Her father does, saying, "Lolly, open your eyes, sweetheart!" Her wet eyelashes slowly pull apart.

"Daddy?"

"Yes, I'm here." He swipes her hair out of her face.

"Where am I?" Her eyes are filled with tears.

"You made it all the way to the kitchen sleepwalking, Big Pobs," says Josh, trying to crack a joke at the wrong time. His father shoots him a look.

"What?" He shrugs. "I'm just saying, she's sleep walking."

"I'm what?" Lolly asks, wide-eyed.

The next night, Daddy and Josh stand in my doorway, staring at me.

"Are you sure you're okay?" Daddy asks as Josh examines me.

"Stop, I'm okay!" I swipe at him.

"Yep, attitude is back. She's okay."

"Ugh! Get out!"

"Double whammy!" he says, and I throw a pillow at him on his way out.

"Lolly, if you feel anything strange, I'm downstairs right next to the kitchen," Daddy says, as if I'm able to shift my body in my sleep. Wait, that's kinda creepy. "Goodnight." He walks out and shuts the door.

I reluctantly turn off my lights. "Everything will be okay," I tell myself before whisking into dreamland.

I see her again. This time she touched my hand, and I was expecting her. She pulls at it, and I get up. This time she's leading me by the hand.

"Mama is that yo—"

"Let's make something, Babygirl." She turns on the stove again.

I tremble, remembering she disappeared last time. "What are we making, Mama?"

"Whatever you wanna make, my beautiful girl," she says, her voice echoing weirdly through the air. I'm having a hard time believing this is my mother. She grabs a pot, fills it to the brim, and places it on the stove. Then another and another. They sit on the red burners. She motions for me to fill the last one.

I turn the knob, and the pot quickly fills. Mommy is nodding in approval. I smile, happy I'm making her happy. I put it on the stove, and a bit spills out.

"Be careful, Babygirl. We need every bit."

For what? She hasn't said, but I nod. I place it on the final burner and turn to find her gone again. I sob, saying, "Mommy! Mommy! Mommy!"

I wake up to a scared Josh and a red-faced father. Sweat is dripping down my face because of steam beaming from the stove. Water is all over the floor. Four pots are sitting stovetop with boiling water jumping out of them. I faint.

I wake up in the hospital. A tube is in my arm like Mommy had, and I try to yank it out.

"Sweetheart, stop!" Daddy runs over to me just in time. Josh is sitting across the room, staring with tired eyes. I mildly fight with my father, trying to get off the bed.

"Daddy, why is there a tube in my arm?"

"You're dehydrated. They're just trying to get liquids into your system."

"But this is where Mama died, Daddy! Am I gonna die too?" I weep, and Daddy's body droops.

"Of course not, sweetheart." He sits next to me and holds my neck, caressing my cheek with his thumb. Josh shifts in his seat, and the normally confident boy seems uncomfortable.

A nurse walks in and says, "Hey, Babygirl, I see you're up now." She checks the bag connected to me.

"Don't call me that!" I say sternly.

"I'm sorry. Her mother use to call her that," Daddy says. I look at him. He doesn't need to tell her our business. He doesn't need to tell her about Mama!

"I'm so sorry, Lolly. I'm just gonna swap out your bag, and I'll be on my way, okay?"

"No, I don't want your bag! Daddy, let's go!"

"Okay. We're just waiting on the doctor to release you. Until then, let her change your bag." I nod, holding onto his shirt.

After a while, a beautiful woman with short blonde hair comes in, and I cross my arms.

"Lolly, you're awake, beautiful," she says and comes to my bedside. Daddy backs up.

"You're a healthy one," the doctor says. "Wanna tell me why you're fainting on your dad, giving him the spooks?"

I look down. I can feel my eyebrows fold into each other.

"Okay," she says and looks between Daddy and me.

"Lolly, we have a wonderful counselor working late tonight." She's treading lightly. "Your dad told me about your Mama, and I think that maybe she can help."

"No, I just wanna go home." I pull the sheets over my shoulder and lay sideways.

"Okay. We won't force you. But we'll be here if you change your mind, all right?"

I get emotional. She's really nice and somehow reminds me of my mother. I nod and close my eyes.

I get out of my bed the next morning. Daddy had driven us home last night, but not before Dr. Beauty told him to pump me with plenty of liquids and make sure I was well-rested. She explained that exhaustion caused me to collapse, and I needed to take it easy.

Daddy and Josh left, but not before Daddy made me promise to call him every hour. *It's not happening.* I'm fine, I already have to suck down Gatorade and water all day. *Oh, Mommy, why'd you have to go?*

I go into my parents' room and look through her things. Daddy hasn't moved anything, and I'm happy about it. I open up a drawer she's always in and swipe my fingers across her blouses.

I see an envelope with my name on it and pull it out. "For Lolly's next birthday," says the writing, her handwriting, on the envelope. My hand covers my mouth.

I sit on their bed and flip it around to the back. It's sealed shut. I pout. My birthday isn't for weeks. I shake it and hear something inside. Like gold, I take the envelope with me, tucking it away. I'll try my best not to open it before my nineteenth birthday.

Addison calls again, and I ignore it.

A text comes in. "Lolly, I know you see this! Lemme in, babe!" I smile at it but don't respond. I know it'll be good to talk to her, but I don't *want* to be happy, and playing girl chat will imply everything's good, and it's really not. I'll give myself some time and then reply.

The Third Night

I see my mother. We're in the kitchen with the burners on, and I see her smirk and feel my reluctance. One single pot sits on the stove. I look at the floor, and the awful dirt fills it. The stone is present, and Mama's gone. I find the strength to read it: "Here lies the beloved Elizabeth Ann Pobs, a true angel on earth." Tears fall as I get up.

"Ready, Babygirl?" I hear her, but I don't see her. I nod.

I take the boiling water off the stove and turn around to take it out of the kitchen. I see Daddy's door.

"Lolly, stop!" The small nudge I've been feeling now loudspeakers in my heart, and I realize what I'm doing. I gasp, turn off all the burners, and pour out the pot's contents. I step over the dirt and turn on the lights, and it disappears. I pray as Mama told me to: "Jesus, I need Your help."

Daddy comes into my room the next morning and says, "Still

in bed, huh?" I nod. "Hmm, maybe you were just dehydrated."

"Hey freak," says Josh, who has also come into my room. "You okay?"

"Whatever, Josh." He smiles for the first time in a while, brightening my day. If my sleepwalking caused him to smile this big, I'd do it again.

I later catch Daddy before he leaves for work. "Daddy, about the shop. Can we reopen? It's not like it's gonna pay for itself." I beg with my eyes.

"We'll talk about that after a few more days of you waking up in your bed, young lady." I nod.

I cook tonight, well, not exactly. I make TV dinners and line them up on the kitchen counter, "Dinner's ready!" I call, and Daddy and Josh run out like they're getting a home-cooked meal. I shove each box in each hand and take mine upstairs to my room, ignoring their sour faces. *Hey, it's a start!* I finish eating, dump the evidence, and decide to never make TV dinners again! I surprisingly see that the contents of both meal boxes got eaten. They were pretty bad, but guys will eat anything if they're hungry enough.

I lay in bed that night and wondered why she'd come to me that way. It's so creepy, it prompts me to pray, "God, if you can hear me . . ." *Ugh, of course, He can. He's God, Lolly!* "God, was that you last night? If so, thank You for helping me. I want to help like You do." *Where did that last part come from?* I wonder as I fall asleep mid prayer.

The wind wakes me as it sends chills up my legs. I throw my blanket over me and snuggle back into a comfortable spot.

"Lolly?" I hear a voice and open one eye. *Who?* It's all foggy. "God has heard your prayer and has favored you amongst this generation."

Half sleeping, I stare at the figure with flowing white clothing. "Hmm," I say before closing my eye. After nights of sleepwalking, I'm exhausted.

"Have you heard, Lolly? God has favored you."

"Yes, yes favor," I reiterate.

"The Lord commands you, fight in His army, and through you He will be glorified."

"Yeah, I will . . . do it," I say, almost snoring.

"He will send you a guide and equip you with all you need to fight the battles at hand. And remember, He is with you always."

"Yes, always. Thanks, God." The light finally disappears, and I drift off to sleep once more.

I dreamt of a guy in a tunic. He introduced himself as Michael, and he was pretty hot. He seemed super sweet, like he was a close friend I'd always known. He called himself my guide.

"Like a guidance counselor?" I asked.

He smiled awkwardly and said, "Sure, like a guidance counselor." His smile was amazing.

I wake up, rub my eyes, and get up to brush my teeth. I accidentally tumble over something very hairy and spin, landing on my bottom. My eyes dart to a furry mass.

"Good morning, Lolly!" says an Old English sheepdog. I faint. He comes over and licks my face. I squeak at His divine choice of a remedy.

"Excuse me!" I back away and pull up. "How'd you get in here? Did Daddy bring you in?" Did I just ask a dog a question, awaiting an audible response?

At that very moment, Daddy walks in. "Lolly . . . Oh? You got a dog?" Daddy pets him, and my eyes say danger.

"No, Daddy. He bites!"

"I do not!" says the dog as he's being petted by my father.

Don't faint, Lolly! Or Daddy won't let you open Mama's shop. I hold myself up.

I look at Daddy, expecting him to be in some sort of shock, but he isn't.

"Did you hear that?" I scan his face.

"Hear what?" Daddy asks confidently, chewing on his biscuit.

"He can't hear me. Only you can, Loll," says the dog. *How comforting.*

"Nothing. Don't you have to go to work?" I push Daddy out of my room.

"Wow, you're really strong. Feeling better, huh?" Daddy asks, but I close my door and press my back to it.

I say to myself, "Okay, last night I prayed, I heard some creepy guy, and—"

"Hey, watch it! You're talking about the Holy of Holies here."

"Right, an angel talked to me, and then I dreamt about the other angel . . . Michael?"

"Present!" He stands up tall.

"Wait, wait, wait. You're Michael?"

"In the flesh. But you can call me Arch."

"Arch? Like Archangel Michael in . . . *the Bible!*" I freak out and yell the words.

"Like Archangel Michael in the Bible, Loll."

"Ugh!" I throw my head and hands up, falling onto my bed.

17

When Push Comes to Shove

Rachel's phone rings for days with no answer, and worry bubbles in Grand's gut. He turns on his fan, trying to stay calm. Maybe her parents took her phone again? He waits a few more days before trying again, but the line's not allowing him to make calls. He hears his mother in the kitchen and says, "Ma, what's going on with the phone?"

"I know about the girl."

Grand steadies his breathing. "So?"

"She doesn't know what you are." She walks up to him, and he's surprised that she's not afraid anymore.

"What I am?"

"I told her don't call this house anymore! And you are *un monstruo*!"

A monster? His eyes get big as anger sets in. "You did what?" he roars as his figure lengthens and is humped over his mother.

Her eyes blink rapidly, and her head swoops back further than it's capable. She gets down on her knees to pray. He's heaving, and a drool of acid oozes from his mouth, falling near her, and it steams. Her tense frame causes his eyes to grow gentle, and he reduces back to his original self. He goes into the room and tugs at his hair, looking down at his torn shirt.

How is he able to go into another form? His insides felt stretchy.

"I need the police! My son, he's out of control! He's a monster! Bendito Señor!"

His mother's words alarm him; he grabs his suitcase and stuffs it. Grand pauses for a moment. She had always been such a hard mother, but he still loved her. The thought of leaving frightens him, and tears run down his face and onto his suitcase, making small circles in it. He's tempted to chuck it across the room. Could he ever just do anything normal again?

He climbs out of his bedroom window and sneaks through the back of the house. Sirens blaze behind him, and he begins to sprint. He goes through the gate of the old military base and spits on the chains, securing it. When he enters the room, he immediately spots the label on the tank he was in with this description: "Z71, an Acid Chemical Compound. Caution." He backs up. *Acid?* He touches his arm. *If it's acid, why didn't it eat him alive?*

Grand gets comfortable on the hard, cement floor with a pillow and blanket, looking up at the stars through a small window. He thinks of Rachel, and he weeps and shivers from the cold floor, or the cold night, or this cold world that's been unfair to him since he came into it. He looks at the out-of-state section in the *Minnesota Daily* he took from home. Rachel dances across his mind, but he burns her image into ashes as Washington, D.C. sticks out on the page. The ad said there were a lot of job opportunities.

He cries all day. It all happened so fast and wasn't even his fault, none of it was. How could God allow this when he was blameless? He spits acid onto the tank room lock, so no one else could get to the chemicals, and says goodbye to his grave. He leaves for D.C. "Look, Mommy, a real superhero!" says a kid on the train. Judging by his power, he doubted that's what he was.

WASHINGTON D.C.

Grand found work as a janitor at a small family-owned restaurant and inn. The owner offered him a room at a discounted price that was instantly taken out of his pay every week. Grand bought a laptop from a pawnshop to finish school. It only took him a year to graduate, and he received his diploma in the mail. He thought about calling his mother. Maybe one day he'd get a good job to help her pay bills after all, and maybe he could even go to college. Should he tell her the good news?

He goes to a pay phone midday and shook as it rung. "Hello?" He doesn't recognize the woman's voice on the other end. "Hello, is Rosa Turosi there?"

"Rosa Turosi is in George Ward's facility. I'm Barbara, her primary nurse, here to pick up a few things she requested."

"Is she sick?"

"Um, sort of. George Ward's is an asylum for the mentally ill."

Grand's heart sinks. "Hello? Hellooo . . ."

The nurse buzzes in the background, and he fastens the phone onto its latch. He had driven her to the crazy house. She had always been so uptight anyway, she might've even sent herself, but he still blamed himself.

He now slept on a large concrete bed held up by a wooded platform and used cardboard from the empty boxes of food deliveries the restaurant received. He replaced pillows, sheets, and blankets on a weekly basis. His AC is set low so he won't sweat at night, but nightmares about the night he was almost killed trigger it. Mr. Johnson, the restaurant owner, often comments about the electric bill being too high. Grand just tells him to deduct it from his pay. Sometimes he throws a very thin mattress above the cardboard, lowers the temperature to forty degrees, and prays he doesn't wake up to a fire. Those nights are the ones he cherishes.

He ate with metal dinnerware and had bathroom cabinets filled with toothbrushes. One would last him three days, if that. His lips would chap because of fumes within him and from licking his lips. They always healed but left behind a very stiff surface, so he had drawers full of blue ChapStick.

He got two Labrador puppies to keep him company, one black and one gray. "You two don't care how I look, do you? As long as I feed you." He pats them, and they race to their bowls. "I gotta go to work. Don't go anywhere." Grand locks the door and walks across the parking lot and through a side door.

"What's up, Grand?"

He looks over to see a waitress with a bright smile. "Daisy, what's up?"

"Nothing much going on with me, but you know Mona's in the back waiting for you."

"She is?"

Daisy nods. He looks at her beautiful long hair and slender figure. She reminds him of Rachel, but his heart still only belongs to her. He goes to the back, and the girl jumps.

"Grand! You scared me."

"Sorry. Daisy said you knew I was coming."

"She did? Big mouth. You know, I like this coverup more than the other black ones. The stitching is different, isn't it?" She places her hand on his arms and smooths her thumb over the ridges.

"Really? Thanks. I didn't think anyone noticed." He chuckles.

Mona had short black hair that reached the bottom of her neck, rounded specs, and a mid-sized figure. She wasn't his cup of tea but was beautiful in her own way. She's the boss's daughter.

Mona snaps her fingers. "There's something going on with the toilet in the women's bathroom. I put in a request this morning. Did you see it?"

"Not yet, but I'm on it." He explained to his new bosses that because of his skin condition, he couldn't work outside. They agreed to hire him on with no problem. He didn't like it, but the inn allowed him to have a home and work.

He got home and showered, it had been a long, dirty day. He digs a hole in the ground and relieves himself because the piping wasn't that great. He looks up at the stars and thinks of Rachel. He lets out a deep breath. Will he ever get to be with anyone? "Is this what you want for me?" he yells to the heavens. "Why'd you save me if you knew this would be my life? You should've just let me die!" He falls to the ground, yelling, "I can't be with anyone! My mother is a lunatic, and I'm sleeping on a cement bed! You're merciless!"

"Has he said anything to you?" asks Daisy.
"About what?" says Mona.
"You two hanging out again."
"No, and we didn't hang out! I went to collect rent from a check that didn't direct deposit, and he had to give me cash. He invited me in to pick ice cream from his stash. That hardly counts!"
"Okay . . . but he could've just said goodnight."
"That just proves he's a decent individual. We flirt, that's all." Mona's eyes widen, and she taps Daisy as Grand comes in.
"Hey."
"Hey, Grand."
"Can I have a breakfast platter and a coffee? Two pumps mocha, five sugars, two pumps cream."
"Sure can," says Mona. She puts in the order and makes his coffee. He thanks her and looks at the staring customers, hoping the cooks hurry. He's not used to being up front. He watches Daisy go to wait tables.

"One platter and coffee with two pumps mocha, five sugars, and two pumps cream," says Mona.

"You're the best," says Grand.

18

A New Tribulation

"So, God is gonna give me superpowers?" I ask.

"In time, you're going to be able to do supernatural things, yes," says Arch.

"What kind of things? Being able to hear and talk to a dog? Even though that is cool and all. And why me? What did I do to deserve it?"

"You didn't earn it. This was always your destiny. It's what He imagined for your life when He made you."

"I was always meant to be a superhero and save the world? From what or whom? Like five hours ago I was just a regular girl!" I say and groan. "Nope! No . . ." I shrug. "I can't be this 'superhero' thing God wants me to be. First of all, I've never been in a fight in my life. Second, I'm trying to show my dad I can run my mother's shop, who just died by the way, and I have to cook instead of making TV dinners, so I just can't."

"Change it, and make time for your destiny."

I laugh. "My mom's shop *is* my destiny! It's pretty clear she left it for me to . . . to . . ."

"As a cover-up so you keep your divinity a secret?"

My mouth drops open. "My what?"

"You said it yourself: 'My mom's shop.' That was her destiny. You are just trying to run from yours!"

My jaw drops even further! "You say that like it's so easy!

Maybe because you never had to give anything up. It's pretty clear you live and indulge in divinity!" I gasp and cover my mouth, not believing those words came out of it.

"You're right, I do live in a divine realm, filled with majesty. There's so much peace, love, and joy. It's surrounded by heavenly beings and the Most High God. There's no fear and no evil. So, I guess I am giving up a lot leaving there to be here with you."

"Arch, I'm so sorry, I didn't mean—"

"But this is my duty, and I live to serve my Master, the King of Kings and the Lord of Lords. It's a pleasure, not a burden, and until you see it as such, you won't be ready."

"Arch, I'm gonna be nineteen in a few weeks. I don't wanna die. I've never even had a boyfriend. I don't wanna be some martyr who never even kissed a guy."

"That's not what you said last night."

"I was asleep, halfway anyway! Who asks someone to go out and save the world barely conscious?"

"God, obviously," he says, and I get off the floor, dusting the back of my shorts.

I don't know why they're doing this. I just lost my mother. I already have the world on my shoulders, and now he's actually asking me to put the actual world on my shoulders! Not. Happening. "I can't do this right now, and maybe I do have a lot to think about," I say.

"Your mother, wouldn't she be proud?"

"Oh," I say and laugh. "My mother? You mean the one who was trying to make me burn up what's left of my family in their sleep?"

"Things aren't always what they seem."

"What do you mean?" I ask, leaning in.

"That wasn't your mother. It was an attack on your mind. Satan knows you're about to become something great, and he wants to put doubt in your mind using your mother's image."

"That's cruel, Arch," I say with a strained voice.

"Lolly, this is real! The earth is worry-free right now, but something disastrous is coming in a few years that you need to be prepared for. This is just the beginning. So seriously think about it because you need to be all in." He walks off towards his comfy space, yet looks back at me and says, "But think quickly. We're crunched for time. If you won't accept, God will have to find a more willing soul to complete your destiny."

Arch makes it all sound so serious, and I can't help but think I've been acting like a spoiled princess. Arch is a mighty warrior, and I let his cutie, furry, harmless appearance make me feel like he's asking when really he's telling.

Later, Daddy gives me back the keys to the shop. "Daddy, I thought you said—"

"I trust you," he says, interrupting.

They sit in my hand, but why now? Could it be another scheme from the devil? I know my dad, and he wouldn't have folded so easily. So now he's using both of my parents? It creeps me out. Nonetheless, I thank Daddy and drive to Pob's Pop Antique. When I open the door, it smells just like her. I touch all the tables, picking up every other trinket. I miss her so much. I sniffle at the fact that she'll never be here again.

I open the door to the Lolly Pobs Collection room. I feel bashful about it, *but I'll do it for her.* I almost cry but have a feeling the sleepwalking may return if I don't pull myself together. Or maybe I was completely healed by God. I focus on the mint walls and how the Italian customer felt at home while he rode. It seemed he missed home but was content being here. I could find contentment while waiting on happiness.

"Hi, Lolly," a customer says. "I'm sorry about Lizzy. She was such a beautiful person."

All I could do was nod at the customer and say, "Yes, and thank you." I had to repeat this often with others during the day. I don't know if maybe they all thought they *had* to say something, anything to show me they cared, but it wasn't helping. I know how special she was. But I couldn't help feeling jabs at my side knowing how long I'd taken that for granted.

This kind of conversation went on and on, and when the day was done, my head was spinning. Maybe Daddy was right. Maybe I did need more time to heal. No, I can do this, for her. I leave for home and ignore my guide at all costs. But felt an urgent need to pray about the situation, so that night I prayed for strength.

The next day, I felt a surge of energy and felt better prepared for their remarks. "Oh Lolly, you must feel terrible, sweetheart! Lizzy was a jewel," says Mrs. Lucas.

"Yes, she was, but I know she's in heaven with God now."

"Yes, that's right," she says quickly, apparently shocked. I guess she expected me to be sad and weak, but I was the opposite. Maybe I *can* be strong, *strong like a superhero.*

I close shop for lunch and walk the strip. I go to Surreal Play because they have a super cool menu. I order a Pretzeled Sandwich. I love how the owner, Charlie, cuts his cheese, turkey, and lettuce to precisely fit the huge, hole-filled pretzel. I look down and notice a glass elephant with cherry blossoms on it. It's gorg. Mom would've loved to have this in her shop.

"Hi, Lolly! How's it going?"

"Hey, Charlie."

"How's the food?" he asks about the grub I haven't even touched. We both look at my solid sandwich and curly fries with blue cheese sauce.

"Good." I take a fry and put it into my mouth. I can tell he was just prepping me for the real conversation.

"Good, good." He breathes in deeply and sits at my table. "Lolly, I'm sorry about your mom."

I think about the way I handled Mrs. Lucas and sit up straight. I'm prepared!

"I know that no amount of words can make you feel better right now." He looks at me for confirmation. I nod, finding myself leaning in, wondering if he'll say something different from the others, something worth hearing.

"When I lost Cindy, Jason's mom, to cancer, nothing would cover that wound. No amount of 'I'm sorrys, 'Everything will be okay' or 'In time you will heal's could touch it. I found that the only thing that kept me going was prayer."

I nod, and tears build in the corners of my eyes.

"Trust God, Lolly. Know that He's working His plan out in your life and that He is in control."

I don't understand fully. I think about the change Arch was talking about and the destiny part too. I blend their talks together. So, God has a plan for the way my life should go, and I should trust Him with it. *Okay.*

I head out for fresh air, thinking about my findings. A guy abruptly bursts out of a door and almost bumps into me. I back away, stumbling into the street.

"I'm sorry," he says with piercing eyes. I breathe heavily but nod. I look up and notice he came out of "Supreme Boxer."

Anna runs out of the shop, saying, "Eric!" She places her hand over her mouth.

"Anna? Are you okay?" I go to her and place my hand on her arm. She nods, saying, "My father disapproves of Eric."

I go inside, and she tells me that her father, Mr. Van, a Chinese man, wants her to date within their heritage, and because Eric has fair skin and green eyes, he wasn't going for it. But like my black mother and white father, multiracial couples are accepted more than ever these days.

"He can really fight. I can beat almost every man in here except him, and I like that!" We giggle. This is a true forbidden love story playing out before my eyes. I wonder how I'll find *the one.*

I look over at her brother, Lem. He's nose deep in a novel, laid across waiting chairs. I hear plenty of guys go over to him, saying they're ready to start their training. I giggle as he puts his finger up every time, saying, "Wait, wait, wait . . . Lemme just finish this last chapter!" And, "One more page, one more page!"

"Man! Come on! You're reading girl books!" say the trainees. I'm tempted to laugh hard, but I get serious remembering Anna's sadness.

"I believe in true love, and I think what you and Eric have is beautiful."

She cracks a smile. "Really?"

I nod, she hugs me and gets her phone. *I hope she will call Eric.*

"Hello, dove?" she says, walking away.

Yes! I smile big, then realize where I am—in a man-filled, sweaty, full-of- mats fighting ring. I see that Lem finally got out of his book zone. His moves draw me, and before I know it, I'm front and center of the match.

Watching them sends tingles through my body. *Could I do this?* I gasp as Lem kicks the man's side. This is so intense. I look over at Mr. Van watching them, and somehow his tight body language is more intimidating than the fighters. I gulp, momentarily looking in the direction Anna went, wondering if encouraging her toward love was the best idea. The bell rings, and it startles me. I look back at Lem and his not so skilled opponent.

They quickly clear out and Anna swoops in, her legs long and sharp. It happened so fast I couldn't even catch how she did it! She's fighting a guy! I look at Mr. Van and Lem, who are not fazed by it. The bell rings, and I look back at diabolical Ann. She's so comfortable and commands the stage. I panic for her.

They take off at each other, and right from the start, the dude has no chance. She strikes him down and puts her arm around his head and neck, then squeezes. He wails but she releases and jumps up, ready to go again.

"Ah, come on, Anna, stop playing with the food!" calls Lem. She grins and salutes her brother.

Her opponent is angry and charges at her. She full-fledge beats him up.

"Anna, chill," says Lem, and I wonder which one he wants her to do! She lets the guy get a breath in at Lem's request, but in the end pins him down for the win. I'm amazed that a girl could do all this! I look at Mr. Van's unusual crooked smile, then watch Anna quickly exit stage left. The men around cheer for her. I walk out of Supreme Boxer inspired, adrenaline pumping through my veins.

19
I Will Say Yes

"I'm in! When do I start?"

"It should've already started. You don't feel different?" says Arch.

"But I didn't accept until now," I say.

"God just needed you to agree with Him."

"So…" I get up and face the sheepdog. "God knew I would say yes?"

"Yep."

"Some free will," I say under my breath.

"Okay, Jonah."

"Who?" I ask.

"Never mind," he says while examining me, picking my arm up with his harry paw.

"Oh, stop it! I'll do it myself." I slap his paw away. I try to move my dresser, but it doesn't budge. *Nope, no super strength.* I do jumping jacks. Nothing happens, so I get up on my bed, hop off, and fall on my behind. "Ouch!" *Nope, can't fly.* Arch painfully watches me destroy my room.

"Nothing's different, Arch!" I say.

"I see. Maybe you should've stopped at the dresser."

I peer at him. "Some guide you are," I mumble and plop down on my bed. My phone vibrates. It's Addison, and answering her call versus dealing with real life right now seems like a vacation.

"Hello?"

"Lolly? Oh my gosh, Lolly! Why haven't you been picking up, babe? Are you okay? I called your dad and brother. I'd call your sister if you had one. I was gonna call the shop, but I realized you closed it since, well . . . do you even have a phone in the shop? I know that—"

"Addison?" I finally interrupt through clinched teeth. Okay, so not the vacation I paid for.

"Yeah?" she says calmly.

"Hi, it's Lolly, and I hold the answers to your questions." I clear my throat. "My father and brother never told me you called because they're guys. Guys don't think girl problems are spectacular or serious. So by now, I could've been missing or worse, highjacked by Jesus and His guard to be shipped off to superhero boarding school, never to be seen or heard of again! Or changed to be a different Lolly."

"Wait, you're what?"

I mumbled that last part, and it only needs to be shared with my inner self. I clear my throat again. "We don't have a phone in the shop, although maybe I should get one."

"You *should* get one."

"I will, I'll get one." This is all beside the point, and what I'm really doing is dodging telling my best friend about my powers that I don't have as of yet, but will.

"Well, Josh never answered, and Dad said to give you some time. But I know you. You need me, and we never miss a beat." She stops for confirmation.

"Yeah, yep . . . never." I say and put my hand to my mouth. If I don't tell her, this is about to get weirder.

"Is it your mom? Oh, you miss her bad, don't you? Oh Cher—"

No, it's not that . . . I mean, I'll always miss her, that's a given, but right now it's about my destiny. "Not really, I kinda want some Cheerios."

"You don't . . . you don't miss your mom?" she says, puzzled.

"Nope." *Of course I do? I sound like I plotted her death!* "Yes! Yes, I do . . . I just have someone else on my mind."

She gasps. "A boy?"

No! Meeeee, I want to scream! "No! Not a boy," I declare. I look at Arch, cover the phone, and try to whisper, "Arch, I am different; I don't miss my mom!" He tilts his head in confusion, and I quietly say, "I'm not sad!"

I can hear Addison ranting as I try to describe to Arch how I feel. I let her until she screams, "Lolly!"

"Okay, kinda a boy," I say, eying Arch.

"Oh my gosh! Is he cute? What's his name? How'd you meet? Why didn't you tell me?"

This is going sideways. What would be the right words to tell my best friend I am now a superhero? How does one reveal her identity? With no proof . . . *Ugh!* I decide against it. It would be super embarrassing, and would she even believe me?

"Can we not talk about the boy right now? Oh, let's talk about the shop. My dad let me reopen!"

"I see what you're doing, but drop the deets on the guy, right now! Is he sweet?"

I look at Arch. "Ummm so, so?"

"I heard that," he barks.

"Lolly, is that a . . . dog?"

Yes! The dog! "Yes, he's the new dude I was telling you about!" Awesome save. I wink at Arch, and he cries. I ask him why in sign language.

I tell her about the new pup, of course leaving the talking part out. She can't believe I picked out an Old English sheepdog, "Okay, not your style, but I get it. Dad is busy selling somebody a house, Josh has football, and you have . . . a big dog."

She's gonna think I'm crazy! "He was a stray." Okay, now I'm pushing it. I need to tell her now, because lying is not okay.

"What? Cher, it could have rabies! Ugh. Hold on," I hear her back away from the phone. "No, I don't want them. They're so last summer!" She comes back on, saying, "Cher, lemme call you back. I'm helping Mom clean out this junky garage. ANSWER THE PHONE!" she says and hangs up.

I look at Arch and he seems to be staring right through me. I freeze. "What?" I manage to say.

"Why didn't you tell her?"

"About?" I shuffle through my dresser, trying to find an invisible Q-Tip for a unicorn's ear.

"You're ashamed."

"Excuse me?" I try to sound offended, but it's not working.

"Maybe that's why your powers aren't starting. You don't believe."

"How can I? I've never experienced anything like this! And I don't know how to say it, okay? I was trying to the whole time, but it's weird."

"Jesus said, 'But whoever denies Me before men, him I will also deny before My Father who is in heaven, Matthew 10:33."

"You're being too hard on me, Arch." He lifts my chin with his nose.

"You don't have to have it all figured out right now. He equips you, so declare it!" He jumps on my bed, I smile and join him.

"What should I say?"

"I am Lolly Pobs, the superhero called by God!"

"Oh my gosh, for real?"

"Don't think about it. Just do it."

"I am Lolly Pobs a superhero" I say a bit blandly.

"Let heaven and the angels hear it! And most importantly, let

God hear it!" He jumps around, and I giggle.

"I am Lolly Pobs! The superhero! Called by God!" I say confidently with my fists balled up.

"That's it!" says Arch.

I decide to let my friend in on my secret.

"Hello?" Addison sounds like she's throwing things around the room.

"There is something I didn't tell you."

"What?" she says nonchalantly. "Ew, dirty socks. *Ugh* they stink!"

This doesn't seem like the best time to tell her, but no excuses. "God gave me super powers, well not like right now. But I'm a superhero, *now.*" I close my eyes. I completely messed that up.

"Hmm, you mean like helping you through your healing process?" I can hear her switch into another room.

"Addison, we are not done!" I hear her mom in the distance.

"Sorry, Mom." I hear things fall to the floor and a door shut.

"Is your mom okay?"

"Maybe, what are you saying?"

"I'm saying like real powers," I say softly.

"I don't understand, babe," she says gently.

I put my shoulders back. "I was having nightmares of Mommy, and sleep walking until I sort of *defeated* my dream Mom . . ."

"Okay?"

At least she's listening. "And one night, an angel told me God would help me fight battles so He could get the victory . . . oh, um, the glory." I look at Arch, and he nods. I'm eager to hear her thoughts. Words aren't coming fast enough.

"Hmm, and why does He need you? Can't He fight these battles Himself?"

I smile. *She believes.*

"He can, but it's my destiny to fight them." I inhale and exhale.

"Wow, Lolly, this is different." It didn't sound like a *good* different. "I told you, you could tell me anything, and *this* definitely falls under the category of *anything*." We giggle.

"But are you like, in any danger, babe?"

"If God is for me, who can be against me?" I put my hand over my mouth. I dunno where that came from!

"Oh my gosh! Is that like your slogan?" We burst into laughter.

"No, I just somehow know He's protecting me."

"Yeah, for sure, I love that."

I leave the fact that Arch is a special dog out. I don't think she can handle more right now. Little by little I'll tell her everything.

I wake up the next morning and go into the bathroom. I must've slept good because my hair is sticking up on my head, which is strange. I yawn, pick up my toothbrush, and turn on the faucet. I wet it, put toothpaste on, and start brushing. I've never seen my hair this wild, and I look closer. A gold spark erupts with a crackling noise near my mouth. I drop everything and faint. *Am I like dead by lightning strike?*

"Mommy?" I blink rapidly, looking around to see if I'm in heaven.

Still in my bathroom, I freak out. "Arch!" I hear him yawning. "Arch!" I get up and look in the mirror, my hair is definitely bigger.

He drowsily walks in and says, "What's going on?"

"Sparks, gold sparks just flew out of my mouth!" I gasp. "Am I like, a dragon?" I cry out.

He has me try it again. I flash my teeth, open my mouth, stick out my tongue, and twist it around. I get nada.

"You're definitely not a dragon." He sits in the doorway, examining me. "What were you doing when it happened?"

"Nothing special. Just brushing my teeth." I shrug.

"Do it again, exactly like the first time."

I turn on the faucet, dip my fingers into the water, and sparks fly. I back away, shaking my hands and breathe heavily.

"You okay?" Arch asks.

I nod, then our panic turns into cheer. I try it again, *sparks*. My fingers glow until the electricity soaks up the water.

"Can you do it on your own?"

I close my eyes and lift my hands.

"Concentrate on the gold spark," he says and I do. No matter how much I push, it doesn't come. We walk back into the room.

"Why is it only working with water?"

"It seems water's your source, and God could be using it to train you. When you trust Him more, He'll become your source."

I pout. "But I wanna do it now."

"Be patient. It won't be too long. You're ready to receive it."

"I am?"

"Uh huh."

Everything is happening at a pretty fast pace. I can't help but feel a bit frightened and something else . . . "Arch? Yesterday, about Mom . . ." He stands in full attention. "For the first time since she went away, I didn't miss her. Not, not at all, but it didn't hurt so much to talk about her. Is that okay?"

"Of course it is. Jesus is giving you a special strength to fulfill your assignment. That doesn't mean you don't love her or won't miss her ever again." I nod and wipe a tear before it falls.

"Also, yesterday I saw these fighters at a boxing ring."

"Yeah?" Arch hops up on all fours.

"Something woke up inside me. It pushed me to want to say

yes to Jesus." I chuckle and shake my head. "It's silly now that I'm saying it out loud, but I was kind of thinking I could learn to fight? For God?"

"That's a great idea!"

I feel my eyes brighten, then dim. "But is it God's plan . . . for my life?"

"Lolly, God communicates with His people in all sorts of ways. Most times, it's to your heart, and other times it's in the form of an inspiration like what you experienced." I think Arch is an inspiration all by himself.

I open Mom's shop and in between customers stare at "Supreme Boxer." It strikes my curiosity, and I make plans to go on my lunch, despite the fact that I wore my mother's heels. I lock my door and make it midway into the street before droplets of rain fall from the sky, and my hands light up.

All the people around me come to a halt. "Lightening! Get out of the rain!" they say. I hide my hands and run back inside the shop. I lock the door and head to the restroom to dry off.

I hear my door clapping and realize I hadn't locked it, so I run to the front. It's blowing in the wind, and I catch it and lock it back. Light fizzes around my hands. *Is this safe?* The lights go out, and it's out in most of the buildings.

I turn to go report the power outage and run into something or someone. I feel hands around my arm and waist as they catch my fall. He has on a hat and light eyes. *All I see are his eyes.* He came out of my room . . . Seconds turn to minutes, and it seems as if he's as stuck as I am. If I don't stop this, it'll be hours.

I stand up straight, wiggling his hands off, and clear my throat to say something, anything. He tucks away a certain device into his jacket pocket, nothing we sold, and scans me once more. It makes me sheepish, but he just rolls his eyes. "Excuse me," he says, then goes around me as if none of it ever happened.

I chuckle. *Seriously?* I watch him dart out of my door without unlocking it. I'm flabbergasted. I go to it and assess the damages. Nothing seems to be popped or broken. I push at it like he did, even put my back to it, but it's sealed.

By the end of the day, I call the company that installed our locks. They assure me the lock they placed on the door not even five months ago was of high quality and built to guard a store. I think about the timeline and remember well the day my mother and I watched them work on it. It reminded me about how long she'd been gone, and I shake my head.

"I saw him push through it while locked. I need a replacement." I touch it, and it seems legit, but either way I don't wanna lose Mom's valuables to a thief.

"Understandable, miss. We'll have a team out in the morning."

In the morning, I watch them install a double lock at no charge. The boss was sympathetic when I told him about my mother's passing. They shared laughs the day he came in and said if I had any more problems, he'd come running, no questions asked. I sit in the dark at lunch time, door locked, wondering if I should go over to Supreme Boxer. It's around the same time the guy was in here wandering around, but he could've just been a customer I locked in unknowingly, even though I checked before I left.

I should stop my accusations because he may not be a thief. Besides, I can defend myself. I have powers now. All I have to do is . . . get water and . . . I'd be dead before I got to a faucet. I roll my eyes and strut to a table, grab old century gloves, and put a fifty into the register. I slip them on and run water over them. When nothing happens, I grin. I open my door, lock both bolts with emphasis, and chuckle. *Get in now, stranger!*

"Lolly?" I turn around, plastering myself on my door. It's

Mrs. Lucas. I breathe. "I'm sorry dear, I didn't mean to startle you. I wanted to get one of those zebra candleholders I saw the other day."

"Of course." I smile, deciding to keep the lights off so no one else will come in. Boy, it's getting harder and harder to get to Supreme Boxer. Arch says I'm supposed to do it, though, and he also said the devil sometimes uses people to get in the way.

I look at Mrs. Lucas in a new light. For one, she was buying one of my mother's infamous animal candles, and I could feel emotions rising up. Then, she stopped me from going to the ring, a destiny step. She's not an enemy per se; the devil is just using her again to stop me, I get it. I suck in my breath and clear my throat as she comes to the register.

"Thank you, Lolly. You're such a doll."

I put on the brightest smile in my closet. "Sure, Mrs. Lucas."

"You're such a strong girl, running your mother's shop like this. Good for you!"

I run the pad of my thumb across the stripes on the glass zebra. "Thank you. You picked a nice one," I manage to say.

"Thanks, dear." She pays and I let her out. Her words were tough on me, and I decide to let myself cry. My mother, mixed with these powers, was enough to drive anyone mad. Arch didn't say I wouldn't be sad sometimes, but he did say God would give me the tools to get through.

Chin up, I lock the door behind me. It's drizzling, and tiny sparks spurt. I forgot I took off my gloves to give Mrs. Lucas change. Once again, I unlock the door and lock it back so no one will come in, determined to make it to the ring. I go to the register, grab my gloves, and hear my door open. My heart sinks as my eyes lock on the ball-capped guy from yesterday. He's searching my tables in the dark.

I say, "Lights off means store's closed."

"But you just took that other customer," he says. *Touché.* I plant my bottom on a stool, let him do his thing, and pout.

If I didn't know any better, I'd say he was laughing at me. How rude! I look at the time, and it's like I can hear every minute pass. He goes into my room once again, and I groan. What could he possibly want in there? He comes to the register and puts down a simple silver beaded necklace. I raise a brow.

"It's for someone special. Do you think she'll like it?" His voice holds a really nice tone. He leans on the counter, looking away, then darts his beautiful blue eyes at mine. *Beautiful?* Yeah, beautiful, ones you can see even in the dark.

I wake up. "I'm sure she will." I grab a small bag for his special gift, and he puts his card in the machine. So, he has a girlfriend then? *So!* I yell at the top of the lungs in my head.

I grab the necklace, he places his hand over mine, and says, "Careful." If I didn't know any better, I'd think he just wanted to touch me. I pull it away.

"Of course."

He's watching my every move, his eyes stinging me like a bee. I carefully pick it up and place it in a gold box. It's heavier than usual and looks shinier, more expensive. *Strange.* I move his bag toward him, and he licks his lips.

"Have a nice day," I say. He grabs it and walks out. And I thought the me before was rude. I clear my head of fizz, make sure to grab my gloves, and stomp to the door. I almost ram my face into it. *It's still locked?* This is a new lock! I'm frustrated because he just pushed through my locked door again! Once again I call and complain to the key maker, and they say they'll be here tomorrow.

I stomp all the way to Supreme Boxer. "At least he paid for something!" I mumble.

I look into the windows of the gym, then back at Mom's shop, making sure he isn't breaking in again. I think about his gaze and get lost in my thoughts. I shake my head as Anna waves for me to come in. I never noticed any girls in here . . . *What am I doing? Are they really gonna train a girl with no experience?* The guys are staring at me, and I shrink.

Anna gets out of the ring and walks towards me, breathing heavily.

"Intense, huh?" she asks.

"Yeah."

I smile as we look at them.

"Are you on lunch?" she asks. "We can go grab something." She points to the door.

"Actually, I wanted to ask you something."

"What's up?"

I summon the courage and go for it. "Can you teach me how?" I ask, pointing at the fighters. Her brows draw together, and she glances down at my high heels. *I knew it.*

20

Jailbreak

After Deylou greets her parents, she disappears into the crowd. She spots huge creatures going into double doors and runs in. Tremendous champions making the floors quake walk by. She asks a Red Sensei lizard, a bald eagle who has a yellow mouth instead of a beak and short feathers for skin and hair, to fight. He's very noble, but says he's on parole, and his only duty is to fight in The Games.

She asks a zebra woman with long, silky hair that stands on two hooves, "I need the prize money to provide for my kids, sorry about your sis."

Deylou asks twin cows, a girl and a boy. They need the prize money as well. "Sorry," they say in unison.

Defeated, she takes a break and peeks out into the arena. Two girls are fighting. One of them turns into a wolf, and her eyes light up. She gasps at the vampire's teeth, and relief comes as the wolf girl surrenders. A man announces the next two. One has gold hair and the other is just a human? She squints to see if he might be a Similory? No antlers. She thought her people too fragile anyway, always needing the protection of others. They are like slugs.

Deylou smiles as they commence, watching in horror as wood is placed into the vampire's body. It makes her step back to catch her breath, but then a girl's scream makes her run back.

The fighter, Ore, whom she thought was human at first, put

out the fire he created as the other surrendered and was on his way to the doors. Her eyes lit up at his power. He could be a worthy subject for the forest! She'll find him, although him winning means he'll advance. *He may not be willing to come,* she thought, but she'll try anyway.

Deylou creeps out, Du'Jomi snags her, and she struggles to get out of his grip. "You wouldn't want your family to be incarcerated with you, would you, thief?" She stops her movement, and he drags her onward. A robot girl overhears them and follows them down a dark staircase.

Du'Jomi sniffs around. "Where fresh air flows through . . ." he mumbles. He comes to a halt. "Ah, flowers." He orders his minion to move loads out of the way. The small goblin struggles to do so and finally finishes. Deylou sees a very tiny crack in the wall.

"I have a source who cleans the place. Says behind this area," explains Du'Jomi as he taps it, "there's a gap between the wall and the forcefield. The walls stop magic, and the forcefield prevents anyone from leaving. So we get in the gap and use my power to break through the forcefield." He swings his wand, and the hole widens. "You will test the gap," Du'Jomi says, and Deylou steps back.

"Bot?" A voice comes from the entrance. The silent tips of the robot's soles jolt upstairs, and she puts her hand over the rock giant's mouth.

"How did you find me?" Loud thumping comes from below.

"I saw you."

"I know you wouldn't approve, but someone is down there trying to break out."

"It is forbidden!" says the giant.

"I know, but I can't go back to Coron. If I stay here, they'll force me back into the portals, and I'll die on your planet," says the robot.

"You can tell them you are from earth, but if you go back to Coron, I will help you."

"There's a warrant out for my arrest here, and I'm tied to Lemon. Besides, they don't treat you like the prince that you are on Coron."

"We must do the right thing. God will protect us."

"My prince." She puts her head down and moves out of his way.

"Your friend," he says, putting a hand on her shoulder and passes through. Bot sits on a step in defeat.

The wizard and goblin kick at the hole in the wall, but it's not growing.

"The king will not like what you are doing here," says Deylou.

"How do you know he's not in on it?" She gasps.

"This'll take all night! We need something sharp!" says Du'Jomi.

Gem's feet hit the ground. "I will not let you leave."

"What is this *sharp* figure?"

All Du'Jomi sees is a diamond, measured and weighed. He grabs Deylou and says, "She's a hostage" and drags her backwards.

"Release her!" Gem calls. Du'Jomis' hold grows tighter, and Deylou struggles to breathe. Gem snatches Deylou out of his clutches. Du'Jomi smirks and pushes Gem into the wall, his rock body shattering it.

Du'Jomi steps out onto the grass after nothing happens to the prince and stares at the colorful forcefield separating him from his freedom. He looks at the unconscious rock on the ground and raises his scepter, "Ánoixe, Ánoixe, Ánoixe!"

Gem's body is dragged, and the forcefield is now bouncing off of his crystal. The wizard chants and walks to the iridescent wall, lifting it like a blanket. "Ladies first," he says.

Deylou fights, but her feet slide towards the hole. She's thrown onto the other side and falls on the grass, breathing heavily. When he sees no harm came to her, he and his goblin cross.

Bot peeks along the cracked wall and sees her motionless friend on the ground. She immediately runs to Gem and uses her strength to pull him from underneath the wall. She stops. What if she pulls him into earth and helps him find a way back home from the lab? She hops through in one piece and pulls Gem in, and the forcefield locks. "Prince Gem, please!" The robot sheds tears.

Breath fills Gem's lungs. "Bot? What happened?"

"You slammed into the wall and broke us all out of The Games. Du'Jomi used your body as leverage."

"Lord forgive us, we didn't mean to break forth!" Bot hangs her head. "I pulled you through, Gem."

"Good, let's rescue the girl." Bot hugs him.

Into Earth

"You! Human, tell me where the witch Gavenla resides!" The wizard demands as the man walks past them. "You!" He tries to grab the woman walking on the sidewalk, but his hands go through her. "Mecees, why can't we communicate with them?"

The goblin shrugs. "I don't know, master."

"What do you know?"

"The law states we cannot show our power on earth. Maybe the Mighty One blocks us."

"I need to break this bond. We must find mother so we can take this planet." Deylou's eyes widen.

"Let her go!" Gem yells, and Robotka's hands dissolve into guns.

"You live?" asks Du'Jomi. "How annoying." He puts out his scepter, and the crystal on top glows. Deylou runs and doesn't look back.

21

Daisy high-fives Grand and gives him a genuine smile. Rachel comes to mind. She probably never thought of him.

"Son, the trash man called. He's not coming. I know you got that skin thing, but I could use your help. Trash is out back," says Mr. Johnson, leaving before Grand gets a word in.

He goes to the back, and he can see six big bags of trash and a dozen little ones. He opens the back door. The walk in the blazing sun to the Dumpster across the way devastates him.

He notices the wheels on the Dumpster. He grabs the small bags and walks across causally, feeling a slit in his mask but continues. He throws them in and pulls at the Dumpster, which is heavier than it looked. He can hear his clothes ripping all over. He manages to get half in before holes start to form. He pushes the Dumpster away from the doorway and runs to his apartment. In his haste, he falls and cuts his hand on a broken bottle. He finally gets in to happy pups.

They cry for food, and he goes into the kitchen, grabbing a kitchen rag to cover the gash in his hand. He tears open new dog food and pours it into their bowl. The pups devour it. The towel around Grand's wound melts, and drops of his blood go into their water.

"No!" He tries to push the pups away, but they're too thirsty. He gets down on the hard floor and watches them closely. When they don't melt, he finally breathes. After a while, Mr. Johnson knocks at his door, but he doesn't answer. He'd left half of the trash and the back door wide open. Would Mr. Johnson continue to give him those types of jobs?

The next morning, he goes to the diner while it's still dark and grabs the newspaper located up front. His liquids jab at him, and he decides using their bathroom one time won't hurt. He passes the girls' bathroom and sees a hand on the floor through the cracked door. He opens it and finds a barely conscious Daisy with a cut on her wrist and blood pooling around it.

"Daisy!" He gets on the floor.

"Grand?"

"Why did you do this?" he asks as her eyes are fading out. "Daisy, no."

He searches for a solution, then takes his mask and gloves off. He hesitates for a moment before licking his thumb and swiping it across her injury. Her skin glues back together before his eyes, leaving a blue seal. But she doesn't awaken.

"Daisy?" He puts his coverings back on and then rocks her back and forth. Her head goes from one end to the other, and her eyes glow blue, drenched in Z71. It disappears, and her eyes seal shut.

"Grand?" she says, her tone light.

"Are you okay?" She nods. A customer bursts in and gasps at the blood and a barely conscious Daisy, then runs out. "Can you walk?" asks Grand, panicked.

"I can't feel my legs." Grand picks her up, goes home, and lays her on the couch.

"Grand, I can't breathe," Daisy says, her nails digging into his skin as he props her up. But she breathes her last breath. He watches her for hours with no response. How was he gonna explain this? He searches through the newspaper. *It's getting too complicated here, and New York looks promising.*

Daisy makes groggy noises.

"Daisy?"

"Grand? What happened?" Her eyes flash in realization, and she looks at her wrist.

"You did this!" Tired of hiding and praying, Daisy doesn't react like his mom did, he steps into the light.

"You're really handsome," she says, scanning his muscles.

He laughs, then tells her his story.

She opens up to him. "I only had my dad, and he had a heart attack and left me here all alone."

"I'm sorry to hear that. You're not alone, though. You have me and Mona, but I'm leaving soon."

She nods and a dizzy spell comes. "My head is pounding, I don't think I can go back to work."

Grand's heart races. *Could what happened to him be happening to her?* "Do me a favor?" He gets up and grabs a napkin. "Spit on this." Her eyes widen. "Just in case." She spits on it, and her saliva sits on the thick napkin.

Mask on, they hop in her car and go to the store. Daisy gets drinks and Grand grabs popcorn for movie night. The woman looks at Grand.

"It's rude to stare," says Daisy. The woman starts to ring them up.

"That'll be seven dollars and seventy-one cents."

They look at each other. Grand says, "I left my wallet at home."

Daisy says, "I left my purse in my locker at work."

They laugh.

"Are either of you gonna pay?" The cashier doesn't think this is funny.

"It's okay," says Daisy. "She'll be happy to give it to us for free, right?" She looks at her name tag and adds, "Benetta!"

Benetta nods, puts the stuff in the bag, and hands it to Grand. "Have a nice night," she says and smiles brightly. They're confused. Benetta starts to clean up around her register.

"Come on before she changes her mind." Daisy pulls his arm, moving quickly to the door. He walks slowly behind her, still trying to make sure it's okay. A biker dude walks into the store.

"What's up, hot stuff?" he says, eying Daisy.

"Get lost, creep!"

He immediately turns around and frantically says, "Where am I?"

Grand and Daisy look at each other.

"Please, someone find me!"

"Okay, okay, you're found! Just leave me alone," says Daisy.

He calms down and rushes out of the door.

"What just happened? First the woman? Then that dude?" says Daisy.

"I know, it's like they were under a spell or something," says Grand.

They drive home. "So you have acid, and I can put people under my spell?" asks Daisy.

Grand shuffles through movies. "Maybe." He goes to the action section and scrolls.

"Let me try it on you."

"Okay."

He shrugs.

"No action movies. Go to romance!"

He thinks about it and says, "No." He's pleased his skin isn't the elephant in the room. "Maybe it doesn't work on me because you're my mini me." They chuckle.

"I should come with you to New York. When do you leave?"

"Soon. I bailed on Johnson last night; can't go back. So, you coming with?"

22

Jesus Is the Answer

Anna walks quickly towards the ring, and I follow.

"You don't know what you're asking," she says.

"I do. I mean, not really . . . but I want to!" I try not to sound whiny, but it still comes out that way. She turns around and looks at my skirt. I flatten it out and gulp.

"Why?"

I'm stuck. I can't tell her the truth, but I gotta tell her something.

"Martial Arts has heart," she says before I can think of a response. "You can't do it for the wrong reasons, and you have to be committed. It's not for everybody."

Wait a minute! That was a little harsh, but I know she's trying to say it's serious. I just nod.

"I like you, Lolly. You're a sweet girl, but doing what I do isn't easy. Once you go that route, there's no going back. So when you can tell me your *why,* I'll consider it, okay?"

I nod, and she swoops around me. I panic. I gotta convince her that I need this, and I need it now! "Lord Jesus, help me." I march towards her, feeling my skirt swaying, heels stomping on the ground like combat boots, 'cause I'm going to war!

"Anna!" She turns and faces me, and I suddenly get nervous but blurt out, "I want this, okay? I wanna fight! When I think about it, it's the only thing that's brought me joy in a long time since Mom."

That was a little too deep, but it's true. "I'm sure when I'm in the ring I'll be blowing off a lot of steam too." I say to myself really, looking at my nails.

It must've worked because she picks me up and hugs me. She's strong, geez. "Lolly! That's a great why! Tuesdays six p.m., okay?"

I squeak! Wait, Tuesday? That's a week away. "I'm kinda crunched for time," I say.

Her eyes scan the place. "Okay! Tomorrow at 6 p.m. I have a friend that owes me one, and it'll be a fast track lesson!" she says while running to the back.

"Um, okay! Thanks!" I have no time to ask her questions. *Ugh.*

The next day, I close up shop, looking around for Cap. When he doesn't show, I head to Supreme Boxer at 6 p.m. When I walk in, all the guys are staring at me and my gym bag big-eyed. What? I didn't wear a skirt and heels this time! I have on jeans and a cute flowery crop top, but still, I met them halfway here! I ask Lem for Anna, and he tells me to go to the back room, the same one she went into yesterday.

I walk back. It's a huge room with a punching bag. I don't see Anna yet, so I go into the bathroom and change into a T-shirt and tights. I put on tennis shoes and walk onto the mats.

"No shoes!" Mr. Van catches me off guard. I scurry back onto the wood floor to take them off. *What's going on?* My eyes follow him. He's walking back and forth in front of me, analyzing me.

"So you want to learn martial arts?"

I nod.

"Yes?" he says, looking into my eyes like he wants me to speak.

"Yes, Mr. Van, sir," I say quickly, afraid he may bark at me again.

"Are you shy?" I think I hear a bit of humor in his voice. I briefly scan his face, but he's so intense I'd never call him out on it. I shake my head no, then change my mind assessing the circumstance.

"Yes," I say timidly, which has never been me.

"You cannot be shy if you're going to kick someone in the face, Ms. Lolly."

I clear my throat and nod.

He says, "Follow me." Anna did not tell me *her friend* was *her father.*

He teaches me how to block in so many different ways and how to create a stance, which feels super funny to hold my legs this way. "You will be here tomorrow at 5 p.m. for three weeks."

"Oh no, Mr. Van. My mom's . . . my shop doesn't close until 5:30."

"Five p.m.," he says before walking out of the room. I get dressed and walk out.

"How was it?" Anna asks.

"Killer!" We giggle. "I didn't know your dad was gonna teach me."

"Yes, let him. He's the best for quick results. He can be hard, but in the end you'll be ready for anything."

I get home and shower. Mom is on my mind. "Mom, you would be so proud . . . I mean, I'm not some strong warrior. I'm just your daughter. But God is changing me, Mama." Tears mix with water, and it's hard to tell them apart. "And I'll never let you go. I'm just fulfilling my destiny," I say because I'm closing the shop earlier than usual. It feels so wrong, but I know it's right because God told me to do it. I sob and say, "Make me strong, God."

I'm forced to close shop at 4:45 p.m. for the next three weeks. I hang the new hours, and people look at me disappointedly. I think they wanted to say, "Your mother wouldn't approve." But God is calling me to go outside the norm, and I'm here to answer that call. Mr. Van makes me run around a track, then teaches me how to jump kick. I fall and fall again. I then punch at his mitts, but I'm not doing any damage. I burn out and find myself on the floor, heaving.

"I can't, Mr. Van!"

"Push yourself past breaking point. That is how you will succeed. 'I can't' is only up here." He points at his temple, but I know he's talking about my thinking. I yank myself up and punch his mitts harder. I learn Taekwondo: how to punch, kick, and guard. I learn the Roundhouse kick, but it's super difficult to hold my leg up that high. I kick myself in frustration. I gotta get this right!

Three Weeks Later

Today I go head-to-head with Mr. Van. I feel super strong and fit. I know Anna said this would be a quick course, but there's no way I could've done this on my own. I felt God pushing me, giving me the strength and the ability to keep going. I stare at myself in the mirror and say a prayer, "We got this! You got this," I say to heaven, knowing I can't do anything without Him. I walk out and into the ring with a quick drawback of the elastic and fling my body forward. I watched Anna do this a few weeks ago. Back then I thought it was difficult.

Mr. Van warned me he wouldn't take it easy on me, but I welcomed it. The bell sounds and we put up our sets. My stance is strong, feet planted to the ground. He right hooks. I block, see an opening, and punch him in his mid-section. He takes it no problem, then left hooks. I block, grab his arms, pull him forward, thrusting my knee into his chest, and back away. He shakes it off and grabs at me, I swoop around his arm, and back sweep him off his feet. He falls onto his bottom and I have an itch to help him up, check on him. But he taught me to stand my ground, so I let it be.

He pulls back and pushes onto his feet and everyone ow's, including me. I go in for a right hook, and he grabs my arm and flips me, slamming me onto my back. My body aches, but I get up anyway. The pain subsides, but there's something about that pain that pushed me to the edge. He comes at me, and I block every hit. I hit him in the face with a flick of the back of my fist, immediately wrap my arm around his neck, then use body weight to sandwich him down. I put one arm around his leg and lock my hands together, putting him in a monkey hook. I tighten my grip, roll him over, and pin him down then get up.

"Oh my!" yells Lem.

"Yes Lolly!" yells Anna.

He gets up once again. I raise my fists as if I'm going to hit him in the face, he goes to block, and I side kick him straight to the body. He flies back. I run to him, kick spin, and hit the final blow to his chin. I twirl around on one foot then stop, removing my hands from my ankle that's above my head. I come back to reality, realizing I just did a move from my ballet class when I was seven and let my foot descend slowly to the ground. My cheeks are flushing in full bloom of embarrassment. Mr. Van's on the ground. This time he doesn't get up. I put my hands to my mouth and say, "Mr. Van!"

Me and Anna rush him, "Who taught you that?" he asks, and we laugh at him.

I'm in disbelief at what I just did so naturally. Looking in the mirror and not recognizing myself feels horrible. I don't know if I want to be a fighter, *to hurt people.* Anna's words ring in my ear: "Once you go that route, there's no going back."

Mr. Van puts his hand on my shoulder. "You did very well, Lolly."

I wipe my tears. "Thank you, Mr. Van. I'm sorry. I didn't mean to hurt you."

"It came from inside," he says, pointing and smiling. Very rare. "You surpassed my expectations. Elizabeth would be proud." I hug him. He doesn't know how much that means.

Anna follows me out. "Lolly, you were made for this!" My mouth drops. *I'm like her biggest fan and she said that to me?*

"Thank you, Anna!" She nods and looks as if she's going to cry.

"What's wrong?"

"Eric says I have to talk to my father, but I know he won't change his mind."

"Aw, Anna, he will. I've learned he has soft spots, especially for you." Her head lifts, "Try to show him that you're serious about Eric, and pray about it, of course."

She smiles. "You're right. Jesus is the answer." That rings true for my situation too.

23

Jesus' Super Lolly

In my backyard, I try to spin kick again, but my leg won't get high enough, and my turn's not as swift. Maybe Arch can tell me why? I go to my room, and Arch is windowside, talking to the sky.

"Yes, Almighty One."

Whaa? He's talking to God? I don't want to snoop, but my curiosity gets the best of me.

"Lolly, it's time," I almost fall on my head at his discovery of me.

"I'm so sorry, Arch . . . "

"The sparks, can you bring them back?"

"Uh, ye . . . yeah." I go for water.

"Try it right here!" He's on edge, rushed. I thrust my hand out in front of me and try.

Arch paces back and forth, I try even harder. "Concentrate!"

"I am! You're distracting me." He stills.

"Rely on God being your source and not the water." I close my eyes, not wanting to let God down after He chose me, and think about how powerful He made me in the ring earlier, and how I wanna make Mama proud. My hands pull together, I grunt feeling the energy leaving my insides, and flowing through my arms.

My eyes open, and a big gold electric power ball is glowing proudly, "Electo Pharim!"

"You summoned Electo Pharim!" He jumps up in excitement.

"What's Electo Pharim?" I whisper it, but no matter the volume, it's foreign on my tongue.

"Electricity from heaven, different from the one seen on earth."

"It's heavy," I pump my hand, it disappears and comes back.

"You got it! Now you have to learn how to throw it."

"Throw it where? This thing looks like it'll take out a building,"

"Back yard it is."

"What no! Daddy's here! No Arch!" I eye him.

"After God instructs us, we only have a certain timeframe to accomplish it.

Supernaturals came into this world without permission, and we have to send them back." I gasp.

"Lolly?" Daddy knocks on my door, "I'm going to the market. You need anything?"

"Umm hmm . . ." Arch says. I can't believe Daddy just gave him the opportunity to destroy our house, *or maybe it was God.*

"No, thanks, Dad." *Ugh.*

"Okay, see you in about thirty minutes." And now he gave Arch a time limit!

"Ha ha!" Arch exclaims and goes towards the outdoors. This is really about to go down! I peek into Josh's room. He has headphones on, munching on snacks.

Outside, I look at my cozy house that I now love but once hated, that is about to be gone in two seconds, with *my brother* in it! And Arch doesn't care. "What if I hit my house?"

"You won't."

"How can you be so sure?"

"Because your brother's in it." My jaw completely drops. I

pout across the grass away from him! Although I better watch the way I'm treating a holy citizen of heaven. Well, he's here now, and he's being rude! Thunder roars out of nowhere, and I ask for forgiveness faster than you can say a one-letter word.

"Bring it back."

I concentrate, and it appears. I'm so frustrated with Arch it's easy to aim. I press my hand up.

"Fire!" Arch yells, expecting a killer release, but it doesn't go anywhere!

I shake my hand. "It won't!" It blasts out of my palm toward my house. We look at each other and run for it, then it disappears. We roll on our backs in laughter and breath heavily.

"You knew it would do that!" I say.

"I didn't," he says, and I narrow my eyes at him.

I'm at the other end of the field, agonizing trying this again! I summon the heaven ball, trying to concentrate on anything other than my father returning to a hole in the ground, Josh gone, and me soaked in tears.

"You're in so much trouble!" says my brother, staring at me and Electo Pharim, *or whatever,* in my hand. I put it behind my back.

"What are you talking about?" I protest.

"You, you . . . the ball!" He points and walks closer.

"Ball? What ball? I don't play games, you do." I look at Arch. "I told you!" I whisper loudly.

"Do it again!" says my brother, obviously in some type of distress because he's digging his nails in his hair. I can't believe I'm exposing him to this.

"Josh . . ." I look at Arch, and he nods. My eyes widen and I say to Arch, "Okay, but if I get banished, I'm telling God to bring you with me so I won't be lonely!"

It's back up.

"Super cool!" says Josh. "I knew you were weird, but this is mad whacko! Even for you!"

"Whatevs. Don't tell dad or whatever, Josh. Don't tell anyone!"

"I'm not! I'm actually a cool little brother. What else can you do? Do I have powers too?"

"No lame-o!"

"Who says that anymore?"

"Be quiet or go back in the house."

"I knew you weren't normal! You're always in your room talking to yourself."

"Actually, she talks to me!" says Arch. Josh eyes Arch, goes behind me, then moves back up to my side. *Too late!*

"Wait, he can hear you too? I thought only I could!" I say in a whiny voice.

"He can talk?" I look at my sophomore of a brother.

"Duh! Are you scared, little brother?"

"No!" he says, blinking really fast.

"Right. That's why you just jumped . . . Now, step aside." My confidence grows. I'm a big sis after all. I aim again, and it slowly comes out and disappears. *Ugh,* so much for that.

"You gotta believe and throw it out fast," says Josh.

"For real! I see it on the game all the time." *Tsk the game!*

"Try it, Lolly," says Arch. I cannot believe I'm taking lessons on fighting from a fifteen-year-old. I breathe, do it fast, and fly over to the other side to catch it.

"Whoa! You can fly?" Josh asks.

"Yeah!" I say matter-of-factly and breathless. "I can fly?" I ask Arch.

"You can fly!" Arch exclaims, and we cheer. I do it over and over again until Daddy gets home.

"Lemme know when you practice again. I have some ideas,"

says Josh. I nod. I never thought this would be a family affair, but at least now I don't feel like a total outcast.

It's me and the stove tonight, and it seems like we're going head-to-head. I take out pots and want to karate chop them because of the nightmares. Before I know it, I'm setting the table, and we stare at Mom's empty chair.

"This is our first dinner without your mother, but we are still counting her in. We love you, Liz," says Daddy. He looks up to the ceiling, and I clear my throat.

"Should we taste the lasagna?" I say.

Daddy nods.

"It probably sucks!" says Josh. Of course, he says exactly what I'm thinking, and we laugh. Do we finally have something in common? *Fighting.* A bond even?

We dig in to the layers of pasta. "Umm, sweetheart!" Daddy says.

"This is good! What'd you do, summon Mom?" asks Josh, and we both pause. *He's doing a really great job at keeping me a secret!* We burst out in laughter.

"What'd I miss?" says Daddy.

"Nothing," I say.

"Yes, I did!" He gets up, and me and Josh shrug at each other. Daddy brings out a birthday cake. *I forgot.* The number 19 sits at the top of the pretty pink cake. Daddy is not a stylish one. That was Mom, so he must've had help!

"It's pretty, Daddy."

"For my pretty princess." He kisses my forehead. They sing happy birthday, and we cut the cake. Needless to say, Josh eats two slices.

I clean up the kitchen, and Daddy and Josh make me promise not to make any more TV dinners. I third that. I see Josh hanging with Arch and for some strange reason feel Arch was not only here to help me fulfill my destiny but was here to help us get through losing our mother. We're not so bad the four of us. We're actually doing pretty darn good!

I go to my room, slowly stepping towards my mother's envelope. It's the only new thing I have of hers. Everything else is history. I press it to my heart. "I'm not gonna cry. I'm strong," I blink away tears. I tussle with the flap, "Just open already!" I put my hand over my mouth, tears unwrap themselves, pouring out like a broken beaver dam, and my vision gets blurred.

"Arch . . ." I say, my voice barely audible, and I feel like I'm drowning. "Jesus." My voice trembles, and though I know Arch will never hear me with my voice being caught by emotions, He hears me. The Creator of the universe, the One who knows me by name, the One who will never leave me no matter who else does. I feel a warmth that presses me to get up and take that envelope with a steady hand. I tear it apart, a locket falls out, and I find a picture of all of us within. A smile, *finally*.

The next day Arch, Josh, and I work on my powers. "Aim and keep shooting, Lolly. Don't give up!" yells the gamer in my brother. He's so good at this my blasts are coming out in different forms, and I actually learn how to fly higher with Arch's help. Days pass, my moves have gotten faster, I can control my lightning balls, and I can reach the clouds now. I get down from the sky with a whisk.

"Whoa!" Josh says in surprise.

"What?"

"Your hair!" Arch is amazed as well. I comb it up. *It's purple!*

I run to the bathroom. "Arch! My mother told me to never dye my hair!"

"It's okay. Trust God, even with your hair." Josh and he laugh, but it's not funny. I eye them, and they stop.

"I understand, Lolls. But this is what He pictured when He made you. It's not dyed, it's just . . . *changed*. No damage included, so you're still getting what Mama wanted."

A bit of relief comes. I kiss my locket. "Love you, Mama." I'm content *and* I didn't get banished.

24
High Priced Vacation Days

William gets released from hell after getting a pile of missions stacked on top of him for bad behavior. Satan decided he needed his best assassin on the surface, regardless of his insubordination. William walks on the sidewalk of the attached stores with his device, trying to find his first hit, a con man who delves in dark magic. *Should I check out the antique shop again?* he thought to himself. He looks at it and sees a girl locking the door. His eyes dance. The girl that'd been snippy with him a few weeks ago had brown hair. He enjoyed their back-and-forth, but this girl has purple hair. Could she be the power source drawing the Talis?

He moves towards her but spots antlers and iridescent skin running down the sidewalk, *a Similory*. He grabs her wrist before she's able to flee. "How'd you get out?" says William.

"It is you! Ore, from The Games," says Deylou then asks, "You can see me?"

William answers, saying, "I'm talking to you, right?"

"The wizard, Du'Jomi, took me as his prisoner out of The Games. Five escaped. He plans to take earth for himself with his mother," says Deylou.

William's eyes widen. "Where are they?" William scans the area and snarls.

"I do not know. I ran."

"A wizard, huh?" He lets go of Deylou and puts his hands in

his pockets while he thinks. She studies his chiseled features and long torso. She couldn't see how good-looking he was from afar. "I've killed one," he finally lets out.

"You have?" Her face brightens. "Their magic makes them hard to locate, but it's doable."

He smirks.

"I came to earth for help," says a desperate Deylou. He lifts a brow.

"My sister was taken in a dangerous forest by a people that threaten mine." Her face is drawn, and she sobs.

He scans her, finally getting to see one of them up-close. She's exotic. Her sandy hair is bone straight, her cheekbones highlight her round face, and she's thin, very thin. He wants to help, but he can't do whatever he wants, let alone leave the planet. "I'll see what I can do. For now, we gotta catch a wizard."

"I do not have much time."

"I get it, I just can't leave extras to roam my planet."

He teleports her to his home; a green ring circling Deylou's body flashes.

"What'd you do?" asks William.

"I did not do anything."

"I pulled you in from the spiritual realm, then?" William pulls the Talis from his pocket.

"What is it?" asks Deylou.

"A magic tracker," says William. "It senses power on earth, especially new power since there isn't a lot here. It looks like a wishbone, right?"

Deylou nods. He's trying to practice gentleness, but it goes against his nature.

He touches the burn marks on it. Yeah, the tracker Satan gave him was directing him to target, but there was a gnawing present, an emotion he'd never felt before bringing him back to the girl at the shop.

"Let's eat," he says to clear his thoughts but still thinks about the way the brown-haired girl blushed. Then he thinks about the purple-haired girl and gets confused as to why he was.

Hell

"You called?"

"William, you're in a chipper mood despite just being released from prison."

"Hope you're not about to ruin it." He knows his captor has power over him, but he won't be a slave in the small freedom he's awarded.

"Hope is futile, William."

"So you say . . ."

"Lolly Pobs."

"No thanks. I don't eat candy."

"That's her name."

"Whose name?" He thinks about *her*. "Your next hit. But be careful with her. She's almost your equal." William chuckles.

"She can defeat you, not because of her amateur power, but because of who she walks with."

"No one will ever defeat me! And when I kill her, *which I will,* I want something since she's so valuable to you."

"Oh? You attempt to bargain with me, which is futile as well, but I'm intrigued."

"I want a vacation. Every job has benefits."

"Why, William, you desire to be far from me?"

"Yeah, I do," He looks at the cage he was in just yesterday.

"As you wish, but I expect all your other hits to be done before you go. Especially your extra credit." He's shocked it actually worked, and he starts walking away.

"Oh, and William?" He stops with a clenched fist. *Is Satan going to change his mind?*

"What?"

"I need you to start gathering stone to build our bridge into the Spiritual Realm."

William's stomach turns. "But that would be going against—"

"Yes, if that troubles you, maybe you should reconsider your vacation days. The girl walks with the Holy One."

He's taken aback, *Lolly Pobs* walks with God? The vampire bite didn't get him, but if God is with her, *will* he defeat her?

"No matter," William shrugs, his competitive side, Ore, getting the best of him. "I picked the right boy."

The devil's laughter fills hell, and William exits.

25

Topsy-Turvy

In New York, Daisy goes into a store and grabs a newspaper.

"Got it free," she says.

"Again?" says Grand.

"Had to test it out." Grand shakes his head. He takes off his mask to read, then looks at her.

"What?" she asks, drinking a bottled water.

"The 'No judgment's' nice."

"None here," she says, and he smiles.

"Everything's so expensive," says Grand.

"We can't depend on jobs for money," says Daisy.

"What are you suggesting?"

"I could use my power to suggest. Starting with robbing a bank or two."

"You're joking, right?" asks Grand, bamboozled.

He thought the move would be as smooth as Washington, but it's proving otherwise. He thinks about praying but won't. God hasn't done things the way he wanted Him to anyway. And if this was God's plan for his life, it was too hard.

"One bank and not here. It's too crowded, and we're trying to live here," he says.

She gives an infectious smile. "Where?" She pulls his arm and lays on his shoulder. He narrows his eyes; she never acted like this at the diner.

"Pennsylvania. It's three hours away. It'll give us room to get away. Let's get a home first," he says.

They find a privately owned apartment overlooking the city. "It's three thousand dollars a month. Will you be able to make rent?" The lady in a suit sticks her nose up at Daisy, peering at her ripped jeans and plain T-shirt.

"Yes," she simply says, feeling suit's eyes.

"I'll need to see credentials. You'll need to sign paperwork and—"

"No need for that," says Daisy.

The lady's head whips up. "Of course not."

Daisy turns to Grand and pumps her fist. "Also, rent is free for two months. After that, we'll start paying." Grand nods in approval.

"Of course, dear. Here are the keys," the realtor says politely.

They bring their bags into their furnished home.

The day of the heist, they park Daisy's car away from cameras. Daisy puts on her big empty purse.

"You ready?" Grand asks.

"Yes, getaway driver." She's way too calm.

"Have you done this before?"

"Never, scouts honor." She throws up two fingers.

"Okay, I'll be waiting. Remember, unmarked cash."

"Got it."

"I hate that you have to go in alone." He knows his mask will put them on alert.

"It's okay, boss," she says before climbing out.

"Boss?" He curls his lip, anxiously watching her walk into the bank.

"I wanna open up an account." She raises her hat and sees there's only two ladies working.

"Sure. What kinda account, sweetheart?"

"Checking."

"Hey, Martha. You gotta come show me how to sign her up for a checking account." She smiles at Daisy. "Sorry, it's my first day."

Daisy nods. *It's about to be her worst day too.* The other woman comes over from the drive thru. "Sure, you just go in here."

"Stop," Daisy says, and the two women look at her. "Go in the back and get the unmarked cash now!" she says in a menacing tone. In a trance, they go back one by one. Daisy looks around, hoping no one will come in.

Back home, they throw money all over the carpet in awe. It takes them all day, but they count out *one hundred thousand dollars*.

"We're rich!" says Daisy.

Grand wonders if he can buy new skin. He goes in the kitchen for dinner and sees his dogs laid out. They haven't eaten in days. "You guys okay?" He pats them deciding to watch them over a few days.

They watch the news to see if they'd be a feature in it. The reporters talk about a war hero that got burned alive inside of a building in Iraq, and the news crew stands outside of his home. "We're just hoping he pulls through. No more comments," says his wife.

"She's pretty," says Daisy. Grand nods. The young wife goes to her toddlers that wait at the front door. "Adam Frank is only twenty-five years old," says the news reporter.

"So young," says Daisy before she takes a huge bite of a turkey leg. Grand looks at it and the other two that are meatless in her huge bowl. She's been eating nonstop since they got here and hasn't gained a pound.

"I wish I could help him," Grand says.

"Maybe you can help him like you helped me."

"I could but look what it did to you. What if something worse happens to him?"

"So? I'm sure his family will take him however he comes *and living.*"

"How will I do it?"

She says, "A syringe?"

The reporter announces, "In other news, an annual giveaway going on today . . ."

"Nothing about us!" They relax.

Daisy goes to the hospital's check-in desk and uses her talents to find Adam Frank. She lets Grand in through a side door. The room is dark, and a beeping sound is the only thing heard, as Adam is sleeping. He puts the injector they found into his own arm with a quick suck of air and starts to withdraw fluids. The needle is thick, and the hole makes his insides melt, but this wasn't about him. Judging by Daisy's healed wounds, Adam should heal just fine.

Daisy paces back and forth, walks over to him, and places her hand on his shoulder. "That's enough. Take it out!" she demands, and he nods. He waits to see if the metal will hold. *It does.*

He goes to Adam, looking for a place to put it. Adam's eyes are blinking slowly in between the wrapping around his head until they're wide open. He sees the contraption in the masked man's hand, then starts to squirm and grunt. Grand takes off his mask. "Hey man it's okay. I just wanna help."

Adam cocks his head back in question as he looks at Grand's marked skin. He tries to move but cries out in agony, the noise clipped by gauze. Adam looks at the morphine drip bag and fades to sleep once more. Grand quickly sticks it in his arm, figuring he won't feel it because of the meds, and squeezes the blue in. When he pulls it out, the gash closes up. They sneak out.

For the next few days, they watch the news. "It's a Miracle!" is plastered on the headlines. "Our top story tonight, folks. Adam Frank is expected to make a full recovery." Cameras flash as he leaves the hospital and when he arrives home. They look at his face and new skin, not a blemish in sight. "Doctors and nurses that aided Frank in recovery are astonished, saying they've never seen anything like it, calling him a 'present-day miracle.'"

"It has to be the Lord's work. That's the only explanation we have," says a nurse. The culprits smile. "Adam Frank came in with third-degree burns covering his entire body. Doctors said he wouldn't survive, but when nurse Abagail went in to change his bandages, she found new skin and that radiant smile we've all come to adore."

The camera shifts to Adam. "I'm just happy to be going home to my family." He waves.

"We need to find him," says Daisy.

"Why?"

"Maybe he'll help us rob the banks."

"Daisy, we agreed on one bank," says Grand.

"Well, he can help with something else. He didn't do that himself. We did, and he needs to know!"

"I just wanted to help him."

"Just in case." She shrugs. Daisy calls the operator and finds out Adam's address.

They go to his house, and after opening the front door, Adam's eyes all but say he remembers Grand.

"Be right back, love," he calls behind him and shuts the door.

"How's the family?" Grand asks.

"Great. Thanks for everything. How'd you do it?" Adam asks cautiously.

Daisy grins. "I'm glad you get to enjoy your family, and I hope you live a full life. Before we go, what's your power?" asks Grand.

"Power?" asks a puzzled Adam.

"I can make him tell us," says Daisy.

Adam rolls his eyes, "How do you even know about it?" Adam hesitates but sees he has no choice. He touches a flower in a bush and it turns to frost. His audience claps.

"That's cool man. All I ask is if I need something in the future, you return the favor. For now, enjoy the second chance at life," says Grand.

They drive home. "You think he'll really help?" asks Grand.

"He's a soldier. He'll keep his word," says Daisy.

Seeing a familiar face walking down the street, Grand says, "Pull over!" He rolls down his window. "Ci! Ci! . . . Jessica!" She stops, keeping her distance from the masked man.

"How do you know my name?" asks Ci.

"It's Grand!"

"Yeah, and my foot's gold," she says and continues to walk.

"You helped me with Rachel in tenth grade!"

She looks at his mask.

"You switched schools and never called!" Ci says. Someone honks their horn. "Can I get your number?" he asks.

"Better. I'll come with." She hops in the back seat. "Hi, I'm Jessica," she says, but Daisy ignores her. "I thought you went by Ci?" asks Grand.

"Jessica's more professional."

"And Cali?"

"Things change. I'm here for college. I graduated early." He wonders about Rachel. "What's up with the mask?" Ci asks.

At the apartment, Lucy and Latch instantly jump on Ci, kissing her up. She gets down and pats them.

"You two feeling better, I see!" Grand says.

Ci goes to the window. "I love your view! It's sparkly." She rocks from side to side.

"Where'd you find this chick?" asks Daisy before sitting on the couch.

"Be nice. She was my only friend in high school."

Daisy rolls her eyes and chomps on a bucket of chicken wings.

"You can come see it any time," Grand tells Ci.

"Don't tell me that! I'll be here every day!" Daisy jeers, then covers it up with a cough.

"I know you wanna know about Rachel." She looks away from the city. Her hair is still long and red. She has on a long black dress, with red flowers around her chest, and a thin beige shawl that looks like it was borrowed from a painter.

"Sure," he says.

"I know you have a skin condition, but do you really have to wear that mask in the house?"

"Yes, he does!" Daisy snaps.

"My bad," says Jessica.

"It's okay," says Grand, glaring at Daisy. "It's pretty necessary."

"Cool. I'm glad you have new friends."

"Yeah, me too," he says but isn't sure at the moment.

"Rachel was doing fine before I left. She's still single . . ." She waggles her eyebrows and he laughs. "She graduated early too but didn't go off to college yet. Said something about helping with a girls' home or something."

"Yeah, she put together a fundraiser for it the year I went."

"She cut her hair. It's neck length."

"Why?" All the images he kept of her blow away like leaves.

"Probably to donate it to the less fortunate. You know Rachel."

Daisy laughs, and Grand clears his throat so he won't join her. "Probably," he says.

"You kissed any girls lately?" She looks at Daisy.

"No," he says, laughing. They talk awhile then drop Jessica off at her dorm. Grand tries to picture Rachel with short hair and knows she's still gorgeous no matter what.

They spend weeks blowing money and gambling. Grand looks at tags to warehouses. "What's that?" asks Daisy.

"A warehouse I wanna buy for five hundred k."

"Um, that's a pretty penny." Her eye twinkles.

"It comes with two trucks. I wanna get the acid and start a business."

"Smart. Ci influenced you, huh?"

"She always does."

"We'll need to pull a bigger stunt. They had more money, but I couldn't carry it all. Maybe we can ask Jessica to come with."

"No, no, no! I don't want her to get involved."

"Look, we can do it, and I can make her forget."

"Go get fresh air. You're not thinking straight!" he says, agitated.

"Right now? I don't really want to."

"Yeah, you need it," he says. She calmly walks out and is gone for hours. He waits for her with his hands banded around his neck. He gets up to go look for her, but she breaks through the door.

"Where were you?"

"You told me to cool off. I finally did." She's shivering. He stares at her. Does he have her power?

"Jump up and down," he commands.

"I don't really want to. Do I have to?" She said that earlier, and he told her yes before.

"No."

She nods. "I'm gonna shower." *What's wrong with her? First the food, now this.*

They sit on the couch and watch a vampire movie. She doesn't seem bothered about what happened earlier, but it's bothering him to the moon and back. In the movie, a girl vampire is drawn to the vampire dude that changed her. She can't get enough of him, does whatever he wills, and is super protective of him. When Daisy exercises her powers, people automatically do what she commands. But when he tells her to do things, she sort of has a choice. It seemed she wanted to please him.

"Daisy is sired to me," he says, thoughts swirling.

Jessica sits across from them. "Do you wanna rob a bank with us?" Daisy blurts out and Grand peers at her.

"Seriously?" Ci asks, her eyes widening.

"Does it look like I'm kidding?" says Daisy.

Jessica studies her for a second. "Sure."

They drive three hours to the bank. Daisy painfully smiles at the two women, a man comes out of the back, and her fake smile drops. A customer comes in the door and stands behind them. Daisy swallows hard then walks backwards to the woman.

"Go home," she says. "Forget you needed to come to the bank until tomorrow." The woman leaves.

"How can I help you?" asks the teller.

"Tell your coworker I need her and then get me two bags of your unmarked cash."

Ci gasps.

"Why certainly."

Martha does as she's told. The lady at the drive thru has cars backed up and takes her time coming. Daisy sweats.

"It's just that easy?" Ci asks.

"I know them," says Daisy.

The other teller finally comes over, and Daisy instructs her to help Martha. The man is nowhere to be found, and she tells another customer to leave.

The women return, and they shove the cash into their bags. "Forget all of this!" she says to them, and they bolt.

"Stop right there!" Police officers point guns at the girls. Daisy looks over at her car just around the way. *Grand, stay where you are,* she thinks.

Grand gets out and runs to them. "No!" Daisy calls and extends her hand. The officers shoot their guns at them. "Take a nap!" Daisy shouts to the officers and they fall.

Blood is running down Daisy's arm from being grazed, and Ci lays on the floor unresponsive.

"No, Ci!" Grand holds her.

"Grand, I'm so sorry, but we have to go. More will be here soon," says Daisy, pulling at his jacket.

He snatches away, grabs a bag of money, and picks up Ci's lifeless body.

26

Heart Bells Ring Too

My alarm wakes me up for work, and I head in, still embarrassed about my new hair. Yesterday, people stared at me big-eyed. Today is gonna be a long day.

Anna walks by. "I love the new hair, Lolly!"

"Thanks, Anna." I have to go by and ask about Eric soon. To my surprise, I get so many compliments on my hair, but I'm still trying to get used to it.

Strangely, a shipment comes in, and I run to the delivery guy before he wastes his time. "I didn't order anything. You must be at the wrong shop."

He looks at his little machine. "Delivery for Elizabeth Pobs?"

"Oh, yeah, that's us," I say and chuckle, but I'm confused.

"I'll let you know now, you have deliveries for months down the road, all paid for."

I get excited looking at all the boxes he brought in. I thought the locket was the only new thing from Mama! I grab his machine and sure enough I see a ton of dates for upcoming deliveries. I sign the machine and say, "Thank you!"

"Your hair's gorgeous by the way," he says.

"Thank you," I say shyly. His smile is pearly, his dark skin is dazzling, and he's maybe six feet tall. *Will he be delivering all my mother's packages?*

Most of the boxes contain glass vases and more candleholders, but there's a long box that calls for my attention. I slice it open with a box cutter and feel a handle. I pull it out and look at the gold in my small hand. I remove it completely, *a sword in its sheath*. Wow, she really wanted to change the style of the store. I look at all the empty boxes, eager to see future orders. Bells I added atop my door jangle, my head springs up, and my heart leaps. They're there so Cap won't catch me off guard again, but he hasn't been in lately. I sigh when I see it isn't him and shove the sword back in its box.

"Do you think she knew?" I ask Arch.

"Anything's possible."

I get an idea and call Addy. She three-ways Leena into the call.

"Hello, MADE here!"

"Leena? It's Lolly!" Never knew I'd miss her voice so much, but we practically lived in her store.

"Lolly! Hey! How's New York?"

"Very interesting, but better than I thought. I miss you."

"We miss you too!"

She talks to her mother. My excitement is on pause and I see nothing's changed in LA.

"I'm sorry, you need something made?"

"Yes! By the one and only!" Leena giggles. She tells me she'll stop all orders to make my costume and will overnight it. Halloween had already passed, but Leena asked no questions. I'll order from her on a weekly basis if possible.

She cries when I tell her about Mom. She didn't know her, she just related to me because of her crazy relationship with her mom. She says, "Maybe I should be nicer to my mother."

I agree, we should cherish the people in our lives while we still have them. Plus, there's nothing like sharing a testimony that'll help someone. Addy and I cry with her.

The next day, it arrives at my shop before closing time. At home, Arch and me surround it. I call Addy and put her on speaker.

"Open it now! Leena let me see it before she shipped it, and it's gorg! Thankfully she knows your measurements by heart!" says Addy.

I pull the thing open, and pink paper's on top, *so girly!* After all this karate stuff, pants, sweat, and tears, this is very much needed! I peel back the delicate paper, snatch it, and come alive. Her stitching is just like I remember it, never missing a beat!

I put it on and go to my infamous body mirror, I haven't felt dressed up enough to twirl in it since LA.

"You can look now, Archie."

"You sure?"

"I'm sure!" I am so excited! He peeks with one paw uncovered, and when he sees it's safe, he comes over. Long sleeves run down my arms, the sides of my stomach are out, and the bottom sways so elegantly. Shorts are connected for fighting. It's perfect. I admire the vinyl lining she put along the stitching, her style all the way. I put on my white go-go boots and grab my sword.

"Lolly, you look heavenly!" Arch affirms.

"What does Jesus think?"

"Ask Him."

I get a little shy but close my eyes. "Jesus, do you like my dress?" In the mirror, I see a golden glow around me.

"He sealed it! Now it'll come on automatically!" says Arch.

I am in shock. "I picked it out, and He let me!" Happy tears well at the corners of my eyes. "Thank You, Lord," I whisper and old fashioned bronzed metal appears in the middle of my dress. Two metal plates to match wrap around my wrist, and tiny bells fall from them.

"Arch, what's this?"

"Righteous Bells." He sounds puzzled. "He gave you the Righteous Bells!"

"What do they do?"

"He sanctified you. It's a *vow of love*. And they tell you the difference between good and evil."

"Do you mean I'll know when someone is good or evil?"

"They'll sound when evil is around," he rhymes and bounces on his bottom. I giggle. I run my fingers on the rhinestones located on my wrist plates and wiggle the bells that fall like charms but don't make a sound. I'm caught in a trance as I look at the finished product. My purple hair makes so much sense now. I see that sometimes we can't see the whole picture, but God will bring it together in His time.

I shower and sit at my vanity, trying to see if anything else has changed about me, but I'm still Lolly. I splash lip gloss on my lips and add a little eyeliner and mascara. I tie my long hair into a ponytail with a pink ribbon and make kissy faces in the mirror. Who am I kidding? *Makeup me* is history! I grab a makeup remover pad, then spot Arch talking to himself in my mirror.

"Lolly, we got a lead. Suit up." I get up and immediately see myself transform in my body mirror. I gasp. I could have sworn my eyes were just glowing. Arch cries as my sword pops up in my hand, and I quiver in delight.

"Josh!" I shout and my brother runs into my room.

"Whoa, Geeka!"

"You're the geek!" I say and tell him about the radicals.

"I wanna go!"

"It's too dangerous, Josh."

He groans. "Okay, but tell me all about your first time using Electo ball."

"Promise!" I think about telling Daddy bye just in case something goes wrong. He's been putting in overtime, and I know he's just trying to stay busy to keep his mind at ease. So I just let him rest, remembering my bells. *I'll live.*

Josh watches me take off, and Arch carefully follows on the ground. When we get there, I glide down. "Why didn't you tell me it was at Barns, Arch? What if someone sees me?"

"Because no one's gonna see you." Again with the *just trust me*'s like when I was about to blast my brother down.

"You still could've told me!" I whisper to my double-crossing dog. We're on a long sidewalk.

"Wanna race?" we say together, giggle, then take off. We stop at the edge of the pavement before the street.

"Shhh!" I say so the enemy won't hear us, and he nods.

We look on both sides of the street, stare at each other, and nod. I balance on my tippy toes, putting one hand over my head, gracefully extending the other in front of me. Arch gets on his two back legs, I know he wants to bark so bad right now, but he contains it. My years of ballet as a child are now really paying off. I make sure my legs are in tune, and we start across.

Midway, I pirouette and extend my foot to land.

"Whoa! Nice skills!" says Arch, and I bow. A huge truck flashes its headlights and honks. We zip to the other side. I think we need a respirator at this point. We giggle silently.

We get a grip and Arch nods towards a dark alley. We approach it, but for some reason, he starts to draw back. The wind blows heavily and snatches the ribbon out of my hair. I reach for it, but the pink just laces around my fingers and escapes. I grunt and turn back to target, getting around the corner now. There's barely any light back here, but I see a figure in the air conducting rocks from one end to the other. In my old life this would've been weird, but now it's not much weirder than a flying girl and a talking dog. I hide behind a nearby car. Arch has just made it around the corner. I roll my eyes. *What's he doing?* I slightly stand and pull out my sword, not believing I'm really about to use this thing.

Lights turn on all around me and I hear a metal-y *smack!* I stand up straight, and my eyes dart to the now-revealed figure sitting on the hood of the old school I just hid behind. He has on a blue suit that fits him just right. *It does?* A perfectly crowned flame blazes on his head, his teeth are a pearly black, and a gold chain sits on his neck and wrist. I breathe heavily. Something in me doesn't wanna show him what I've been learning. My heart's beating unnaturally, like it's about to roll off its tracks. *I notice my bells haven't rung.*

"Umm, milady," he says sizing me up. *Wha?* He turns from this thing into normal and is now even more handsome. He has beautiful, straight, neatly combed black hair and piercing blue eyes. *Those eye*s. I know them, but from where?

"Arch?" I call out. My dog cries. He obviously doesn't know what to do either; some crew we are.

All of a sudden, I'm being pulled in blue suit's direction. My sword scrapes against the ground in protest. I have zero control and am now in his face. I try to swing my sword, do something, but I can't move. I stare at the character before me, and know he's doing it.

"Let me go!" I yell. He studies me, then gets closer and looks as if he is going to *kiss me!* "You wouldn't dare!" I say through clenched teeth, trying to loosen myself from his grip. He sweeps my hair out of my face, then places his hand on my cheek. I'm already stopped, but I grow still, and my heart quiets. His eyes deeply plunge into my eyes before pressing his lips down on mine. I close my eyes at the feel of soft tissue and think back to my ninth birthday party.

I had friends over, and my parents were in the kitchen finish-ing up the last touches to my cake. We played a foolish game where we had to make another react in some kind of way to win. But if they stayed completely still, you lost. My cousin Suzzie always won! She stood there with unshakable crossed arms and a smirk to match while little Anna Jack jumped in her face, waving her hands for ten minutes straight but couldn't get Suzzie to flinch.

Because I was such a happy child, all someone had to do was make me laugh, and I quickly lost. But there was one time I decided to mimic my cousin. I lasted *five whole minutes!* I was so proud. Little Brandon Armstrong from next door marched back and forth in front of me, hands balled up at his side. I was so tempted to laugh, but I held my composure. *So much for that.*

"Come on, Armstrong!" hollered his best friend, Billy Wing, as he adjusted his cowboy hat on the sidelines. I looked at it, his cowboy boots, and the tiny straw between his teeth he sucked on from chocolate milk Mama handed out earlier, and *knew* I was a goner. Brandon kissed me, and I screamed. My parents ran into the room, and I lost. *That* kiss didn't count, but this kiss? Counts!

Our eyes fling open at the same time, and we stare at one another, both chests pumping. I gather up all my strength and slap him *HARD!* His face shifts to one side and stays there. I'm tempted to put my hand over my mouth and apologize but stand my ground, not fully sure what I should do next. He turns back into flame man, then roars, *literally roars* at me. I step back, he eases up, and he puts both hands in his pockets.

"Love taps. I like it," he says, looking at the whole of me. I put my sword in its sheath and turn to kick him. He grabs my ankle just before his face and pulls, bringing me into his arms.

"I didn't come at you once, yet you keep attacking me. What's up with that?" he whispers, humor in his voice. His voice makes me blink repeatedly; *I know it.*

"Is this what you do? Freeze girls to win a fight?"

"Nope, just you,"

Liar! I break free, pivot, and kick him for real this time. He catches himself in the air, and I quickly fly to him, pulling my sword out. With one glance, he makes my sword evaporate before my eyes. *No,* Mama's sword! My eyebrows draw together, and I charge at him. I throw hook after hook and foot after foot, but he catches every one and won't strike back. It seems he has great ability but isn't using it.

What frustrates me is I'm using most of what Mr. Van taught me, to no avail. Enraged, electricity pumps within my hands, I raise my knee to throw it, but he simply blows it out like a birthday candle. I heave and look at his hair. Fire is obviously *his* thing. *Okay I'm done!* I sweep over to him, and he instantly puts my hand behind my back, holding the other. He swoops us to the ground.

"Let me go!" I kick my feet out, glad that at least I'm not frozen. I feel him power down.

"Are you done?" he bluntly asks, and it burns at my confidence.

"No!" I declare. I look at my dog. He's just sitting there, watching calmly.

Is something going on that I don't know about? I try to break his hold, but he's too strong without even trying.

"If you stop, I'll let you go. You're gonna burn yourself out," he says softly in my ear. I melt and nod in defeat. He lets go. I'm happy to be free, but why do I feel like a puzzle piece, getting disconnected from its whole?

"Are you the wizard?" I ask.

"Do I look like a wizard?" His tone is a little harsh, and I'm having trouble going back and forth between his sweet and sour. Still, I analyze him.

Suddenly, my bells angelically chime like Christmas Day. We

look at them, then he looks behind me. Before I can see what or who he's looking at, I'm lying in the back seat of a car, unable to move. He opens his car door and lets Arch in. I'm super confused. Who does flame dude think he is! More importantly, did the wizard set off my bells? I try to listen to what's going on outside. I hear voices, but they're muffled. *He kissed me.* I lay my head on the seat.

In that very moment, he opens the door and I'm able to climb out after Arch. In outright disbelief, I'm watching Arch allowing this person to pat him, and he's doing tricks for him now. I quietly laugh and cross my arms.

"Arch, let's go!" Obviously, we're done here, and he's not a real threat. A waste of time *and kisses*. Okay so I did not just think that last part.

Arch paddles to me. "What's going on?" I whisper and he cries. Flame blower appears in front of us. I roll my eyes.

"What now?" I haven't been this agitated in a long time. Well, not since I was like this with my mother.

He looks around. "Can I bring you somewhere?"

"Can you what?" I say harshly. "After all that, you think I'm gonna trust you to take me anywhere?" I think about Carter and the small amount of trust I can place in guys these days.

27

Meet Your Match

William thinks of ways to get just a little more time with the purple-haired girl that *is* the brown-haired girl. That's why he was so drawn to both. *But was she always on earth?* Had he missed her like Von's family?

"I'm looking for the wizard too, maybe we can help each other?" he asks Lolly. *Please?* He hopes.

"How do we know . . ." She pauses and looks at her quiet dog. "How do *I* know you're not working for the wizard?"

"Because I'm telling you I'm not."

"Very believable," she says before walking away, her dog following her.

"I have proof," he says loudly.

She talks to her dog while walking back. "What proof?" She crosses her arms.

"Get in and I'll show you," he says, looking at his car.

Lolly laughs. "I heard that one before!"

His brows draw together. *Was she talking about another guy?* Jealousy rises up, but he places his hands in his pockets and shrugs to hide it. "I dunno who lied to you, but I'm not. Stop acting so tough and come with me. We both know it doesn't work for you." He tries to say it softly, although he doesn't know if he picked the right words.

"How rude!" she says, confirming he hadn't. She turns away

and he panics, instantaneously appearing in front of her again.

"I'm sorry. I'm telling you the truth, okay?" Her shoulders and eyes ease. She whispers something to her dog.

"Fine, but if you try anything, my dog will bite you." It looks as if even she doesn't believe her words.

He grins and says, "All right." His picture-worthy smile causes her to freeze, but she reloads and nods. He relaxes.

They sit in his car quietly.

"Can I at least know your name?"

"No," she says firmly.

"Well, I'm William. William Blue." He puts out a hand for her to shake, but she doesn't. He shakes his head at her stubbornness.

Suddenly, hers pops out of the darkness. "I'm Lolly Pobs," she says sweetly, seeming apologetic. He thinks back on how he knows that name, but an assassin never forgets *a hit,* especially not *the one* that was gonna allow him to go on that trip to help Deylou. He plays it cool and shakes her hand.

His face twitches. *Great,* this girl had his heart without even doing much, and now she's about to be dead. He wipes at his lip in frustration and shifts in his seat. It was said she was his equal. He looks at the beautiful girl, *Lolly,* and can't picture himself testing it out. This might be the mission he won't go through with, and he never missed one. Although, it intrigued him how easily the prey came to him. It could be a simple assassination, *so it seemed.* He'd do it fast. She probably wouldn't even feel it. He'd snap her . . . He shakes the thought that somehow crept into his mind and clicks on the radio.

They pull up to his gate and it slowly opens.

"You live in a mansion?" Lolly asks, surprised.

"Yeah, c'mon," he says nonchalantly, still in limbo about his findings. They go upstairs. Lolly treads lightly.

"William, would you like dinner? Your lady Deylou has

already eaten," says Eloise, short of Deylou's door and greets his guests, distastefully peering at Lolly.

"We ate on the way, thanks, Elo." William gulps; his eyes dart to Lolly. She smirks and licks her lips, wondering who Deylou is.

"Very well." The maid departs.

"I miss my home" says Deylou. "William said he will help, but first we must find the wizard." Lolly stares at her glowing skin and antennas, then at William's *I told you so* smile, and rolls her eyes.

"Aw, I'm sorry you got stuck here, Deylou. I believe God can help us get you back successfully."

"I believe He brought you two to me," says Deylou.

"Any idea how we can get to her planet?" Lolly asks William.

"Not yet."

Lolly nods. "Okay, it's pretty late. We're gonna go home," says Lolly.

"I'm taking you," says William.

"No, you're not." She tries to sound firm but yawns.

"I brought you here. Let me take you home . . . *please.*"

"Okay." She rolls her eyes, but he smiles in victory.

"Goodbye!" Deylou says, putting a hat on William's head.

Lolly glares at him, realizing who he really is.

The ride home is quiet at first. "So, is breaking and entering one of your specialties?" Lolly says sarcastically.

"Oh, you remember that?" he says nervously.

"*I do*, so what exactly were you doing in my shop?"

"I bought something, didn't I?" he says dryly, in complete change of character, fighting compulsions to attack.

"Did you take something?" she asks.

"The only thing I hope to steal is your heart," he says, grinning playfully. The line was too good to resist.

"Really? That's where you're taking this?"

"Yeah."

William Blue doesn't have a clue on how to chase after girls. They always came to him. They're both at a loss of words.

"So, are you gonna apologize?" he finally says through a smile.

"For what?" Lolly asks.

"For calling me a thief and kicking me in the face earlier."

She giggles. *Score.* "I'm sorry for insinuating you were the bad guy, which doesn't fully check out yet. Especially after that car thing you pulled, throwing me in it like that."

"I didn't throw you . . ." *Had he?* He scans her face but can't read her.

"So you think I'm a bad guy?"

"Yep," she says, snickering.

"C'mon!" he says as if rooting for a football team. "I'm helping Deylou, that has to give me some kinda points!"

"Points?" She looks back at a sleeping Arch. She doesn't know if this is flirting, but if it is, she doesn't want him to hear it. Although, God can hear all of it.

"Yeah. How do I get 'em?" William asks.

"You don't!"

"Really?" he asks woefully.

"Really!"

"Okay. Let me just take you on a date then." He's trying his hardest at this thing.

"What! No, not happening."

"Why not?"

"I dunno! Because I don't know you."

"You can get to know me."

"I don't think so." They get to her home, and her dog runs inside.

"Can I at least have your number then?" She looks at him as if she's pondering it. "To call about the wizard," he adds.

"Fine! Only for the wizard!" she says and pulls out her phone.

"My number's already in there."

"Seriously? How?" she asks and looks through her phone.

"You better answer. If not, I have other ways of getting to you."

"Whatever!" she says and he laughs. He walks her down the path to her front door. "Just so you know, I had to get my lock replaced two times."

"Ouch. This is gonna hurt then. I control metal."

"What does that mean?"

"That your lock was perfectly fine."

She shoves him and says. "The poor locksmith said that!"

"Your jabs could use some work, though."

"Stop! I'm really sensitive about my fighting," she says, her head dropping to her chin.

"I can teach you."

"No thanks. I have great teachers. *Now good night,*" she says.

"Can I have a goodnight hug?" She crosses her arms.

"C'mon, after a good beating, a hug is always nice." He holds his stomach.

"Whatever! You didn't even flinch!"

"I was about to."

"Not true!" She pushes him again.

"See? You're so aggressive!" he says, straining his voice. If he could be here all night with her, *he would be.* It felt good, aside from being so vulnerable with her.

"Fine!" she says. He sweeps her into his arms and somehow feels complete.

28

Bell Pepper Warlock

The first thing Arch is gonna see when he opens his eyes is me. We both fell asleep fast last night, and it's the only reason he got away. He peeks at her.

"You have some explaining to do, mister!"

He says, "Can I have breakfast first?"

I'm still caught on cloud nine from yesterday *and not the Carter kind as* I float downstairs to breakfast. *Who needs feet?*

"He works for the devil!" I yell. *Okay,* never in a million years did I think this would be the explanation I'd get!

"Yep," Arch says calmly, "And you or God didn't think that was important enough to tell me?"

I want to crawl in my bowl of cereal and slowly drown in the milk. He says nothing, just licks water.

"So why didn't God stop it? Why didn't you stop it? Isn't he the enemy?"

"Some things aren't as they seem."

"Again with that phrase, but the devil can't be influencing William, right?" *Right?* seconds my heart.

"Lolly, that's all I'm allowed to say."

"It's okay. That's all you need to say." I stomp through the kitchen and up the stairs. The only animals coming up with me

197

are my bunny slippers. "All I'm saying is I was in full conversation with a demon, and you let me be!" *Why me?* I can't help but feel betrayed by my best friend. I know he knows best, but what could possibly be the best in this?

William *is* evil. But then again, my bells didn't ring for him. They're obviously working, as they rang for his uninvited guest. *Wait.* What if his guest *was* the devil? I get lost under my thick purple blanket. This doesn't make any sense! Why aren't God and Arch freaking out? Why aren't they telling me what to do?

With God permanently in my life, I clearly see our human ways are not His ways. Just because it's not happening the way I think it should doesn't mean He's not in control of my situation. Most of the time, He's trying to teach me something, even when it's hard. Maybe I was mean before to learn what it is to be kind. Maybe I had to lose to appreciate what is gained. And maybe I had to know good to understand what evil really is. I may not know much, but I know William isn't evil. I don't have all the answers, but I know they're gonna come. For now, I have to stop thinking about him.

I realize I haven't checked on Daddy. I've been wrapped up in my mission. Thankfully, he's outside picking bell peppers from our garden, and I help. "Your mother made the best stuffed peppers," he says. The sun is scorching. I listen as I wipe my forehead, making sure to dodge the glove. I can feel some dirt on me, and I pout. "Do you think you can make her stuffed peppers?" he asks me.

She didn't teach me how, but I know they'll cheer him up. "Sure."

I retrieve Mother's book, tracing my fingers over her writing. It seems so magical that she was once here holding it. One by one the pages sway, and worry pierces my heart as I almost reach the back with *no bell pepper recipe!* Then I see a drawing of a bell pepper with a heart. I hug it and relax. I scan the page and see "Tim's favorite" written at the bottom. She's still taking care of him even from heaven. My eyes try to tear up, but I sniffle it away. I open the small red book wide on the pepper page and put it on top of the microwave for Daddy to see I found it for dinner.

A knock at the door startles me. I go peek through the blinds. *It's William.* A weight drops to the bottom of my stomach. I can't decide if it's fear, butterflies, or both. I fix my crazy hair in the small mirror by the door before opening it. I see those eyes and try to pick myself off the ground . . . *because he's a demon.* I gulp, looking at the thing glowing in his hands. He looks at my filthy clothes, and I shriek, agitated that he feels so comfortable coming here.

"So, now you're showing up at my house!"

"You didn't answer," he simply says.

"Hi Lolly!" Deylou comes out of the woodwork, her smile just as big as last night.

"Hey, Deylou," I see her shiny skin and big clothes, must be William's. We creep upstairs to my room. I have Deylou sit on my bed and whip out my makeup kit.

"You said you can make your antennas disappear?"

"They are antlers!" Deylou corrects and sucks them into her head. I jump. Realizing I may be being rude, I smile.

"We need to go," William interrupts, examining things on my dresser as if he's at a science fair. I snatch my perfume as he goes to smell it.

"A little privacy," I say. He realizes what he'd been doing and nods. A demon is in my room. I back away, and he steps towards me.

"We're gonna miss the power surge."

I gulp at his closeness and hidden agenda and say, "It'll only take five minutes!" I give Deylou one of my long-sleeve crop tops and pair it with sweats to cover her arms and legs. I retrieve Arch from Josh's room, bashfully promise I'll tell my little brother about last night's fight, then head out in the direction the wishbone sends us.

We get to Barns.

"Again? Why do bad guys always end up here?" I ask without thinking. William's face turns red. "I mean—"

"Let's just get the lizard," he interrupts, all hot and bothered, and walks ahead. I feel my cheeks turn red now. I watch him. I adore his determination and admire his white dress shirt, red vest, and slacks. How could someone hold that much handsomeness? Arch's bark breaks my concentration. "In the alley!" he says.

We run in and spot a cloaked figure on the ground. The tracker begins to radiate, telling us he's the one. William blows on it, and it stops. He then motions for us to stay put. Thankfully, no humans are around. "Hey!" he calls, and the being rises.

"You can see me?" he asks.

From here, his skin looks translucent. "Yeah, that's why I'm talking to you." William turns on his flame.

"I mean no harm. I didn't mean to escape," he says.

I examine William closer. This must be his demon form, and a stroke of nervousness comes.

William takes off the giant's hoodie with a whip of his hand. He resembles the crystalline pitchers we sell at the shop. His soft hair is twisted into dreadlocks. He straightens out, and he's huge—way taller than William. His eyes dart to me. William turns around, and I look away.

"I got more food . . ." A blonde girl walks around the corner and freezes, saying, "My prince!" He's a prince? From where?

She comes undone, and her green lasers are aiming at us. Deylou and I back up.

"Bot, put down your weapon," says the prince calmly.

"I'm not going back! They can't make me go back!"

She's frantic.

"I see you're gonna make this hard. No matter," says William with a whole new temperament. They have a story. We can't just crucify them.

"I won't hurt you and neither will he." William smirks, and I try not to let his sour attitude affect me.

"Why don't you wanna go back?" I ask.

"I'm from here."

"And why should we care?" asks William, I look at him in disbelief. I'm trying to deescalate the situation, and he's making it worse.

The robot takes her pointers off of us, aiming them only at William. I caught my breath. *Is she going to shoot?* He chuckles as if he's enjoying this, and it puzzles me.

"Your energy's too low to use those. You won't last long if you do, and if you don't put them down now, I'll disarm you." William's smug smile is so deep it's creepy. Bot cocks them anyway, but just as fast as she did, they deactivate.

She falls to the ground, turning back into a human. She was all metal before.

"How can you breach my system? Only Robert Lemon can do that!" She's glaring at William.

"Not that I need to tell, but the name's Ore. Which one of you is the wizard?" Did he just call himself, *Ore?*

"Neither," says Deylou.

"Waste of my time," he says. William turns back to normal and says, "As protectors of this planet, we intend to investigate your claim. For now, you're coming with us," he says cordially. "Gemwyn, nice to meet you. Ore," William shakes the giant's hand even though he was just being mean.

"You drive, right?" William asks me. I nod. "I texted you an address. Take my car and meet me there." I didn't see him text anything and more importantly, his demanding is throwing me off. I grab the keys anyway.

"That's my baby. Don't wreak her, okay?" he says in a softer tone and smiles. I think my whole world just went black with butterflies covering my sight, and nodding is the only thing I can do. I leave him with the fugitives and take Arch and Deylou to this infamous address. I noticed that Arch didn't intervene like last night.

We get to an old-looking convenience store. Did he really just lure me away? *Oh no.* What's he gonna do with them? "Lolly?" says an older man behind the counter.

"Yes?" I'm confused.

"Go on the side of the building, into the shed." I open the thin, dark brown shed attached to the store. There's no way they're all in here. All we see are mops and brooms.

"Huh?" I say.

"Let's go in," says Arch. We do, and the door closes behind us. I try to push it open. but it's bolted.

We feel a rapid downward motion that takes our breath away. It dings when it stops, and the fact that we were just in an elevator throws me. We have to look like plastered bugs because when the door opens, William is smiling from cheek to cheek.

"You could've told us that was an elevator!" I say.

"That would've ruined it." There are words I want to use other than his name, but I leave them in my thoughts. I roll my eyes at him instead, but it only amuses him.

I then see cages and barred rooms everywhere. "What is this, prison?" I ask.

"It used to be an underground animal testing site." Arch whimpers. I look over at a cell our new friends are just sitting in and run to it. There's a forcefield around it.

"Is that necessary?" I say and walk up to William.

He says, "Have you ever dealt with people like them?" I cross my arms and shake my head. "Okay . . . so I get that you *just* want to trust them, but that's not how it works, Lolly." Did I say butterflies were flapping around? I meant bees, a swarm of bees that want to attack him and his rude behavior.

"I gotta connect. I'll make sure their stories check out." He's moving stuff off the receptionist desk.

"When, William?" I say.

"Do you have to say my name like that?" he says mildly, but it's still blunt.

"Like what?"

"Look, my family calls me Liam. Just call me that, 'cause the way you say my government . . ." He mumbled the last part, and I could have sworn he rolled his eyes. If he thinks I'm ever going on that date with him, he can forget it.

My thoughts haunt me because not so long ago, I had the same attitude with my mother. I decide to give him a break like Mama gave me. He walks to their cell, and I follow.

"Do either of you know where the wizard is?" The robot looks way from him at the wall.

"We got separated," says Gemwyn.

"We need to get you back to your planets." After catching my reaction, he whispers, "I got this."

"I told you I can't go back to Coron!" says the human robot.

"Care to elaborate?" asks William. He's so bittersweet like the bell peppers I'm about to cook for dinner.

29

A Squeezed Lemon

"I died in a car accident and my husband couldn't let me go." We gather around and dig into Bot's story. "He was a scientist, working on experiments for the government. He thought they didn't know about the robot he'd been working on, on the side." She stops a moment to compose herself, and I can relate.

"I was in a coma for months," she continued. "They said I would never regain consciousness. He had hope at first, but after two years grew restless. I was twenty-four then. He thought it a waste of life, and he missed me." She clears her throat.

"There's a chemical named *Merth* he was testing. It's only available on planet Coron, and top rank classified. It came to earth within a rock that fell into our atmosphere. He found it triggered the radio in his office and any other device that came into contact with it. Since I was already gone, he took a chance and placed my organs inside of the robot infused with Merth.

"My husband was a praying man, a genius, and his want was big enough." She bites her nails. "I woke up with wires everywhere, thinking I was in a dismantled car because that was my last memory." She sheds a tear, and we're in awe. "Robert Lemon was his name. I'm Rebecca Lemon, and Robotka is the name my husband gave me."

"How'd you end up on Coron?" asks Liam.

"Merth can only exist on planet Coron. Robert said the only

thing holding it here was the rock it came in. When he worked on me, he had to use restraints so it wouldn't take me like a magnet back to its source. My husband designed a directory within my systems, setting its coordinates to earth but . . ." she wipes her eyes, "the government found out he used the Merth on me and came to take their property. During the struggle, my coordinates went to manual, and the Merth sucked me back to Coron, a planet with rock dwellers that eat metal."

What? She's made of metal.

"When I arrived on the planet, my system set new coordinates, making me a prisoner. I tried to reset, but it wouldn't budge. I was on the run every day, feeding on plants that were scarce there. The hardest part was having to turn off my system to recharge by solar panels. I hid myself, hoping they wouldn't find me while I was down. They have four suns surrounding their planet in a sort of arrangement, *four suns,* and they don't even equal up to the warmth of our *one sun.* Their planet is gloomy, cold, and black."

"This is true," says Gemwyn.

"So, instead of charging for an hour to operate for two days, I had to charge two hours to operate for one day, for six months." She wipes the liquid from her nose. It's surreal how she has everything a human has.

"How'd you get back?" I try not to giggle at Liam's curiosity. He believes her, and he better not say otherwise!

"I found a river of Merth, but I was too far for my system to trigger it. As I got closer, I saw the Obsidian guards everywhere. They were even bathing in it." She looks disturbed.

"But before I could make a run for it, they got me. I screamed but couldn't draw my weapons. My power was drained. That's when they brought me to Prince Gem and his two brothers. His oldest brother, *the king,* threw me in prison. His youngest went with it, but Gem was the only one that came to my rescue." She smiles at him. "He took me toward the river, but his brother's guards detained us. This time, I quickly realized they were going towards Merth. I looked at my system thinking, *Jesus, if you don't get me out, I'm done.* Then a new setting popped up. I used all my strength to pull one arm out of their clutches and set my coordinates for earth. I wiggled a bit more, and off into space I flew to the nearest frequency, Scoffs Arena."

Everyone breathes. We'd been on edge.

"How'd you get here?" Liam asks the prince.

"As punishment from the king."

"Figures," says Liam.

"William! You rang?" A female voice comes from the elevator. Liam goes to it. I look, and he hugs a girl tightly. I wonder what they're talking about. My life was so much easier when I didn't have feelings for . . . *feelings?* No way! I decide to calm down but can't deny the ease I feel when he calls me over.

"This is Tammy. She's gonna help get us to Deylou's planet."

"Howdy." She glares at me as if I'm going to steal her prized possession. I look at her curly blonde hair and cowboy boots, deciding she's definitely *friend zoned.*

"Hey," comes out sweeter than I intended after finding a friendly vibe between them.

We run down everything to her. "This is tricky, Billy," Tammy says, "but I think I can get you in. There's just a teeny tiny problem,"

I mouth the word *Billy* while she's distracted. *Why did she call him that?*

"You'll have to go through the Spiritual Realm to go that far."

"No one can go into the Spiritual Realm," says Liam.

"I know. I wish there was another way," she says.

"What about the teleportation pods at Scoffs?" asks Liam.

"Those are specially reserved for the fighters and antler people to be able to get back home. No offense, hon," she says, looking at Deylou, who nods.

"Lolly," Arch whispers, and we walk away from the group. "The Spiritual Realm is God's territory. It's the purest of places, where prayers are heard and battles are fought on behalf of God's people. It's unseen by human eyes. What goes on there directly affects what happens in the physical world. Who knows what would happen if it were breached."

"Why'd she even suggest it?"

"It seems she just wanted to help." He looks away. "The Similory people are God's people too. I have to consult with Him in prayer. Please excuse me." He scurries away.

Gosh, I want to help Deylou, but not at the expense of our God. "We'll find another way," Liam says, putting his hand on my arm. His touch electrifies me, and I back away.

"I know. Are you gonna let Bot and Gem go?" I ask.

"Tams?" He calls her name, and I cringe. Her boots thud over.

"Whoa, you have prisoners?"

"She murdered my husband!" Robotka yells.

"Rebecca Lemon?" Tammy's surprised.

"Murderer!" Robotka yells.

"I work for the government, hon. I follow orders, but I'm no murderer. You and your husband, on the other hand, are thie—" William covers her mouth and carries her away.

Before Liam can say anything, she asks, "How'd you get Rebecca Lemon? She's been MIA for months!"

"Why were you after her?" William asks.

"It's classified."

William points at himself. She rolls her eyes and deflates. They laugh, never acknowledging I'm there.

"Robert Lemon, her husband, used a trial chemical we hired him to test to create miss thang over there. Every bit of it! Sarge was heated, and we tore the whole lab apart looking for it!"

"Did you . . ." he asks, and her eyes widen.

"Of course not! Brown accidentally pulled the trigger. We were supposed to bring him in for questioning and bring his bride to confiscate the green stuff. We'd been watching him on his private cameras."

She looks in the direction of their cell. "We would've helped further his research. I mean look at her! There's no one like her around. He's a genius!"

"That's what she said," says Liam.

"Well, he is. But he's just as mad as a hungry coyote!" She waves the absent man away.

"He was in love," Liam says, and Tammy and me are blown away at his use of the word. She would know him better than me, *so I am reading him correctly then.*

"You need to tell her what happened," says Liam.

"What?" we say in unison. He looks at us, and we look at us.

"Look, we can't have friction in the camp."

"Fine, but I ain't gon' like it." She stomps over to the bars, and I take a second to pray. Liam said this could cause friction. I ask God to allow Rebecca to have an open heart and open ears to listen to Tammy. I ask Him to allow Tammy to have kind words and an understanding spirit. She tells Robotka everything, and Robotka cries. Tammy even apologizes, and that wasn't in the script at all.

Afterwards, we're back in our corner. "Did you get information on Du'Jomi?" Liam asks Tammy.

"Oh yes!" She takes out her phone. I'm surprised at all the stuff the government actually knows. "He's a traveling wizard and has connections to a *Gavenla* on earth. She lives here in the mountains."

30

Defuse Me

"I have to go. My *boss* is calling me." William twitches at his choice of words.

"Okay, I'll be here," says Lolly and William nods. He hates walking away from her. All day he'd been uptight, resisting the revolting impulse to hurt her. Not more than usual, the fuel just burned differently. Instead of being conflicted about hurting others, he was fighting himself to defend her. He could never hurt her, not when she has his heart in her pocket.

He looks at his wrist. If they even found a way to leave, would he risk it and go? If he risked it, would his chains hold him back? These questions were playing on his mind all day like a broken record, adding to the tension.

Tammy follows him out. "Boss is calling, huh?"

"He's not your boss. You're free to leave."

"None of us are free to leave. You just have chains, that's all." She touches his bracelet, and he shakes his head.

Hell

"What is it now?" William says harshly to his opposer.

"Oh, nothing, I was just checking on your progress with Lolly Pobs, the bridge, the other assassinations . . ."

"It's good."

"Details?"

William rolls his eyes. "I got the stone needed for the bridge, as you saw. It got delivered last night and is ready for construction."

"And Pobs?"

William hates that he even has her name in his mouth. "I got a lead on her."

"A lead? You got Scoff like meat ripped from a chicken bone. Are you losing your mojo?"

"No! You said yourself she's my equal. So it's taking a little longer, but I got it."

"Hmm, if I didn't know any better, I'd think you were trying to get me off of your trail."

William starts to panic. He has to think of something. "Do it yourself, then!" He hopes the reverse psychology works.

"No, no. I'm busy preparing to break into the Spiritual Realm. Up until now, I've only been able to trick them. But when I reach the Tree of the Knowledge of Good and Evil, I'll cut its branches and feed each person's soul a leaf. It will open their eyes to see their royalty now when they're supposed to receive it in heaven through Him. They'll be a haughty people, and the world will be filled with castles in the place of houses. They will choose me instead of Him, forever breaking His heart."

The rueful look on William's face causes him to look away. He burns with anger at the devil's disgusting words. And the thought about going against God Almighty nauseates him.

"There's a cherubim guarding the trees," the devil says. "I want you to take him down. All your assassinations were just training. I've been preparing you for such a time as this." William's eyes widen, and the horrifying news shakes him to his core. He thought the devil just needed slaves to carry out his handywork, but no, Satan was scheming all along.

"No one knows where the trees are!" William says.

"Oh, you forgot? I do. I deceived the woman there." William's body radiates with rancor. "On earth it's invisible to the naked eye, but in the Spiritual Realm it's as ripe as a fresh peach."

"How will you get past Him?" asks William.

"Who, the Son of Man?" Laughter fills hells walls. "I did it before, and I'll do it again," he says arrogantly. "But I need you to eliminate Pobs first, so stop with the questions and get her!" Satan demands, turning into a large red horned tower and eying William. The amplified sound of William's heartbeat can he heard in his own ear.

A woman's agonizing screech breaks through the tension, and William looks in its direction. Satan follows. "Quiet witch!" he roars. "A newcomer, she's going to help me bring extras into the realm. Now GET . . . OUT!" he blusters, pushing William out of hell.

"What'd I miss?" he says as he walks into the room. Lolly's and Deylou's faces brighten.

"Not much," says Lolly. He longs to be close to her but keeps his distance, knowing Ore's activated to harm her. As she talks, he looks over her olive skin, radiating so wonderfully. Her lips are beautifully made, and *he got to experience them*. It bewildered him that it wasn't Ore that stole the smooch. He was guilty of the menacing behavior this time. He wants to have it once more. Could one more time be enough?

His eyes plead with hers to notice their outcry, and he yearns to make her heart his. If she said no, his would break, never allowing another in again. But if she said yes, his feet would walk bountifully to meet her side, his hands would work relentlessly to hold her up, and he'll protest outside of heaven's walls until the Creator heard his plea of release to be with her.

Lolly's voice pushes him out of his thoughts. "Can you let Bot and Gem out now?" He walks to their cell, and the robot is weak. "Bot!" Lolly calls. "Please, I need the sun."

Liam opens the bared door. "We're at sunset. Open your panels," he demands. "You stand outside the cell, and if you try anything, you'll never make it to be a crowned king," he says to the prince. The girls gasp, and Gemwyn ducks to go out.

William turns into Ore and ignites his power.

"I can't charge on fire. The sun is the only source that radiates the right temperature to fuel me," says Bot.

"Good to know. Now take them out. I won't ask again," Ore says sharply.

She breathes one last breath before opening her system. Her tiny platelets are visible, but so is her brain and heart. Ore takes off his shirt to give off a bigger amount of light. He shuts the prison door with his mind, and his eyes dart around her being. *Marvelous* he decides. He scans every weapon she owns and reads her coordinate history. She was indeed created on earth and spent six months in a different location.

Gemwyn sits on the ground eating a paperclip, and Ore appears outside of the bars, pushing Lolly and Deylou behind him. Lolly peeks around it and sees a raised lava ring sitting in his palm ready to fire. She looks between Liam and the Ore in the cell. *There are two of him,* she gasps.

When he sees there's no danger, he disappears, and now there's only one in the cell.

Shortly after, he wakes Bot. She looks at the screen on her arm. "It's only been ten minutes, and I'm fully charged!"

"I'm closer than the sun."

"You hold the sun's power?"

"Just say thank you and move on," he says sharply.

"You have to hold its—"

"I said, let it go!" He snarls, his eyes and nails turn dark, and the circle of those surrounding him grows bigger. He breathes heavily but calms himself and clears his throat. "I brought food. We're gonna need our strength for the mountains," he says and walks away.

31
Evil Begets Evil

Ci's blood mixes with water as Grand holds his hands under the faucet. He'd tried for most of the day to bring her back to life with his powers, but she never woke up. He realized he wasn't in control after all. God was. "You take everything from me!" He looks to the sky.

"But I won't be a slave to the life you gave me anymore!" the devil whispers the words in his ear. "I'll take the world before I let you take anything else."

"Hello, Grand," the whisperer finally announces himself.

"Who's there?"

"They say the enemy of an enemy is a friend, and I my friend, am in need of Daisy's services. I can give you what you desire, but you'll need more recruits. I have one in mind." Grand agrees to the devil's bidding.

They rob a string of banks in Pennsylvania and by the end of the week have keys to the warehouse. He weeps while setting Ci's body ablaze behind the building. His liquids were within her, so he couldn't just leave her anywhere. He slung her ashes into the sea alone and watched the waves rave as she did.

Grand orders a private room in the fanciest restaurant in town and requests blue lighting. They order lobster and champagne and keep the plates coming. Daisy appreciates it.

"She was a good friend, Grand," says Daisy.

"And all I did in return is get her killed," Grand says bitterly. He swallows the drink down and continues, "I don't wanna talk about Ci. We're rich," he snaps, throwing a bundle of money on the table. Waitresses stare at the wad. "That's what my friend was worth," Grand says. Daisy looks at the servers who may be listening, but they depart.

She tries to comfort him with a hug, but he pulls back. "It's God's fault anyway. He won't let me be happy. He won't let me just be free for once in my life."

"I'm not religious, but maybe the universe has a plan. Let it take its course," says Daisy.

"The universe? It's easier for people to say it's the universe because it won't talk back to tell them their faults. There's only one God, one Being orchestrating this whole thing. It's not the sun, not stars, not the moon, not a crystal, just the Trinity."

"Where'd you learn this?" asks Daisy.

"Bible camp."

"Do you want me to believe in Jesus?" asks Daisy.

The sire-ship is starting to rock his nerves. She needed to believe on her own, not because he demanded her to. That's free will. *Maybe I should give God a few pointers.* "You can believe what you want, but it's the truth."

"You're mad at your God, yet you speak His truths?"

"Because they're facts, not fairytale." He throws on his mask and walks outside, leaving the money on the table. Daisy quickly counts it and leaves more than enough for the tab and tips.

"Grand!" She follows him down the street. "Grand you're going the wrong way!" She panics, watching him stumbling. "Grand, please! I don't want you to get hurt!"

"Yeah, only because you're sired to me!" shouts Grand.

"Sired?" She's confused.

"My juices got you doing whatever I say like Simon Says." He pokes her nose.

"That's not true," says Daisy.

"Stand in the road until a car comes and let it hit you," Grand demands.

"No, do I have—"

"Yes, yes, you have to! Just like Ci had to die, so do you." Tears fall as she backs up into the road.

"Who'll take care of you? If I die I can't take care of you, Grand," Daisy says, sobbing.

Take care of him? Is that what she'd been doing? Furthermore, she wasn't pleading for her own life to be spared in this dire moment, she's concerned about his. He sobers up quickly as headlights appear.

"Come to me!" he yells, and she runs into his arms.

"Grand, I don't care what it is. I just want to be with you."

"Daisy." He grabs her by the shoulders. "Don't do anything you don't want to do. Do what comes from your heart. That's an order." She nods.

"You cheat! Get outta here!" A commotion gets their attention. Men playing cards push another man away. He stumbles over his feet going downstairs.

"I'll show you! I'll win one day playing straight! They'll be no cheater in me no more!" The man falls from above behind them and doesn't move.

"Should we call 911?" asks Daisy. Grand thinks about the new recruits Satan said he needed. Another addition wouldn't hurt.

"I need more people."

"I don't think that's a good idea. He was a cheat."

"And what are we?" She doesn't answer. He grabs a glass bottle nearby and cuts himself.

An hour and a dozen explanations to passersby later . . .

"Who is you's and what happened to me?"

Daisy says, "He sounds like a criminal, great." They explain his fall.

"Do you feel strange?" asks Grand.

"I just fell off a flight of stairs. What do you think? This hurts worse than when I got beat up in prison."

"Ha," Daisy says, and Grand clears his eyes.

"I gotta get back to my pad."

"Where do you live?" asks Grand.

"Up the road with my ma," the man says, and Daisy rolls her eyes.

They pick up Chinese, and at home watch him devour his food in record time.

"Super speed," says Daisy.

"I'm so hungry all of a sudden," says the man. Daisy looks at the bald spot on the top of his head. He looks like he could be in his mid-forties. A blue squiggle is also on his forehead where Grand put in his blood, like the one on her wrist. He disappears then zips back. "Sorry, had to use the potty. I looked in every room, and it was just right there." He points.

Daisy rubs her temples and says, "Yeah, he's gonna be a problem."

"What's your name?" Grand asks.

"George, but my friends call me *Wildcard*, 'cause I'ma whiz on the deck." He clicks his teeth.

Daisy is not convinced. "Cheater . . ."

"Aye, don't judge my sin. You sin just like me. I'm unpredictable. You never know what my quick hand's gonna do. That's why they call me that. But I went to jail for snatchin'. I'm a thief." He shrugs. "That's my sin. What's yours?"

"Same," says Daisy. Deciding she's had enough of George, she gets up from the couch.

"See," he says, pointing at her. "Everyone sins. She can't judge me, but I can do better."

Grand smiles at his honesty.

"Boy, I'm pooped," George says. He takes off his tux, then his shoes, and lies on their couch in under a second. Before Grand can look up, he's snoring. Grand shakes his head and walks into his room.

"He fell asleep before I could talk to him," says Daisy.

"Get him in the morning." He doesn't look at her.

"Will you ever forgive me?"

"Yeah, when I stop seeing my best friend every time I look at you." He shuts the door in her face.

The next morning, they rush into the empty living room and panic until they hear rummaging in the kitchen. He's taking out all things that make a sandwich.

"Of course he's not going anywhere. He has it good here," Daisy says, leaning on the wall next to the kitchen.

"Oh, good morning you two. I helped myself. Figured you wouldn't mind. Sandwich anyone?"

Daisy says, "You didn't steal anything, did you?"

"For your information, miss, you have nothing I want."

"If we did, would you have?" Not waiting for an answer, she crosses her arms and goes to sit on the couch.

Grand chuckles at the man and says, "Your ma won't miss you?"

"Uh, I think she'll be happy to have an empty nest for a little." He slaps mayonnaise on the bread. "Do you have jalapeños?"

"No."

"Thought so. When you have cancer, you learn to enjoy the little things, ya know?"

"You have cancer?"

"Gotta doc appointment today." He chomps on his newly

made sandwich, grabs a grape soda, and fast forwards to the table. "I don't suppose you can give me a ride, huh, toots?" He breathes down his drink. Grand nods and Daisy rolls her eyes.

"Sure."

Grand sits by her, and she says, "He's a liability."

"You two whispering about me?" asks George. "Whatever you gotta say, I can take it. Did I overstay my welcome?" He zips to the kitchen and puts his plate in the sink.

"Your ability, you didn't have it before, right?" Grand asks.

"What ability?" George stands before them, taking food out of his teeth with his tongue.

"The speed?" Grand motions.

"Speed?" He tilts his head.

"Did you really not see how fast you gobbled down that drink like it was just a drop!" Daisy snaps.

He looks at the kitchen. "Now that you mention it . . ." Daisy lets out an exasperated huff.

"Last night you could've died, but I gave you some of my blood."

"Wha? Like a blood transfusion? In the street . . ." Daisy grunts, and Grand holds her back.

"You could say that, but you got your speed from me."

"Are you some kinda god or something?"

"There's only one God," Grand says plainly.

"True, do you two have abilities?" George asks.

"Don't tell anyone about your power, and don't use it unless Grand gives you permission," Daisy demands.

"No powers, got it. So can I use it to go to my appointment? That way you won't have to, toots?"

"Yeah, then go home, get some things, and come back," says Grand.

Daisy and Grand walk in and out of rooms at his new warehouse. "These were offices. I want to make them into rooms for all my new recruits, so they can live here with us."

"How many do you plan to make?"

"As many as I want. I was thinking of calling myself Grandfather."

"But you're young."

"Eighteen, but I got all you kids under my belt now. You don't have to live here if you don't want to, though."

"I don't want to leave you." He stares at her. She rolls her eyes, smiles, and says, "I'll think about it."

They go downstairs to the semis and hear Lucy and Latch viciously growling. Liquid is bubbling around their mouths.

"No!" Grand yells. They growl and run toward them. Grand somehow forms an acid barrier. They start to cry, he puts it down slightly, and they bow in surrender. Grand lets it down and glares at the pups' large size and metal fur. He approaches them carefully and pats them. They shrink, then jump and play as usual. He grins at his newfound weapon.

"It's time to get Mckenzie Alexander," says Satan.

"The boy in the facility?" asks Grand.

"Yes. It's army guarded. They might have a supernatural or two." Satan's voice is eerie. "He's gonna get us into another realm, and we'll have access to God's people."

"Christians?"

"Precisely."

"Then what?" Grand asks.

"Whatever you want," Satan says. *You want to kill them, like he took the people you loved from you,* Satan whispers to the unsuspecting, unguarded child.

"Yeah, exactly," says Grand, as if he's seen the light. "They can also be slaves along with the nonbelievers."

"No, I want them gone because they serve Him. You can have the rest."

"Sounds like a plan."

"Now get me Alexander," says the manipulator.

That night, Satan provides the floor plans for the government building.

"We stepped it up a notch, huh? Now we're stealing people," says Daisy, smirking.

"Guess so. He said the room's right here."

"Who said? You haven't told me who we're dealing with. How do we know we can trust him?"

"It's the devil."

Her eyes widen. "Grand, you can't be serious!" He continues to look at the plans. "Grand, if you're telling me the truth, there has to be a downside to this. That kid must be dangerous or worth gold. I don't think you're *really* talking to the devil, but this is..." Her head sways from side to side.

"Don't agree? Leave!" His voice echoes.

"But I don't want to."

"Leave now!" he orders, and she walks out of the room. *So much for free will.*

Grand pulls up to a pawn shop and steps out of his newly purchased all-black Lincoln Navigator SUV that he paid cash for. He rings the buzzer to be let in, and a voice breaks out from a tiny black speaker.

"What's with the mask?"

"Skin condition." He lifts his shirt and turns to show his waistband. After a while, the buzzer sounds, and Grand goes in.

"Don't try anything funny." The long-haired man holds up a Remington 870.

"It's not like that, man." *If Daisy were here, this would've been easier, but he had to dump the broad.* Now he has to take things into his own hands.

He removes his mask. "I need machinery."

$$32$$

The Heist

The man backs up, his whole body quakes while letting out a single round. It hits Grand's shoulder, and blood gushes out. The bullet is instantly ejected, and the hole closes up. A thin layered forcefield pushes him back and sweeps over the entire area. He gets a nagging in his side to put his mask back on, so he pulls it over with one stroke. Grand looks up at the pawn man. He stands back in his original spot.

"Don't try anything funny," he says a second time, or a first. "I need Ghost guns."

After, he's shaken up. He touches the area where he'd been shot. Even his shirt was knitted back together. "What are you doing?" he asks God. Was He not allowing his form to be seen? Does the Lamb of God know what he's up to? The evil he was plotting . . . For a hot second, shame flushes him, but he pushes it back.

He picks up Wildcard. He got him set up in the warehouse and stuffed the fridge with sandwich stuff.

"Grandfather, I was just fixing myself a sandwich. Want one?"

"We gotta go," Grand takes off his mask.

"So that's what your hiding?" Wildcard laughs. "I'm not gonna lie, boss. I wasn't expecting that. but it's you. You're gorgeous with your green skin."

Grand smiles. "Check this out." He pulls out a device from his side. "Grandfather," the tiny black device calls out in a soft female voice.

"It announces you! Where'd you get that?"

"A whiz kid online."

"Genius boss."

"Pretty soon, the world's gonna know who I am."

They finish and go out to the SUV while eating sandwiches. Daisy climbs in. "I'm coming."

Wildcard moves over in the back as the SUV stops in an alley to let Adam in.

"Today was laundry day," says Adam.

"We got better things to do," says Grand.

"Yeah, whatever you say, Grand."

"It's Grandfather now."

"Grandfather," repeats Adam.

"Superhero names, let's hear 'em," says Grand. Daisy scoffs at the idea.

"What about you, Daze? You think a'one?" asks Wildcard.

"I guess you did," says Daze. "You ever sweet talk me, toots?" When she doesn't answer, he moves on, deciding she had. "What can you do?" he asks Adam. He turns an empty container of soda into ice then crushes it. The blades drop like shattered glass. "Ow, Adam Freeze," says Wildcard with sparkling eyes. They speed to Boston, Massachusetts.

The military hospital is located within city limits and is guarded. They park behind nearby buildings. Grand steps out without a mask.

"What are you doing?" asks Daze,

"Being myself. No more questions."

She nods, then makes her way to the center first as they planned. They're dressed in black clothing, stuffed hoisters hang all over, and they creep a ways behind Daze. A. Freeze pulls a beanie over his blonde buzz cut, hoping his brothers inside won't recognize him.

"Hi, boys," says Daisy.

"You lost, little lady?" asks one of the soldiers.

"No, but I would like to be let into this wonderful building."

"You have to have clearance to get inside these walls." He narrows his eyes. "But *you* . . . you're not ordinary. You thought you were just gonna say the word and get in, didn't you?"

She backs up. "Code rufous, we gotta *code rufous*," he says into a headset. "This hospital blocks mental manipulation frequencies. It's obvious you didn't plan properly." A dart hits her shoulder, she falls to the ground, and soldiers come get her.

"Daisy!" Grandfather runs with his super pups, and Wildcard is already in the building.

"Grandfather," the device calls, getting the attention of the soldiers. Rings of bullets shoot out at him and Adam Freeze. Lucy and Latch run ahead, shielding them with their metal bodies. Their sharp teeth sink into the soldiers, who holler as the blue acid pours out from their saliva. Grand goes inside. Adam Freeze follows behind guarding but not letting out a single round. Daisy's wound heals, and she wakes. Wildcard zooms around her captors, knocking them all out. "I got you, Daze." He lifts her, and they go find Grand.

An alarm goes off. "We have a code indigo, code indigo," says a soldier. His comrades suit up to look for the supernatural break-in. The puppies run at Grand's and Adam's side, and soldiers roll out a huge revolving weapon. A general leads the troops, they stop short of Grand, and the frontline men go in with their guns.

"I'm General Reynolds. What are you?" he asks, eyeing Grand's blue skin. His eyes dart to Adam in an attempt to remember who he is.

"A monster," Grand answers.

"Tell me, monster, what do you want here?"

"We want the boy."

"What boy? We hold tons of patients."

"Mckenzie."

"Oh, Mckenzie . . ." Reynolds nods.

"Yeah, we're delivering him to the devil." The general's eyes fling up at Grand.

"Grandfather," calls the female voice box.

"You dare go against the army of the Lord, Grandfather?"

Grand gets angry at the mention. "Yes!" His body stretches and he hangs over. He wore bigger clothes so they'd grow with him, and he makes the acid soak into the material. Shreds at the bottom of his long sleeves hang over his hands, and minimal holes tear in random places. He looks at himself, realizing he's able to control his ability more now. Acid fountains around him, and his dogs walk up.

Reynolds had been watching to see what the supernatural could do. He places his hands behind his back and says, "Ready!" They fire up their weapon, the frontline soldiers shoot the creature, and Grand's wings of acid engulfs the bullets. A. Freeze is behind a thick rock shield of ice. Daze and Wildcard are wide eyed as they examine Grand's new form. Daisy holds her head as Grandfather's pointy claws and animalistic features make her droopy.

"Fire!" calls Reynolds, and they discharge the small newt gun. An orange blast fires away. They take cover but watch as the water around the blue man dissolves their missile. It twists and combusts like a firecracker, then goes out like a light. General Reynolds face stiffens. "Release the Garitooc!" he yells into his walkie. Grand's gaze turns into an eldritch glare, and he moves forward, passing them through his rivers. Wildcard wakes up and shoots at the soldiers Grand can't see.

Daisy and Adam approach Grand. "Are you okay?" Daisy asks the ghoul, her eyes scanning him in terror. Daisy peels her eyes away, watching Wildcard shoot aimlessly. "Grand, stop him!" she says.

"He's free to be himself too," Grand says. Daisy glares at him, thinking he's lost his marbles. He scoops Reynolds up.

"Where's Mckenzie!" Grand says.

"I recognize the floor plans!" Daisy yells.

A. Freeze takes Reynolds per Grand's instruction. "What happened, soldier?" Reynolds asks, while normal-sized Grand and Daisy are up further.

Adam sighs. "I have to do what he says."

"You under control?" asks Reynolds.

"Not exactly . . . "

"If I live, report to me when this is over," says Reynolds.

"Yes, sir."

"Aye, no whispering!" says Wildcard, his sprayer pointed.

"Dr. Lemon, intruders have come into the building. We must evacuate," says a tall woman with a black braided ponytail.

"Will you be putting cuffs on me then, Dakota?"

"Yes, of course, doctor."

"Very well. Let me get my son."

"I have orders to escort you out immediately. The team is getting Mckenzie as we speak."

They wake the boy, and Grand breaks through the bulletproof glass. Dr. Lemon and the guards turn around.

"Mckenzie!" Lemon shouts.

"Take him to the island," says Dakota. They whisk him away.

"No!"

"Who are you?" Grand thinks Mckenzie's British is funny.

"I'm Grand."

"You're blue, Grand."

"It's a part of my power. Can I borrow yours?"

"Father says I shouldn't use it. I don't, but he still won't take me to see the grass in the meadows outside."

"If I take you, will you help me?" The boy nods. Hand in hand, Grand and the boy in the white robe walk out.

When Grand's team hits the entrance, two large iron bolder beasts stand in wait.

"Garitooc! Garitooc!" they cry as they walk around on hand and foot like gorillas.

"Take cover!" Grand points to the wall. Daisy takes Mckenzie, and Wildcard and A. Freeze stand by him. Lucy and Latch paw up, and he extends his liquid border.

"Let's get 'em boss!" says Wildcard.

"Go with Daisy. I can recover, but I don't know if you two can." Ci runs through his mind.

"But, boss?"

"Now!" he rumbles. Wildcard hesitantly walks away taking Reynolds with him. A. Freeze was already almost to Daisy and Mckenzie.

The Garitooc skip toward Grand, playfully swinging their arms. The room quakes, and Grand wonders if the glass windows will break. He sends chemicals towards them, but they bust straight through it. Their skin is a dark marble that doesn't have the slightest crack. The twin dogs run for the monsters but are immediately knocked away.

Grand sweats, not knowing if they'll make it out free, or alive. The first Garitooc grabs Grand's body and slams him against the floor like it's playing with a toy soldier. They take turns pounding on him with clenched fists. Grand tries to get up but can't, and his memories take him back to his beating.

Wildcard walks up and shoots every round he has. The bullets bounce off of their skin, sending them flying in every direction. Adam Freeze shields the crew. The Graitooc slowly creep to Wildcard. "Come on!" says Wildcard as he runs but gets trapped between the beast's arms like a pinball machine. It lifts its large arm and backhands him, sending him off to dreamland.

Reynolds slowly backs away, disappearing into darkness. The Garitooc doesn't see the trio behind A. Freeze's ice and runs back to his Grand toy.

"Garitooc! Garitooc!" They jump in excitement, grabbing each side of Grand's body, pulling and twisting, playing Ring Around the Rosie. His stretchy insides break in half, and water rolls onto the floor. "Garitooc! Garitooc!" They splash in the puddle. Grand touches his goopy insides and goes into shock. It's hard to breathe. Chunky acid filled with blood falls out of his mouth. He closes his eyes, remembering a girl . . . *Rachel,* her smile flashing.

A light beams from the heavens. Grand looks around, and everyone's eyes are only on him. His head falls to the side, making bubbles in his own fluids. He feels the top half of his torso slide down, stitching together with his lower half. The light draws back, and his chest rises with lungs full of air. His hands search him, and he's whole. He jumps to his feet and tackles a Garitooc that had been playing in his waste. It squirms in agony and starts to smoke beneath an ample amount of acid. The other knocks Grand to the ground.

"Enough!" says Mckenzie. Everyone comes to a halt, and he lifts the Garitooc into the air with his hand. "Have you not seen God's work?" So the eyes of a child did see. "Go back to your chambers!" he commands, and the Garitooc run down the spiraling passageways. "Grand, I'm ready." Grand grabs his hand.

"Kid, if you could've done that the whole time. Why didn't ya?" says a limping Wildcard.

"I'm not on anyone's side. I just favored Grand this time."
They're surprised by his wisdom.

"Well, good for us," says Wildcard, and Grand drives off into
the night.

33

See Through

We go deep into the trees and see a lovely lake. Even at night it's beautiful and calm. Further up, we see an orange beam of light stretched up into the sky we didn't see from the city. We break through the trees. The illumination is shooting out from the chimney of this creepy, old-looking cabin. Chill bumps raise as a howling wind gusts our way, causing its wood to screech. All of a sudden, we hear feet land nearby.

"Ore!" A girl with curly brown hair and a plait skirt walks towards us. Liam looks annoyed. A bit of worry flashes in his eyes, but he grins. A stroke of territorial blood runs through me as she twists her way over to him.

"I thought I'd see you here," Liam says. She peers at me.

"Oh, you were thinking about me, baby? Funny you haven't called."

My heart drops. *Say what?* What is she anyway?

"I don't have time for this right now, Von," he says assertively.

"The witch is dead," she says, pointing to the cabin with her chin.

So this indeed is Du'Jomi's mother's house. Liam looks at me like he's connecting the dots too.

"What do you want, Von?" Her face transfigures, her sharp monstrous teeth visible.

She is undeniably a vampire. I'm tempted to flee, scream like

231

the girls in the movies, and hide my neck. But, like, I'm standing before a lion. Threatening we've stumbled across its den, I don't move. "Did you kill my brother, Ore?" she asks dejectedly. I thought, *Of course not!* But he pauses before so boldly answering, "Yes."

My knees are threatening to give out unless I find steady ground. How could he so coolly admit to taking someone from their family? Her elbows draw back, and she rams her hands forward, ringing them around his throat. My foot moves in position to strike, my hand twitching to blast her away. I can hear the whole crew follow, but Liam puts up his hand, stopping the cock of our gun. We retreat.

Her sharp, pretty pink nails burrow into his flesh, shivering with readiness. Her grip is so tight, it looks as if she's going to dig through. I don't know how much longer I can stand for this, him being wrong or right. With that, I tell myself I don't know the whole story and don't draw any final conclusions. Her eyes instantly turn to puddles, her face falls like melted marshmallows atop a campfire, and her arms go limp. She then wails, and my own heart cries.

"Why?" she whimpers. I turn to him wanting, no *needing* a response myself. He uses some quick technique to lay her head on his chest, wrapping his arms around her. I'm completely bewildered, trying to suppress a shooting pain that suddenly rushes the veins in my wrists. I've never felt the sensation before I look away.

"He wasn't the best person, but he was my brother," she says, sobbing.

When he speaks again, I can't help but look up. I'm drawn to his voice. "I know, kata put him on my list. I'll come explain everything later, okay?" She nods and he kisses her on her forehead. *How intimate.* She takes one more look at us before swiftly running into the trees. Only then do I let myself breathe.

Liam opens his mouth, but chanting gets our attention. I can't help but wonder if he was going to explain himself, or better said, explain *them*.

Liam kicks open the door, and we rush in. Bot draws her guns and aims. Two stand before us. It's surreal. The Wizard has on a blue-hooded robe full of stars that turns into pants, and his shoes are that of a genie. A ring of necklaces are around his neck, and he holds a short wooded wand that comes to a peak.

"Robot, Rock, who are your friends?" the Wizard asks, his voice steady. He's standing at a giant book, flipping its thick pages. At the fireplace, a witch's pot sits above the fire. The orange light shooting from it is creepy and vile.

"We're sending you back to your planet," Liam says with his usual demanding tone. Du'Jomi stops flipping and looks at him. Du'Jomi is spooky. His skin is dark, with slashes of green light running through. His nails are long and twisted, and nothing about him is humanlike.

"He is the leader of the Megalo Army and not very nice. Papa said he protects us from outsiders with his barrier."

"Thank you for the introduction, Deylou. Allow me to introduce myself further. I am Du'Jomi, the wizard with no true home." He aims that statement at Deylou. "And have no intentions on returning."

"Back in chains it is," says Ore.

"That fire is calling mother," says Du'Jomi. "She's most powerful. When we join forces, we'll be unstoppable!"

Liam laughs and says, "Your mother's dead. I heard her cries in hell."

"Liar!" Du'Jomi screams. I gasp. *He heard them where?* Ore smirks. "Now she's the most powerful witch in the underworld." He laughs like a child. Evil seems to amuse him, like he enjoys it.

The wizard tosses the book he'd been reading to the red and purple goblin. "Run!" he says. The goblin catches the book that's almost his size with no problem and stuffs it in his bag. He then bolts into the fireplace, dodging the fire but tipping the pot of boiling herb. Smoke fills the room. I run outside, happy to get away from the demon Ore, who isn't *really* evil, according to my bells. But when I see Arch, I'll have them checked for manufacturing issues after everything I've just witnessed. Bot follows, and I hear Liam tell Gem to help us. *So he's fighting the wizard alone!*

We rush back after capturing the goblin. Outside, the Wizard is doing some kind of fancy dust show, then forms a rocky shield. William's eyes are dark. It looks as if he knows no defeat as he pushes harder with a shield of his own. It's the shape of a large half-moon but shines like the sun.

He goes more and more into Du'Jomi's barrier. They're both grunting, pushing their power forward. Du'Jomi looks over at our retrieval of the book and goblin. "Mother's book!" he yells, losing concentration. Liam breaks the border and instantly paralyzes him like he did me. I roll my eyes at the memory.

On the ride back, so many things run through my mind, especially his confession of killing Von's brother. I think of Josh. *Could he do that to him?* I know he's the devil's henchman or whatever, but he wouldn't, right? Then, I think about how affectionate he was towards her. I can sense he's just trying to make things right by her, but it still messes with me.

At the lab, Liam puts a forcefield around their prison, and a lit rope restrains them. "We're going to Planet Vaimos in the morning," says Liam.

"How?" I ask.

"Tammy's driving ship."

"But we can't without God's permission."

"We can!" says Arch, running towards me.

"Arch!" I almost cry. I've been feeling so out of place lately, and he's the anchor pulling me back to a happy place. Arch says he'll be transporting us in a van so we don't contaminate spiritual boundaries, and it's gonna be shielded from our eyes. It's intimidating. Could we see God himself? Arch said humans aren't supposed to because we'd surely die.

It's weird to talk to Liam now, but at the end of the night, I find myself wanting him to walk me to my door. However, when he says, "Can I walk you?" I answer with a sharp, "No, I'm perfectly fine!"

"I'm not gonna let you walk to your door alone at this time of night," he says.

Arch runs in, having full faith that Jesus will carry me through safely wherever I go. I can't help but think he may be leaving me alone with devil boy on purpose. I roll my eyes and allow Liam to walk with me.

34

The Spiritual Realm

The next morning, I kiss my sleeping daddy. His alarm is due to go off in thirty, so I hurry. Arch's head is bowed when I go up. "I was just asking for His covering, knowing He's in control," he says.

I walk over and pat him. "Arch! That's really sweet."

"And it's important to ask for God's guidance. He's strategic."

"Definitely. I mean, look at me. I would've never come up with this."

"God's dream for your life is always bigger than your own." *Bigger* is right.

I hear a muffler outside and go to my window. *It's Liam.* He's leaning against his car in his phone, probably texting me. I suddenly get super nervous. He's wearing a shirt that reveals the whole of his arms. I've never seen him this casual. Arch's words are being blocked out by my sight.

"Umm hmm," I say to whatever he wants. Suddenly, Liam looks straight up at me, smirks, and waves. I dart away from the window big-eyed.

After doing breathing exercises, I go downstairs and get in the car.

"Watching me?" he asks.

"You randomly show up at my house . . . *again.* I had to see who was outside."

236

"Randomly? You know we have a mission," he says sternly without even looking at me.

I'm the one that should have an attitude. He kissed me, then was all over Vamp Babe! He buys breakfast and coffee for everyone like the gentlemen that he is . . . *not!*

"Thanks," I tell him as I gently snatch the cup. He and I notice.

Tammy, the other suspicious subject, is at the lab going over safety precautions. I find her voice annoying. I contemplate cutting her off or laughing at her. Then, to top it all off, Liam goes and stands so close to her. I half-grunt but those thoughts come to a halt as I twirl my locket. I've come too far from the person I used to be to allow myself to go backwards. I close my eyes and ask Jesus to quiet my thoughts.

The elevator sounds, and a human comes in. My eyes dart to Gem and Deylou in their natural state. The human and Liam clap hands. When we all don't combust into a million pieces, I wonder if he's a supernatural. The tall, brown- haired, brown-eyed guy greets us. Luca is a pilot for the army and is accompanying us to Vaimos. Liam says they've been friends since they were kids.

Liam proceeds to load the prisoners into the back of the van. A barbed wire wall separates us from them, and he secures it with his powers. The van's dark windows are colorfully blurred out like a channel with no signal. I look at the super dark windshield, wondering if they'll be able to navigate. Robotka is beside me, and Tammy is beside her. Deylou and Luca are behind us, and Gemwyn is all the way in the back by himself, slouching because of his large size.

Liam opens the door to let Arch in the passenger's side, and he sits in the driver's. I lean forward into the cockpit and can see outside perfectly now. Liam and Arch are focused on the GPS.

"So where are—"

"Sit back! It's dangerous for you to see what you don't understand!" Liam says. "That goes for everyone," he adds, and we nod.

"Chill, bro," says Luca. Everyone laughs, including Liam. Arch looks at me and cries. I wonder how a full-on devil's minion is sitting side by side with Jesus' angel? That speaks volumes, never mind the fact that he's about to see the purest of purest places. I'm super confused, and my heart aches at his use of the word *dangerous*. So, you mean to tell me he's in *danger?* Was this a suicide mission? I look at him with anxious eyes.

We drive for a bit, and the only excitement is every bump Liam hits on the road. Light conversations erupt between pairs and triplets. I'm sitting directly behind Liam, and I am focused on him, even if all I can see is the back of his head with the tilt of my head. I see an eye or two, maybe a nose sometimes in the rearview mirror, and it's enough for me to keep calm. There's times he looks at me too. It seems we're looking out for each other. I hear rain but can barely make out the tiny droplets falling on my window. I put my hand on it, thinking of my mother. It seems her memory now calms me instead of haunts me.

The car stops and so does the chatter. Arch and Liam whisper to each other. "You think she can?" Arch asks Liam. *Are they talking about me?* I find myself wanting my best friend back. The one before Daddy, Josh, and Liam got their hands on him. Liam nods, and my arms cross.

"Lolly, c'mon." Finally seeing his full face and smile brightens my current mood, and I clear my throat.

"Where?" I give him attitude, but his smile doesn't move.

"You'll see," he says all wonder-y. I roll my eyes and grab the door handle, but it won't budge. He opens it.

"Child lock!" I say. The whole car laughs.

"Maximum security," says William, and we boo him.

We're still in the back alleys of Barns, and this is the place to be, obviously. I follow Liam and Arch to a large dark space. "There's a sensor if we just walk in the right . . . section," Arch says, maneuvering around. I wonder what's happening but know better than to ask these two questions about anything right now. My heart still aches from the night I met Liam, and Arch decided to be a switch out. I guess favor doesn't play favorites, supposed demon or not.

A once nonexistent place in the wall of this building pops out, and I wonder if my eyes are playing tricks on me when I see tiny aliens walk out. They're a dark pearly blue, have rectangles for bodies, and squares for heads. Their eyes stick out of their heads like snails, and they have tiny arms and legs. They walk toward us squeaking, as if they're polishing something with every step. I step back, and Liam puts his hand on my back. "It's okay," he says.

I nod, nervousness causing me to step away from him. Confusion flashes in his eyes, but he focuses back on the little guys. It bothers me that after all I've seen, I'm still afraid of this stuff. *This is what God called me for.*

"We are the Thrice Eminence Overseers, in complete obedience to the Trinity. That is God the Father, God the Son, and God the Holy Spirit. He who is wonderful, He who is seated in majesty on the right hand of the Father, commands us. May He be glorified, may He be praised forevermore."

The little guy throws his hands up in praise. "You are able to be in our presence because you know of our detectors." He looks back at the area Arch located. "Because the King of Kings and the Lord of Lords decrees it, now state your business."

"Amen," says Arch.

"Amen," Liam and I say in unison and try not to giggle.

"We've come to pass your land and board a ship in the realm

for the safe return of God's servant to Planet Vaimos. We have authorization."

Three of them bring up floating transparent screens. "Planet Vaimos . . . archangel Michael," they say.

"Yes." Arch is so professional and honorable. They clear the screens away.

"Kérdos, Kérdos, Kérdos," they say. A crowd of them steps back, but three remain center stage. One hops until he gets enough momentum to get up on the other's head, and a third one follows.

"Kérdos, Kérdos Kérdos, Kérdos," they repeat and are now perfectly structured, I see why they were created in this shape. They melt before our eyes, and we all step back. I chuckle at the fact that now we are *all* on board, that this is some freaky stuff.

A man in a long trench coat and hat appears and creeps me out. *Why do they have to do this in a dark alley?* "So God is allowing you to go into the natural realm, uh?" he says. We nod. His sombrero and upped collar hides half his face, and his voice is low like the people in those black and white soap operas. "Unheard of, but it's like Him to do something . . . *new.*"

He finally looks over at us. "I'll be escorting you to the Spiritual Realm's version of your ship, found on classified government premises, prepared by Tamron Malcom." He focuses on Liam and me. "Understand this isn't your actual world. Your world is a shell compared to where we're going, very sensitive bounds."

"We understand," says Arch.

"Oh, I know you do, Michael. Good to know there's someone here on the spiritual side."

"Nice to see you too, Profit." *Of course Arch knows him.* Profit seems to have great respect for him.

The Thrice scatter to each side of the alley, and a few pile up, molding into tall trolls with wacky hair and spears. They don't look so humble now. Now they look like they're protecting something! Light suddenly shoots out of nowhere, and a tremendous gust of wind explodes, threatening to blow us away. We evacuate.

The Profit rides out on a motorcycle. We follow, but it feels like we're pressing through something that's forcibly holding us back. Everyone is quiet, awaiting the results.

"C'mon, William!" Bot says, and Tammy and I shush her. I roll my eyes at our exact response. It sounds like someone sliced two swords together and like we're on steady ground.

"Wooooo!" Liam yodels, which makes us giggle. Tammy puts her elbows to her knees and stares at him with heart eyes. *Does she like him?*

The van starts to shake vigorously. Something is pushing at it and bumping into it. Liam's eyes look like they're in distress. They don't have their same steadiness, same light, and cool texture. They look like they're seeing ghosts, ghouls, and yucky goblins, ones that stare at you from the darkness of the closet, threatening they're indeed *real*. Like they're witnessing wars of terror, blood, and agony.

"Jesus please help us," I silently pray. The turmoil goes on for a few more minutes, then settles. Relief flashes in Liam's eyes as beautiful light falls onto his face. It now penetrates our dark windows and despite the AC, heat radiates through the car. We moan in displeasure and are tempted to sweat right before the temperature changes and our skin breathes.

Everyone's talking, but I just want to look at his stupid face again, wanting to know how he could be that horrified when he's from hell. A light bump under a wheel allows the front mirror to catch his smile. The peace he's found makes my heart sing. I hated seeing him in trouble. I look over at Arch. He's confidently standing like a valiant steed, seatbelt on of course. A shadow washes over them, and my smile disappears. Liam speeds up, his eyes are large and focused, barely blinking. It seems like he wants to close them but can't.

"Please! Please! Help me! By the blood of Jesus!" Voices cry out, and we get uneasy. People are also speaking weirdly. I think in church they called it *speaking in tongues*.

"It's spiritual warfare!" Arch calls over them and gusts of wind pound at our doors.

"I know that you hear me, God! You always hear me," says another. We hear singing and clapping. They sound so eager, and now I see why it's such a sacred place. This is for God's ears alone. It's raw and incredible. Arch said there's a purpose for us being able to experience this. Still, it feels wrong hearing their supplications to Christ. But is this really how He hears us? Every word, loud and clear?

35
All Aboard

We reach a breaking point of silence and I wonder, *If our van experienced that much pounding, how was The Profit doing on that motorcycle?* We come to a stop. Liam rubs his eyes, and Arch looks around. Liam gets out of the car and opens both doors quickly. I instinctively jump out and hug him with some will that isn't my own. He takes it in, pressing his head into mine. We stay there a while, and the world seems invisible.

I come back to reality after getting a glimpse of Tammy's dropped lip and clear my throat. We reluctantly let go. I'm too bashful to see if anyone else was looking, but maybe they're checking out the scenery or talking amongst themselves. Well, whispering because I don't hear anything. We finally look, and they are *all* looking at us like we're the aliens back home, *including Arch.* Yes, Arch, the one that was so adamant in minding his own business before. "It was a long ride," I say.

"Yeah," Liam seconds. Most of them grin. Tammy looks hurt.

Liam gets the struggling prisoners and hands the goblin to Gem. There's a glow around both, keeping them secure. We finally look at our surroundings.

"Well I'll be, it looks exactly the same," Tammy says. She walks through the garage and puts in a code at the door. Then a little light turns green.

"It isn't. They can't see you, but they can hear you. Speaking to anyone can disturb the balance," says The Profit.

"No prob. It's just a walk down, elevator up." We relax. "I'll take you up," he says.

A legit soul in the form of a soldier walks down opposite of us. He looks like a white ghost with a pink nose, ears, and mouth, indicating that he's still . . . *alive?* I think of my mother and stiffen.

"Ummm!" Although Du'Jomi's mouth is locked, he still makes noise through his nose. Liam jacks him up on the wall, and Du'Jomi's nostrils disappear before our eyes. We look at the guard as he comes to a halt, raises an eyebrow, and inspects the place. He shrugs, continuing his stroll as if he's not paid enough. Du'Jomi struggles to breathe, and William asks him, "Are you gonna shut up?"

Du'Jomi nods, and Liam lets him breathe.

We move forward. Soldiers line every part of this main hall. We get to the elevator quietly, and a woman spirit with short brown hair, a skirt suit, and pink features stops with us.

"Oh, mornin', Shannon," Tammy says quickly, as if it's just another day at the office. She looks at her watch, slowly realizing what we've already caught on to. She looks at us first before looking at her coworker in dread. Shannon's face scrunches up as she looks around and sees no one.

"Tammy?" she questions. The elevator opens, and we quietly breathe in relief. We climb aboard, making sure to give her plenty of room. No telling what would happen if we touch them.

"Hold the door!" We panic as a man spirit sprints in and greets Shannon. We huddle together in a corner, then he asks her, "Have you heard about the new boss?" He sounds like he's under water.

"I've heard," she replies.

"Do you think he's gonna make it? The last one didn't last a month."

"I don't know, maybe." It seems she doesn't want to talk to him. "Leave me alone; you're so irritating," she adds. We can't believe she actually said it. We look for his response, and he's surprisingly unbothered.

"Are you doing anything tonight?" the man asks her.

"Yes, I'm doing everything if that keeps me from hanging out with you!"

We smile, and I put my hand over my mouth to keep from giggling. Liam's trying to do the same.

"Yes, I'm really busy, working on a new project for my art gallery," she says, then we realize we'd been hearing their inner thoughts.

"Liar," he says. We're entertained and realize we're hearing his thoughts too. "That sucks! We gotta hang out some time," he says for real.

"Change the subject," she says within. "Yeah. Hey, did you see Tammy when you were coming up? I thought I heard her, but when I looked, she wasn't there."

Tammy looks down.

"No, nor do I want to!" the man says.

Tammy's head springs up in shock. "I concur," says the woman, and Tammy steps back in outrage.

"Now there's something we can agree on," the woman spirit says without opening her mouth, and they exit.

"Uh! I'm gonna have them fired!" says Tammy, outraged.

"Tammy, whatever happens in the Spirit Realm stays in the Spirit Realm," Liam jokes. We snicker, not wanting to hurt her feelings.

"Be quiet, Billy! I thought Shannon was my friend!"

"Not anymore. This place is *the truth!*" he shouts. Now we're really laughing. His playful side is back, and I'm glad he didn't let what he saw affect him much. What else has he endured for him to be so strong?

Tammy mopes while unlocking a door. We plunge into the gigantic room, the lights go on, and the beautiful black shiny ship sits before us. Tammy and Gem escort Du'Jomi and the goblin in as I watch Liam talk to The Profit.

"Are you gonna get back okay?" Liam asks.

"God willing," he says and walks us to the huge open door. Our feet click on the lit floors.

"William! You traitor!" We turn, and I look in horror at the creepy giant black figure with no face clothed in brown tribal clothes. He's rushing out of a dark corner toward us, pushing everything out of its way. Even with no features, I can see he's peering at me. *Is that the . . .*

"Go, William! I'll hold him back!" Liam is stuck looking at a bracelet on his wrist. It goes from red to black, and he is smiling big. *His smile is a bit disturbing.*

"Go!" The Profit's voice echoes in the distance.

I rip my sockets away for a moment and see The Profit has turned into a large brown figure with a lizard-like tongue whipping out of its mouth. He has the evil thing pushed back. I gasp and run to press the close button, dragging demon boy back until we're secure. He's still stuck.

"Liam? What was that!" I say and lift his head by his chin. His eyes glisten like they've seen gold.

"You don't understand . . . I've tried for years to break away from them. Never could until now." I look at the black mesh on his neck and wrist.

Ship Arnáki blazes into the sky, set for a galaxy out of ours. Liam's pulling at his bracelet that's extending like a rubber band.

"I still can't take it off, but it's not turning into chains," he says.

"That's a chain? How'd you get it?" I ask.

He hesitates. "Long story."

Obviously! He's so secretive. "So, Satan can come here too?" I ask to clear the air.

"He causes the evil things in the world. Bad thoughts, sorrow, pain. But he can't reach past a certain point. That's why people can decide whether or not to do the right thing, think a good or bad thought."

Bad thoughts? I think about my nightmares and can imagine him watching me in my sleep, using Mama to drive it.

"So the devil has power?" I ask, freaked out.

"Not like God, not even close. I think God took the chains off, even if *it is* just for a little while."

"How do you know it's not permanent?"

He laughs. "They'd be off. I might be free to do this because it's God's will or something, but that's all."

Whoa, he knows a lot about God. It's lovely. I wonder why God is allowing him to be under the devil's lock and key. I will never understand God's ways, but I'm not God, so there's just trust. It seems as if he's caught on to something and moves away from the closeness he'd just given me. The air now feels chilly.

"God . . ." he whispers as we walk toward everyone.

It's still morning, but we retreat to bed. The journey took a lot out of us. There's four bunkers in each room. The girls sleep in one and the guys in another. Later, I awake hungry and walk Arnáki's floors barefoot, not wanting to wake anyone. When I reach the deck, I admire the stars burning brightly out of the huge glass up ahead.

Then I see Liam laughing, and Tammy pushes him. My smile disappears, and I move behind a panel.

"Don't push me! You know I'm stronger than you," Liam teases.

"Wanna bet?" she says. Are they really flirting? I peek, and she grabs his shirt and pulls him toward her lips. I quickly turn around with stinging eyes and run, praying I remember where my bunker is, deciding to keep my distance from the ambiguous *William Blue*.

36
Do Ore Don't

"We are in Viamos' atmosphere!" says Deylou. Lolly now stands expressionless on the other side of the window, looking at Vaimos. William hears her tell Arch that she loves the pink lit forcefield surrounding the planet. He wants her to say it to him. She scans over to where he's standing next to Tammy with narrowed eyes, then rolls them. He doesn't get it. She jumped on him when they got through the Spiritual Realm, and now she's acting strange. He could tell she sensed he needed comfort, and he did, so much.

All the hurt and pain he saw out there was heart-wrenching. He could see people's defeats and failures. Their giving up and refusal to try. He saw demons surrounding them, attacking them, the devil's handiwork in its simplest form. He saw things he couldn't figure out in his mortal mind or vocabulary. One thing he remembered so vividly was that some people were almost to their victory, just one more push to their breakthroughs, when some of them forfeited the battle. He wanted to reach out to them, tell them to keep going, just a little more! But it wasn't allowed, and that's what hurt the most.

But others did go the distance! They didn't give up and got what they were praying for. That was the brightest part of the Spiritual Realm, where people lived in complete peace. Even if it was just for a week, a month, a year. The way angels cheered for mankind when they prayed confirmed that God inhabits all praise, all worship, and hears all. Even though William was exposed, God covered his eyes to a lot of it, keeping His territory full of wonder and mystery.

William's thoughts are interrupted by hearing Deylou say that Du'Jomi being on the ship was the only way they got in his temporary shield. He thinks of Lolly. He has to stay away to protect her. *It's the only way.* For a moment, he'd gotten close to her, thinking the chains were off for good. When it hit him that they weren't and probably wouldn't be, he had to distance himself. Why try to belong to someone that'll only be hurt when she finds out he's not completely hers? Also, she can't let her guard down around him. There's no telling what could happen if he's not careful. But could he stay away from her? *He wasn't sure.*

They land on Ládi mountain by the instruction of Deylou and bring the prisoner out. An army of Similory awaits them. The king runs through the soldiers that are ready to attack.

"Wait, wait!" he calls, his arms flailing in the air. "Jomi! Is that my servant I see?" He's pushing muscle out of the way, then waves off a mighty crocodile on the front line. "Oh, stand back you horrid creature! Can't you see it's Du'jomi? He has returned from holiday!" He throws the bottom of his robe at his face, and the croc rolls his eyes at the silly king who hasn't seen the wizard's bonds yet. "On a strange ship . . . instead of the portals" he says slowly.

He finally takes in his surroundings. "Guard me, you scoundrel!" He throws the crocodile in front of him, and the croc gurgles in annoyance at the king's indecisiveness.

"What is the meaning of this? Why do you have my pet in ropes?" he asks.

"He came to earth to take over. Did you know about it?" asks William.

"Of course not!" he declares, peering at the wizard. "I know he guards your planet, and that's why he's back but can't remain free," says William.

The Similory people have come out of the city and gathered around, and the earth crew looks back at them.

"Yes, we're defenseless without him, snails really . . ." says the king, then looks at his audience. He puffs out his chest. "You have no right!" The king stomps his foot.

The ground rumbles, and Du'Jomi's knees go to the floor. He cries out in agony, "You can't kill a wizard! That's ludicrous!"

"Watch me," says William through a clenched jaw.

"But the other kingdoms will attack us!" The king's face melts in realization he's revealed too much, and he adjusts himself.

"Hand over the necklace!" William demands. The Megálo Army draw their spears, and the earth crew get ready for a fight. William smirks. The necklace that controls the wizard has to be given freely by the holder or taken from their corps. While either would do, he can't continue on the path he'd been on. Not after what he saw in the Spiritual Realm and not after the devil used him for destruction alone *for so long*. He had to do some good. It wasn't an option anymore. He had to change, even if it killed him. He didn't know it, but accepting that truth into his heart was the first step to his freedom.

"If you want an army leftover to protect your planet, I suggest calling them down now!" says Ore. His hair now floats above his scalp, flaring with captivating fire. He feels different but can't describe how.

"Down boys," the king commands, glaring at Ore's appearance. The hard body crocs hesitantly retreat, hissing in disappointment. Ore's eyes ease but drift, wondering why it was so easy. Nonetheless, he puts his fire out when the king places the piece in his hands.

King Vasiliás leads Liam to a cell and binds Du'Jomi in it with his power. They allow his goblin to return to his duties. He now stands with the other different colored goblins. William looks at them.

"They make for good pest control," says the king.

"One more thing, King Vasiliás." The king sighs. "Tell me, Ore."

"We came to help Deylou find her sister. We'll be out in the forest." Asking instead of demanding feels foreign to him, especially because he'd learned it from his captor, but he's determined to make a change.

"Why, you've lost your sister, dear?" Deylou nods.

"Oh my. Well, you have to go find her," the king says with compassion.

"Thank you, your majesty," says Deylou and bows. They dispatch to the forest.

The king's face swirls with fury. "Go and warn the Greta and Howla of what's to come," he whispers to the goblins. "Tell the creatures not to let the earthlings get too far," he demands.

37
Vai Forest

The buzzing coming from the boat's motor pulls me, but not as much as *he* does. No matter how many times I try to blink away what I saw on that spaceship, I can't. Even seeing them talking makes my stomach and chest churn. Are they a thing?

We set foot on Vai Valley, and it gives me the heebie-jeebies.

"Home!" Deylou says with wide open arms. She takes us to her house to change. Inside, Bot and I walk around her humble abode. We ache when we realize how little she truly has. When she comes out, we try to hide our sadness. She has on a short tunic.

"Deylou! Super cute!" I say. I think of Addison and miss her dearly. That ten-minute call I made to fill her in wasn't enough. She'd know what to do about Liam, but why am I still thinking about him?

Deylou hands Bot and I an outfit each. "Mama washed them. Please wear it for the forest." We thank her. I'd be a fool to turn away vintage! I have on a tunic skirt and shirt that only has one sleeve. Bot has on a dress that looks like she's on an episode of *The Flintstones*, and she's gorg in it. I put my hair up in a messy ponytail as we go outside.

Liam stares at me in a way that makes me feel like the jungle version of Cinderella stepping into the ballroom, and I get shy.

"Hey, where's mine?" asks Tammy.

"I am sorry, Tammy. I only have these cleaned."

"Awww shucks!"

"You look really beautiful in your native clothing, Deylou," says Luca. She blushes. Those two definitely have a thing for each other. We walk towards the forest. Liam, who's aways from me, won't stop looking at me. I feel sheepish. He seems to notice and pulls his gaze away. An unexpected sigh comes out, and I reprimand myself. I could really use a furry hug right now, but Arch stayed behind to guard the ship.

We pass the line of separation, then go through a pretty leafed wall. It seems to have a different sky. It's dark and moist in here. We immediately hear a high-pitched call from some sort of animal. I look to Deylou for an explanation.

"It is the Greta, but they are only drawn by noise." She looks confused.

We push on. I admire William's stylish black jacket over a ripped white shirt, black pants, and low-cut boots. I try to look away because I need to be watching for Grina's or whatever they call them, especially after that scream, but I don't want to. I manage to look over and see Tammy watching him the same way, if not more on the desperate side. That immediately makes me look away, trying to erase the last episode of *Tammy & Liam*.

"Be careful. Greta travel in groups and are poisonous," Deylou says. We continue with caution.

A stunning sunflower wakes and follows Liam's movement from sun up to sundown. The petals on her flower elongate, like luscious hair. She plucks her gorgeous petals and sets them as her arms. She has almond-shaped eyes and pink-painted lips. She pulls a nearby vine and swoops her hair into a ponytail. This is all really happening before my eyes, Deylou's, and Bot's. The rest pushed passed the extraordinary in plain sight. The sunflower clears her throat, and the others turn around.

She's only looking at Liam. "Do you know of my master?" she says, fluttering her lashes. She even has a calming voice that sounds a tiny bit robotic. *In a forest?* After I shut my mouth and Bot's, I notice Deylou's angry glare.

"No, we just got here." Liam's so tickled, like a child snickering at a goofy cartoon. It makes me laugh.

The flower turns to Deylou. "Deylou, I'm sorry about Nelly."

"Do not say you are sorry! You did not help, Vema!" The flower searches for answers, and colors dance around us.

"Deylou, I tried. The Arkin intervened. I'm only charged to preserve the forest and hold information." Deylou walks past all of us. We follow her, and Vema's flower slumps in sadness. My eyes watch in amazement as she plucks herself out of the ground. Her stem separates turning into legs as she ducks and runs into the forest. She has to be at least six feet tall.

We hear branches and leaves moving and put our backs to one another. A Greta jumps out at Prince Gem. He hovers on a carpet, pulls out a sword the color of his skin, and slashes it in two. We duck, blocking the liquid it sprayed. I want to cry. I notice he made away with his cloak. He has on pants and a long red and beige vest to match. The top portion shows nothing but his gemmed chest, and I blush at his bareness.

"Well done, my prince," says Bot.

"I told you I'm your friend." His eyes go from Bot's to mine for just a moment, and I feel self-conscious.

"You will always be my prince," says Bot. How sweet! I feel a strange pull and happen to look over at Liam. He's glaring at Gem and me. I gulp.

Movement crackles all around us, tree branches fall from afar, and we see two jungle men running for their lives.

"Morro? Lei?" Deylou says. The guys with long ponytails and tan shirt and pants stop shy of us, chests pounding.

"Deylou? A herd of Greta approach! I have never seen so many." His eyes swing to us. "Humans?" His gaze warns that we aren't allowed here, and we sink back.

"They are here to help," says Deylou.

"There!" Lei says, pointing. Suddenly, tons of Greta break through the darkness.

I wind bow string in the air. It arrived at the shop the last time I worked and was another piece mama ordered. I throw it at two of them, instantly severing their heads from their bodies. I cover my mouth. *Did I actually just . . .*

"You're good at this." Liam smirks, and my shock falls into annoyance at the thrill Ore gets out of this.

"No, Liam. Just no." I walk away.

"What?" He's clueless.

The Greta are awfully ugly. Their green skin is dark and bumpy. The hair around their head and neck exceeds far beyond their bodies and sticks out unevenly down their spines. *Bizarre.* I see Bot jump in the air and smash a Greta's belly in. The white puss rolls out, and I gag. Deylou somehow has a bow and arrow and shoots a creature dead center. *Impressive.* The two male Similory are swinging hammers at Greta that Gem is throwing their way. My eyes meet Ore's. Then I see a Greta fall out of a very tall tree, going straight for his head. I fly towards it to get a better aim, position my hands like Josh taught me, and blast away. It all happens so fast, the impact of the blow pushes me backwards.

Familiar hands hold me up. I turn to find Ore smiling at me. Curiosity gets the best of me. Wondering if it's Liam's hologram, I poke at his side. The brute puts his hand over the spot in disbelief.

"You're gonna pay for that!"

"Liam, I'm sorry!" I put my hands up in defense as he comes

closer, and tickles me! In the middle of a war, he tickles me! "Liam!" Laughter erupts from a hidden compartment I didn't know existed. My back hits the trunk of a tree, and his pointy fingers dig deeper into my sides.

My head hits the trunk, forcing me to look into his eyes. Their blue color stuns me. Ore brings my chin up, scans my reaction, and gets closer, saying, "Would it be wrong if I said I felt that little monster coming for me but knew it would bring you close?"

I'm shocked. "You want me close?"

He exhales. "Obviously." *He's frustrated?*

It seems Ore is blunt, so I ask, "What about the vampire?" He grins. "What about her?" He says it like she's a nobody.

Creatures are burning all around us, and with no one else in sight, I know he's doing it. Before I can ask about Tammy, he looks at me in a way that carnivores look at their prey. He then runs his fingers along my jawline towards my neck. "No!" Liam says and shakes his head, turning back to normal and breathing heavily. My heart is beating against my chest like it has drumsticks.

He huffs and raises his hands before dropping them down to his sides. About a hundred Greta fall from the branches and onto the ground around us. My eyes blink profusely at the infestation.

He waves two fingers, creating a massive fire ring, and blows it out with a single puff. Smoke builds around us. I cough, and he whisks me through the tree into the sky. Clear air fills my lungs.

"I'm sorry, I'm so sorry," he whispers, a melody I've come to adore. *But why does he sound so upset?* He just got us out.

"I'm fine." I grab onto him tightly, placing my head against his chest.

We land in the middle of everyone, and someone shouts in agony. We run over. Luca has been bitten on his abdomen, and he's turning red all over.

"Luca!" Deylou cries. She and Liam teleport him to a doctor in town. We wait on their return with only a few sightings of Greta. Her people don't have the power to fight these things on their own. Something has to be done about the unfair treatment happening on this planet.

Deylou and Liam return. They say the doctor is doing everything she can for Luca. Before I can ask what that means, the ground begins to shake. Liam huddles us together. I'm near him, but he seems uncomfortable. *Didn't he just say he wanted me close?* His feelings are so unclear. He forms a bubble around us and says we're invisible, so we wait quietly. The giant creatures run out, and I put my hand over my mouth to keep from screaming because they're hideous! They look like they've been in hiding for ages. Their faces are yellow and crooked. They have winged arms and stand up on their webbed feet, moving their heads about like owls.

"Howla," Deylou says, her eyes twinkling. "They are scarce," she says.

I feel a surge of power run through me as I begin to walk toward the Howla, completely absorbed in power. My eyes glowed they said. I can still feel Liam's fingertips as he tried to catch me before I broke out of his protective bubble and revealed myself to the wretched owls. *But he couldn't stop me because God was in control.* Not him and not me but Almighty God.

I felt my arms open. Fire, hail, and lightning fell down from heaven as two mouths longing to eat my flesh surrounded me. Their beaks only hit the rumbling ground beneath me. *I was impenetrable.* I saw . . . I saw angels come to our aid. They were the ones throwing elements from above. The creatures squealed in distress. I could hear the hail hitting their bodies—thud, thud, thud, and their struggle to take another breath. Then I felt my body go limp. When I opened my eyes, the creatures were dismantled at my feet. I kicked dirt to get away from them as Liam pulled me into his arms. I couldn't hear what he was saying, as my hearing hadn't returned. All I knew was we didn't have to fight because our God fought for us.

38
The Fight to Victory

"Lolly? Talk to me, beautiful. Please?" Liam pushes back the few strands of hair that blew out of my ponytail.

"I'm okay."

"I didn't know you could do all that," he says.

"I didn't."

"What do you mean?"

"There were angels up there. You didn't see them?" Deylou, Bot, and Liam all shake their heads. I see the gang checking out the pieces of the bird-like creatures, and I'm amazed at how God just used me like that. "You're amazing," I whisper to God.

We confidently go deeper into Vai forest. It seems we've fought the worst around, but we could be wrong. Deylou directs us to where she last saw her sister, but everything looks familiar.

"Guys?" I say, and we realize we've been going in circles.

"This was the way," says a panicked Deylou.

"It's okay, Deylou. We'll find it," I reassure her. I hear a shooting sound then feel an awful sting coming from my neck. I touch the long, thin thorn.

Liam sees it. "Get down!" he yells to the others. More thrones fly, and large flowers with teeth and no eyes are throwing spikes from their mouths. Liam burns them up, and they wither.

I try to swallow, but my throat is extremely dry, making it difficult to speak. I carefully make my way to the ground. I look over and see Tammy and Marro have fallen too.

"I'm gonna pull it out, okay?" Liam asks and I nod. When he does, I can finally breathe, and my throat is moistened again.

"That's better," I say, snuggling into the dirt.

"I'm gonna go help the others," says Liam. "I'll be back." I nod with closed eyes.

"A lot better, huh?" Bot asks.

"Yeah, I just . . . I can feel my chest warming and feel liquid filling my lungs quickly."

"Don't pull them out!" she yells.

My skin is clammy. I can't smell and feel really hot, but the sun is nowhere to be found.

"I shouldn't have done that," says Liam.

"You were helping." I lay on his chest.

"Don't close your eyes, baby. Please don't close your eyes."

"Okay." If I am thinking straight, I'd say he just called me baby. Bushes shake and everyone gets ready to fight.

The long sunflower emerges and we relax. She looks nervous but is still so beautiful and tall. She approaches me. "I'm Vema, may I?" Liam nods. I see her circled head moving to each side as she examines me. Her petal flyaways tickle me, but I'm too exhausted to laugh.

There's a gnawing at my stomach and I begin to moan, burrowing into Liam's chest.

"Dili flowers," says Vema. "Their stingers are very poisonous, especially when pulled out. It quickens the process."

I swear she has a computerized voice. I'm tempted to snuggle up against Liam and fall asleep where I feel protected, but he wakes me. "You can't do that, okay?" He sounds shaken, and I nod. "Vema went to find the antidote, and she's coming right back."

"Marro? Tammy?" I ask.

"She gave them leaves to chew for dry throats." He gets really close. "As soon as Tammy got a chance to speak, she said they tasted like pigeon foot." It makes us both laugh. "Because how does she know what those taste like, baby, right?" We laugh louder. I put my hand on his cheek. I love him like this.

Vema comes back with a basket. "Okay, you just have to . . ." A blank gaze falls on her face, and she drops to the floor like a dead flower.

"Oh, for crying out loud!" says Tammy, and we giggle before hearing more wrestling bushes. Gem and Bot stand, drawing their weapons, but it's Vema again. We stare at her green crops.

"My apologies," she says and proceeds to drag her old self into the bushes, grunting and panting. When she returns, we stare at her cycle of life. "It will decompose and soil the planet." She walks back to her basket and picks through it like nothing just happened.

"Ballies," she says, holding them up in her petal hand.

"Ballies?" everyone says in disgust.

I extend my hand. "Me please." I hold the small gray marble in my palm. It's transparent and rubbery. "Manducate them for a small duration, and you will perceive them to be quiet objectionable after your taste immediately commences. Then you ingest it."

"English please!" Tammy shouts.

"Chew for a few seconds. It will be disgusting when your taste returns, similar to rotten eggs on your planet. Swallow."

We do and she pauses as if she's about to say the hard part. "It will turn into small balls in your stomach, rolling around absorbing the poison. When the process is all done, you will throw up." *Okay not so bad.* "For ten minutes."

"Oh, heck!" Tammy says, and I cover my mouth so I won't spit this disgusting thing out from laughter!

Those of us infected moan with distastefulness and force ourselves to swallow. It's a gag fest for ten minutes as Vema said as Marro, Tammy, and me throw up in our own area. Vema comes over. "Lolly? Will Deylou forgive me?"

"Yes, especially if you help her find her sister. We've been lost for at least an hour."

"The forest's protective mechanism is on high alert. There are rules here, and I can't overstep my boundaries."

"Yeah, but you can do something."

The sunflower nods. "I will take you as far as I can. But we must watch for the Arkin, who are hierarchy and possess strong power of fire and blue light. They can shut down my systems." She's whispering and looking around. "We are in wait of our true king, and they command the forest until his arrival." I wipe my mouth and was so plugged into her story that I didn't notice I stopped throwing up.

We crowd around and tell everyone about our plan. Deylou still seems upset, but she smiles at the development. Fully nursed back to health, we march forward. I hear Vema talking to Liam.

"What are you called?" Vema asks.

"William."

"William? A common earth name." She seems to light up while speaking to him, yep the *William Blue charm.*

"I guess you can say that," he says, unaffected.

"But you're not common. I feel your energy."

"You can feel? Does it hurt when you . . ." He looks at the ground, and I'm tempted to laugh.

"Not at all. I just stop and start again." She jumps and twists in the air, fluttering her petals to help her ease back down. "But there's something about you . . ." she says before gasping and turning to me. "Lolly, the Arkin." She backs away slowly.

Two dark animals that resemble large panthers with beautiful, prickly manes come out. Their flat pink noses illuminate their features and glowing blue eyes look fierce and territorial. They have two thick, partial black antlers and entangled copper wiring coming out of them. Blue electricity sparks in between the metal as they make their way to us. They send voltage our way, which Liam blocks with his shield.

He does something next that shocks all of us. Using the same energy they are, he pushes back. Strings of blue light tag each tree. Some stretch as far as the sky. Our heads rise as they do. The crackling sound pops in our ears, and the air smells burnt. I barely hear Vema from afar say, *"Master?"* Deylou and Tammy's hair swish around from the breeze the surge is creating. Liam walks forward, and we follow cautiously. He grunts, and it turns into a forceful shout. I can see slashes building on the skin of his arms from the sparks coming out of his hands. How much more of a beating can we take? I close my eyes and pray.

The sound suddenly stops. William and the Arkin are just staring at each other. They finally turn and walk away. Were they just challenging him to see if he was strong enough? Liam falls to the ground, and his fingernails scrape up dirt.

"Liam?" I put my hand on his arm, and tears well in my eyes.

"Don't," he says, and I pull back. I can see his teeth are clenched. He's shivering, and his breathing is irregular.

The lashes on his arms are slowly diminishing, but only one at a time. His burned hands are turning back to their original color, and the scratch on his head where it looks like a bolt hit disappears. Deylou holds on to me, and I grip her arm, trying to compose myself. I hate that he's in pain. What did they just do to him? Or take from him? He gets up and wipes his whole face.

"Keep straight. You are on the safest route," says Vema through flashy lights in the trees.

"Let's move," says Liam.

This place is a constant threat and tiring. A chilly wind blows out of nowhere, and I cover up, watching trees sway with every push and pull. It's so wet and gray here, I can't wait to get home to a steaming hot bath. Liam sweeps his jacket around me. I look at his bare arms.

"No, I don't want you to be cold," I say, then see three stones sitting at the fold of his elbow I hadn't noticed before. One is ruby red, the other a sapphire blue, and the last a shimmery gold. Tiny ones sit at his wrist. *Is he royalty?* Does this happen only in the form of Ore? I've been close to him plenty of times and have never seen them. Before I know it, they're gone. *He has the ability to hide them!*

"Keep it," he whispers with an icy vibrato and walks away, leaving me feeling colder than before.

We come up to a sign. "Mudwor," says Deylou, penetrating my compilation of thoughts about William. I look behind me to him. He'd separated from us a while ago. I feel a sadness building in me, thinking about all he's been through until I hear giggling and turn again to see he's now laughing with Tammy. I huff *'cause all I got was the cold shoulder*.

Bunches of craters, filled with gushy mud, are everywhere. Mud rivers flow, and soft sand in the distance is definitely quicksand. I see chunks of shiny metal all over the floor. The Similory rush to pick them up. Is this the trade Deylou was referring to?

"Trespassers!" a Mudwor says. He whistles and more arise. Liam turns to Ore and whisks a black and red disc at the Mudwor. It coats his being, he trembles, and cries out in pain. Ore flinches as if he felt it. All I see is lava burning brightly, seeping out of cracked clay the mud man turned into. *Ore's power is extraordinary.* The other Mudwor are stuck, gaping over his appearance.

"Stay here," Ore instructs and jumps down into a Mudwor hole. Strangely, they run after him, not caring one bit about us.

39

Restlessness

"I love the smell of fresh air. Father thought it best I stay in my room."

"Yeah, it's pretty great out here," says Grand. "My real parents used to bring me to a similar place back home until I hurt them by accident." Grand looks at his small friend sitting in the grass, wondering what he'd done.

"What are your plans for me, Grand?"

Grand is shocked at his maturity. He takes out the needle, but the boy isn't afraid. "I don't know exactly, but the guy I work for does."

"I can feel your broken heart. Are your actions in anger?"

"I'm not angry." Grand laughs.

Mckenzie picks a daisy and gives it to Grand. "They make me happy. Maybe they'll make you happy too," he says. He thinks about Ci and puts the daisy in his pocket. As pretty as this daisy is, the Daisy back home isn't as pretty inside.

The boy grabs the needle and cuts himself. Grand flinches. "Go on," he says, handing it back. Grand follows and hovers his arm over the boy's cut. He can feel a different chemical release when he's about to turn someone. It's the soothing feeling of menthol. Grand carries the sleeping boy to the truck and takes him home. He's asleep for hours.

In the morning, Grand stares at the grown boy in the refrigerator and smiles. "Mckenzie?" The teen gives a toothy smile. "How'd you grow so fast?"

"I'm seventeen. Your blood helped my body mature out of that ten-year-old body. I knew it would, and I know about the Spiritual Realm too," Mckenzie says before downing a sandwich.

Daisy walks into the living room. "Who's this?"

"This is Mckenzie."

"The acid? Are you okay?" she asks Mckenzie.

"Never better," he says, keeping his eyes on the game. "We're leaving for Minnesota, and Wildcard is missing. We need to go pick up A. Freeze. He needs to know he belongs to me."

Daisy crosses her arms. "Since when did you start saying we belong to you?"

"Since you do. Now get dressed."

She obediently walks away, grumbling. "Okay, Grandfather."

They knock on A. Freeze's door, and his wife answers.

"Adam home?" Grand asks.

"May I ask who's looking for him?"

"No." Daisy peers at him through sunglasses and sucks her teeth.

"Hon!" The woman calls and closes the door.

"You were rude to my wife?" A. Freeze gets in his face.

"We're leaving."

"Leaving?" Adam asks.

Grand walks away, expecting him to follow. They leave for the old military base and collect the acid. Grand drives home all day and all night as his crew sleeps.

He can feel darkness growing inside of him. The fight made it come out. He craved the action and wanted more. "We got the kid, now what?" he asks Satan.

"Yes, I see." He looks at Grand's strained eyes. They're no

longer lit. "You're looking better and better every day," says the evil one.

"I like the change," says Grand.

"If only my son, Ore, had as much potential as you." Satan hums. "I'm waiting on a witch to get her hands on a certain book. Then we'll be ready."

"Take some time off. You've been busy, Grandfather," he hisses.

"I don't need time. I need payback."

The devil laughs. "Yes, we do. For now, do what I tell you, boy, but the time draws near."

Grand pumps acid into one of his underground gas tanks. A rasp in his voice mixes with every other breath he takes. Everyone is aware of this except him. He's constantly doing, pacing, and feeling uneasy. He still hasn't heard from Wildcard, and it enrages him.

Adam shows at the warehouse. "A. Freeze, let me show you your room." He follows Grand.

"I'm married, have a home, and kids. I don't need a room here."

"Okay, just an option, although I would like to have all my juniors here."

Grand's itching all over, and Adam looks over at him. "Dude, you cool?"

"Yes, why do you ask?"

"You're acting weird."

"You can live with your family for a little while. Then I want you to move in, you got that?" Adam hesitantly nods.

Grand sets up a refrigeration system in his room and has A. Freeze build stacks of ice in it so he can sleep in a normal bed. The plan is successful. He should be able to have restful nights, but they're still restless.

"We're going out," Grand yells to Daisy and Mckenzie as he and Adam leave.

"I have a funny feeling I'm gonna find Card here." They climb the stairs. They watch Wildcard rapidly move around the table of an unsuspecting crowd, manipulating the game as he pleases.

Grand observes for a bit and Adam laughs. "Come on, we don't need to do this here," he says. They wait for Wildcard to stumble down the stairs. "When I say, freeze him."

Adam nods. "Card, this is where you've been, huh? Old habits never die."

"Grandfather? You know I gotta get my game in." Wildcard looks around.

"Now!" Adam creates a rock border around his feet.

"Were you not coming back?"

"Yeah, I was celebrating, boss. Doc says I'm cancer free. Plus Daze said I was free to be me."

"Daze? That suits her! Well, allow me to put your hold back on since that's the only thing keeping you in line." He looks back at Adam and nods. He calls Daze.

"You told him to do what?"

"That's what you said."

"I told you that, not for you to release him, but for you to know!"

"Boss, are you really gonna put it back on me?" asks Wildcard, and Grand ignores him.

"Well, I'm sorry," says Daze.

"You're always sorry. I should tell you to jump off a building." She gulps so loudly it's heard through the speakerphone.

"Grand . . ." she says, sobbing, "you're letting him get into your head. Fight him."

"Now you believe?" He scoffs. "Tell Wildcard to chill and

make us all twelve sandwiches each. I want them ready when we get there. I'm hungry!"

"I like that one, boss," says Wildcard.

"Oh, and feed the puppies until they're satisfied." She does as she's told, and he hangs up on her.

Grand rubs his eyes and thinks about her words. He hasn't changed much. He just has to get this job done to get revenge. He can't deny his exhaustion, though. It seems going against the Lord was indeed wearing him out. But something was pushing him to keep going. He wondered if it was the influence of the devil like Daisy said. He presses on to bring his people home for dinner.

40
Triumph

Liam retrieved Pinelle successfully. Deylou hugged and kissed her and praised God for her safe return. *Mission completed.* We walk back to Deylou's house, making sure to keep our guard up. She says as long as we make it past the rock barrier, they can't harm us. Liam hasn't said a word to me. He's still aloof and quiet. A tribe of Mudwor appear before us, and our chatter ceases. *But we're on Greta land!*

"Let us through," Liam orders and turns into Ore.

"This! This is who we seek," the chief says, his gaze directed at Liam. "Our king."

"Your what?" Tammy says.

"Their what?" I second.

"Come with us." We hesitantly follow. They lead us to a cave, shining their torches at the scribbling on the wall. "My people have long told stories about a great man that would come and change our land for the better. That he would come with fire worn as a crown." He waves at a Mudwor. "The gold and jewels belong to you as well, oh king." A metal tin filled with sparkling diamonds, rubies, and gold chunks sits in their hands. "This isn't even a third of what's yours," says the chief.

Liam briefly looks in my direction. "I can't be your king. I'm going back to earth."

"You must stay," says the chief.

I bite my lip and say, "I need fresh air." I walk away. When wind hits my face, I finally breathe, feeling the familiarity of anxiety crawling up my arms. I'm trying to remember, what caused this last time? *Goodbye.* It was the feeling of goodbye. I lean on the rock wall. Maybe his chains were off so that he could stay. *Maybe he could be happier here.* Realization hits me . . . but I don't want him to stay.

After a while, Bot speeds towards me. "Lolly, are you okay?"

"Yes, it was a little too small in there."

"Okay. We're heading out."

"Is Liam staying?"

"No! But they did say he had to come back." I think about this while Liam is setting regulations in the castle. The king isn't happy at all, especially when Liam takes a trunk of their money, *Vairos*, and gives it to Deylou. Gem is staying to make sure the king follows orders. Luca isn't coming back either. The doctor says he'll survive but needs to be on their meds for at least a month, and Liam okayed Bot's return to earth.

I hear the chief telling Liam about all the creatures of the forest, and I'm glad we didn't meet them all. Liam disappeared into the forest and returned with galactic phones he made with Vema to be able to communicate with our friends. He's still not speaking to me, and the *"But I don't want him to stay"* eats at me as I try to make sense of my feelings.

"Deylou?"

"Mama?" Deylou is completely surprised. Her parents walk up, and she and Pinelle run and hug them. Deylou tells her parents everything and explains Liam as their long lost king. Her mother cries for Pinelle's sake but is happy the girls are safe and won't have to worry about the evil forest now that the creatures are at peace because of Liam. I could've sworn there was a mist above the forest when we got here, but it's gone. Her mother is now overjoyed about the Vairos and says she knew God was in control and says something about *more than enough.*

273

41

What If I Said I Was Rotten?

Ever wake up in the middle of nowhere, wondering where the sun went, super hungry, and out of your mind? *Currently me*. I accidentally roll off the bed and into Arch's comfy bed *that he is not in*. I feel betrayed. So you mean to tell me he wasn't guarding me as I slept? Greta, Howla, or Arkin could be at my window just waiting to get me! "Some guard dog you are, angel!" I shout. I get no response. Instead, I hear the TV blasting downstairs.

I go down wrapped in my comforter. Daddy and my brother are on the couch. And traitor Arch is on the floor at my daddy's side. I raise my brow at him, and he cries, "Switch out."

"What's going on!" I put my hand on my hip.

"C'mon sweetheart. We're having a movie marathon, watching the best movies ever created." This seems like a guy's night, but I wouldn't mind interrupting it, although I know *best movies* means action movies. *Ugh* . . . I sit down anyway. I would love to be normal for a few hours and erase a certain someone from my memory.

Back to the Future flashes on the screen. That title doesn't make any sense. I guess that's why it's a movie. "Wait," I say and spring up to pop two bags of popcorn. *Men . . .* they dunno how to do things right!

"Oh yeah!" says Daddy after I bring in the freshly popped snack. Josh grabs two handfuls. Between these two, these bags are gone within minutes. I should've made three bags or more.

"How was the mission?" Josh asks. Daddy looks over casually.

"Not now, Josh," I say dryly, especially when all I can think about is Liam, and his inscrutable eyes, walking me to my door earlier. *Impeccable blue eyes* they are. For some reason, I ran upstairs and watched him ride off.

"Have you thought about a superhero name?" he had whispered to me.

Not really, I thought. After today, I'm not sure about it all. "I'm an original," I said, shrugging, and he nodded. I think my name is pretty darn intimidating anyway.

The movie starts, and Daddy tells us to be quiet. He's such a child. He's the one who ends up explaining every part, and I'm all into it. So much so that when I dig into the popcorn bag, I just touch the bottom of it. *Seriously!* I am ticked.

"C'mon, Marty!" Daddy yells. The main character, Marty Mcfly, gets punched trying to save the younger version of his mom. I put my hands over my mouth and narrow my eyes at a sleeping Josh who is missing it. *Weakling.*

My phone vibrates, and I casually look at it. Liam's name is slapped across the screen, and I almost bite my tongue off.

Liam says, "You up? I need to talk to you. I'm outside."

He what, where?

"Look, look, look!" Daddy says, and I put my phone down. He *needs* to talk to me? I roll my fingers around the remote to see how much time is left—just under five minutes. Although a nervous hammer drops to the bottom of my stomach, I text back,

"Ten minutes?"

That'll give enough time for the living room to clear. I eagerly wait for his text back.

"I'll be waiting."

I throw my head back. Why did he have to say that? It makes me even more nervous. At last, the credits roll and we retreat to our rooms. The movie was awesome, but I didn't get to fully enjoy the ending since I was thinking about what Liam could possibly want to say to me. My bunnies run downstairs and make it out of the door without getting caught. But I'm nineteen. Even if I get caught, I'll be crying like a baby 'cause Daddy doesn't play.

I hear a motor turn off. I choke and gulp at the same time, which doesn't make for a good mixture. I lightly cough away the strangulation and watch a serious Liam walk up my driveway. I cross my arms and wait. I never noticed how effortless his stride is. He has on a varsity jacket, pants, and tennis shoes. *Casual again.*

"What's up?" he says after I step on the front porch, closing the door behind me.

"Hey," I say sheepishly. He seems as nervous as me.

"Hope I didn't interrupt anything."

"No, is everything okay?" *You know, since you weren't talking to me on Vaimos.*

"Yeah . . . no . . ."

"Wait, which is it?" I ask, giving a confused smile.

"You have such a beautiful smile. You know I'd never hurt you, right?" Liam gently runs his thumb across my cheekbone.

My cheek sparks under his touch. If he's referring to my feelings, he already has hurt them so many times. But here I am, on my mama's porch with a boy I met a little while ago. All I can do is nod.

"Lolly, you don't know a lot about me. I never let anyone in like I let you in, and that's dangerous." His choice of words makes me want to look under my bed to see if there are any monsters.

"How so?" My curiosity makes me take a step toward him. He backs up and laughs.

"See, you like me like I like you, but you don't know what I'm truly capable of."

Well, that was brave of him to say. Ore is a little wild, but the *realization* I had on Vaimos when he almost stayed there tugs at my heart.

"It doesn't matter," I say, and it shocks me like it shocks him. If he's here to get down to what's been going on between us, I'm open.

"You don't know what you're saying . . ."

"What's wrong?" I put my hand on his forearm.

He very calmly says, "The devil put you on my hit list."

What? A numbness rushes over my body, and my fingertips get icy. I back away from him with crossed arms.

Suddenly it's super dark out, and he really does look like an assassin. I'm all alone with a killer, *my killer*, and I came straight to him. "Liam . . ."

"You don't have to say anything. I see it. You're afraid of me." He chuckles like Ore, which disturbs me. "I just didn't know it would feel this bad," he says, sounding defeated. My heart goes out to him. He takes out his keys and starts to walk away. I don't have the words. To say his confession didn't affect me would be lying.

He turns around. "At the tree on Vaimos, I almost lost it. I almost . . ." He shakes his head, and his eyes gloss over.

Ore almost killed me. I tremble thinking about how devilish he gets. I want to tell him to stay, that I don't care, that even now when he's just a few more feet away than before, I miss his aura.

"Just know I'll never hurt you. I'd let him destroy my body before I ever let him touch what feeds my soul." He sounds so vulnerable. *Don't go* I think as I watch him speed off. I run to my bed and cry. He was honest, but I was not able to take what he dished out. I blow up Addison's phone, but she's not picking up. I stay up for hours, asking God if Liam is supposed to be in my life, awaiting an answer.

In the morning, my phone's buzz wakes me. For a second I think it's Liam, but it's Addison.

"Hey babe!" Even in the morning, she's lit.

"Help!"

"Oh my gosh, spill! Is it Tammy?"

"Not this time . . ."

"I'm listening!" She shuffles around and gets comfy for the new series of the Lolly Pobs Show. "

Liam told me something last night when he came over." I crash my head into my pillow. She's not gonna take this well.

"You had a boy in Papa Pobs' house late at night? Who are you and what have you done with my best friend?"

"We were on the porch," I muffle through my pillow.

"Even worse, you could've gotten poor Liam shot, even if he heals!"

"I know. Can we get back to the part where I found something out?"

"Listening . . ."

How do I ease it on her? "He said . . ."

"Umm hmm?"

"I was on his hit list." I close my eyes, she bursts into laughter, and I'm so confused. This is the girl who always defends me and takes everything seriously. I pout. "Addison?" She's finally coming down from her laughter rush, only for her to start again. I wait.

"I'm sorry. I'm sorry," she says. If I know my best friend well, she's crying right now. "Okay, I'm done. That boy wouldn't hurt you!"

That's what she has for me? The same exact thing he said? "Best friend? How can you be so confident?"

"Because of the way he acts toward you. It's obvious." I smush my hand into my face.

I explain all the things that happened at Vaimos or anywhere else for that matter.

"Are you blind! Tammy is drooling over him, but he doesn't like her like that, babe." I breathe at the clarity she's providing. "He definitely wants *more*, regardless of the danger, but he's still trying to protect you. *So romance novel worthy.*"

"More?" I ask cautiously.

"Like date *more,* like be your boyfriend *more. OMG* your first boyfriend, Lolly!"

"Ady, let's just take a few steps back . . ."

Right then, I get a text from Liam. It just says my name, and my heart jumps off the cliff that is my chest. Then my alarm clock starts switching radio stations, and my eyes dart to it. "Here's 'Unforgettable,' folks, by Nat King Cole," the radio man announces and music starts playing.

"I love that song!" says Ady, hearing it in the background. "That's Nat King Cole, right?" She has no idea what's happening right now.

"My mom plays it like all the time," she says, but I'm too stunned to answer, remembering the day Liam said he had ways of getting to me if I didn't answer. I put my hand over my mouth.

"I didn't even know I had a radio on my alarm clock! I think he's playing it." She gasps.

Just when I thought she'd finally grasped the seriousness of the situation, she says, "So romantic!"

"Ugh! says the hopeless romantic that you are . . . it's creepy!"

"Of course you think that. It's only because you know someone likes you, like for real, for real this time!"

"No."

"Yes!" she counters.

"He texted me."

"What'd he say?"

"Just my name."

"Text him back. Talk about it."

"To talk about the devil, Ad?"

"Why are you over-thinking? You know what this says to me?" I sigh, knowing most times she's right. "That you like him too, and that's okay, Cher. Carter was a joke. William isn't. And did you pray about it?"

I hear a knock at the front door, and alarms go off in my heart. "Someone's knocking at my door!"

"Daddy!" we say in unison, hoping my dad doesn't answer the door. I look outside, and sure enough, it's Liam.

"It's him!" I don't see Daddy's car in the driveway and remember Josh had an early practice before a huge game this weekend, Daddy must've taken him. I go in my room, shut my door, and look at it as if he's going to burst through.

"Lolly?" I hear him say. I slowly turn around, and he's standing by my window. I put my hands up for protection but don't want to hurt him, so I put them back down.

"Addison, I'll call you back."

"But, Loll—" I hang up and drop my phone.

"Are you scared? If you are, I'll leave and never come back. I promise." He doesn't mean it, I can tell. And even if he did, I don't think I could handle him being gone.

"Why'd you come back?" I rub my arm to keep from shivering.

"I panicked and . . . just needed to be close to you again." My eyes flutter. "I know what I told you wasn't easy to hear . . ." I search his face. It almost looks like he's in pain, but I don't see a wound. "But The Profit told me the chains would come back, and I just want to spend the time I have left *with you.*" It feels like every word in that sentence shot me.

"But what about Tammy?" *That's what you ask?* Instead of *Are you gonna assassinate me when my back is turned?*

"Tammy?" He lowers his brows in question. "Why are you bringing her up at *this* moment exactly?" I roll my eyes. "*Say it.* Whatever it is. You always have anyway," he says tenderly.

He's so caring, unlike Ore's destructiveness. "I saw you kiss her."

"I didn't kiss her!" he says so fast and takes a step towards me. "If you're referring to what happened on the deck, I stopped her. I didn't know you saw that. I would've explained." When I look away, he darts over to me. "I know she has some kind of crush on me, but I don't feel the same."

He delicately places his hand on my cheek and whispers in my ear. "Now are you afraid of me?" I shake my head. "But you're shaking." He grabs my hands. I'm only shaking because he's this close to me.

"I'm not," I say softly.

"Good, then come with me. Let's get away from it all, even if it's just for a little while."

"Now?" He nods.

"Okay." He walks out of my door like a normal person and gives me a chance to get myself together, my outfit, and my heart.

42

What If I Trusted Your Sweet?

As soon as I hear the front door shut, I call Addison, and she makes mention of Liam being, *the one*. I tell her to come back to one from ten because I may very well be dead by tonight. And she tells *me*, her best-est friend in the world, to shut up.

"Mommy, what do you think?" I pose in the mirror, wearing a white lace dress with a small split on the side and sleeves that hang under my shoulders. My hair and makeup are perfect. I picture Mama looking at me in the mirror as she always did, and I can't help looking behind my shoulder. Oh, how I want her to barge in without knocking *just once more*. I wipe tears.

Still shaking from earlier, I walk out. Liam is scrolling on his phone, leaning against his car as always. I can imagine my tapping shoes quickly caught his attention, *him being an assassin and all*. I shake my head of the thought.

"Wow," he says. *My heart is racing.* He has on a plain white T-shirt, jeans, and a black leather jacket that fits just right. His hair is combed back to perfection, and as always, he's super cute. I stand there awkwardly until he snaps out of it.

"You're gorgeous!" I smile. *OMG!*

We're quiet. I've ridden in his car a thousand times, and *now* it's weird.

"You comfortable?"

"Yes."

"That's . . . that's good," he says, straightening up in his seat, tapping his thumbs on the steering wheel. I clear my throat as we pull up behind an old building with shattered windows that looks as though it could collapse at any moment. *Is this where he's gonna do it?* Is this where they'll find my body? All of a sudden, a clear bubble surrounds us. The car lifts and glides slowly into the sky.

"We're going to New Orleans," he says.

"Isn't it really far?" I ask.

"A day away, but we'll be there in an hour, tops. I want to enjoy the view," he says, staring at me. I look the city over. It's extravagant up here.

"Can they see us?"

"No."

How romantic, I can just hear Addison say. "What's in New Orleans?"

"A surprise," he says with a captivating smile I've never seen before. "What do you usually do for fun?" he asks.

When I think about it, I realize *nothing.* Most of my enjoyment comes from hanging with Arch. Embarrassment hits me. "I'm always working, and my best friend is a million miles away."

"Working at the shop?"

I close my eyes, knowing I'll have to share the story of my mother once again. But I feel safe. Even though I may be far from the word. I nod. "It belonged to my mother before she passed from Lupus a few months ago."

"I'm sorry," he says. I wonder if this'll turn into one of those sad songs I've been hearing for months now. "I can relate. Both my parents passed in a car accident when I was fifteen. But we should change the subject before this day goes differently than what I had in mind." *He understands.*

"Agreed. I'm so sorry about your parents."

"Thanks." He looks at the hand I'd placed over his, and I take it away.

"But like your mom, they left me a few businesses I run. My dad wanted me to take over one day. I guess he got his wish." *Thus the suits he wears.* "I own this Italian restaurant I want to take you to one day." His words come to a halt, his situation bouncing between us. "God willing," he adds, and I smile.

We talk for the rest of the way, until an indictor sounds, and he pulls a lever. We descend, his car hits the middle of an empty highway, and he speeds away.

After eating at a nice restaurant, he pulls up to a crowded area. "We're going to a masquerade ball."

"You mean, like, with masks?" I ask.

"Yeah. May I?" he asks with his hand extended. I'm not sure what he's going to do, but I nod. All of a sudden, I have on a sparkly black dress and black heels. I look around, but there's no one in sight. Then I look at my reflection in the window. I have on a shimmery mask with an overflow of jewels.

The necklace he places on me is mine but different. I stare at it. *The diamonds are real.* So, does he have the power to summon any object?

"I told you it was for someone special." I'm floored. He repeats the technique on himself, and suddenly he has on a black tux that fits him nicely, a crisp white dress shirt, and a gold mask. I try not to drool. "Shall we?" he so charmingly asks.

We walk into a large noisy room, instantly noticing a security guard eyeing us a little too hard. Liam scans him.

"I think I know him," I say.

"He does look familiar." I never thought we'd know the same people. He dismisses it after a while and comes close to whisper in my ear, "You're stunning, my Juliet." I melt. I played Juliet in my school play. I bat my eyes at him as a tall woman with red hair pulls me back. We're both caught completely off guard.

"Now, dear, men over on the left, women on the right. If he's yours, he'll find you." *If he's mine?* I look back at Liam. He looks displeased, hands in his pockets, as I'm whisked away.

I stand with a lot of women on a long case of stairs leading up to a singular upper level. The men's side is the same. My head peeks over all the different colored hairs and masks, trying to spot Liam, but there's too many of them. I finally just lean up against the wall, pouting. "Did you see the guy in all black with a gold mask?" My head turns to attention. A girl in a pink dress and white mask says she has to be talking about Liam.

"I think he's Romeo," says one with a black dress, black mask, with green peacock feathers sticking out of it.

"I'll be his Juliet," says the third wheel, and I find myself examining my nails to decide which one I'll scratch first. I think about all the girls that have tried to come between us now, and it's exhausting. I look carefully at them and decide they don't have a chance . . . *right?*

Man over speaker: "Ladies and gentlemen, the moment has now arrived for you to find that special one! Whether you came with them, are trying to find a date for the night, or seek a soulmate for life, now is the time to do so."

All the ladies around me are excited, and I'm sweating.

Man over speaker: "If you saw that pretty lady walk in, go talk to her! The good Lord once said a man that finds a wife finds a good thing, but be warned. You officially seal the deal on the dance floor, so don't go stealing someone else's date! Mingle if you will, but you only have ten minutes to find your soulmate. On your mark, get set . . . Booooyyss!"

He points at his band and they start playing. The piano keys roll over the board so fast and sharp as everyone makes their way down to the floor. I realize I had been standing there in thought. The three stooges are already dodging past people and made it midways to the guys' side. "Great!" I gather my dress and run down.

I spontaneously spin around. *Liam? No,* a red-masked guy with all red on stands before me. I panic when I realize we're on the dance floor by design, so this is my soulmate? *I think NOT!* Where is my Romeo? "OMG!" I am a mess. Disbelief hits me when Red whirls me to the middle of the dance floor. I look around the room but don't see Liam at all.

"Lolly?" I hear him in my mind. I look around, and he's across the room.

"Liam!" Then I spot *the three.* They've found him and are pulling him between the crowd. We're both spinning around with different people, and I can see Liam is upset I'm with Red. The girls all talk to him at once, moving his hands around, forcing him to dance.

"What's your name?" Red asks, but I'm searching for Liam, who disappeared. He twirls me and our hands break as Liam grabs mine and brings me in.

"You okay?" he asks and I nod.

"Aye man, what's the big idea? She belongs to me!" Red says, but the human being has no idea what he's getting himself into. I can feel Liam's temperature rising. I'm terrified for Red. *Liam can't bring Ore out.* I want to calm him, but I don't know how.

"Liam?" I call, but he answers the guy instead.

"Oh, yeah?" He lets go of me. I put my hands over my mouth and want to cry as he walks towards him. I can hear Liam chuckling, or is it Ore?

"Liam!" I call, going forward and grabbing his arm before he gets too far.

Two guys run up alongside *Reddie, the Red Masked Don,* their fists balled up. "Yo, you a-right, man? Or do we need to handle something?"

"Let's go. I'll take all of you," says Liam. I feel rattled, wanting to throw a hand over Ore's fly mouth, pulling his arm with two hands.

The two guys jump forward, but Red stops them. "No!" he says.

"Man, just give me one hit, and I'll knock him out clean," says one of Red's friends. I wrap my arm around Liam's, and his temperature steadies.

"Shut up!" Red yells like a child, and they relax.

I giggle behind Liam's shoulder, and I can tell Liam wants to too, but he keeps his composure. "Waste of my time," he says, and I shush him. "Look, I don't want any trouble," says Red. "We came all the way from Charleston to have a good time!"

Red has words with his friends, pointing out their struggle. "Is this your man, pretty lady?" Red says. "Because me bringing you to this dance floor sealed the deal like mic man said."

"Who said you could talk to her?" Liam says sternly. It seems he's used to fighting all his battles, but sometimes you have to let things go.

"I'm with him," I say before this transpires.

"Okay then . . ." They all walk away, mumbling, still watching Liam.

"All this for a chick, bro?" one says.

Liam shakes his head, annoyed. His eyebrows are still lowered long before they've vanished. I put my hand on his handsome face, and his features refresh. I get super shy and drop it. "Sorry."

"Don't apologize." He sweeps my hair behind my ear and stares into my eyes. Is he going to kiss me? Suddenly, Liam is pulled back.

"Come hang out with us." I look around Liam's shoulder and see the three stooges.

"I'm good," Liam says and grabs my hand. They're bickering as we walk away. "I knew that was his Juliet!" We laugh in disbelief. Why did I think it would've gone any other way?

Liam whirls me around and pulls me close. "Unforgettable," the song he played on my radio, is now being played by the jazz band, and he rests his head on mine. I remember the way Bryan pulled me around at prom, but even our slow dance wasn't as intimate as this. It's the way his hand rests at the small of my back, the way he seems to adore being this close to me. I imagine his eyes are closed like mine. Liam sings to me. I smile. Is he saying *I'm unforgettable?* If I weren't oblivious to love, I'd think I was falling in it right now. *And if he were truly my assassin, I'd go freely into his trap.*

43

Tête-a-Tête
{A Private Conversation}

He looks up as if something's caught his eye. "C'mon," he says. I lift my head off of his shoulder and feel the difference when I detach. A gust of confusion hits as he pulls me up the stairs. We go through a locked door and are high above ground, standing on a bar of concrete with no way down. I scan the room and see paint buckets spread throughout the room atop their sheets, showing this room is under construction.

The room starts to clear of debris, and buckets get dragged until they disappear into the wall. Sheets dance as if they have feet and twist into nothingness. Caution signs vanish and then everything else until there's just a glistening marble floor. A thick gold railing starts to build right in front of us, bar by bar sparkling in the air. Liam lets go of my hand and stands dangerously close to the edge. I catch my breath, forgetting he can hover. He puts a foot out, and a brick of marble forms to catch his step. He grins at me before going down quickly and easily, steps appearing as he goes.

I don't breathe until he's on solid ground.It's funny how gravity can trick the mind. When he goes to the center of the room and looks up at me, I know exactly what this is. I'm completely fascinated. I can't hide that his ways are like shooting stars to me, *astounding*. I go back to my memories of Romeo and Juliet, trying to remember the lines as Liam dims the lights. Looking down at his gazing eyes, I start:

Juliet

O Romeo, Romeo! Wherefore art thou Romeo? Deny thy father and refuse thy name

Or, if thou wilt not, be but sworn my love. And I'll no longer be a Capulet.

'Tis but thy name that is my enemy.

Thou art thyself, though not a Montague. What's Montague? It is nor hand nor foot, Nor arm, nor face, nor any other part Belonging to a man. O, be some other name! What's in a name? That which we call a rose By any other word would smell as sweet.

So Romeo lose your name, trade it in Which has nothing to do with you and take All of me in exchange."

Romeo

I take thee at thy word.

Call me but love, and I'll be new, baptized. Henceforth, I never will be Romeo.

I know not how to tell thee who I am.

My name, dear saint, is hateful to myself

Because it is an enemy to thee.

Had I it written, I would tear the word."

Juliet

My ears have not yet drunk a hundred words Of that tongue's uttering, yet I know the sound. Art thou not Romeo, and a Montague?

Romeo

Neither, fair maid, if either thee dislike.

Me

Are you not Ore? And my assassin? I whisper to myself.

"But the chains," I say. The room slowly turns back to muck at his sadness.

"I'm still here." He smiles and I nod, grateful he's still free and here with me. Outside there's a Mardi Gras parade, and we join it before leaving.

We now speed down the highway to home, Liam's hand in mine. "Did you have fun?" he says.

"Lots."

"Better than fighting a forest full of creatures?"

"We did that?" I ask. We laugh. That seems so unreal now. I'm loving the calmness of a normal, quiet life. Liam then stops abruptly. The security guard from the ball is in the road, in the middle of nowhere. We get out of the car. Right before our eyes, he melts into The Profit. They clap hands.

"What are you doing here?" asks Liam.

"Watching you two," says The Profit.

"What? Why?" asks Liam.

"Can't say. You need to get to Tamron. An enemy is among us."

We arrive at the heavily guarded government building. Liam rolls down his window for the guard at the gate. "Sir," says the man in uniform. He nods at another guard peeking out of the guardhouse, and the gate begins to open. I look across the area. I see it looks just like it did in the Spiritual Realm but is even more guarded.

"Lieutenant Blue," says soldier after soldier as we walk into the building. He nods at them. I look at him. *Lieutenant?*

"I was just about to call you! Why'd you bring her?" says Tammy as we walk in. *Well, excuse me!*

"Chill," says Liam.

She clears her throat, looking at our date attire. She spreads blueprints on a huge round table. "This, is the realm bridge Satan has been building with Du'jomi's mother, the witch."

"He finished it?" says Liam.

"Yep, with the black pixie coal you transported."

Liam quickly looks at me. That has to be the rocks he was collecting the night we met.

"To get into the Spiritual Realm?" I ask.

"Yes," they say in unison, although Tammy sounds annoyed I even asked. Liam sounds shameful, maybe even disappointed.

"Recently, kata teamed up with a supernatural named Grand." She opens a folder and hands him a paper off the top of a thick stack. I get on my tippy toes to look at it. "According to an inside man working for Reynolds, Grand fell into a tank filled with Z71 that was just sittin' at some old military base in Minnesota. Remember that acid chemical we created to fuel military weaponry."

"Ouch . . . That was what, two years ago?"

"Right, but when we put it in the guns, it was useless. What we didn't know is for it to be effective, it needed to be combined with human blood. That's how he got supernatural powers." She spreads out numerous printed sheets of him using his power. I study them. It looks like he's melting people. Horrific.

"You know the witch, Gavenla, Du'Jomi's mother?" Tammy continues, "I've been reading her book. It says the bridge needs someone who's connected to the Spiritual Realm on the livin' side to open its gates." She picks up a long black book. "And in *Galein's Book of Sorcery*, it says that when a witch dies, her power isn't as strong as it was when she was livin'. So she needs to combine her power on the Realm's side, with a living being, for the bridge to work. So, they'll be beating at the door on both sides."

I sigh. We just got back from Vaimos, and my body is still sore from fighting and my skin parched from the atmosphere there. Couldn't they have chosen a different time to attack?

Tammy tells us about all of Grand's mini-me's. About some kid named Mckenzie who was under the care of a *Dr. Fischer* and how they were gonna use him as the link to the Spiritual Realm because of his mental power.

"Daisy's father died a few months ago, and they say he was killed by the devil," says Tammy. She and I look at William.

"What was his name?" he hesitantly asks.

"Christopher Flores, Washington, DC."

"Can we just move on . . ." says a grumpy Liam.

Tammy slaps down Galein's book to a page. "The Stone Dagger was taken from the base they broke into a few days ago. It converts anything it cuts into stone, but we dunno how it connects."

"Why are they trying to get into the Spiritual Realm?" I ask and we look at Liam.

"He's trying to turn people against God. He said if he can't change God's mind about us, he'll change our minds about God. What better way is there to corrupt someone than from the inside out, where they're most vulnerable?"

His words almost sound poetic had they not been a monstrosity. Imagine being asleep, then waking up a mindless zombie, hating God. Not because you decided to, but because someone programmed it into your mind by default? That's not fair. Even God gives us free will, but He desires for all of us to love Him. And I do, very much.

"Is that even possible? God has guards at the gate? What about us? God Himself?" They're quiet.

"We have to check the gate," I say, and Tammy grabs her coat.

"Not you. If kata finds out you've been helping me, he'd bring you down with me." Then she changes her mind, saying, "Fine. But let me give you somethin'."

She takes us to garage doors. Inside there are two motorcycles, one metallic black and one blue one. They're thin in structure. "I designed these with you in mind," she says all chipper.

"They're incredible!" He's so into it. "The fastest in the world! I tried to top the Tomahawk's 420 mph. I'm pretty sure it's illegal." The helmet is almost nonexistent, and a black strip is in front of his forehead with a piece by his mouth.

"It protects with less coverage, so we can still see your beautiful face." She taps it, and the full helmet comes into display, then disappears again.

"Thanks, Tams."

"It has lasers, activated by Merth core, and it is solar powered."

"Did you say Merth?" asks Liam.

"Yeah, somethin' wrong?" We both shake our heads, knowing where Merth comes from, and how it goes back, then look at the metal beneath him.

She turns the helmet into a small gadget and presses it into a missing patch in the bike. She pulls at it like a handle, and the bike flips and bends around her hand until it clamps to complete a watch, then fastens it on his wrist. "All yours. If you ever need the other one, you know where to find me. I doubt anything can destroy it, but remember, *we have the only two on the planet!* Later Cowboy," she says before exiting. He looks like he has candy, *actual candy,* in his possession.

44

My New Normal Isn't

We drive through the streets on his bike. He informed me this was only his second time riding. I held on for dear life, but the ride was smooth. Being so close to him makes me feel a connection I want to protect with all I have. When we get to the gate, it's all clear.

"We are not in the dark of such allegations. We have doubled our watch but trust that the Mighty One will complete what is written," say The Thrice, and we make plans to help guard it too.

The next morning, my alarm goes off, and I struggle to get up from body fatigue. My life was so much more simpler when it was just me and the shop. I finally get in my jeep today and turn on my colorful radio. I close my eyes and let the colors splash on my eyelids. My space feels good but somehow so ordinary without all the hype of superhero-ism. *Would I go back to normal if I had the chance?* Instead of pondering things I have no control over, I put the gear in D, hoping I remember how to drive.

At the shop, I sit in the parking space me and mama use to park in. I know what The Thrice meant when they spoke of trust. We don't have to fight every battle because there's a power at work here that reaches far beyond our comprehension. Yes, things are going on in the dark that no preparation can get you ready for, but that's where prayer comes in. Jesus can reach places we could never reach, speak to those whom we could never persuade with our own words, and end wars with a mere insect because He is in control. *Wow, Arch has really rubbed off on me.* I'm amazed at how much I've changed. I grab my locket and say, "You would be so proud, Mama."

My phone vibrates. *It's Liam.* "Hey," I say, not knowing if I can breathe right now.

"Sup?"

"I'm at the shop. How was first watch?"

"Working? At a time like this?" I can picture the look of annoyance on his face.

"I haven't been. People are gonna start to protest. I can just feel Mom cringing at my business decisions lately," I say.

"You should *try* to live as normal as possible. The stakeout went good." *As possible* is right. So he agrees life's never gonna be the same.

"Listen, I apologize for what happened in New Orleans. I promised myself I wouldn't behave that way anymore, and I guess the old me just came out." I am surprised. His owning up to it is refreshing.

"I understand. There's an old me I try not to let get out either. We can just try our best."

"Yeah," he simply says.

"But last night was really nice," I say.

"Glad you enjoyed it." I did, besides all the drama that comes along so easily these days.

"So you're in the army?" He sighs . . . *oh no.*

"I am." *He's being short with me.*

"Are you serving now?"

"Yeah." *I've never seen him in uniform.*

"Do you work with Tammy?" I roll my eyes at the mention of her name and eagerly await an answer.

"No, I'm stationed in Vermont."

Vermont? That's so far away. "Do you like it?"

"Yeah, I can't really talk about it, that's all." I wonder why he's in the army if he can do extraordinary things. And more importantly, the fact that he's a supernatural and still feels the need to keep government secrets is admirable.

"Oh, I'm sorry."

"Can I ask *you* something now?" His question surprises me. Did he answer mine because he had one of his own?

"Yeah."

"I'm guessing you said yes to a date because you don't have a boyfriend?" Does he think I'm the kind of girl that would go out with him if I did?

"I don't . . . have a boyfriend."

"Could I be?" He did not just say that! Suddenly my lungs feel vacuumed tight, and my cheeks tingle.

"Liam . . ."

"I know it's not a good time, but if I can't have anything else, my freedom, my life, *give me you. For as much time as I have left.*"

My jaw drops, and I hold on to my heart that has suffered too many emotional tugs, hoping it won't desert me for abuse. He exhales as if he's pushing himself to say these passionate words: "I didn't think I could bring someone into my jacked-up life, but you make me feel like you can handle me and my... *situation.* I hope I'm not being selfish, but you're everything I never knew I wanted and more."

"Liam?" I'm overflowing with emotion, and I have to tell him that he doesn't have to say more because *I'm his.* I have been since day one and have a feeling I'll always be.

"Yeah?" He finally gets the chance to breathe.

"I've never had a boyfriend, but I would love that."

Finally, an authentic *normal life* moment.

"Never?"

"Yes," I say coyly.

"So yes then, despite everything you know about me?"

"Everything and anything, Liam," I say straight from my heart. I guess my ticker decided to stick with me after all.

I check on Bot at the gate. She's now living with Liam, and I think it's a great idea. Then I head to the shop to do some cleaning.

"Oh hey, Lolly doll," says Labelle from Pin It Up Hair Salon.

"Hey, Bell." She tells me my ends look terrible, and it'll bother her all day if she doesn't snip them.

"Okay," I say. I often wonder what would've happened if I never accepted her offer. It was such a small thing, but it changed everything. And maybe, just maybe, if I wouldn't have done it, *they* would still be here.

The customers bombard me with questions about my absence, and I apologize all day. I planned to take a lunch to check on Liam and Bot, but I didn't get a moment to spare. I now clean the glass of a broken vase someone's wild child dropped. *Will I be able to handle both worlds?* The door bells chime. Another customer . . . I inhale and exhale. Shyness overtakes me as Liam walks through the door. I'm stuck. He zooms over to me and leans on my counter like he'd done when we were strangers.

"Liam," I say in a panic, knowing he'd been blowing me up with no reply.

"Baby," he says. I can't ignore the pull his eyes are inducing. I feel so guilty.

"It's been such a long day. I'm sorry."

"Is everything okay?"

"Yeah, I just . . . thought maybe you were having second thoughts about us."

"No! Of course not. I've just been so tied up, and now I'm freaking out even more because of how I made you feel." He grabs my wrist and pulls me around the small counter, straight into his arms, and I fall like a baby into his embrace.

"I love your haircut." He noticed, and it makes me smile. He helps me close up shop and walks me to my car, insisting I go home and rest. That he and Bot had the gate under control. I hesitantly depart.

I get home, carrying extras from the shop and drop them as I see Arch running down the road. I run after him. "Arch?" We are on an empty street, and two puppies, one black and one gray, are challenging Arch. The dogs grow, and their fur turns to metal. How are they able to show themselves in the middle of the street?

"Oh my gosh!" I say.

"Stay back!" says Arch. "They're Grand's mutts."

"Oh! *Oh* . . ." They charge at Arch, and he doesn't back down. I watch Arch, who is ten times smaller, bite one of the dog's neck. Then he tosses him to the side like a sack.

"Fire fall down from heaven!" Arch says and puts his paw out in front of him. Lightning inflamed with magenta streaks strikes them, rusting their shiny tin.

They cry and Arch growls, his paws apart in attack mode. They get up, and I feel my chest pumping as I watch my friend run towards the scrap hounds. He jolts from side to side, and I can barely catch up. He jumps up and pounces on both their heads, ramming each into the ground. *He's killing it.* They fall, shuffling their legs to get up. A car drives by, and they leap on to it to get to Arch. Their spit drips on to the hood of the car, and it steams up. When the dogs are finally off, it scurries away.

A flash of light ticks, and I cover my eyes as they grow sensitive. When I finally look up, two men in white tunics appear, standing strong and fierce. One has long blonde hair and the other short brown hair.

"You are in direct violation against the kingdom of God," he says to the dogs. "You have shown your power on earth with no cause. You are now banished to the ends of the earth." They take out swords and zap the two pups, and the angels disappear along with them.

I run to Arch. "You did great. I thought God . . ." *was going to take you.* I don't finish that sentence. I look over and see someone watching us. His skin is blue, and I recognize him from the pictures. "Arch?" My dog growls, and the figure runs and gets into an SUV that speeds off.

"You're next!" calls Arch, and I can't believe I actually saw *Grand.*

The next day is Josh's big game. Daddy took baby bro in early to practice. I have to call my best friend to fill her in on my new life, but even that feels like a task.

"Hellooooo! Earth to Cher!" *Oh gosh,* attitude on ten already.

"Hey, best friend," I sweetly say, hoping for mercy.

"Don't you *best friend* me! What's going on!"

Ouch. I lean against my wall. My life is changing, and it seems out of control. But really, I am now in God's hands, and *He is in control.* I don't call the shots, and I don't have the luxury to just sit around and tell my friend every detail about my life anymore. But that doesn't mean I shouldn't try. I tell her about Liam and me and end with, "He said I was everything he ever wanted."

"He did?" She turns into butter on a skillet.

I tell Addison about my new mission, and she says she doesn't want to be a zombie, so fight hard. *I agree.* I promise myself to fill Josh in on everything and pray for Jesus to help me balance out priorities while waiting on Liam to meet me outside of Josh's game. He gets out of his old school, and I get shy all over again.

I admire his burgundy jacket and all black underneath.

Nervousness kicks in. We sit mid-crowd hand-in-hand. Daddy looks up at Liam and me. He's sitting near Josh. While smiling, Daddy nods at Liam, who nods back. *Very weird.*

Josh's team is now down four points. "C'mon Josh!" I get up and yell. Arch jumps beside me, and I can tell he's trying not to bark. Liam smiles at me. He's not very animated, although very outgoing.

"Josh! What was that!" I yell.

He throws both hands up, probably telling me to shut up. I sit down, realizing my competitive side is getting the best of me. Liam is focused on the ball. *What is he doing?* Josh kicks the ball, and it goes into the goal. We jump up and cheer with everyone.

"Wooooo! Let's go!" Liam finally shouts. I giggle.

My excitement takes over, and I push him. He grabs my arm. *Lolly, haven't you learned not to poke at him?* Our eyes meet, and we're so close that what happens next is inevitable. Our lips lock and everything around us gets lost—the noisy crowd, the bleachers bouncing as people jump in excitement, the announcer announcing the gain of three points, and even the fact that Arch is sitting right next to me. It's just us and the starry sky above. *Our second, first kiss.* It's even better than the first, and that one was breathtaking. Is it possible to do this, *just this,* for a whole day?

Everyone starts to get quiet, and we break. We look around and sit down with the people looking at us. I dig my head into his shoulder and giggle. He laughs with me. At this point, I think we're both embarrassed. Never would I have imagined when I first met this flame of a boy that I'd be kissing him *as his girlfriend* instead of kicking him in the face. But I did kiss him, and I believe I always wanted to, even the night we first met.

Josh's team is finally up one point, and we're waiting to see the next play.

"Did you um . . . help Josh score back there?"

"No," he says, blowing into his hands. I realize that the wishbone is going off. It must've burned him. He puts it inside his jacket and gets up.

"We gotta go." *Now*? I look at my brother on the field and hate that I have to leave like this, but duty calls once again.

We run out of the stadium gates. By the time we get to a spot we won't be seen, Liam's jacket is smoking. He takes the Talis out and shakes it. I look up at light rain sprinkling in the air. "It has to be them, the spark is too powerful. Let's go," says Liam. I nod.

We look around first, then Liam takes off. Arch runs under him, but I can't move. I stand on my tippy toes to start flying, but it's not working! Liam notices and comes back down, and Arch follows. This is so embarrassing.

"What's wrong?"

"I can't fly."

"Why?" Arch asks me, and I don't have an answer.

45
Another Way

I try everything, but nothing's working.

"They must've done something," says Liam.

"No, you still have your powers," I'm almost in tears. The time finally comes for me to be ready, and I'm not.

"Okay, we have to figure this out. Did you do anything outside the norm?" asks Arch.

"No," except the fact that Liam is now my boyfriend, but that couldn't be it, *could it?* I look at him and can't believe what I'm about to suggest. "Maybe us?"

"What?" Arch says, and it hits Liam. We're legit angel vs demon.

"No, that's not why," Liam protests, and it hits me in my heart. "That is not why, okay?" He grabs my hand, but why does it sound like he's not convinced himself? I play along and nod.

"No, you two are destined to be together," Arch says.

"What?" we say.

"What else? There has to be something else, Lolly," Arch says sternly. Liam exhales as if he was holding his breath this whole time.

My eyes blink, trying to remember anything *different*, because if we don't figure this out and reverse it, I'll be useless on the battlefield. I close my eyes and hear Bell's scissors that now sound like weapons. "I got a haircut yesterday."

"Lolly, I told you not to do anything drastic."

"How was I supposed to know doing an everyday thing was considered drastic?"

"I said anything, *a-n-y-t-h-i-n-g* that changes you. But it's done now, and we're not gonna have your power to fight against Satan, the one thing we've been working on for weeks." My spirit is completely crushed, and tears roll down my cheeks. I look away, wiping them quickly.

"Arch, I'm sorry." Liam squeezes my hand.

"Everything counts, even the small stuff when it comes to God. And just in case you aren't realizing it, it's gonna take all of us to beat this. God is strategic, and we can delay things when we take a different route. *But,* He can turn it for our good." I know Arch is serious about God's business, so I can't be mad that he's upset. "We have to go," he says, and we run to Liam's car.

When we pull up, The Profit stops us. "We have reinforcements for you, but we have to hurry." He takes us to a part of the alley we've never been. Flashes of light fill a large gap in the wall, and three warriors appear. A beautiful girl with bangs and a sword taller than her sticks it in the ground, and she leans on it.

"Blee, Chan, and Ahor," says The Profit, introducing them to me. They don't speak. They're serious like Arch.

"Nice to see I'll be fighting with old friends," says Arch. I sigh.

"And—" says The Profit, when he is interrupted by the sound of heavy feet running towards us. It's some sort of lion man.

"Cannon!" says Liam.

"Sup, Ore, you mangy mutt!" His country accent is so thick.

"They brought the best out, I see," says Liam.

For the first time, I feel as though I'm out of the circle, all because of a haircut. I look at Blee. *Is she supposed to be my replacement? I try my hardest not to walk away like the old me and start to wonder if they'd be here if I could fight.*

"Glad everyone is well acquainted," says The Profit. *Yeah, everyone except me.* "They attacked the other side of the realm. It's been sealed for years in Central Park. Civilians are being evacuated as we speak." *There's another side! Furthermore,* no one is supposed to know we exist! "All they see is a huge storm, focused on one part of the city," he says. I'm grateful God is still in control. I text my dad and tell him to stay away. "Now go. They'll lead the way," he says, pointing at the new shiny crew. They fly into the night.

I look at my dog, and he transforms into a cutie right before my eyes, the angel that properly introduced himself to me in my dreams. "Wow," I say out loud. *He's magnificent.* He smiles at me and soars away. Liam and I are left. He turns into Ore and is still intimidating, boyfriend or not. He puts his hand on my shoulder.

"Maybe it'll be better if you take my car and go home?" I pull back from him.

"I'm not leaving you or Arch."

"I know, but it was worth a shot." We laugh. "You can come. I just need you to stay away from the fun. I don't want anything to happen to my first girlfriend."

"I'm not your first girlfriend!" Before he can confirm or deny, he whisks us off.

Now that we're in the sky, I can see the storm swirling around in a ball and hear people screaming. We see a big truck that must've transported the bridge. He glides down speedily and drops me off by a tree. I can see everything clearly now. The whirlwind was just a cover.

"I put a forcefield around you. Please don't move. I mean it." I nod. *Ore* kisses me on my forehead, then flies away so fast I didn't see where he landed. But what's up with him? Liam is so romantic, but I never thought Ore would be mushy. I look around, and I start to get uneasy about the chaos afar.

I see Bot. She must've gotten here first. She's fighting Wildcard. He's moving quickly, and there's at least three of him. Cannon is fighting winged demons. They're dark brown with mini horns, wrinkled skin, and bright red eyes. *Gross.*

I see Liam now, talking to the infamous blue-colored dude, *Grand.* Could Grand's chemicals hurt him? I would like to think nothing could after what he endured in the forest. There's a big light radiating from a gap in between trees. The bridge on the floor is flat but arches a little off of the ground. There are thorn-like designs rippling throughout it, and I see a glowing boy. *That has to be Mckenzie.* I see a dark figure in the corner with Mckenzie, *the devil.*

As my eyes go back and forth between friends, I see someone land that could be the enemy. *Vonvex, he called her?* I stand there cold as ice, thinking about what he could've said to persuade her to even step foot on ground shared by him. The thought sets my own skin ablaze, and my fingers grow numb from the hot and cold I'm experiencing. I see her twist over towards Liam. It sickens me that she's here helping him and I can't.

"God, if you can hear me . . ." I look up to the sky, and my eyes widen. An army fills it, and swords fly. Angels are being led by Arch to slay flying demons. I gasp. I can't just stay here doing nothing. If my hands can't work, I know my prayer will. "God, I'm sorry for cutting my hair, but this is why you gave me power. And if you give it back . . ." I look around, "I'll win. I'll make sure I close the realm and put everything back in its rightful place."

"*Move.*"

"What?" Did I really just hear that? My eyes search for someone who could be nearby. "Was that you, God?" I hear nothing. Liam told me not to move, but those are the very words I just heard. I try to fly, but I still can't!

"God, help me please," I say silently. "*Move first.*" I hear it even clearer this time. Like God talks to Arch, He is now talking to me! I take off towards them, trying to spark my electricity up, but it isn't coming.

My eyes go to Liam first. He's juggling black rings in the air and throwing them at a stretched Grand. They spin around his neck and wrist, holding him in place. Liam holds Grand's head, hovers in the air, and places his feet on Grand's shoulders as if he's going to snap it off. Like clockwork, he looks over at me running into battle. He shouts my name. Then I hear, "What are you doing?" in my head. I shake it off and continue to run, trusting God will show up.

I see a demon creeping up on a distracted Vonvex. I look around for help, but everyone is tied up. I look down for a weapon, but the floor is clear. Then I spot Cannon ripping a monster apart, and its jawbone gets thrown nearby. I pick it up and throw it like a boomerang. It tears part of his neck off, and I jump on a bench and roundhouse kick it like Mr. Van taught me. His head spins, and he falls to the ground stone still. Von grins at me, then turns back to Daze. Von is holding a strap tightly behind her head that stops her from speaking, and she is trying to snatch the dagger with the other.

Mckenzie has stepped on to the bridge. The devil whispers to him, and the witch is chanting, disappearing, and reappearing. Could she be going in and out of the gate? Mckenzie's eyes look gone, like he has no control. *Daze.* I am sure of it. Remembering what I promised God, I run to Mckenzie and somehow successfully push him off of the bridge. I pushed past a tough-looking forcefield.

"How did she break the barrier?" thunders Satan to Gavenla, a slender woman with long white hair.

"The child has no powers, and the barrier blocks supernaturals only. I didn't know a human was among them," she says. I realized then that Jesus had in fact worked my misfortune for my good like Arch said, even if it didn't look like it at the moment.

Gavenla walks up to me and says, "Who are you, child?"

She asks in an authoritative way that's still smooth, so I answer, "Lolly Pobs." I hear Daze chanting and look her way. Mckenzie is on the ground, fighting the trance. I look beside her at a stony figure next to Daze. It can't be! She turned Vonvex to stone. I begin to breathe heavily. Daze extends her hands out to pierce the stone.

"No!" Liam shouts and freezes her. Grand grabs a handful of Liam's hair and punches him over and over again. His concentration is wavering, and Daze is slowly moving out of the restraint. I sniffle because I don't know what to do.

"He's the one you love, isn't he?" the witch asks.

Without thinking, I say, "Yes."

"Tsk, tsk, tsk. Yet he calls out to another." I stare at her. I didn't confess to loving him before I even knew I did, for her to throw that in my face. I don't really know why I told her. Maybe because right now I'm emotional. I ignore her.

"Tell me, do you know of my son, Du'Jomi? If you give me this information, I will tell you the fate of his and your love." *Our fate?*

I look around at the pain going on. How could I be so selfish to worry about my relationship right now when I have to find a way to help? Plus, I get instruction and the like from God, not from some witch using her talents in a dark way. I look at Liam. No matter what our fate is, right now all I know is I love him, and we're destined to be together.

"You don't have to tell me anything. He's fine, back on Vaimos." Breath isn't coming into my lungs fast enough, but *I am not about to have a panic attack right now.* I go to the ground, and Gavenla rubs my back.

"Easy child, nothing tea won't fix, a cup a day." She calms me even though my skin crawls at her hellish appearance. She's very pale with dark shadows over her features. The death-look is the only thing taking away from her beauty. I pull away, but she gets closer. "The boy will drag you down with him to the depths of hell. You will ask yourself if love conquers all. It does child, but it also changes."

A gust of wind blows, and leaves sweep over my face. I throw my hands up. When I come out of the spiral, she's gone. *He'll do what?* My mind is racing, my blood is rushing, and my knees are weak. At the same time, I'm trying to pull myself off of the ground.

Back onto the bridge, Daze is trying to talk Mckenzie. I grab the dagger from her side. "Give it back!" I don't. "A. Freeze!" she yells, and I hear feet hitting the ground behind me. Someone detains me, and she tells them, "My powers don't work on her." I look back, *it's the soldier from the pictures.*

I try to break away, fly, or do anything as I look at Vonvex. She's as blocked as bricks, and I don't want that to be me. Daze snatches the dagger.

"Liam! Arch!" I yell. I hate that I need to call for help.

"Lolly!" Liam's voice sounds strained, and I look over. Grand has Liam's arms behind his back and is creating an acid tornado around them both. *Are we losing?* I really look at Freeze. It seems he's under a spell himself. I feel a sharp pain on my shoulder, and I see blood running down my arm. *Did Daze just stab me?*

"I like her purple hair," I faintly hear Daze say. My vision is blurred, going in, and out. I look down and see my feet turning to stone, and the gray is now crawling up my thighs.

"Liam . . ." I whisper.

I look over and see Wildcard rip off Bot's arm, and green liquid squirts out. She retrieves it with the other. I see Daze pull back the knife and break Vonvex's stone. Each piece hits concrete to concrete. We *are* losing. *Jesus, are we losing? Is it my fault?* Tears stream down my face. I feel Adam rush back and a light sting from William's fire is felt on the skin I have left. The stiffness is now felt on my stomach. It's *growing, growing.*

I hear my love say, "Lolly, I'm gonna . . . I'm gonna do something." He seems unsure as he touches the stone on my arms and looks at Vonvex's remains. "Lolly I . . . I'm sorry. I love you." I can hear his throat trembling, and he puts his forehead on mine. I look into his eyes and see his heart, but before I can say it back, the stone covers my mouth, my cheeks, and nose. Then everything goes pitch black. *I love you, William Blue, my first and only love.*

46

Home to You

I wake up on an empty street. It's black with freshly painted yellow lines on it. I like the smell. I suck it in and rub my fingers over it, then feel a rumble indicating a car is coming, *maybe two.* I pick up my tired body and run out of the way, then unexpectedly bump into a guy taking out his trash.

"Hey! Watch it," he nicely complains.

"I'm so sorry!" I look around, trying to figure out where I am. The street name isn't ringing a bell.

"You lost?" he asks.

"Sort of."

"You're sure wearing funny clothes." *He's talking super funny.*

"I'm Martin, Martin Mcfly. Pleased to meet you. This is my house," he says. Why does that name sound familiar?

"Can I use your phone?"

"Sure." Something about his old-fashioned demeanor compels me to feel safe.

I call Daddy. I hear distorted noises on the line, and I have the very strange feeling his number doesn't exist yet. I look at the calendar hanging on the fridge. It says *2005.* "What year is it?"

"2005." Can't be. I'm barely a toddler in *2005!*

"You said Mcfly . . . Is your dad Marty Mcfly?" I ask. He looks at me strangely.

"Yeah, you know him?" I try to put everything together before I lose it. So . . . Daze put me to sleep, *or in a trance*, and now I'm in the *movie* my family and I watched the other night! But I somehow ended up in their future. I sit at their table to think.

"You okay?" he asks. I am at a loss. *He has no idea! Wait, maybe he does.*

"Is your dad available?"

"My dad?" Brimming with hope, I nod and shoot up from my seat. If Marty still has that futuristic car, I might be able to get back to the future. *From a dream, Lolly? Get real,* you're dead. *Am not!*

"My mom is in the other room. Are you a groupie? Did you follow him home or something?"

"Oh my gosh, no!" I put my hands up in surrender. *Now I have to tell the truth, hoping they let him in on their travels.*

"I'm from the future. I need his help to get back to my time!" He stares at me, and I just know he's gonna think I'm a nut!

"You're Lolly Pobs? The purple-haired girl."

Hooray! wait . . . "How do you know my name?"

"Doc told us about you. Said you would need help getting back to your time. He said you're from another frequency or something?" I nod. This is the coolest thing I've ever done.

"In the flesh!" I say. Mind blown. *Back to the Future* is really turning into my favorite movie.

"Can he help me get back to my frequency?"

"Nope, he's touring with his band."

I freak out. "So, can you? I kinda need to get back *now!*"

"Never did it before."

"What? Aren't you guys supposed to be, like, waiting for my grand entrance?"

"No."

Ugh. What is my world coming to? "Can you call your dad?"

"It's really late, but judging by the circumstance, sure." Could this kid be anymore cringey? I laugh to myself.

Martin dials his dad's number. "Wait," I say, "put it on speaker. He's like my favorite actor now."

"What?"

"Nothing." I wave him off with a smile.

"Hello!" It sounds noisy. Marty is living a rockstar lifestyle. Martin explains the situation, and his dad tells him what to do. I say hello and start to ask about the next movie but decide against it. We hang up, and Martin takes me to the car in the garage.

"He said it's fueled up and ready to go." I nod. "I always wanted to do this," he says.

"You don't want to play like Marty, *your dad*?" I am not trying to be disrespectful.

"No, I wanna be a scientist like Doc."

"Doc? Like the one in the mov—" I stop myself, knowing that if I say a bit more, I'll rock this boy's world when he finds out he's a fictional character.

He tells me to put in my year of destination, and I start to plug it in. "Wait, we're in California, right?"

"Right." I was born in Cali. Daddy used to drive by the brick house we lived in all the time, and I wonder if I can find it. *Mommy,* a sting hits my veins. This is a movie. *Could she exist here?* "Could we make one pit stop before I go home?"

"Where to?"

On our way, I think about what I will say or do. Another chance at seeing her is like a dream come true. Will I tell her who I am? I stiffen as I remember the weaponry that's coming into the shop. Could she have known about me because I would tell her right here and now? Tears flood my eyes. I find the house. I hate I'm knocking on her door at this time of night, but I have no other choice. Hoping I'm not a sleeping newborn, I take a deep breath and knock.

She instantly opens it, and I just stand there teary-eyed, staring at how beautiful she is.

"Yes?" she says casually, looking past me at Martin, wondering if she's in any danger. She looks worn out as if she's been cleaning and taking care of a baby all day, well *me*.

"Lolly?" says Martin, and I snap out of it. She's looking at me *like she knows me*. I'm sure she's thinking of Granny Lollian, my twin.

"I'm sorry. I was in town and I . . . wanted to see you."

"You *do* look like family." She smiles.

"I know you're probably putting the baby to bed, but could I possibly come in?"

She looks at us, then looks back at her baby girl. I can see her heart is telling her to do so. "Sure, come in."

Martin and I sit in the living room. She finally gets little Lolly to bed and joins us. I giggle at endless pictures of us. She looks as if she's seen a ghost, holding something to her heart. She lightly laughs as she hands me the picture of Granny Lollian Jones at a mic. *We look identical.*

"Oh Mom, she looks just like . . ." I pause and her smile disappears. "Me," I finish. She gets up from the couch.

"Why'd you call me that?"

"She meant—" Martin starts, but I butt in.

"I'm sorry. I didn't mean to . . ." I stand up and without thinking, wrap my arms around her.

Tears stream down my face. "I'm sorry, Mama, I'm just so happy to see you. I never thought I would ever see you again." She rubs my back like she always had and allows me to hold on but sits me down with her on the couch. I lay my head on her lap and hug her knees.

"Tell me. I'm listening." She's still so sweet. I pour out my heart, tell her about her passing from an illness she asked me not to tell her about, said it would disrupt God's plans. I even show her my birthmark so she'll believe.

"That birthmark's my favorite thing about you." I smile big. *Yes!*

She asks about Daddy, then about how I am. Here's my chance to say what I didn't get to before. "I miss you so much. I wondered, if I had a question no one could answer but you, how would I get the answer?"

"Aw, you seem like a very smart girl. I'm sure I gave you all you needed to be able to continue on with life." I think about how I'm running the shop and making good decisions, and she's right.

"Yeah, and God helped me too."

"I'm happy you trust in God, Lolly."

"I just wanted you to be proud of me, but I messed up . . . I was so into school, and I didn't get to spend a lot of time with you. I just couldn't. I dunno why." I'm all over the place.

"It's okay. We all mess up. All I know is, you're mine, and nothing you could ever do would change my love for you."

"Mama, I'm sorry for everything I will ever do."

"I don't know what you're gonna do, but I'll always hold on to what you just said to me." This really did happen, and she really lived her life by everything I said. That's why her words were so final. *She knew.*

I have to show her my powers somehow. I stand up. "Lord, please let me show her the gift You gave me." I look at my feet and she follows. They hover over the floor. She gasps and pulls me down to the floor.

"Don't hurt yourself!"

"Whoa!" says Martin and looks afraid for all of us.

"Amazing," she says. "And Josh?" I open my locket. She cries when she sees him and can't believe how handsome Daddy looks when he got older. I tell her everything about them.

By now the whole realm is probably under reconstruction.

Liam is probably being pulled through it, forced to watch the devil's handiwork. The rest are probably still fighting through their minds being taken over, and we don't have a future to go back to anymore. I get it. I finally get it. *Back to the Future*. I look at my beautiful young mother and am trying to find ways to say goodbye *again*.

"This isn't goodbye forever," she says. Maybe not for her . . . "You have to trust that God has a plan." *True*. I have to know God knows best.

"I loved spending time with you," I tell her. I fight tears and hate the funny way it makes me sound.

"Me too. Come back any time." I seriously think about it. I need to figure out how Daze did it. She sees my expression. "Lolly, I don't mean literally, because even if you don't come back, I'll always live in your heart. And we will meet again in heaven just like this." She hugs me.

"Bye, Mrs. Pobs," Martin says and waves.

"Bye, Marty. Thank you for bringing her and for not thinking we're crazy!" He laughs but doesn't confirm or deny. After what goes down in his household, he has no room to be freaked about anything.

"I want you to have this." I take off my locket. I saw how happy it made her.

"Lolly, I couldn't."

"You can and you will." I signal for her to turn around and put it on her. She looks beautiful in it.

"Thank you, puddin'. I'll cherish it forever." *I'll cherish you forever, Mama. Until heaven and into eternity.* She stays at the door until I get in the car and closes it slowly as we ride off

47
The Clean Up

I wonder how she'll sleep tonight. I know I won't, and I thank Jesus for that miracle. Once again. He turned tragedy for my good. We're always winners in Christ.

"Alrighty!" Martin says, and we're back on the black road. "You all good?" he asks.

"Yeah, thank you." If I really think about it, I may not be. He hits the gas. "See you later, Mommy," I say, and just like that we're off in a *zap!* We come to a screeching stop.

"Whoa!" we say together. I sit up straight and see blasts going off in the distance. I put out my hand, and electricity sparks.

"Whoa again," he says, gulping. He looks starstruck.

"I know right!" *Faith brought it back.*

I see my statue turn to dust before my eyes. I guess since I'm here, we can't stand together.

"Thanks for all your help," I say. He gives me the same look I've seen Liam give. It's *the kiss look.* My eyes widen. "See ya around, MJ!"

"Totally," he says, and someone swings open my car door. *It's William.* I almost fall out of my seat when he looks inside between us, then helps me out. I peek back in and say, "Sorry. Boyfriend's here. Gotta go!" MJ waves sadly, and Liam dramatically shuts the door in his face. Martin races back to his own time in a jiffy.

"I can explain," I say, but he just holds me. I squeeze back. After a while, Liam stands, waiting for my explanation. "He helped me get back from the past," I say.

"I'll need more details later. For now, get back over here," he says and makes my sword pop up in my hand then disappears before my eyes. OMG I missed it! Something in me hoped we'd won, and he was over here to tell me the good news, but nope. I bend my knees and whip into the sky. *Yes!* When I land I feel something shake on my chest. *My locket is back!* She gave me the locket I gave her. I kiss it and look to the sky. "You're awesome, God."

I look over on the floor where Vonvex was standing, and she's still a rock pile. My bottom lip shivers. I look to the right and Satan, the witch, and Daze are watching Mckenzie trying to pull the doors to the Spiritual Realm open. I try to get to them, but I can't break the barrier anymore because I'm supernatural. I see Cannon being bombarded by an army of demons and their leader. Could that be Ashaka? I go into the crowd of demons and slice away. I wrap my arm around a demons neck, using it as level ground to kick in a circle, bashing about five heads in. Then I flip the demon on the ground and pierce it. They're scary to look at, but I think Satan was counting on their quantity not quality.

"You turned to dust! Didn't you?" says the lion.

"Peekaboo," I say and he laughs. "I went to the past, just came back."

"The past? You were rock all but five minutes." I hear gunshots. It's Tammy, shooting demons from left to right.

"Where have you been?" I ask, although I can't believe I'm talking to her.

"Cleaning up y'all's mess." She's a good shot. A big gun hanging on the side of her thigh catches my eye; it's exquisite.

Bot grunts on the floor. I forgot about *her arm!* I run to her.

I see wires hanging from the tear, and the metal on her knee is dented.

"Bot!"

"Lolly? I'm so glad you're okay." She looks at Vonvex's dust.

"Well, well, well, more women that want me?" says Wildcard, and my lip tightens. *Ew.*

"I do! I got a present for ya," says Tammy and switches guns. She fires away. His eyes roll to the back of his head, and he falls.

Bot starts to cough. Liam could help. *Liam!* It's been too quiet. I get up with Bot to look for him, and Tammy follows. He looks worn out. Grand is suspended over him in the air.

"Tammy, we need help."

"I came to help, Liam." She starts toward him.

"You know that I can help him in ways you can't." I'm speaking of the supernatural and the fact that he's *my* boyfriend!

"I don't think so, hon. See this?" She points to the see-through gun. "This is an antidote to stop Grand." She turns and runs away. I'm shocked at how she could just leave us like this!

I look back and hear monsters snickering, headed toward us. Bot's metal is weighing me down. I'm not sure if I can get us both to Liam. Bot's rockets fire up, and I'm a boot scrape away from the ground.

"Bot, you'll hurt yourself."

"I can do it. I can do all things through Christ who strengthens me."

"Well, then I can too!" I add my thrust, and we move faster. I think about my love. I need to see him, and I need to be near him. That hologram wasn't enough. I need him close as he's been since I met him.

"Back off!" Tammy points at Grand and huffs. I sit Bot down on the floor. Liam looks at us. His once flawless face is scratched up, and his clothes are all ripped from the acid. Grand's rivers flow, and he's bloody. His scarred bare chest is out. They're heaving. I thought Liam looked bad but . . . My bells go off, but I sense it's *one for salvation for Grand!* Grand extends his waters towards us, but Liam holds it back with his blue light. Tammy's fingers squeeze to shoot.

"Tammy, wait!" I call, but she fires anyway. Grand instantly falls to his knees.

"What's this?" he asks, and saliva falls out of his mouth before foam does, then falls down face first. Tammy blows at the opening of the gun. I see Mckenzie look over slightly, and the forcefield over the bridge falls. The hackers don't notice, though.

I run to Liam, who looks like he's taking a moment to rest. I put my hands on his face and touch the scratches with my thumbs. They're slowly healing. I kiss them as they go.

"Hey," I say.

"Milady . . ." *How enchanting.* "Don't leave me like that again," he says softly before sweeping me up into his arms. He's so tall and definitely has his strength back.

"I won't," I say, but he pulls back.

"Who was dude?" he asks, alert now.

"A guy from a movie. I'll tell you about it later! Bot needs you." He repairs Bot and tells Tammy to take her home. She's weak from the missing Merth.

I suddenly remember something. "The forcefield is down!" I yell. We run to it. I hear Arch call my name and stop.

"Arch?" I fly up, and he reaches out for me. Blee defeats the last of the demons in the air, and everyone starts to disappear. Her first, then Chang, Ahor and *then* . . . I try to fly faster, but Arch vanishes right before my eyes. I'm left hovering in the air, spinning around. He has to be here somewhere!

"Arch!" I whimper and go down. "Is Arch down here?" I'm panicking. Liam shakes his head. "Arch!"

48

Adonai
{The God Who Rules}

A big light shines from a distance. Did they get in? We grunt at the piercing brightness coming from the Realm. We hear a wooden stick hit the ground and can see everyone near the gate flying back.

"We rebuke you, Satan, in the name of Jesus!" say The Thrice. Satan dives onto the floor, desperately crawling away. When the light dims, the witch is gone, and The Thrice seal the Realm.

"Took you long enough," says Liam.

"We were delayed. Satan set off a rebellion in the Spiritual Realm, but the demons were in over their heads."

My bells ring and we put Daze, Mckenzie, and Wildcard in a row. A. Freeze had taken the first opportunity to repent and left. I didn't think he was a part of their group anyway. I look over at Grand. He's still motionless. I close my eyes and think of Arch.

"You are in complete violation of the Lord's decree to keep the use of your powers unseen from the world. *And* you tried to break into the Spiritual Realm," says The Profit, sprinkling on the last part. "You will be shown mercy according to the loving-kindness of our Lord Jesus Christ. Repent and turn from your wicked ways."

"I don't know what all them words mean, sirs, but I ain't doing it!" says Wildcard and spits on the ground.

Suddenly, vines grow through the ground and wrap around his legs. They pull at him. The ground opens up and swallows him whole. Liam and I flinch. Wildcard is screaming until the ground closes and silence fills the area. I look at Daze and Mckenzie. They gulp, and so do I. *He's really gone? Like forever?*

"I just want to go home to my father. I repent, God. I'm sorry!" Mckenzie yells at the sky and then disappears before our eyes.

"Daisy?" Grand wakes from his slumber and reaches out for her. He seems weak. I wonder if the antidote worked?

"Daisy?" says The Profit, looking for a response.

"I'm not bowing down to a God I don't know." She looks over at Grand. "What has He ever done for me!" We wait for her to be pulled down, but nothing happens. I hear whispering voices all around me and listen up. It's *The Holy Spirit.*

"Liam, put her in a cell in the lab please." He looks at Grand, who's in a fetal position before walking over and putting his hand on her shoulder.

"Don't touch me!" she yells, and they disappear.

I think about Arch. He's really gone. I could see it in his eyes that he's not coming back. Liam returns and sees the sadness in my eyes and pulls me into his arms. "It's gonna be okay."

"He's really gone, Liam," I sob.

"I know, baby. I know." He just holds me. He stiffens. I look up and find that a blade has pierced his chest—The Stone Dagger. He falls to the floor, and we look to see that Ashaka had thrown it before disappearing. My hand quivers as it hovers over his wound, not knowing what to do.

I look at the rock pile that was Vonvex. I came back, but she never did. What does this mean? Suddenly, The Profit and Thrice get splashed by Grand's venom. "Stop him," says a groaning Liam. The skin around the blade is pulsing with the stone that he's fighting. My breathing stagnates, and I am trying to fight a panic attack.

"Go," he says, cupping my cheek. I hesitate and stumble over my feet.

"Jesus," I call to the One who can end this all with one word, *His name.*

I weakly fly into the sky, form Electo, and throw it at Grand. He dodges.

"I'd hate to burn your pretty face off, but I will, Pobs." He's trying to get to the gate. I hear my bells ring again. How am I supposed to defeat him when Liam was trying to this whole time? He grows his fountain and extends his hands, throwing it towards me. I dodge and he follows behind me. I can hear his rugged breathing and see his demented eyes below me. *Super creepy!* I reach for my bow string and whisk it. They whip around his upper body, and the spraying stops.

I look over at Liam, reaching to loosen the dagger. "You have us in the palm of Your hand, Adonai," I pray. Out of nowhere, Grand kicks me to the ground. I crash into the earth, and my muscles ache all over. I struggle to get up. I'm hoping the enemy doesn't reach me in this state and makes the ditch my body created a bowl of soup. "No matter what comes," I say to finish my prayer to the God who rules.

I feel a strength pulling me out of the hole. A surge of energy blazes through me, and I rush Grand, thrusting my fists into him. I hit my kick spin, *finally,* and tilt and kick him straight to the ground. I zip down, punching him into it further and further. My blows are digging into his flesh. I come up for air, then whisk back in but feel hands wrap around me and pull until I'm looking directly into Liam's renewed eyes. I sob.

Grand is now before the same counsel his mini's were in, and the restored Profit reads him his rights before God. "Grand, what do you say? Will you turn from your wicked ways? Come back to the Lord? He's waiting for you."

"Is He now?" asks Grand,

"He is," says The Profit.

"Well, then why does He cause so much pain?"

"God doesn't cause the evil in this world, the wickedness in it does. But one day, we'll live in a place so beautiful there will be no more suffering. Grand, I know you've endured so much, but we must pick up our cross as Christ did and run our race so that we may hear *well done*."

Grand lets out a tired breath. With his head down, he humbly says, "I repent."

Right before our eyes, Grand's skin turns back to normal, his hair still a very light brown. We cheer, and I nuzzle into Liam's chest. We won!

Thank You, Jesus.

Epilogue

GRAND

Grand walks into a familiar DC diner. "Welcome. What can I get for you?" asks Mona.

"A coffee please. Two pumps mocha, five sugars, two pumps cream." She examines him for a second but turns to make it. He watches to see if she'll recognize him. She sends a flirtatious glance at Grand, but it doesn't click.

"One coffee."

"Thank you." He looks at her nametag. "Mona," she nods shyly and turns to wipe the counter.

He takes a look around and breathes in freedom. He feels stronger, more confident in who he is. A woman comes in and hands Grand a piece of paper, then proceeds to hand them out to other customers. "Oh no, you can't do that here," says Mona. The woman places a small stack on the bar next to Grand.

"God bless you," she says. He nods, and she walks out. Mona snatches the papers and mumbles under her breath before dumping them in the trash bin.

He scans the paper. It says, "Accept Jesus into your heart today by saying these words: Jesus, I know I'm a sinner. Forgive me. I believe You died on the cross for me. I accept You and invite You into my heart as my Lord and Savior." At the bottom it says, "*Starting* today*, you are made new.*" He needs more, so he turns it over. It says, "*God loves you.* 'Now to Him who is able to do exceedingly abundantly above all that we ask or think, according to the power that works in us' (Ephesians 3:20)."

He feels a tug in his heart and repeats the words, *"Jesus, I know I'm a sinner . . ."* and formally turns his life over to Christ. "I want everything You can give me, God. *I want it all.*" He prays and feels at peace.

"Can I get you anything else?" He snaps out of it. Mona looks as if she's hoping he'll ask for her number.

"No thanks."

"K."

"Is Daisy in today?" He gets the nerve to ask. She looks puzzled, almost like she's gonna ask, *who's that?* Does Daisy not exist to begin with?

"She's off today."

That's all he needed to hear. After paying, he heads for the door.

"Hey, you remind me of someone," Mona says.

"Later, Mona!"

"Grand?" He turns back and smiles but doesn't stop. She's left staring, wondering about what could've been.

Grand races to Daisy's home. She's at her door with grocery bags, and she knocks.

"Daisy?"

She turns abruptly. "You scared me," she says, staring at him.

"It's Grand."

"Grand? No way! I thought I recognized your voice!" she exclaims.

"I got better." He smiles.

"I see, and you're a hottie. Has Mona seen you?"

He laughs. "Yeah."

"Sweet." She smiles brightly, not like siren Daze.

"Daisy, I'm sorry about everything."

"What's everything?" He grabs her wrist, but there's nothing there.

The front door opens, and an older man stands in the doorway. "It's about time!" Daisy says.

"I thought you had a key?" says the man.

"It's getting old, and I need a new one. Oh, Dad, this is Grand."

"Hello, Grand."

Grand smiles. "Oh wow. Your dad's here now too?" They look puzzled. Grand hugs her. "Are you okay?" asks Daisy.

"I wanted to give you this," he says, handing her a duffle bag of money. "Don't open it until I leave, okay?"

"Okay." Her father takes the groceries inside.

Grand grabs her key, licks his fingers, and smooths them over the ridges of the metal.

"Yuck, Grand!"

"Try it again."

She puts it into the keyhole with no problem and says, "All it needed was a little elbow grease! Thanks, sort of." She really doesn't remember anything, but he's glad she still remembers him—not the wicked creature he'd become, but the innocent one he was before. *Jesus restored him.*

"Can I call you sometime, D?"

"Of course, but not tonight. The neighbor won't stop inviting me to church, so I'm just gonna go." He beams. He had forgiven Daisy, just like Jesus forgave him.

He leaves to return to Minnesota. By nightfall, he reaches all the banks they'd hit to return the money. The drive back home is filled with hope. He imagined his mother in the kitchen, awaiting his arrival, memories erased of him just like Daisy. When he arrived, though, the house was empty. He realizes he has to go to the asylum to see her. After arriving, he walks in, teary-eyed. "Turosi," he says to the receptionist, and a nurse escorts him to her.

"She never gets visitors. She'll be happy to see you." He's not so sure, but he smiles anyway. "Hello, dear. Your son Grand is here to see you."

Her head snaps to him. "Grand?" she says in surprise, looking up at him from her chair.

"I'm her head nurse, Barbra. Call if you need me," she says and walks out.

He falls at her feet. "Ma, I'm so sorry,"

"For what, my son? It's not your fault the monster took you." She rubs his hair. "Your hair? What happened to your nice orange hair?" She pulls her hand away. "You're not my son! The devil has you still!" She pushes him and screams for help at the top of her lungs. Grand rams into the dresser. He wails in pain. A tiny knob made a gash on his forearm.

Her nurse bursts in, saying, "I'm sorry. This was probably too soon," Grand can see sympathy in her eyes.

"He is the devil! A blue devil!" his mom cries out before Barbra gives her a sedative.

He dolefully goes to a drugstore for medicine for his wound. His eyes dart to a girl on the same aisle with short hair and beautiful pink lips. "Rachel?" He didn't mean to call her, but he couldn't believe his eyes.

She stops reading a box and looks over with a neutral face that soon lights up like a Christmas tree. "Grand!" She leaves her cart and runs to him. "Where have you been? I can't believe it's really you!"

"I moved to New York. I'm here visiting my mom."

"How is she? Look at your hair. I love it! Did you dye it?" She runs her fingers through it. Grand is glad God saw in his heart that he loved his hair and let him keep it.

"No, all mine."

"It just turned brown?"

"Something like that, yeah." She touches it once more before tucking her hand into crossed arms. Then it feels awkward between them.

"I got myself good," he says, showing her the cut.

"Oh, crap! Here let me help." She picks out a few things and puts it in his basket. "I can help wrap it if you want." They bop each other with balloons that have sticks in them at the register. Laughter fills the space, and cashiers and customers stare at them. Grand pays for her things after she fights with him not to. He loads her car, and she goes with him to his SUV.

"What happened to you back then?" she asks, opening gauze. "Your ah . . ." she pauses and smiles. "Your mom told my parents you attacked her, and I was in danger. They took my phone, and I never heard from you again. I mean, I knew it wasn't true." She looks into his eyes for confirmation, but he can't give it.

"Then after, we heard she went to that home, and I knew she was wrong about you." She folds the gauze and places it on his arm.

"What if it were true?" he asks.

"Grand, you wouldn't hurt a fly." She places her hand on his heart. He doesn't know what to say. He is filled with sorrow thinking about all the people he hurt, *including Ci.* "I'll be seeing you, ya know. I'm going to college in New York to be a social worker, starting next month." His spirit lifts as she puts surgical tape around the gauze.

Could this be the *all* he'd just asked God for? He takes a risk and draws closer to her, and she looks into his eyes.

"Grand?"

"Yeah?" He looks at her lips, then at her amazing almond eyes.

"Kiss me." He doesn't wait for her to change her mind and crashes his lips into hers. And everything that happened to him—

all the scars that crippled his heart, suddenly dissipate.

He pulls away and looks into her eyes. He hesitates but needs to say these next words: "I want to tell you everything."

One Month Later

Grand's apartment door swings open. He carries in loads of suitcases, the door slamming behind him. He managed to get most of the things from his old room since he won't be there any-more. He tried to visit his mother again before he left last month, but she refused to see him. Eventually he planned to move her to New York so he could continue to try to rebuild their relationship. God willing, she'd come around. *And he never stopped visiting Ci.*

He runs back to the front door just in time to open it for Rachel, who was holding a few things. He plants a small kiss on her lips before going downstairs to retrieve the rest of her things from the car. Their drive up had gone fast because they'd kept each other laughing. He told her everything . . . the good, the bad, the ugly. The acid, the deaths, the robberies, even about Ci. Even about the battle at the gates of the Spiritual Realm that seemed so evil now. They cried and laughed. She'd walk away, and he'd go get her.

With God's help, she accepted it and he showed her the power he still held. It wasn't a burden anymore, and his liquids didn't affect everyday material. It was just sweat, just urine, just tears. Like the ones he shed the day he married Rachel, just days after he'd found her again. He couldn't risk letting her go anymore. *He got the girl* even after everything he was. She wiped his tears at the courthouse, and now she laid beside him as his wife. He mar-veled at the promise God kept of abundance, and promised to serve him always.

LOLLY

That Night

"You're never gonna let me walk this path alone are you?" I ask Liam as we walk down my driveway.

"Not a chance," he says. I laugh, then look down at my nails, thinking about my dog. "I'm sorry about Arch, but we gotta trust God knows what He's doing," says Liam.

I nod. "I just don't understand how God wants me to do this superhero thing on my own."

"I know, baby, but you know God is always with us. And you have me." He cups my cheek.

We both look at the mesh bracelet that's still black and instantly melt. He pulls me in, and we sway to nonexistent music on my porch.

"I'm so glad you're mine," he says. "All mine." He stops and turns into Ore, whipping me behind him. I look over his shoulder.

Ashaka stands there with a devilish grin. "And you're mine," he says to Ore.

Fin

About the Author

NATALYE BENITEZ is a follower of Christ, first time author,, singer/songwriter, and mommy of a princess. "One day, my sister asked me to go to the library with her. I said, 'Haven't been since school but LET'S GO!' When we got there, I was amazed. I didn't see books, I saw small trunks containing jewels to uncover. But God totally shocked me when He said, 'You're an author'—with zero experience! And I just want to thank Him." - Nat

To contact the author, use her email: natalye@tgslpmeplz.com